JILL McGIVERING

The Last Kestrel

blue door

Blue Door
An imprint of HarperCollins*Publishers*
77–85 Fulham Palace Road,
Hammersmith, London W6 8JB

www.harpercollins.co.uk

This paperback edition 2011
3

First published in Great Britain
by Blue Door 2010

Extract of 'Report on Experience' by Edmund Blunden from
Undertones of War (© Edmund Blunden, 1928) is reproduced by permission of
PFD (www.pfd.co.uk) on behalf of The Estate of Edmund Blunden

A catalogue record for this book
is available from the British Library

ISBN: 978-0-00-733815-3

Set in Minion by Palimpsest Book Production Limited,
Falkirk, Stirlingshire

Printed and bound in Great Britain by
Clays Ltd, St Ives plc

MIX
Paper from
responsible sources
FSC
www.fsc.org
FSC® C007454

For my mother

I have seen a green country, useful to the race,
   Knocked silly with guns and mines, its villages vanished,
   Even the last rat and last kestrel banished –
   God bless us all, this was peculiar grace.

      'Report on Experience' by Edmund Blunden

Prologue

The line was taut. The cord circles tightened into handcuffs, burning his wrists. He was propelled forward, dragged on the rope, stumbling over sand and stones on the leash. His neck craned backwards, his face towards the sky and the glare of the sun fired the cloth of his blindfold. His tongue flickered to his lips, tasted their dryness. Sweat blossomed on his scalp, trickled down his temples, stung chapped skin.

He was sick with shock, his limbs convulsing. The man had jumped him from behind, from nowhere, and knocked him to the ground. He had pinioned him, his knee hard in his back, and bound his eyes before he could twist his face to see. Who was he? He caught the stink of male sweat; his own, bitter with adrenalin, and, overlaying it, the thick meaty smell of the man.

He stretched the tendons of his neck and managed to move the cloth a fraction. The material was wound tightly round his head, pressing into his eyes and, as he lifted it, he created a narrow slit of light at the bottom. Light, there, below, just beyond his vision. His eyes bulged, forcing themselves downwards, straining towards his chin, to focus on the paper-thin line of brightness. Was that a blur of sand he could see, dancing with pinpricks of colour? His head was bursting with effort and fear.

He tried to take control of his body, to steady his breathing and, with it, his mind. This man is taking me somewhere. He has a plan for me. With this thought, hope rose. He almost giggled, intoxicated with it. If he were going to kill me, he would have done it by now. Wouldn't he? Yes. *Alhamdulillah*. Thanks be to God. He grasped this hope and hugged it to him, a lifebelt thought. Yes. If he—

A sharp rock at his toes and he was tripping, his feet splayed. The cord closed its teeth more sharply round his wrists, biting into the skin. The rope jerked. Pain through his hands, a sudden white heat in his shoulder sockets, his arms. A rush of air on his face as he fell forward, crashing, bouncing hard against the ground. Air struck out of his chest, leaving him gasping. Fine sand rose in a cloud, filling his mouth, his nose, making him choke. The stink of grit close to his face, a smell of dead sand and desiccated dirt.

A pause. He was alive, breathing noisily in, out. His nostrils ran wet with mucus or blood. He tried to lift his head and opened his mouth a crack to speak. His eyes, encrusted with sand, were trying to force themselves open beneath the cloth. His tongue was thick. He held his breath to listen. He heard the man, close to him, exhale.

His head was held down, his face pressed into the sand. A weight on the back of his head. A foot. The hard sole of a boot. He bucked and twisted, trying to flip over, to turn his covered face to the man, to beg. The boot held him firm, standing on his skull, grinding his nose into the dirt, causing a hundred minute sharp stones to embed in his forehead, his chin. A wave of nausea brought bile into his throat, riding a swell of panic.

A metallic click. A gun being cocked. He opened his mouth to shout but no word came. The sharp stink of piss, hot and steamy. The sudden wetness in his groin. A searing flash of white light. Cleansing and bleaching everything in an instant. The halo of the gunshot Jalil didn't live to hear.

1

The room was shabby and hot. Ellen, sitting cross-legged on the threadbare carpet, tried to shift her weight and ease herself into another position without attracting attention. Her knees were aching.

Dust hung heavy in the air, suspended in the shafts of early evening light which were pressing in through open windows. The furniture was sparse. Just an old-fashioned television on a stand, a vast dark-wood dresser, scraped and scuffed by several generations, and worn cushions scattered across the carpet and against the walls.

Jalil's mother was kneading her hands, rhythmically squeezing one through the other, back and forth. Her head was bent, watching her fingers as if their restlessness surprised her. The skin was papery. The veins along the backs of her hands stood full and thick with purple blood, part of the map of her new shrinking self.

Her scarf was pulled forward, screening her face, although the only male present was her young son. He was squatting on his haunches beside her, pressed against her body for comfort. He was a thin boy of ten or eleven with protruding ears and a scab on his chin. He was too young to understand he'd become the man of the house.

The daughter, embarrassed by her mother's silence, tried to take control. She leaned forward to Ellen to whisper. 'You understand,' she said. 'A very big shock.'

'Of course.'

The daughter pushed a dish of greasy long-grained rice towards Ellen. It was laced with flakes of nut and plump stock-rich raisins. Ellen added another spoonful to her plate. She broke off a piece of fresh ridged bread, warm and spongy, and wiped it round, pinching a piece of lamb and rice together with her forefingers. She leaned forward over the plastic cloth. It was spread out between them on the floor, dominating the room, covered with cheap glass dishes of home-cooked food, a litre bottle of Coca-Cola and a smatter of shot glasses.

She brought her hand to her mouth, pushed the food between her lips, even though she had no appetite. The lamb had been marinated in a pungent sauce and she chewed slowly. She knew the rules. They must press food on her even after she was sated, to show respect, and she, to show thanks, must eat it.

'He has a friend there.' The daughter's voice faltered as she corrected herself. She was fiddling with the fabric of her head-scarf, playing it between her long fingers, shading her eyes. 'Had a friend.'

Ellen looked up. The daughter was nineteen or twenty, a little younger than Jalil. Her nose was broad and prominent, as his had been. Sitting so close to her mother, she looked a younger, less broken version of her, with clear olive skin and expressive eyes ringed with kohl. She'd already lost her father. Now she'd also lost her older brother, any uncle or cousin could push her into a hasty marriage.

'His friend,' Ellen asked her, 'is he also a translator?'

The daughter nodded. 'His name is Najib,' she said. 'An old classmate of his, also from Kabul.'

'And he's still in Helmand?'

'Yes. Maybe now he can help you instead of Jalil.' She breathed heavily. 'With your reports.'

The girl attempted a smile but looked away and it crumpled. Ellen pushed a piece of lamb round her plate with her bunched fingers, struggling to find the will to eat. In four years of coming back and forth to Kabul to cover Afghanistan for *NewsWorld,* this

4

was the first time she would work without Jalil. He'd been full of life, of talent; exactly the sort of man his country needed. His death sickened her. He should never have turned to the military for work. She looked round now at the faces that mirrored his.

Jalil's mother lifted her fleshless hands and ran them through the boy's hair and along the contours of his face, as if she were a blind woman, learning him. He wriggled, sighed, scratched himself around the ribs, then settled against her again and submitted to the hands without protest.

'It was Najib who told us.' The corners of the daughter's mouth were tight with tension. All this was just a week old and they were still in shock.

The daughter leaned forward automatically to press on Ellen the dish of meat and rice. Ellen forced herself to take a little more. The lamb split easily into pieces on her plate, releasing aromatic steam. It was good meat. They must have paid a lot of afghanis for it. Without Jalil, money would be tight. She was very conscious that she was the only one eating. The family sat round her, dull-eyed, and watched. This evening, she knew, they would pick at her leftovers.

The daughter was educated. Some course in management or teaching – Ellen couldn't recall what exactly. Her neat gold earrings, her shoulder-length bob and the tailoring of her Afghan kameez gave her a hint of Western stylishness.

'What will you do now?'

The daughter shrugged. 'Find work.' Her tone was lifeless.

'I could ask around,' Ellen said. 'The aid agencies might need someone. Or the embassies.'

The daughter kept her eyes on the plastic cloth between them. It was dotted now with stray grains of rice and wet circles of water and Coke where glasses had stood.

Jalil should be here. Their visits to this small family room, with its bare walls and peeling white plaster, had become a ritual whenever she'd worked with him. He'd always invited her home for a special evening meal, planned for the end of her stay once their work was done, and hosted by his mother. It was an honour to be welcomed into an Afghan home. His family had been proud that Jalil had an important English friend who paid him well in dollars.

Without him, the air in the room was stale. She had done the right thing in making the effort to come, dashing from the chaos of Kabul Airport to these hushed rooms, but their grief was drowning her. She tore off a final piece of bread, ran it round the congealing sauce on her plate. Another few minutes and she'd have to head back to the airport to report for the military flight south to Helmand Province.

The daughter had lifted her eyes to the television and was staring at it sightlessly. The sound was muted but the images flickered on, splashing colour and light into the room. From the heavy dresser, Jalil's face stared out. It was a black and white photograph that Ellen had never seen before, framed in black. A spray of plastic flowers sat in a small glass vase beside it. It was an old-fashioned studio portrait that looked several years out of date. Jalil was wearing a pale kameez with a stiff collar. His hair, usually so unruly, was combed severely to one side, glossy and fixed in place, perhaps with gel. His expression, straight into the camera, was serious and subdued. She bet he hated that picture. It wasn't at all how she wanted to remember him.

When she looked away, she saw him as he used to be, sitting opposite her, stooped over his food, his long legs crossed, his back pressed against a cushion and the wall, his hair flopping forward over his forehead. His mother, shyly triumphant, would have fussed over their meal, pressing too much rich food on them both. She and her daughter would have cooked all day in readiness. His little brother, adoring, would be horsing around, overexcited. Climbing on him until he was pushed aside and told to behave. She looked over at the boy now. He had Jalil's delicate features, the same long black eyelashes and large eyes that would break hearts. Now, though, they were red-rimmed and anxious as he pressed his cheek against his mother's side for comfort, like a much younger child.

She turned to the daughter. 'On the phone,' she said in a low voice, 'you said something. About the way he died.'

The daughter tutted under her breath, gave her mother a quick glance, then lowered her eyes to her lap. Her fingers plucked again at the hem of her headscarf.

Ellen persisted. 'What did you mean? What makes you think you weren't told the truth?'

'They said he was killed by the Taliban when they were out on patrol. An ambush. That's what they said.'

The daughter unfolded her legs and brought herself to her feet, crossed to the dresser and opened a drawer. It was crammed with yellowing papers. She picked out an envelope near the top, withdrew a single sheet of thin paper and spread it out on the floor between them, smoothing it with her fingertips. The writing was neat, covered in the ink squiggles of Pashto.

'From him?'

Across the room, her mother had lifted her head to watch. Ellen felt the weight of the silence, of the room's holding its breath.

'This is the last letter we received from him,' the daughter said. She traced the writing gently with her finger. 'He says he is leaving Helmand, leaving the job with the military. We should expect him home.' She paused, blinked, continued. 'But he sounds upset. "Things are not as I thought," he says. "Not at all." He writes to Mama not to worry. He'll find work in Kabul.' She glanced up at Ellen. 'He means some work for foreign journalists, like he did with you. Translating.' She paused. 'He liked to work with you. Always when you came here. He looked forward to it.'

Ellen nodded, holding her gaze. 'I did too.'

The daughter sighed, turned back to the letter. '"Don't be angry. I cannot stay here any longer. It is not honourable." This is what he says.' She looked up again and Ellen saw her hesitate before she decided to speak. 'I think he sounds afraid.'

Ellen let her eyes fall to her own hands, limp in her lap. She forced herself to face this new thought of Jalil's fear. It sat heavy in her gut. Was it fear for his life that had made him decide to leave? A wave of nausea took her. She clenched her hands into fists, resisting it, and saw her knuckles whiten. It is not honourable for me to stay, he'd written. Honour. A cornerstone for him, she knew that.

It's my fault, she thought. His death. I could have stopped it. She closed her eyes, screening it all out, digging her nails into her palms. Her breaths were coming in short bursts in the quietness and she tried consciously to slow and lengthen them. The family mustn't see her distress.

A splutter of static and microphone squeal broke into the room from outside as the dusk call to prayer began. It filled the silence, shimmering in through the open windows and across the room, a young male voice of sad sweetness. Ellen sat, rigid, feeling the blessing of prayer wash over them, low and melodious in its devotion. She concentrated on breathing. The room was soft with memories.

The first time she worked with Jalil, they'd embarked on an intense ten-day road trip, interviewing dozens of Afghans about the forthcoming elections. What did they expect from their politicians? Who did they support? They'd asked shopkeepers, housewives, farmers and traders, piecing together material for a four-page spread on the general mood and how Afghans saw their future.

She'd been given Jalil's number over lunch in Islamabad. A friend on *The New York Times* had just come out of Afghanistan. With so many journalists swarming through Kabul, decent translators were thin on the ground.

'Kinda young,' he'd said, scribbling down the mobile phone number on a paper napkin. 'But good. Smart as a whip.'

For the first three days of the trip, she'd wondered. Jalil had been nervous, stumbling over his English. He seemed shy. He was little more than twenty and she was used to working with older men, canny operators who were usually ex-journalists themselves.

They could be cocky and not always trustworthy but they brimmed with confidence and they knew a story when they saw one. By comparison, Jalil seemed naive.

On the fourth day, they turned off the road and bumped along dirt to a cluster of mud-brick houses. A boy, herding goats, flattened himself against a wall to watch and was turned to a ghost by the fine brown dust beaten up by the wheels. Beyond him a thin man was tugging at a donkey whose body was rendered invisible by a vast load of brushwood. A girl with a dirt-encrusted face ran to the man and clutched at his leg as they passed, her eyes round.

The schoolteacher, a contact of Jalil's, greeted them warmly. They sat cross-legged on cushions in his bare front room and drank green tea from tall glasses. Jalil translated back and forth. Yes, the schoolteacher told them, his voice measured, everyone in the village knew about the elections. He was encouraging them all to vote. But would the politicians help them? He had his doubts. Would they bring electricity to the village? And then, there was the school. He shook his head, his eyes pleading. He hadn't been paid his salary for so long now, for four, five months. How could he—?

The throb of an approaching truck interrupted him. He looked towards the window, nodded to Jalil and, in the doorway, pushed his bare feet back into the sandals waiting there. Ellen sipped her scalding tea and listened to the slam of a truck door outside, then low voices.

The man who entered with him smiled round. He had a short beard and a brown Afghan hat and greeted them with easy confidence. Ellen sat up, interested, to watch. My cousin, said the schoolteacher, and clicked his fingers to his son to run for a fresh *chai* glass. Just a few minutes later, before the conversation had really resumed, Jalil got to his feet, thanked the schoolteacher and ushered Ellen hastily out of the house.

'That was abrupt.' Ellen watched the passing landscape with dismay from the back seat of the vehicle. They'd spent several hours driving out to find the schoolteacher and she'd left with barely half an interview. 'What's the hurry?'

Jalil was sitting in the front passenger seat by the driver. He mumbled something she didn't catch.

'He had more to say,' she went on. The late morning sun was intense. Her head, encased in a headscarf, was already hot. 'We didn't have to leave just because his cousin came.'

'That man he calls his cousin,' Jalil turned back to her and lowered his voice, 'he is not a good man.'

Ellen shook her head. 'Why do you say that?'

Jalil raised his hand and worked it open and closed like the mouth of a glove puppet. 'Blah blah,' he said, snapping his thumb against his fingers. 'He is a man to go blah blah blah to someone. To some powerful man. He came rushing to see us for a reason.' He stared at Ellen. His voice had dropped to a whisper. 'Maybe he is going blah blah to some Taliban.'

Ellen glanced out of the window at the swirling dust, the blank brown landscape. They were in the middle of nowhere. 'Oh, come on.'

When she looked back at Jalil, he was frowning.

'Maybe they're just cousins.' She sighed to herself. She'd hurt his pride. 'He seemed friendly enough.'

'You saw his smile?'

'What about it?'

Jalil pointed to his own mouth. 'So much of gold in his teeth. New gold.'

Ellen shrugged. So what? He had gold teeth.

'His watch?' Jalil ran his hand round his wrist. 'Foreign watch. New.' Jalil paused, watching her reaction. 'Who gave him all this money?'

He faced forward again. His hair was sticking together in clumps along the top of his neck.

Ellen thought about what he'd said. The teeth, the watch. She hadn't noticed them. Jalil had. 'He could be a businessman,' she said. 'A trader.'

Jalil gave a dismissive grunt. 'Business?' He gestured out of the window at the emptiness of the desert. 'Here?'

She paused and considered. Maybe Jalil was smarter than he looked. He just wasn't loud. 'Blah, blah,' she said. She was used to Afghan men with big egos. Jalil was different. She lifted her own hand and opened and closed it like a mouth, as he had done. 'Blah blah, blah blah.'

He turned back to see and she snapped her hand open and closed at him until they both started to laugh, saying 'blah, blah' stupidly to each other as the driver swung back onto the road and they headed through the dry, swirling dust towards the next village.

Now, in this grieving house, the call to prayer gave a final burst of static and came to a close. Silence reached into the room. Ellen shifted her weight. It was already late.

'*Manana*.' Thank you. She placed her right hand on her heart in a gesture of thanks and bowed her head to Jalil's mother. Ellen unravelled her legs and rubbed her ankles to bring them back to life. She reached forward to gather together the scattered dishes and help to clear them. Jalil's sister protested, pushing Ellen's hands away and scolding her softly, as Ellen knew she would.

In the dim hallway, she covered her head with a voluminous scarf, wound the ends round her neck to keep it in place and bent to lace up her boots. Jalil's mother had retreated to the kitchen and only the daughter was hovering, adjusting her own scarf nervously in folds round her head and shoulders as she watched Ellen prepare to leave.

Ellen gestured the girl to come towards her. In a quick movement, she took a bundle of dollars from her pocket, folded the girl's long fingers round the money and enclosed her hands for a moment in the mesh of her own. Behind them rose a clatter of dishes, shifting in the sink. A tap coughed and water splashed onto a hard surface. The girl hesitated and opened her mouth to protest.

'*Balay*,' said Ellen. Yes. Her voice was firm. 'Please.'

The girl prised off Ellen's fingers and thrust the money back at her. Her eyes were proud. She knows what Jalil asked me, Ellen thought. She blames me. The money was thick and greasy in her hands. Dirty. She pushed it back into her pocket. She and the girl stared at each other, unspeaking.

The moment was ended by Jalil's mother who came out to them from the kitchen, wiping her hands on a towel. Her scarf had fallen back to her shoulders. Her hair, prematurely grey, was clipped into a bun, dripping strands.

She embraced Ellen, kissing her on both cheeks, then pressed herself against her body. She smelt of rose-water and spices and her hair was dry and prickly against the soft skin of Ellen's neck. She pulled back and took Ellen's hands in her own. She clasped them, looking up into her eyes. Her palms were hot and firm. Her eyes looked so like his. Deep brown with fragments of light radiating outwards. As she spoke, Ellen read the concern there.

'Don't go, she is saying.' The daughter was standing beside them, her voice cool as she translated her mother's words. 'It's too dangerous. Don't go to Helmand, she says. Go back to your own country and forget your work here. Be safe.'

His mother embraced her a second time. Ellen felt the hardness of the smaller woman's ribs against her own flesh, the compact muscle of years of labour.

'I must go,' she said at last. She put her hands on Jalil's mother's shoulders and lifted her away. 'I've got stories to file.'

His mother was reaching up to Ellen's cheek, patting it with a cupped hand.

'I'll find out,' Ellen said. 'Tell her. I'll find out what happened to Jalil.'

His mother spoke once more as her daughter unbolted the door and opened it. The family's guard, standing outside in the shadows, rushed forward, his rifle glinting in the half-light. He escorted Ellen across the shabby courtyard to the high metal gate set in the compound wall. His mother had used one of the phrases Jalil had taught Ellen in the time they'd worked together. One she didn't need anyone else to translate for her. May Allah bless you, she'd said. May Allah protect you.

2

The C-130 was a whale of an aircraft. It rattled and groaned as it flew them over the desert towards the base. The vibrations trembled through her bones as she sat, strapped in place against the aircraft's outer shell, against a climbing frame of military webbing. The army-issue earplugs had moulded themselves to the inside of her ears, but the noise was still deafening. Too loud to breathe.

All along the edge of the aircraft and down its central spine, sharing a running canvas seat, young soldiers were dozing, their heads lolling forward against their chests. They were solid and thick limbed, prickling with kit, guns upright between their thighs. The low military lights in the ceiling were painting them a ghoulish underwater green, sickly as corpses. She looked down the row of faces. They were hard jawed with sharp haircuts, their skin slackened by sleep, iPods in their ears. The more wars she covered, the younger they got. It was airless. Her muscles were tense with apprehension. She shifted her weight, wiped her forehead.

The two young air crew at the rear unbuckled their lap-belts, clipped on safety lines and started to move round the aircraft, signalling to each other, positioning loads and preparing for landing. The lumbering transport plane slid to one side, then dropped.

She thought of the desert below, endlessly flat and barren and peppered with stones. It would be black there now but when she closed her eyes, she saw it as she remembered it, in daylight, a scarred land, the colour of grey-brown nothingness, a land flayed to its skeleton. Jagged ridges of mountains rising, sharp with shadows and the contours of vast bite marks gouged out of the earth. The only signs of human life were the occasional stick figures of boys, herding goats, and the square compounds of weatherworn houses, their mud walls rubbed smooth like wave-lapped sandcastles, surviving in the middle of all this lifelessness. The only shade was cast by the broad silhouette of the aircraft, running along beneath them, darkening the earth below.

There was a mechanical shudder as the back of the aircraft cranked open, showing dirty night sky. The smell of dust filled her nostrils as it rushed in, coating everything like softly falling brown snow. They were almost down.

As they landed, the dirt rose in clouds, filling the air with fine sand. She ran down the back ramp in sequence, clumsy with the weight of the rucksack on her back and the beetle-case of her flak jacket, into the hot scour of the blast from the aircraft. She followed the dark shape of the young soldier ahead of her, through the swirling sandstorm, over shifting pebbles, to the wire fence that signalled the outer edge of the base.

A young sergeant with a clipboard led her through the warren of structures. Past the NAAFI store where knots of soldiers were sitting idly at Formica tables on a wooden porch, nursing cups of bad coffee. Past the deserted cookhouse and the giant tents, with their male and female ablution blocks, to a small accommodation tent where they'd found her a berth. He unzipped the heavy canvas outer flap and held it for her as she ducked through, her back aching from the rucksack and the cramped journey.

'Scoff from seven to eight tomorrow,' he whispered. 'You'll find the cookhouse?'

The tent was dark. She ran a torch beam along the row of green canvas camp beds to find the only one without bedding, and dropped her rucksack by it. Dark sleeping-bag caterpillars lay on most of the others. She looked quickly over the spaces between the beds, at the sand-coloured clothes-tidies hanging down from the ceiling, neatly piled with socks and shirts and books. At the rows of flip-flops, trainers and army boots tucked below. The camp bed next to hers, against the end wall, had a leaning cork board, crammed with snapshots of party groups, young women with arms round each other's shoulders, sticking out tongues, pulling faces, raising bottles of beer to the camera. They were framed by a mess of greetings cards of cartoon bears and kittens and dogs and a giant cut-out heart, emblazoned with the words: Luv ya loads!

The washing line that ran across the back of the tent was strewn with stiffly dried pink and green towels and camouflage trousers. She sat for a moment on the edge of the bed, aware of the heaviness in her limbs. I wouldn't have lasted five minutes in the army, she thought, looking round. Far too soft. And far too rebellious.

The night air was heavy with stale sweat, overlaid with the perfume of cheap talcum powder and soft with female breathing. The sudden roar of an aircraft engine cut through from outside. She listened, trying to identify it as the sound peaked, then faded away into the night. She nodded to herself. Despite all the discomfort and danger, war zones made her feel more fully alive than any other place she knew.

She dug out her towel and wash-bag and lit a path by torch to the ablution block, where she showered off the dust in a stainless-steel cubicle, punching the valve repeatedly for spurts of lukewarm water to rinse herself off. Army life. She looked at herself in the mirror as she towelled herself dry, taking in the slackness of her skin. One of these days, she thought, I'll be too old for this. But not quite yet.

Her cot would be stiff and uncomfortable, she knew. But she was exhausted. She'd sleep.

At breakfast the next day, she sat at the end of a trestle table in the cookhouse, absorbing the clatter and chat of the soldiers around her and sawing with a plastic knife at a piece of bacon in a mess of cooling baked beans. Printed notices were stuck to the inner wall of the tent with tape. 'Your Mother doesn't work here. Clean up after yourself.' Beneath it was a list of 'Rules of the Cookhouse' in smaller print. She thought of Jalil, wondering if he'd eaten here, what he'd made of life with the British army. It was still hard to believe she'd never see him again.

'Ellen?'

She looked up.

'Heard you were coming. You just in?'

John from *The Times*. She feigned a smile. He was already threading his thick legs through the gap between the chair and the table, dropping his plastic tray onto the table top. It was piled with food.

He looked smug, appraising her instinctively like a circling, sniffing dog.

'How long you here for?' His breath smelt sour with hunger. He tore open his plastic sachet of a napkin and plastic cutlery and fell on his breakfast, a mingling mush of hash browns, scrambled eggs, sausages and bacon.

'A week or so,' she said. He'd put on weight. He was starting to look middle-aged. She wondered if he were thinking the same about her. They were both the wrong side of forty. The hair at his temples was flecked with grey. The start of a double chin was showing in the slackness of his jaw. 'You?'

He was breaking a bread roll in his broad fingers, smearing it liberally with half-melted butter, inserting a sausage. His nose and cheekbones were pink with sunburn, his lips chapped.

'Same. Off to Lamesh today. If there's a place on the helo.' He started to chew, spilling breadcrumbs.

Helo. Just say helicopter, for pity's sake. John was one of those self-important war correspondents who thought they were really soldiers.

'Saw you were in Iraq last month.' He was stuffing the bread and sausage into his mouth. 'You get up to the north?'

She shook her head. 'Just Basra. You?'

'All over.' He swilled down a paper cup of orange juice. 'Bloody hairy.'

She ripped open a plastic portion of margarine and spread it on a round of toast, the plastic knife grating like a washboard. 'How's it been here?'

He spoke and chewed at the same time, swallowing his food in gulps as if he expected to be summoned to breaking news at any moment. 'Pretty good.' He nodded at her. 'Lots of bang-bang.'

'Anyone else around?'

'A newbie from the *Mail*. Left now.'

'Jeremy something?'

He screwed up his face, not much interested. 'Don't remember. And some young kid from a regional. Doing puff pieces on Our Boys.'

They sat in silence for a few minutes, chewing. He was a windbag but he was experienced. He was also a sharp operator and she didn't trust him an inch.

'Heard about Nayullah?' He scraped his fork round his plate, scooping up beans.

She nodded. She'd read the agency reports. Nayullah was a town on the new front line that had been out of bounds until recently. Now the army was trying to establish a presence there. It had just been shaken by its first suicide bomb.

He shovelled in another forkful of beans, staining his lips orange. 'Took out a few ANP. What a shower they are. But civilians, mostly. Women and children.'

The Afghan police. She'd done stories on them in Kabul. Poorly trained new recruits without kit or ethics. She'd heard they'd been the target. The bomb had exploded in the market, a day or two before Jalil died.

'Did you get down there?'

He nodded. 'That afternoon. Not pretty.' He shrugged. 'Hard to get a picture they could use.'

'Any idea who it was?'

He wiped off his tray with a crust and crammed it into his mouth. She waited until he could speak.

'Not much left to ID. Locals, not foreigners, they say. Young lads.'

He drained the last of his tea and licked his lips, his eyes darting round the soldiers as they queued to sterilize their hands or emerged with trays of food and settled to eat. He's looking for someone else, she thought, so he can trade up from me.

'Food's not bad,' he said, 'considering.'

She swished the tea round her paper cup and considered the Nayullah bomb.

'What do you make of it?'

He ignored her. A thought was crossing his face, crumpling his forehead into a frown. 'This new offensive. They letting you join it?'

She shrugged, trying not to give anything away. 'Don't know yet.'

'I've done it anyway,' he said quickly. 'Sent London a piece yesterday.'

He was comforting himself. He pushed away his tray with a lordly gesture and sat back. 'Major Mack. The Commander. You met him? Decent guy. Old school.'

She tried to steer him back to her question. 'So what about the Nayullah bomb? A reaction?'

He nodded. 'Know how much the army's pouring into this? They're knocking the Taliban off ground they've held for years. So, question is,' he brandished a finger at her, 'why aren't the rag-heads putting up a better fight?'

'And?'

He shrugged. 'They can't. Haven't got the numbers. Or the kit. But they can sure as hell slow things up. Roadside bombs. Suicide attacks. Shoot and scoot. Then disappear back into the woodwork.'

She nodded, drank her tea. The fact he was telling her this meant he must have filed on it already. Two soldiers pulled out chairs and joined their table.

'Could drag on like that for years. Thirty years' time, I reckon, we'll still be dug in here.' He pushed back his own chair, tore off a disinfectant wipe from the plastic canister on the table and ran it over the table top in front of him. She did the same. 'The Brits, I mean,' he said. 'God help me, hope I'm out by then.'

They picked up their trays and walked to the dustbins outside to dump the lot.

'Anyway,' he said, 'bugger all to do round here. Coming for a smoke?'

She sat beside him on the slatted bench in the smoking area, a secluded corner set apart from the accommodation tents. The soldiers had knocked up a rough trellis and hung it with camouflage netting for shade. A grumpy-looking soldier was installed in one corner, an ankle resting on the opposite knee, smoking silently and keeping himself to himself.

John offered her a cigarette and, when she refused, scratched a match and lit up in a rush of sulphur.

'That's new, isn't it?' He was pointing at the gold band on her wedding finger. His eyes were keen. 'You got lucky?'

She turned the ring on her finger. 'My mother's.' It felt odd. She didn't usually wear it but, when she travelled alone, it didn't hurt to look married. 'She died a few years ago.' She looked down at it, thinking of her mother. She'd had the same long fingers, a warm, strong hand to hold. 'There's a matching engagement ring. My sister's got that.'

John was laughing. 'Thought it was a turn-up,' he said. 'Always had you down as a die-hard spinster.'

The soldier opposite was looking at them. She wondered what he was thinking. He glanced away again, stony-faced.

'Maybe you'll bag yourself a nice soldier boy.' John was amusing himself, sniggering into his fug of smoke. 'You're in the right place for it.'

She turned to look at his slack-skinned face and managed to smile. Ten years ago, she would have told him to shut up, she had plenty of men in her life. Ten years ago, that was true. Nowadays she was alone and used to it and, anyway, she couldn't be bothered to argue. John wasn't worth it. He was on his third wife already.

He leaned back and drew on his cigarette. 'Anyway,' he said, 'what's your angle?'

'The usual.' She shrugged. 'Life on the front line.'

He nodded, eyes on her face, not looking convinced. 'It's a shit hole,' he said. He leant towards her, lowered his voice. 'One of the world's greatest.'

He drew on his cigarette. The smoke rose into the thick, hot air.

'Corrupt as hell, this country,' he said. He rubbed his fingers together to indicate money-grubbing. 'Can't trust them.'

'You think so?'

'I know so.' He tipped back his head and exhaled lazily. 'Even the uniforms say so. Off the record. Ask Major Mack.'

She wondered how many Afghans John actually knew. He was a master of the hack's instant guide.

'Modern democracy, here?' he said. 'All bollocks. They're stuck in the Stone Age.'

The soldier opposite them reached forward to the sand-filled mortar shell that served as an ashtray and stubbed out his cigarette. It splayed into sparks and died. Without acknowledging either of them, he heaved himself to his feet, all bulk and swagger, and left. A pause.

The morning sat slow and still on their shoulders. The muffled whine of a radio or television drifted through to them from the nearest tent. Beyond the open metal fence, past the parked container trucks and military vehicles, miles of desert lay shimmering in the gathering heat. There's nothing here to sustain life, she thought. No water, no natural shelter, no food. It's utterly desolate. This is an artificial world, built from nothing in the middle of nowhere. The Afghans must think we're crazy.

'It's like we've learnt nothing.' Next to her, John's one-sided conversation had reignited. 'Two centuries spilling blood, trying to civilize this godforsaken land, and here we are, back again.'

She stayed silent, waiting for him to finish. John was a man who liked to talk, not listen. Especially in conversation with a woman.

'Of course it matters.' He drew on his cigarette, snorted, exhaled skywards in a stream of smoke. 'Regional security. India. Pakistan. Securing the borders. All that crap. But these guys we're bankrolling? Money down the toilet.'

He coughed, spat into the sand at his feet.

'All at it. Stuffing their pockets,' he said. 'Bloody narco-state.'

She sat quietly while he cleared his throat and started to smoke again. The heat was gathering. Already her skin was desiccating, scrubbed raw by the fine sand which invaded everything.

'Do a patrol of police stations if you can. Great story.'

She smiled to herself. That meant he'd already exhausted it.

'Used syringes everywhere. Beards sitting around in dirty vests. Half of them stoned. God help us. And they're the good guys.'

She seized her chance to cut in. 'Heard one of the translators got killed,' she said. She tried to keep her tone light. 'Guy called Jalil. You come across him?'

He stuck out his lip, shook his head. 'Heard something about that. Ambushed, wasn't he?'

'Was he?'

He shrugged. 'That's what I heard. Last week? Didn't file. Two Brits died around then. In a Snatch. That was big. You see that one?'

He paused, thinking it over, then turned to her, his eyes shrewd. 'Why're you asking about the Afghan anyway?'

'No reason.' She looked him straight in the eye. 'Just wondered.'

He stubbed out his cigarette, stretched, sighed. The fumes of dying ash mingled with the smell of his sweat. 'Drugs,' he said, 'betcha. He must've been on the take.' He got to his feet. 'Or unlucky. Wrong time, wrong place.'

He coughed, wiped his mouth on his sleeve. His eyes were sunken. The putt of helicopter blades came to them softly from a distance, strengthening as they listened. They peered up into the sun-bleached sky. 'Chinook,' he said.

The throb of the blades was steadily building. She got up too to get under canvas before it came in low and whipped up a frenzy of sand.

'Dying for a drink.' He looked at her. 'You didn't by any chance . . .?'

'Booze? 'Fraid not.'

He tutted, sighed. 'Well, not long to go.'

They walked back together to the main drag, their boots clattering on the plastic military decking underfoot. As they separated, he pointed a stout finger at her, all fake bonhomie. 'I'm moving off again this afternoon. But you keep safe. Hear me?'

She nodded, shook his outstretched hand. 'I always keep out of trouble,' she said. 'You know that.'

'Yeah. Right. Like hell you do.'

She stood for a moment, watching him walk away. The thick set of his shoulders showed just the beginnings of a stoop. Anything happened to me, she thought, he'd be licking his chops in the rush to file. And then probably spell my name wrong. She turned down between the rows of tents towards her own, thinking of the vodka stashed away in her second shampoo bottle.

Inside the darkened tent, she sat on the edge of her cot and listened to the breathing of the women sleeping around her, overlaid with the stutter of the air conditioning. The joys of shift work. She closed her eyes and let herself think.

John was wrong about Jalil. He wouldn't have been mixed up in drugs or on the take. She was sure of that. If he'd been a less principled young man, heaven knows, he'd be alive and well now and far away from Helmand. She ran her hands heavily down her face. There was no escaping it. Whoever pulled the trigger, it was her fault he'd ended up in Helmand at the wrong end of a gun.

Jalil had come to her at the guesthouse in Kabul on the final afternoon of her last visit. They had worked together as usual for a fortnight, companionable but businesslike, sharing long days of dusty travel, conducting interviews in airless rooms across the capital and in hot, fly-thick shacks beyond it. They'd endured running sweat and toxic smells and sat together on filthy floors, sipping *chai* and nibbling on plates of stale sweetmeats and pastry that were barely edible but necessary to consume for the sake of politeness.

Now, on the final day of that visit, she had her story and had withdrawn to write. She was sitting in relative comfort at the desk in her room at the guesthouse, with pots of tea and good food to order and the luxury of empty hours ahead of her. She'd need them. Phil, her editor back in London, was already pushing her for copy, complaining she'd taken too long. He usually gave her a decent amount of time to research each story. A week – or even two, sometimes. But he expected a lot in return. Six- or seven-thousand-word pieces that broke new ground and were carefully crafted. Now she had the facts but she needed to focus on writing and rewriting until she had a news-feature that even Phil would consider strong enough to print.

It was at this point, when she was halfway through her second draft, that she was interrupted by a hesitant tapping at her door. She opened it to find Jalil, looking out of place amongst the kitsch foreign decor and rich fittings of the hallway.

'Come in,' she said, without thinking. Of course he wouldn't. It wouldn't be proper. Instead he stayed hovering there on the public side of the threshold with growing awkwardness. She sighed to herself and signalled to him to wait while she went back to her laptop and reluctantly turned it off. The story had just been coming together. Now her flow of thought was lost and she was irritated.

They sat together in the parched garden on wicker chairs with stained cotton cushions. She tried to press him to accept a drink – tea or fresh juice – and he politely refused. He was struggling, she could see, under a great weight of embarrassment. Her attempts to lighten the atmosphere by chatting to him only prolonged the awkwardness. Finally she fell silent and they sat, side by side, looking out at the darting birds and the startlingly bright colours of the flowerbeds, and she waited until he was ready to speak.

'It is only a loaning,' he said. 'I will pay back everything. More than everything. Interests as well.' He spoke carefully into the still heat of the garden, his voice stilted as if he'd practised his speech many times. 'We will make a proper agreement. I will pay you this much in this year and this much in the next. Like this. Very proper.'

He had the offer of a place at Pennsylvania State University to study engineering, he said. He'd applied there because the distant cousin of a friend of the family lived nearby.

'All the living is no problem for me,' he said. 'I can sleep anywhere. They have some bedroom with their sons. That's enough for me. And I can eat with them at night-time. Cheap food. Afghan food.' He twisted and untwisted his fingers in his lap, still unable to look her in the face.

Once he had his degree, he could get a good job, he said. Then he would have enough money to support his mother and sister and pay for his little brother to attend a good school.

'Everything I will pay back,' he said again. 'This loaning is for the fees.' A hint of pleading had entered his voice. 'The fees are very costly in United States. So much of money.' He tailed off. The quietness rushed in and smothered them both.

She tried to think how to phrase a reply. As she was finally about to open her mouth to try, he spoke again.

'Some of this money', he said, 'my relatives can give me. And from friends of my mother. Men who knew my father also. But not all.'

He hesitated. 'I need still more money. Maybe two, three thousand US dollars.' He was staring at his feet, his long toes, flecked with dark hairs, at the edge of his sandals. 'It is so much of money. I know. It dishonours me to ask. But it is just . . .' He broke off as if his English were failing him. 'This is a very difficult matter . . .'

He left the phrase hanging. A cat, its pregnant belly hanging low, ran across the grass in front of them. It was a mangy thing, flea-bitten and feral. They watched together as it crouched in the flowerbed, hunting.

She had been asked for money several times in her career by people she had grown to know well. People from developing countries who had no one else to ask. It was always for something significant. For a major operation for an elderly parent or for schooling for a child. She was a journalist, she told herself. An outsider who travelled, observed, reported and then moved on. She had to stay separate, to be objective. Don't interfere. Don't cross the line.

'I'd love to,' she said. She too was staring at his toes, at the neat square cut of his nails. 'Really. But I just can't. I am sorry. Perhaps I could—'

'Of course.' He interrupted her at once, nodding and waving his hand as if to bat away the awkwardness between them. 'I'm sorry. Please. Forgive me.'

Suddenly they were both on their feet, making hasty, nervous movements and hiding their shame with a flurry of meaningless arrangements, confirming what time the car would take her to the airport the next morning and discussing the final settlement of the driver's bill.

Afterwards she had gone back to her room, ordered a fresh pot of *chai sabz* and a plate of Afghan bread and jam and immersed herself in her story. It was only later, when her friend at *The New York Times* emailed to tell her about his death in Helmand, that she stopped, shaken, and really thought back. By giving up work with journalists and instead signing a contract to go into conflict zones and translate for the military, he was risking his life. Suddenly it became clear to her why he'd done it. He'd been desperate for the money so he could escape.

'Ellen Thomas?' Someone was hissing her name into the darkness, through the lifted tent flap. The tone was more accusation than question. When she emerged, a young soldier was pacing outside, looking impatient. 'The Major sent me. Follow me.'

He led her across the camp, then turned sharply right into a dim narrow corridor between hessian sandbag walls. Engineers corps, she thought. Build anything. He pushed open a plywood door and ushered her inside, down a hallway and into an office.

26

It had the dead smell of an underground bunker, ripe with dust and recycled air. It was poorly lit by low-wattage bulbs, strung on wires that were pinned in loops along the wood ceiling struts like Christmas decorations. An old air-conditioning unit was panting against one wall, making memos and notices on the board above it flutter and crack.

'Ellen?'

A short, compact man rose from behind a desk and came forward to greet her. His gaze was direct, his eyes a surprising blue. Intense, she thought at once. Intelligent. He was muscular but the creases round his eyes suggested he must be about her age, forty something. His hair was blond and clearly thinning, the dome of his head glowing warmly in the mellow light, offset by arches of thicker growth above his ears.

'Major McKay,' he said. 'But call me Mack. Everyone does.'

He pumped her hand, his fingers hard in hers.

'Thought we'd lost you,' he said. 'Coffee?'

He nodded to the young soldier who bustled about at a water heater with polystyrene cups and powdered milk and handed them drinks.

'Well.' He folded himself onto a chair and gestured to her to sit too. 'The famous Ellen Thomas. I'm honoured.'

'I'm afraid you've been misinformed.' The coffee smelt strong and stale.

He smiled, showing even teeth. Somewhere behind him, a clock was ticking. Civilizing the desert, she thought. War was surreal.

'Read a lot of your stuff,' he said. 'Brave woman. Hope we're going to pass the Thomas test here.'

She smiled back. 'Not brave,' she said. 'I just report.'

His manner was confident. Yes, she thought, in a crisis, this was a man you'd trust.

'Not sure I always agree with you, though.' He tutted. 'That piece on Basra.'

Oh no, she thought. A man with opinions on my work. She lowered her lips to her polystyrene cup and watched his face as he took issue with her argument on Iraq. His look was sharp. He was articulate, clearly. A good adversary. But a debate on Basra wasn't what she needed right now. Iraq already seemed a long time ago.

She pretended to listen, nodding in increments and scanning the room. A war room. Shared and impersonal. Desks piled with folders and papers. Behind him, a flip chart with notes written across it in marker pen in a loopy, sloping hand. 'What are we fighting for?' read the heading, underlined. Then a list: Cathedrals. Real cider. Bangers and mash. Small cottages. Little old ladies in teashops. She wondered which young wags had brainstormed that and from which part of rural England they'd been plucked. She became aware again of the clock's tick. Mack had stopped talking.

'So what's the plan?' she said. 'What's this offensive?'

He paused, watching her, then got to his feet. 'We're about to take new ground.' He drew her across to an area map tacked to the wall and used his pen as a pointer. 'Here's the camp, where we are now. Early tomorrow morning, B and C Company will move into position in this area of desert here.' He pointed to a white space some distance north into the desert. No tracks were marked. The only roads snaked from the camp in different directions, to the south and west. 'The Danes will provide backup here. The Estonians here. Once they're in place, B and C Company will launch a fresh attack here. Crossing the river at this point. Into this area of the green belt.'

She nodded, taking in the distances, the contours. There were several villages marked in the target area, clusters of squares and dots.

'How well fortified is it?'

He shrugged. 'Pretty well. The enemy's been dug in there for more than two years.'

They'll have an established underground bunker system then, she thought. Carefully constructed traps.

'Mines?'

'Almost certainly.'

She looked again at the map, trying to imagine the terrain. 'So you expect resistance. Probably a lot.'

'We're always prepared for contact with the enemy,' he said.

'Any estimate of timings?' She pointed to the first village, high on a ridge above the river. 'When do you think you'll reach here? Noon?'

'Depends.' His eyes were thoughtful. 'Depends how much resistance there is.'

She finished her coffee. She wanted to sort out her kit and repack for the field. Today might be her last chance to eat fresh food, shower and get some sleep.

'Now,' he was saying, 'you need to have a think. I have to make it clear to you: it will be dangerous out there. We can't guarantee your safety. You understand that? So you need to weigh up the risks against the gains. Of course, you're a reporter. You've got a job to do. But you may think it wise to stay in camp tomorrow. I can arrange a briefing for you here. Then the following day we can review . . .'

She dropped her cup into the dustbin and turned to face him. He came to the end of his speech and paused. 'Don't feel,' he said, 'you have to give me an answer now. Think it over.'

'I've thought,' she said. 'What time do we leave?'

3

Almost two weeks earlier

Late in the night, a sound woke Hasina. She opened her eyes with a jolt and listened. Abdul, her husband, breathed heavily beside her. The stale but comfortable animal smell of him filled her nostrils. The room was clotted with darkness. She eased herself off the cot and wound her long cotton scarf round her shoulders and head.

Outside, she poured herself water from the jug, drank a little, then wet the end of her scarf. The night air was fresh and earthy, after the breath-thick room. She crept round the side of the house, scanning the mud yard and the running blot of the low boundary wall. The goats stamped, moving nervously in a half-circle on their tethers. Beyond them, the field of standing corn stretched away in a solid dark block. She stood, hidden in the shadow of the house, and rubbed the damp tail of her scarf round her neck. Nothing.

She looked out across the land. She knew every stone, every ditch of this field as well as she knew the bumps and contours of her son's body, of her husband's body too. It was good land. It rose like a blessing out of the barren desert, green fields made fertile by the sudden appearance of the river. The soil had fed as many generations of her husband's family as anyone could remember. Like the people, it struggled to stave off exhaustion. She ran her eyes along the raised ridge, looking for fresh signs of collapse.

When the rains were heavy, the top layer could lift and run away with the torrents of water. Their carefully dug irrigation channels silted up and, once the rain stopped, they squelched through them, feeling the mud ooze between their toes, to sieve the earth between their fingers and pile it back.

But at this time of year, in the long stifling hope of rain, it was baked hard, a sunken square of land that they struggled to keep moist. The first crop of the year was long since harvested. The second crop – corn for themselves and poppy to sell to Abdul's brother, Karam – was growing higher, day by day. She sniffed the air, tasting the health of the plants. The first harvest had been average. This second one held more promise.

She settled on a stone and rocked herself. Somewhere out in the desert, wild dogs were calling to each other. A low breeze was blowing in from the plains. She wrapped her moist scarf across her face, shielding her eyes from the lightly swirling sand.

Then she heard it. A tiny human explosion: a sneeze. She lowered the rim of her scarf. Someone was out there, hiding in the corn. She listened, her senses raw. After some time, a barely audible rustle, as if someone, deep in the cornfield, were shifting their weight.

She crept forward, one slow step at a time, feeling out the ground with each foot. She made her way, bent double, down the side of the field, balancing on the thin strip between the last planted row and the ditch. Every few paces, she stopped and listened.

Finally she heard breathing. Short, shallow breaths. She turned towards the centre of the corn and reached forward to ease apart the corn stems, as if she were parting a curtain. She let out a sudden cry. Crouched in front of her, looking right into her eyes, so close she could reach out and touch him, was a young man, a stranger, his head wrapped in the printed cotton scarf of the jihadi fighter. A brass talisman gleamed on a leather thong round his neck. It was in the shape of a bird, its wings spread and claws outstretched. The young man frowned. The thin moonlight caught the metal casing of the gun he held across his body, its muzzle a matter of inches from her bending head.

The three young men perched on the perimeter wall and lit up fat cigarettes. Hasina's son, Aref, sat beside them, the only one without a gun propped against his legs. Hasina recognized the acrid smell of fresh hashish. Aref smoked too, when the cigarette was offered, but self-consciously. They were teasing him, laughing and calling him 'little brother'. Such arrogance. Hasina wanted to slap their faces. They thought they were so clever, these boys with guns. They were nothing more than trouble-makers, with their bullets and bombs. Whatever they called themselves, Leftists, jihadis, mujahideen. She'd seen so much death already.

Moving quietly, she poured water into cups and offered it to them. They reeked of stale sweat. She tried not to let her dis-approval show. Even the poorest villager showed respect to his body by keeping clean.

As the young men smoked, she pulled Aref away and took him to the back of the house. His eyes were sullen.

'Who are these boys?' she said. 'Why have you brought them to our home? Have you no respect?'

He scowled. 'They are my brothers.'

'Brothers?' She stared at him. 'How do you know them?'

Aref turned his eyes to the earth. 'Karam Uncle,' he said.

Hasina blinked. Karam? He had dark contacts, she knew that. Selling poppy to them had made his fortune. But fighters, like these?

'You've met them before?'

'Many times.' He gave a thin smile. 'I have trained with them.' He lifted his hands as if he were aiming a gun at her. 'You never knew, did you?'

What a child, she thought. She saw triumph in his eyes. What would Abdul say? Those times Aref had disappeared for two, three days on Karam's business. Was it for this? She wanted to take hold of his shoulders and shake him hard. Instead she reached for his hand. 'Aref, these are not decent boys.'

'Not decent?' He swatted her away. 'These men are fighting. Defending our land. Not decent?'

Hasina sighed. Beside them the goats shuffled and pressed, hot and pungent, against her. She thought of that face, so close to hers in the corn. He looked little more than a boy, but his eyes, hard and knowing, were old.

'Where are they from?'

Aref gestured vaguely. 'Beyond Nayullah.'

'They should go home, Aref. Back to their families.'

Her son was looking at her the way some men in the village looked at their wives, as if women had no more brains than a goat.

'They're fighters. Not farmers.' He spat out the word with disdain. 'They're fighting for Allah.'

Behind them, one of the young men let out a barely stifled laugh. She froze, frightened the noise would wake Abdul.

'Bring them to the back,' she said. She untied the goats and led them out into the clearing. 'I'll fetch food.'

She sat in the shadow of the wall and watched them. They bristled with tense excitement as they whispered and sniggered. They didn't attempt to wash. They kicked the area clean of goat droppings and dirty straw and half sat, half lay on the mud. Once they'd pulled off their boots, they fell on the food she'd given them. Their long-nosed guns lay at their sides. Aref sat with his arms curled tightly round his knees, a look of devotion on his face.

What lives were these boys leading, fleeing across the desert as the foreigners advanced? The boys were settling to sleep now, their arms round their guns as if they were wives. Their faces had relaxed. Sleep was turning them to boys again. She imagined their mothers, lying in the darkness in small mud-brick houses like their own. She bowed her head and tried to pray for them, to beg Allah to give them His guidance and keep them safe from harm.

But all she could see when she closed her eyes was the eager face of her own son, loyal as a dog at their feet.

When she woke at first light, the young men had disappeared. So had Aref. He must be guiding them off the village land. An hour or two, then he'd be back. She waited, listening for his step every moment as she swept and cooked. Morning passed. When she took food to Abdul in the fields, she stayed with him as he ate. Should she tell him? She read the exhaustion in his face and held her tongue. By mid-afternoon, she was desperate. She straightened her skirts and walked through the village to the grand compound of her brother-in-law, Karam.

Her sister-in-law, Palwasha, was lying on her side on a crimson carpet. It was decorated with geometric designs in black, yellow and cream. The colours were strong and bright. Abdul's wealthy brother had sent his first wife back to her family for failing to bear children. Now he spoiled his second wife with costly gifts. Hasina pursed her lips. Before this, only the mosque had been decked with carpets.

Palwasha was pulling at her elder daughter's hair, tugging it into tight plaits. Sima was grimacing. Palwasha's wrists tinkled with bracelets as she flexed her arms.

'I should never have come to live here,' Palwasha said as soon as she saw Hasina. Her eyes, heavily circled with kohl, rolled dramatically. 'I told Karam I would simply die. I'm a town girl. People should remember that.' She looked sullenly at Hasina. 'Why am I telling you?' she said. 'You never understand a thing.'

Hasina settled herself on the compact mud, some distance from the edge of the carpet. Palwasha talked such nonsense. The village women said her family had married her off to Karam because they were in debt.

'Of course, sister-in-law,' Hasina said. 'Life here must seem very harsh to you.'

Sima squirmed, struggling to break free. Palwasha slapped her leg. Sima's breathing juddered as she tried not to cry.

'Primitive!' Palwasha muttered. 'You're so right.'

She finished plaiting and pushed Sima away. The girl crept out into the compound to join her young brother, Yousaf, and sister, Nadira, chasing chickens and setting them flapping through the straw.

'How are your good mother and father?' Hasina spoke the ritual greetings politely. 'Your younger sister? May Allah grant them good health.'

Palwasha didn't bother to answer. A younger woman should show respect. It was Hasina's due. But they took their status from their husbands. Abdul was just a farmer. Karam was rich.

'The village is hard for you,' Hasina tried again. She looked at the thick carpet under Palwasha's thigh, the expensive brass pots and plates stacked in the corner behind her. 'But perhaps,' she went on, 'in these troubled times, we are safer here.'

'Safer?' Palwasha was picking at her polished nails. 'May God help us! If I have to die, please, not here. That would be too cruel.' She let out a sudden laugh.

'The foreign soldiers are advancing, sister-in-law.' Hasina proceeded carefully. 'Have you heard? They're already in Nayullah.'

Palwasha rolled over onto her back. 'What does it matter?' she said. 'No one ever comes here.' She is just a girl, Hasina thought, looking at her long body, stretched out, petulant, on the floor.

'Besides,' Palwasha added, 'my husband has powerful friends.' She sat up and crossed her legs carefully, as if posing for a portrait. 'In another year, the foreigners will be gone. Then Karam and I will move to the city.'

Hasina breathed deeply. She rarely visited Palwasha nowadays. The girl had so few brains. 'Sister-in-law,' she said, 'I am worried about Aref. Have you seen him?'

'Aref?' Palwasha's eyes narrowed. 'Why would he be here?'

'To see your husband, perhaps.'

'Karam's not here.' Palwasha frowned, her mood changing. She languidly stretched her legs, one at a time. 'He'll be back tonight, *inshallah.*' She rose and left the room, leaving Hasina staring at emptiness.

In the evening, when Abdul had eaten, Hasina crept back to Karam's compound. She had barely swallowed a mouthful all day. Her mouth was too dry, her stomach too twisted with fear.

She tapped on the metal gate. One of Karam's men opened the inner door and peered out. She waited inside, her back pressed back against the wall, until Karam's broad silhouette emerged from the house.

'Sister-in-law?'

She bowed low. 'Karam brother-in-law. I am so sorry to trouble you. But—'

'Aref?'

She looked up sharply. 'You know where he is?'

'Of course. He is about my business.'

Hasina felt her knees buckle. 'Your business?' She held his gaze. 'The young men. I saw them.'

Karam's expression soured. 'Some things', he said, 'should be left unspoken.'

She pulled her scarf across her face. Karam looked round, as if for eavesdroppers, before he spoke in a low voice.

'Of course he has gone,' he said. 'It is his duty.'

She looked at the large compound, the servants, the animals. She knew where the money came from. From poppy. Karam was beholden to these fighting men. But Aref?

'He is so young.' She thought of his boyish face, his foolishness. 'If anything happens to him . . .' Her voice trailed off. What hope did these young boys have? She knelt before him and raised the trailing cloth of her scarf on the flat of her hands, beseeching him.

'Go home to your husband.' He turned away, embarrassed at her begging, and took a step back. 'My brother needs to control his wife. Do I need to teach him?'

Hasina tried to steady her voice. 'No, brother-in-law,' she said.

36

Someone moved in the shadows behind her. The bolt on the inner gate slid back, inviting her to leave.

'He has a chance', Karam whispered as he pulled her to her feet, 'to defend his people. To do God's will. You should be proud.'

As she stepped through, the gate clanged shut behind her. Outside, she sank against the compound wall, her face buried in her hands, her scarf stuffed against her mouth to stifle the sound, and sobbed.

The night after Aref's disappearance, she found no sleep at all. The night cries and howls outside were full of menace. Aref was somewhere out there, in a ditch or cornfield. Hungry. Afraid. Had they made him go, those boys? She turned onto her side and drew up her knees. Aref had looked so smug when he spoke of training with them. Training to fight? She wrapped her arms round her body in anguish. Had Karam really sent their boy to these hotheads? Recently, Aref had gone off on Karam's business more often, sometimes for several days. Selling poppy, she'd thought. They hadn't asked questions. But training with these foolish, fired-up boys? She moaned to herself. Beside her, Abdul stirred.

They had welcomed Karam's interest in Aref. They had let him influence their boy. He had power and money. Abdul trusted his elder brother with his life. What would he say, if all this were true?

She twisted on her front, buried her face in her shawl. And now the foreign soldiers were waging war against them. She put her fist to her mouth. She was cold with fear. Abdul would never believe that Karam would put their son in danger. She must tread carefully. Allah alone knew how.

As soon as she saw first light, she got up. She tried to wash the exhaustion out of her body with cool water, then forced herself to start her chores. Abdul emerged, yawning, to find much of her work already done.

'I'll go to the big market today,' she told him while he ate.

'I need spices. And my cooking pot is cracked. These village ones are useless.'

'Cracked?' He looked up. 'But it's new.'

Hasina spread her hands. 'Why quarrel over a pot?' she said. 'Anything you need?'

He shrugged. He was already finishing his bread and tea. He dipped into his pocket and pulled out some crumpled notes. 'Spend it with care,' he said.

She waited until he had set off for the fields. She wrapped her best shawl around her head and shoulders, making sure her hair was properly covered, and picked her way along the edge of the fields, down the hillside towards the riverside track. Her body settled into the rhythm of the long walk to Nayullah.

The big market was held every week but she didn't go often. It took a whole morning and, besides, they couldn't afford to buy much. Today she'd needed a reason to walk. If she stayed in the fields all day, her worry would suffocate her. She looked out across the river, at the thick reeds breaking the water, the flies in a low black cloud on the surface. She'd bought treats at the market for Aref when he was a boy. Nuts and sweets in twists of coloured paper. Cheap plastic toys. How he'd loved them. She wiped off her forehead with the end of her scarf. Now where was he?

She lengthened her stride. The sunlight was bouncing sharp and clean off the water at her side. It was a blessing from Allah, the river. The land around it was green with ripening corn and low foliage. A lizard ran into the path in front of her, froze, then darted for cover. When she raised her eyes to look beyond the river, the desert softly shimmered in the heat, stretching away to the horizon, endlessly thirsty and barren.

A boy came slowly towards her, herding goats along the river bank. He was a gawky child. She nodded to him as he approached but he slid his eyes away, embarrassed. He clicked his tongue at the goats, slapping at them with a long switch. The goats knocked and stumbled against each other. They filled the narrow path and she stepped into the scrub to let them pass. For some moments, the air was suffused with the low tinkling of the bells at their necks and the thick pungent scent of hot goat.

She walked on, thinking. Since she could remember, there'd always been fear and fighting here and restless young men eager to kill. Her own family's village had been razed by the Leftists when she was a girl. The baker and his wife tortured and killed. No one would tell her why. Their children, her playmates, had been sent around the village to grow up with cousins. Sad children, after that, with fewer friends. When would it end? She thought again of Aref. The way those young men had strutted like cockerels, all self-importance. Such foolishness.

As she finally approached the market, she quickened her pace. The stalls were spilling out along both sides of the dirt road and deep into the land behind it. She looked over the hawkers. That was someone she recognized, that farmer. Over there, another. Regulars from a nearby village. She'd bought from them since they were boys. Baskets woven by their wives. Clay pots. Vegetables and fruit. They were seated silently on the edge of the large cloths they'd rolled out over the dirt. Something about their stillness made her uneasy.

She walked further, past a fat row of dented trucks. The metalwork flashed with sunlight. More outsiders. Vegetables gave way to bales of used garments and second-hand shoes, hillocks of garish foreign plastic, buckets and bowls. The old men and boys who sat with these goods, cross-legged, their feet bare, were strangers.

Her head was starting to ache. A volley of cries from crackling loud-hailers. Cages of chickens squawked and clawed. Young men were cooking up snacks in pots, flipping them with flattened knives. The smell of frying oil hung heavy in the air. How Aref loved oily snacks when he was a child. What would those boys with guns give him to eat today?

A young boy, weighed down by a bulging bag, came running towards her. He stuck to her side, brandishing a plastic bottle of juice. He pushed it in her face, urging her to buy. She swatted him away. Across the road, a group of young men skidded to a halt on motorbikes, kicking up dust. They wore dark glasses and faded foreign T-shirts, cotton scarves tied loosely round their necks. They were whooping and showing off. They called out insults to a passing group of mothers and daughters. The young women pulled their scarves more closely round their faces. Hasina hesitated.

A sudden movement caught her eye, down beyond the market, towards Nayullah. There were men in the road, waving their arms and flagging down vehicles. The sun glinted on metal at their chests. She screened her eyes to look. Guns.

They were Afghans, not foreigners. They wore shabby uniforms, bunched in folds at the waist. There was a barrier in the road. They were stopping passing vehicles, forcing them to pull in to the side and be searched. At that moment, a motorbike came roaring through, two young men clinging to the seat. Behind it a battered pickup truck, open at the back like a farmer's vehicle, was forced to a halt. Were the men in uniform asking the drivers for money? Who were they? She frowned. This was something new. It unsettled her.

She turned in from the street and picked her way down the narrow mud aisles between the stalls. The clamour flowed over her. Last time she was here, she'd bought boots for Aref. He'd be wearing those boots now. She looked round, trying to get her bearings. The second-hand shoe stall had gone. Everything looked different. The stalls seemed brasher, the shouting stallholders more aggressive. Other shoppers barged and jostled her, as some pressed their way forward, others forced their way past. Every time someone stopped to examine the goods, crouching down to turn over in their hands a plastic sandal or cotton scarf, they became a rock in the stream, damming up the crowd behind them.

Hasina began to feel light-headed with the noise, the heat and her lack of sleep. Through the crowd, she saw a face she recognized.

A fruit-seller. An old man from a village near town. She pushed her way towards him.

'May Allah bless and protect you,' she said to him. 'And all your family.'

'And may He also bless and protect yours.' He got to his feet, pushed his toes into his sandals. His cap was dusty. He moved to the side, clearing a small space at the side of his stall so she could step in from the thoroughfare.

'So busy today,' she said. She wiped her face with her shawl.

'Yes, so many people.' He gestured to her to sit, then turned from her to his goods. He had arranged a display of oranges in a carefully balanced pyramid, small misshapen pieces of fruit, picked too early in the season. He spent time choosing one, then sliced it open over the earth with his knife and handed her a piece to suck. The sweetness of the juice made her heady. He settled down, cross-legged, beside her, and smiled as he watched her eat, showing, through his grey beard, black stumps of teeth.

She sucked on the orange, pulling her scarf forward round her face. In front of them, the crowd streamed past. 'How is business?'

The old man spread his hands. Hasina saw the bulging veins running along their backs. 'Like this, like that,' he said. 'When the rains come, then it will be better.'

'Yes, let's pray for rain soon.'

They nodded. The fat man at the next stall began to shout through a loud-hailer, urging passers-by to stop and look. The rich smell of the orange cut into the stale sweat all around her.

'I've never seen so many vehicles,' she said.

The old man scowled. 'And those new police, you saw them?' He wagged his finger at her. 'Thugs. The foreigners give them guns.'

Hasina felt the orange thicken in her throat. The policemen's guns must be good then. Better than the country-made weapons of the fighters. She threw the orange peel behind her onto the ground, wiped her sticky fingers on her scarf.

'So much trouble.' She looked round. No one was close enough to hear. 'More killing in town, I hear.'

The old man raised his hands to the sky. 'Every day.'

They sat with their heads close, whispering in each other's ears in the midst of the hubbub, as if they were sheltering together under a tree in a violent storm.

'The foreign soldiers have built a camp in the desert,' he said. 'Just a few miles outside Nayullah. They're trying to shake out all the . . .' He paused, hesitating as he chose his word. '. . . the fighters.'

She nodded. 'I heard.'

'Every day they drive through the streets, big guns pointing everywhere, shouting at us all.' He shook his head. 'The children throw stones. Everyone's afraid.' He coughed, spat to the side.

'First the Russians, now the Americans,' Hasina said. 'When will they leave us in peace?'

The old man tutted agreement. 'Today, even people from town have walked out here.' He paused, gestured about him with an outstretched arm. 'People are frightened to go to market in town in case the foreigners come. How many are being killed?' He lowered his voice to a murmur. 'Killed or just disappeared.'

Hasina closed her eyes. She felt the ground beneath her sway and put her hand to her face. Her fingers, close to her nose, stank of orange. When she opened her eyes again, the old man was looking at her with concern.

She swallowed hard. 'Will we ever see peace?'

'We chased off the Russians. But it cost a lot of blood.' He paused, looked away into the blur of the crowd. 'All the bombing. My old body doesn't matter. But the young people, the children . . .' He sighed.

A passer-by stopped to examine the oranges. The old man got to his feet and invited him to taste one. The man walked on without speaking. The old man settled back. 'These people,' he said. 'No manners.'

His expression suddenly lightened as he remembered something. He reached in his pocket to pull out a grimy photograph.

A cheap studio portrait, creased with wear. It showed a couple, uncomfortable in new clothes, posing stiffly with an infant. 'See,' he said. His face shone with pride. 'I have a grandson now. Finally! After so many years of just girls. Praise be to Allah!'

'What a blessing,' she said. 'I'll pray he grows up safe and healthy.' She got to her feet.

'Pray he grows up safe,' he whispered. 'And not speaking American.'

She bought spices and, at a hardware stall, bargained for a stout cooking pot. She started back along the road. The cries from the market stalls were garish in her ears. Her hand steadied the pot on her head. The young boy, hawking his local juice, ran up again as soon as he saw her, pushing the bottles in her face. She fended him off with her free hand.

'Have you no manners?' she said. The boy paused, backed off a little. 'Weren't you taught to show respect?' He took a step towards her again. 'Well, weren't you?'

She was punched in the back of the head. Struck hard. Pitched forward. Knocked down. A deep, resonant boom. Powerful as thunder. Her bones vibrated with it. Her face smacked into the ground. Deafened. Dust filled her eyes. Her mouth. A wave of sickness. Her limbs were shaking, drumming the ground in spasms. She blinked frantically, trying to see. She managed to lift her head. The broken shards of the pot were rocking from side to side in the road.

She lay still. She must breathe. The world must settle into place again. Alive. Praise Allah. She was alive. She closed her eyes. She was sinking. Her limbs were like stones. Still and heavy, held by the ground. She tried again to lift her head, to open her eyes. She was breathing now. The air stank. Petrol. Burning cloth. A stench of singed meat. Her stomach was convulsing. Around her, a blur of fast-moving shapes. People were running. Arms were waving in and out of clouds of dust. She could hear nothing. Was she dying? No. A pop. She was bursting up from the bottom of a well. Raw sound broke into her ears. Screaming. Men shouting. Feet beating on the road.

The soft tang of fruit pulp broke near her face. Rivulets of juice running in the dust. Bubbling as it sank into the ground, turning it to mud. The small boy. His bottles. Burst. She sensed him scrambling to his feet beside her. He peered into her face. His brown eyes wide with terror. A sweet boy. Like Aref. She shouldn't have scolded. He was staring past her, back down the road, towards the market. Something there. What? She eased her head from the ground. Twisted her neck. Black smoke hung, thick and oily. A tall orange flame. A flame dirty with smoke, bent like a person staggering. She let her face fall back to the dust. Exhausted. Someone was tugging at her. A frightened voice in her ear. 'Get up, Auntie. Get up.' The boy.

Finally she managed to sit. She was in the road. In the way. People were crying. Hugging children. A man, running, stepped on her hand. His arms were brimming with shoes, snatched up from somewhere. A plastic sandal fell in the dirt beside her. Green. Shiny. How stupid, she thought. To steal an odd shoe.

The boy had run towards the smoke. Now he came running back. His face was contorted. He knelt in the dirt, took hold of her shoulders and shook them.

'Get up.' He seemed ready to cry. Why didn't he leave her be? He was pulling on her arms. She got onto her knees, then to her feet. She stood uncertainly. Swaying. Her scarf was in folds at her neck, her head exposed. She lifted it back into place. She felt sick. Her head was dizzy with fumes, with noise. Maybe she should sink down and sit again. The boy, pulling at her, was agitated.

'What?' she said. 'What now?'

He lifted his hand and pointed down the road to the wreckage. 'The policemen,' he said. 'Look!'

She tried out her legs. They were shaking. She took a step. The boy buzzed about in front of her. She was intact. She was alive. He seized her hand and pulled her forward, down the road.

A ring of people had formed. A tight crowd. Men stood, silent with shock. Others draped their arms round shoulders and craned forward to see. Their arms and heads were blocking her view.

The boy had crouched to look through the legs. She sank down beside him. The flame was burning quietly in a sheath of smoke. It was thin and dying, rising from a greasy heap of twisted metal. The fumes filled her mouth. The air was shuddering with its heat.

She twisted to see through the gaps. She could make out the mangled remains of vehicles. She couldn't tell how many. Too many blackened parts. Many were blown some distance. They smouldered where they lay. Scattered fragments of metal, of glass, covered the surface of the road. Dark pools of oil, others of blood, stained the dust. Splashes of black and deep red against brown.

She sat heavily. The boy was pulling at her sleeve, pointing. She couldn't look. The heat of the fire, the press of the men, was making her giddy. She tasted bile and tried to swallow it back. She put her hand to her mouth. 'I'm sick,' she said. No one was listening.

The boy was still tugging. She lifted her head. Through the legs and the shifting smoke, she made out figures slumped along the road. A policeman, his torso drenched in blood. On his side. A woman, her hair blackened with soot. Sitting. Bent over the shape of a child stretched across her lap. A man, staggering, his hands grasping the air. A boy, staring about him in confusion. A police radio, abandoned on the ground, suddenly sparked into life, pumping out voices from far away. She covered her eyes with her hands. Too much. How could this happen? The fading smell of orange was still on her fingers. Dizziness enfolded her in waves. She lowered her head to her lap.

The sounds swelled and faded and swelled again in her ears. She sat. She had to get home. How would she get home? She shifted her feet. The soles of her sandals stuck to the filth in the road. Two men beside her were talking in low voices. She opened her eyes, looked up at them. Their faces swam.

'What happened?' She didn't bother with the customary greetings.

'Bombs,' said one of the men. 'Maybe two.' He gestured towards the debris. 'Suicide bombers.'

45

'Who?' She had clasped his leg, digging her nails into his cotton trousers. 'Who did it?'

He leaned back from her, his face closing. 'Who knows?'

Aref. Could he be . . .? She crawled frantically into the crowd. Pushing herself forward through the legs like a dog. A young man barred her way with his foot. She knocked it away. She was nearing the front. Voices above. Men moved aside for her. Now the heat from the fire was scorching. She blinked, stared in disbelief. The horror. Soot-blackened corpses. Hair burned. Flesh swollen and bubbling as it cooked. A single arm, severed. Lying with its knuckles to the ground, fingers curling. Half a man's body. A pair of trousers still clinging, drenched with blood, to the legs. She moaned. She couldn't look. Her elbows gave way. Her face fell to the dirt. She was shaking too much to move.

Her mind was bursting. Images seared her eyes. Her throat burned with acid. Abdul. I must reach Abdul. She was sobbing, rocking herself. It wasn't true. Couldn't be true. Allah, in His mercy, would never allow it. Such wickedness. Such mutilation. She started to wail. A strangled sound. High-pitched with pain. She had seen another thing. Too terrifying to bear. Limp on the ground, blackened and pockmarked, a brass talisman. Still threaded on a scrap of leather. In the shape of a bird with its wings spread and claws outstretched.

A man was dragging her away, scolding her. The boy's face was in hers, hovering with big eyes. The crowd around her was being broken up. A thickset man seized hold of her shoulders and propelled her forward, away from the flames, the bodies. He was stern-faced. Get away, he kept saying. Go home. The foreign soldiers are coming. Go! A mess of people tugged at her.

She didn't know how she got home. She had a sense of running, stumbling, arms outstretched. Calling Abdul. Aref. She made it just inside the hut, then collapsed on the ground in the cool darkness. She flattened her palms against the mud, clinging to it. The earth was spinning out of control. Her stomach turned. Her body, exhausted, ached. She banged the flat of her hands against the ground. She dug her fingernails into the earth, scraping them along the smooth earth, and howled. Her eyes were already blind with weeping.

As she lay there, pounding the floor with her hands, all she could hear were the voices. A pitiful voice which refused to believe it. Maybe he's safe. Maybe he wasn't there. Maybe he said No and left them. Even as her mind tried to think this, a second voice was louder, tolling like a bell, saying: it's over, it's over, my boy, my Aref, he's gone. The smell of burning flesh seemed to cling to her.

Her face was flattened against the mud. Cool against her cheek. Darkness. After some time, she didn't know how long, she heard shuffling and whispering. A very ordinary noise. It seemed to drift down to her from across a vast divide. She lay still, trying to block it out. The noise grew louder.

A small hand brushed against her hair, tentative at first and soft, then a little firmer as it stroked. Another hand patted her back, light rhythmical taps, the way a child might bounce a ball. She let herself sob a little more, leaking tears and mucus into the wet mud round her face. The hands paused, stopped. There was whispering. She tried to ignore it, to shut out the world, to focus on her grief, her pain. After a few minutes, the hands started again to pat, to stroke.

Something landed on the mud beside her head, smooth skin rubbing up against her temple, nuzzling her. She lifted her head a fraction and opened her eyes. A pair of clear brown eyes were an inch or two from her face, full of worry and puzzlement.

'Hasina Auntie?' Sima asked. 'What's wrong?'

She closed her eyes again, let her head fall back to the wet mud. She could sense the other children as well. That must be Nadira who was patting her back and crooning nonsense in a low voice, as if she were soothing a favourite doll. Hasina could hear Yousaf too. He was out in the back, perhaps, talking to the goats, petting them and setting them twitching on their tethers.

Hasina tried again to lift her face. Her head was throbbing. She should just die here. Coming back to life was too hard, too painful.

'We came to see you,' Sima said. She reached in to Hasina and tried to wipe off her filthy face with her scarf. 'To say hello.'

Hasina couldn't speak. She let the girls prod her into a sitting position, rested her back against the cot. She looked sightlessly at the dead legs stretched out in front of her, worn out with running.

Sima tried to bend herself into Hasina's vision. 'Hasina Auntie,' she said, 'shall I fetch Mother?'

Hasina shook her head. May God protect her from that foolish woman. Sima disappeared. Hasina could feel the warm shape of Nadira cuddled beside her. She was still patting Hasina, now on the thigh.

Sima reappeared with a cup of water. 'Drink this,' she said. She pushed it into Hasina's hands. 'Water is very good for health. You'll feel much better.'

She took the water and drank. It was cool and pure in her dirty mouth. I might get better, she thought suddenly. What if I were to survive and carry on without him? What an insult that would be. She fell to weeping again, her hands to her face. The small arms of the girls hung on her wherever they could find purchase.

The children stayed with her all afternoon. They crouched beside her, gazing at her with anxious eyes, until she finally stopped crying. Then, as she sat there, worn and indifferent, they started to prattle.

'I like your house,' Sima said. 'It's quiet.' She pulled Nadira to her feet, took both her hands and started to turn with her. 'There's always someone shouting in ours. It's too noisy.'

Hasina let her chin fall to her chest. It will always be quiet here now. It is a dead house.

The girls started to spin, bumping into the cots. They fell in a heap, giggling. Hasina watched them dully.

'Will you tell us more?' Sima said. She rolled onto her stomach and kicked up her legs behind her. 'Your story. About the village and the children.'

'Please, Hasina Auntie!' Yousaf had appeared in the doorway. 'No one tells us stories except you.'

Hasina, looking at him, thought of Aref. Aref's face when he was a boy. The long lashes that veiled his eyes, the softness of his skin, his milky smell. She turned her face away from them. 'There is no more story,' she said.

Late in the afternoon, she took the children home. She heard Palwasha scold them as they went into the house, the slap of a hand on bare skin. Where had they been? Thoughtless creatures.

Hasina sank to the ground, there in the compound yard, her legs too weak to bear her. When Palwasha came out with strong sweet tea, Hasina left it sitting beside her in the dirt, steaming, until it was cold and wasted.

Finally Karam came out. He crouched beside her and put his hand on her shoulder.

'I salute you,' he said in a low voice, 'precious mother of a martyr. May Allah bless you.'

Hasina didn't look at him.

'You shouldn't have seen it,' he said. 'That was wrong.' He put his hand under her chin and lifted her face. 'You must keep this secret.'

She stared at him. What could he be thinking? How could she possibly . . .?

'Remember the gossip in the village after the death of Masoud's son.' Karam's eyes were stern. 'He was a martyr.' He paused. 'But not everyone understood.'

Hasina did remember. People said the boy brought danger to the village. No one wanted their own sons to copy him.

Karam took her arm, pulled her roughly to her feet. For a moment, she thought her legs would falter. But Karam's hand was gripping her, keeping her upright. 'Go home,' he said. 'Say nothing.'

She stared, bewildered. How could she bear this loss in silence, alone, without the comfort of her husband? How was that possible? 'But Abdul—'

'I will tell him the boy has gone away. To Kandahar. For now, you must say nothing.'

He was propelling Hasina forward towards the gate. His grip cut into her flesh.

'Abdul trusts me,' he said. He turned her to face the compound gate, to leave. 'You must trust me too.' He opened the gate and half guided, half pushed her through into the road. 'You should be joyful,' he said. '*Alhamdulillah*. Thanks be to Allah.'

4

Two days after the market bombing, Hasina dreamt of Aref and woke, wondering. It was late in the night. In the yard, the stars were strong, the moon almost fully grown. The shapes of the land shone in the half-light. The stones, the ditches, the corn, high as a man. The rich, earthy scent of it. Their home. Their land.

She went to sit on the large flat stone at the top of the fields. The mud was cold under her feet. She drew her shawl round her shoulders. The first chill of autumn. She tried to calm herself, leaning her mind into the scream of insects in the undergrowth at her feet.

The foreign soldiers were coming. Everyone said so. Where would she and Abdul go, if they were driven off their land? She shuddered. Impossible, she thought, that Allah, who had given them this land, this blessing on His people, would force them to leave it.

She closed her eyes. Images swarmed into her head, dancing and weaving. Aref's presence. She could feel him. The warm scent of his body, first as a small boy, then as an awkward young man. This is my grief, she told herself. Grief is making his ghost rise and come back to me. She reached out her hands, imagining her fingertips on his skin.

A stick cracked in the corn. She kept still. Better to keep the dream, she thought, and be slaughtered where I sit, than to lose my Aref, my boy, a second time. The rustle in the corn grew louder, closer. Finally, she opened her eyes.

The air was silvery with moonlight. The noise was in the field, just a few metres from her. An animal, perhaps. Or the slow stealth of a person. Was that a low dark shape, crouching? She crept forward to peer into the corn.

His ghost was haunting her. She blinked. How fat he was, his stomach rounded. Then she made out the rags tied round his middle, stained with patches of black. When he raised his eyes, his face was pallid. The face of the dead. She stretched out her arms.

'Aref?'

He lifted himself to his hands and knees and crawled towards her.

'My Aref?'

He collapsed half at her feet, half across her knee. She buried her face in his neck, inhaling him. She patted him with fluttering hands, her fingers working him as if they were kneading bread. She took possession again of each hollow, each joint, each rib, each knob of spine, relearning his body for herself, the way she'd first learned it when he was put into her arms as a new baby, all those years before. He was moaning quietly. When her hands reached his face, her fingers were black and wet with blood. In stroking him, she smeared his cheeks, his chin.

She rocked him hard, encircling him with her arms to keep him safe. He lay, limp, and surrendered to her.

She expected the dream to end. When her arms began to ache, she pulled back her face to look. His forehead and cheeks were moist with sweat, his skin chilled. She lifted her fists and pummelled him in the chest.

'How could you?' she heard herself saying. His body was jumping, jolted by her hammering fists. 'How could you leave me?'

He raised his arms and groped for her wrists. His grasp was weak. Her anger dissolved into weeping.

'Aref,' she moaned. 'You precious fool.'

'I need to hide,' he whispered. 'Just until I'm strong again.'

Hasina half dragged, half walked him along the ridge at the top of the fields, away from the village. Along the outer edge of their land, Abdul had dug an irrigation channel for flash floods. Now it was dry. She searched for the most hidden stretch and cleared away the stones there. Aref lay on his back in the channel, his eyes glazed. The earth sides were smooth and steep, as if he lay already in his grave.

Hasina cradled his head in her lap. She was afraid to look at his wound. The rags were matted together in clumps, fused with dried blood. When she tried to touch them, he pushed her hand away.

'I could clean it,' she said.

He shook his head.

'What happened?' she said. 'Those boys. I know what they did. But you . . .?'

He looked embarrassed. 'It didn't work,' he said. He gestured to his stomach. 'The belt. It didn't go off.' He raised his head to look at her. 'It wasn't me,' he said. His tone was defensive. 'I did it just the way they taught me.'

'Of course,' she said. 'Of course you did.'

He let his head fall back. She tried to imagine him with explosives strapped round his body, ready to blow himself into pieces. What he must have felt and what madness made him want to say 'Yes' to those crazy boys.

'There was a flash,' he said. 'White light. Then burning round my stomach. I realized I was still alive, on my back in the dirt.'

His voice was trembling. Hasina took his hand and squeezed it. 'How did you get away?'

'I ran. I waved my arms and shouted. There was so much smoke, so much shouting, one more person didn't seem to matter.'

'And you hid?'

'In the fields.' He gestured to a cotton pouch at his side, bulging above the contour of his hip. 'I have a weapon,' he said. 'A bomb.'

'Let me take it,' she said. She held out her hand. 'I could bury it.'

He shook his head. 'It's not for a woman.'

She looked again at the pouch. 'Bury it yourself then,' she said. 'You're safe now.'

He fell silent. 'If they find out,' he said at last, 'they'll call me a coward.'

'No.' Hasina stroked the hair from his forehead. 'They will not find out. God has sent you back to me. He will protect us.'

His eyes had closed. She wrapped her shawl tightly round him.

'You must stay hidden,' she said. 'Your father thinks you're in Kandahar.'

'Kandahar?' He opened his eyes.

'That was what Karam Uncle told him.'

He smiled to himself. 'That would be good,' he said.

'Foolish boy.' She kissed the tip of his nose. 'Get well. Then we'll talk of Kandahar.'

For the next week, Hasina nursed Aref every moment she could. When Abdul went to the neighbour's fields to work, she scraped together leftover food and ran to find her son. She sat close to him while he ate. 'You must get strong,' she said. He pulled a sour face at the sight of food. 'You must get well.'

He could only manage to stand bent double, his arm across his stomach. His wound ached, he said. Hasina saw the colours on the rags round his stomach shift as it bled. She saw the elderly man in him, pushing out through the young skin, and was afraid.

5

Hasina and Abdul were woken early by a strange sound. At first she thought it was Karam's radio set. They went together into the yard. The noise grew, bouncing along the hillside. It was coming from beyond the valley, from the desert.

'Some announcement,' Abdul said. 'Listen.'

An Afghan voice. A warning. Foreign soldiers were coming, it said. They must all leave. No one need be hurt. She groped for Abdul's hand, limp at his side.

They found Karam's compound in disarray. Men were rushing, stacking pots at the entrance. Palwasha was standing at the window, her hands on her hips, her face clouded.

'Don't just stand there,' she called when she saw Hasina.

Hasina looked round at the carpets and cushions scattered across the floor. 'You're leaving?'

'What does it look like?' Palwasha's eyes were blazing.

Hasina swallowed. 'But where?' she said. 'Where will you go?'

'Help me, won't you.' She didn't look up. Hasina knelt beside her, rolling the carpets and stacking them by the door. Abdul must go too, she thought. She must make him.

As soon as they returned home, she packed a bundle for Abdul. Tin plates and cups and bread to eat on the road. From the threshold, she stood and looked back into the gloom. This was the house where she'd first come as a bride so many years ago. A good house. Not rich but honest. She looked round at the empty cots, the blankets, the wooden stools, the battered trunk.

'You must go. Quickly.' She pressed the bundle into his hand, propelled him towards the road. 'Go now, with Karam and Palwasha. It's better for us.'

She was urging him on, her hand on his broad arm. He stared down at her, his eyes bewildered. 'But you,' he said, blinking, 'what about you?'

'I'll be right there, coming after you, won't I?' She tutted. 'Hurry. I've got knives to gather and a pot and blankets and clothes. I need some time. But you must go ahead.'

His feet dragged as she walked with him to the main track. The road was already thick with travelling families, a swarm of villagers pulling carts, carrying infants, pots on their heads and bundles on their backs. Some led a donkey or goat.

'See what they have?' She gestured at the flow. 'I need to prepare more things. Go with Karam. I'll soon catch you up.' Her whisper was urgent. 'Husband, please don't hesitate. Go.'

Abdul looked as lost as a small boy. 'How will I find you?' he said.

'You'll find me.' She brushed her hand against his to say goodbye. 'How could you not find me? I won't be far behind.'

She stood to the side as he turned, reluctant and dazed, and was taken by the crowd.

She had to carry Aref to the house. His eyes rolled sightlessly in his head as she laid him out on the cot and stripped him. His body was hot, his limbs shaking. She took her cooking knife and hacked at the rags. Close to the wound, the cloth had fused with the flesh. She couldn't cut it away. It stank. She washed down his skin with block soap and water and patted him dry with her shawl. She slid a blanket under him and wrapped it round, until he was cocooned. She boiled up sugary tea and lifted his head while she forced it, trickle by trickle, between his lips.

All night she stroked his forehead, fanned flies from his wound and murmured to him. Once, he woke abruptly, as if from a nightmare, and stared at her. His eyes were blank. His face was slippery with fresh sweat. She patted him, soothed him back to sleep.

When he woke again at first light, his fever had lifted. He was weak but he knew her and knew the place. She fed him hot tea and fragments of soft food. A hint of colour was returning to his lips.

A deep rumbling drifted in from the fields. She went out to the yard to look. A fleet of lumbering, metallic vehicles was pitching down the desert slope, making its way from the far ridge to the valley and the river below. The early morning light bounced off the sharp angles. She put her hand to her face. They were closer than she'd imagined possible. She heard a droning and turned her eyes to the sky. Aircraft were twisting there, turning sideways, one wing-tip pointing to the ground, the other to heaven, then righting themselves again with a rush. They dipped and screamed overhead. The foreigners, she thought. It had begun.

She ran back inside and forced Aref to sit, propped up against the wall.

'Soldiers,' she said. 'You must go.'

He stared, his eyes dull. 'Where?'

'Anywhere. Go.' She pulled his tattered, stained shirt back over his head, pushed his arms through the sleeves and watched him stuff his few possessions into its folds. 'If these foreigners find you . . .'

He seemed ready to sink back onto the cot.

'Hide in ditches, in fields.' She tugged him to his feet. 'Use the blessing of the land.'

From deep in the valley, the thick choke of an explosion. Hasina struggled to pull him out into the yard. When she let go of him, his legs buckled. He sank down the wall of the house to the ground. In the valley, black smoke was rising. An aeroplane dived, shrieking, from the sky, and swooped low over the hillside. She fell to the ground, covering her head with her shawl. A moment later, the earth shook. The blast deafened her.

She sat up. Aref was staring at her. Miserable and afraid.

Hasina looked at the pouch. 'Those bombs you have,' she said, 'give them to me.'

His eyes widened. 'They are not—' he began.

She raised her hand as if to slap him. 'Do as you're told,' she said.

Aref ripped open the stitching and eased out two metal objects. They were grey-green, rounded with straight metal levers.

'You twist and pull this,' he said, 'then throw them. They go off like bombs.'

Hasina looked at the smallness of them in his hand. They were dull, unappetizing pieces of fruit. One was scored by a line of rust.

Another jet shot over the valley, cutting through the air. She clamped her hands to her ears. A moment later the hillside shivered. The yard trembled under her feet. She took the bombs from him. The metal was chilled and dirty.

'Go,' she said. 'May Allah in His mercy protect you.'

He pulled himself to his feet, turned without a word and swayed across the yard, lurching at last into the corn.

The dense smoke of the foreign bombs blocked out the creeping vehicles, then, as it dispersed, they reappeared, always closer. Hasina pushed her way through the cornfield to the edge of the poppy below. The valley opened out before her. The foreigners' vehicles drew a defensive circle alongside the river. Figures of men, in light brown clothes, were darting along the bank. Digging machines were throwing up clouds of dirt. Between the crash of falling bombs, she could hear the steady chug of engines.

What kind of men were these Westerners? She wrapped her arms round her chest and hugged her thin shoulders. May God protect us. She looked at the metal fruit in her hands. She must give Aref time to flee.

The soldiers made rapid progress. They slotted metal panels into a bridge and nosed them into place over the river with their machines. They worked without contest, their aeroplanes screaming overhead, deforming the face of the hillside with fire and pockmarks.

When the first men ran over the bridge, her stomach heaved. Her palms were stinging with sweat. She turned and fled back to the house. She dashed round the yard, picking up her old cooking pot and cooking knife and the large water pot. She took them with her into the house.

She pushed away the large stone, which kept the door to the house permanently open in summer and fastened the door shut from the inside. Once it closed, the house became black. She stood quietly in the cool darkness, listening to the bang of blood in her ears. The house smelt rich, of earth and family. My home, she thought. This is where Aref was made and born. She wondered how far from the house he had crawled and what hiding place he'd found.

Her eyes were starting to adjust to the thin light. It was seeping in from the back window, and from the near one, which gave onto the valley. She pulled a stool under the window and sat, looking out over the corn. Halfway up the hillside, there were shots. She swallowed, struggling to compose herself. Behind her a cry, quickly stifled.

'Who's that?' She challenged the darkness. 'Tell me.'

A scramble, a sob and a small figure crawled out from under the cot, catapulted across the room and banged into her knees. It pushed its head at her stomach, almost knocking the grenades off her lap.

'You,' she said. 'What . . .?'

Yousaf, Palwasha's boy, stared up into her face with bulging eyes, wet with tears. 'I'm scared,' he said. He started to sob. His nose was running with snot. 'Where's Mummy?' His breath came in gulps. 'I want Mummy.'

Hasina stared. Behind him, the dark shapes of the two girls rose from under the cot.

'What are you doing here?' Hasina was beside herself. 'Go. Get away. Run.'

'Don't make us, Auntie.' Sima's voice was already breaking into tears. 'Please.'

Nadira pushed past Sima and buried her face against Hasina's thigh. Hasina ran a hand abstractedly over the child's tousled hair. Outside, another shot. The soldiers sounded close to the outer edge of their land. She gave the children a shove.

'Quick,' she said. 'Crouch down. Quiet.'

They ran together, arms churning the air, and crouched in a line against the wall. Hasina turned back to the window, light-headed with fear. She focused her eyes on the veil of corn, feeling the foreign soldiers creep closer and fingering in her wet hands the two small bombs, the only weapons she had to keep them at bay.

6

The darkness was still dense when Ellen followed the young soldier to the convoy, led by a low bouncing shaft of torchlight. She leaned against the steel of the nearest military vehicle, her flak jacket crushing her shoulders, and watched the black shapes of the men move around her in silence as they checked kit and loaded up. The air was cool and dry against her skin.

Major Mack sought her out as the men moved into position and pointed her to a Snatch in the middle of the convoy. She sat squashed up against the heavy back door. It was a tin can of a vehicle, its interior stripped bare. The Snatch shook itself into life and started to pitch and roll out of the camp gates and across open desert. She braced her legs and gripped the roof strap. Her helmet cracked against the metal struts behind her every time they banged into a hollow. She rode the impact, steadied her nerves and said nothing.

She'd never liked Snatches. The rough ride didn't bother her but they were poor protection, nicknamed 'metal coffins' for a reason. If they hit anything now, an IED or a mine, the flying shrapnel would slice them to mince. What was that expression the lads in Iraq used? Everyone gets a bit.

They were wedged tightly into this one, thigh against thigh, knee scraping knee. She'd pushed the team over quota; five, instead of four in the back, sharing the same stale air. Packs and boxes were piled round their feet. The soldiers sat in silence, their faces tight with concentration. The young soldier opposite her, Frank, was looking everywhere to avoid catching her eye. He was barely twenty but thuggish, with the heavy forehead and thickset nose of a fighter. She wondered where in the UK he came from and how much military action he'd seen. Her eyes fell to the weapon, an SA-80, across his lap.

Two more lads were riding top cover, cut off at the chest; head and shoulders sticking up out of the vehicle, out of sight. When she tried to look forward, her view was filled by their broad thighs. Their scrambling feet kicked out wildly for support every time the Snatch rocked and pitched. Dillon, the lad next to her, kept getting a boot in the groin as they felt for footholds. He swore under his breath. She squeezed herself further into the corner to give him more room.

A sudden stink broke out in the hot air. Dillon flapped his hands in front of his face wildly.

'Hold it in, Moss.' Dillon gave one of the top cover guys a sharp poke.

The young lad, Hancock, riding top cover with Moss, ducked his head down for a second, caught the whiff and gave a snorting laugh. Dillon kicked out at him before he straightened up again. Ellen watched the way they argued, jostled for position. They were only kids. She'd spoken to Hancock, the quietest in the group, in the darkness before they set off. He was eighteen, he said, keeping his voice low. He'd joined up in January and been sent out here right after training. He looked shell-shocked already.

'Sorry, Ma'am.' Frank, embarrassed.

She shrugged. 'Don't be.' I'm harder to offend than you realize, she thought. And I'll be safer if you think of me as one of you. 'And call me Ellen.'

The Sergeant Major, invisible to her in the front, barked something into the radio sets. Frank sighed and started scrabbling under the seats, checking wiring or groping for a piece of kit.

Dillon leaned towards her, knocking knees. 'Sergeant Major says you're famous. Like Kate Adie.' His eyes were full of life. A cheeky lad, good humoured and excited.

'Like who?' Frank, pausing in his grovelling on the floor, had lifted his head to listen, watching her with new interest.

'Nothing so glamorous,' she said to Dillon. 'I'm with a news magazine.'

'He said you've covered more wars than he has,' Dillon went on. 'That true?'

'I don't keep count.'

'Cool.' Dillon looked impressed. 'Which ones?'

'Crimea?' said Frank, and sniggered like a schoolboy.

Dillon kicked out at him. 'Don't be so bloody rude, you.' A vicious bounce of the Snatch knocked him off the seat onto the floor. He cracked his shin on the metalwork of the back door and swore. Frank doubled up with laughter. Dillon, trying to regain dignity, crawled through the kicking legs to a box and handed her back a bottle of water. 'Don't mind him,' he said, nodding at Frank. 'Tosser.'

Ellen turned her face to the square of bulletproof window and watched the swirls of dust they were throwing up behind them, blurring the outline of the next heaving Snatch in line. There was a dull red glow in the sky beyond. The night was starting to bleed back into day. It was so cold, it was hard to believe that in a few hours, once the heat built up, they'd all long for the chill of night again. The stuffy darkness of the Snatch, with its swaying, crashing motion, and her nervous apprehension about what lay ahead, made her dull with sickness as they drove on across the desert and the light outside whitened into morning.

They stopped. Frank unbolted the back door and climbed out over her, weapon readied. Then Dillon. A moment later they came back for her. She dropped out of the back, weighed down by her flak jacket and helmet. The dry desert air was a relief. She stood for a moment, enjoying the escape from the petrol fumes, getting her bearings.

'What next?' she said to Dillon. He shrugged, looked away. Frank was already walking towards a mud-walled compound where other soldiers were sloughing off their packs. Dillon turned and followed him.

She put her hands on her hips, breathed deeply and scanned the terrain. They'd stopped just short of a natural ridge. Behind them, the way they'd come, lay a desiccated brown landscape of dirty sand, rocks and low scrub. Its lines were broken by simple mud-brick houses, each set apart from the others and enclosed in its own protective boundary walls. No people were visible. The only sign of life came from a pack of scavenging dogs. They were trotting, lean and mangy, across the plain.

Ahead, far below, the slow snake of a river drew a glistening line through a valley. Beyond it, thickly planted corn waved from fields, scored through by the lines of trees that defined the green zone. She narrowed her eyes against the light. The outline of a village was visible a few kilometres in, high on the hill. That must be the first target.

Thick dust, stirred up by the convoy of military vehicles, was billowing in filthy clouds all around her. More Snatches were pulling up, filling the air with fine grit, disgorging soldiers. The day's heat was gathering. The men streamed towards the compound, bowed under the weight of the packs on their backs, shoving, talking in low voices, lighting cigarettes. She hesitated, watching them, then pulled off her helmet, as they had done, and followed.

Dillon, Frank and the others were settling against a low mud wall, smoking, rucksacks dumped at their feet. They looked tense. Freshly arriving soldiers streamed past them, competing for a place in the shade. To the side, a knot of officers was forming. They were talking in glassy public school voices. Binoculars hung from their necks. Radios squawked like parrots. Behind them, yet more vehicles were coming crashing over the desert, raising clouds of dust.

The young officers straightened up and lowered their voices. Mack appeared amongst them, not the tallest in the group but the oldest and broadest. She noted the way the other men shifted to accommodate him, deferring to him as the pack's Alpha male. Mack exchanged a few words as he passed through, then barrelled straight towards her. Heads turned, following him.

'Enjoy the ride?'

He leaned forward to speak to her. She caught the scent of army soap on his skin, undercut by adrenalin. As he opened his mouth to say more, a jet screeched overhead. A minute later, a flash of fire ignited out in the corn, on the far side of the valley. Smoke rose. A few seconds after that, a delayed boom.

'Five hundred-pounder?' she said.

Mack nodded. 'Air offensive's starting.'

The smoke was starting to disperse in black clouds across the corn.

'Is it clear of civilians?'

'We've issued warnings.' His body was hard with tension, his face serious. She sensed Dillon, Frank and some of the other lads looking over at them.

Mack pulled a satellite map from his pocket and spread it out on the sand. She picked out the villages from the office map, several of them, and, in the fields, dozens of small squares that showed individual Afghan compounds. They'd be good defences, thick mud walls that could withstand artillery. They'd been built for war. The country had seen little else.

Mack started to brief her, pointing with a long finger. 'That's the river.'

She made her own calculations, fitting the map to the scene below them. The distances weren't great but the terrain had its own natural fortification. The dips and ridges. The river and the steep rise beyond. And the scattered compounds. No wonder the Taliban had managed to hold it for the last few years. She felt a sense of foreboding, wondering how many failed assaults there'd been.

Heavy digging equipment was already being shunted into position at the waterside. Soldiers in the tan and brown of desert camouflage were waving their arms, signalling to the men inside the vehicles.

'The engineers are throwing a basic bridge across. Then the men go in on foot.' Mack traced their route on the map. 'Up the far bank, through the fields, storming the compounds, one at a time. Then up there. That's the first village we'll head for.'

'Think you'll secure it today?'

He shrugged. 'Depends what we find.'

He always said 'we', not 'they', she noted. He seemed to be a man who identified with his boys.

'You can watch the progress pretty well from here,' he was saying. He fingered the binoculars round his neck, lifted them to his eyes to scan the valley. He seemed to be looking forward to it, as if he'd bagged her a good spot at the races.

She looked past him. Moss, the fat one, and Dillon were hunched over their mess tins, boiling up foil sachets of food. Hancock, the young lad, was lolling against the wall, his eyes closed. He had an iPod stuck in his ears, his head trailing wires like a badly made bomb. He looked stressed as hell. She wondered why he wasn't eating. No one seemed to have noticed.

'I'll go in with the first wave,' she said.

Mack lifted the binoculars away from his eyes. 'I really don't—'

'My risk.' She looked him full in the face. 'That's fine. I need to be up close.'

His expression was thoughtful. 'I'm not sure I can allow that,' he said. 'I know you're—'

'Come on, Mack.' She nodded at him, trying to camouflage her nerves and sound breezy. He was a senior officer and she was pushing her luck. 'Sure you can.'

He paused, considering her closely. 'I'll see,' he said at last, and walked off.

When Frank and Dillon stubbed out their cigarettes and got to their feet, she crossed over to them. The Sergeant Major appeared, fastening his helmet. He looked at her for a second, then pushed his eyes past her.

'Lids on, lads,' he said. 'Time's up.'

'Fucking hope not,' said Dillon.

Hancock, beside him, looked grey with nerves.

They tightened their body armour, fastened helmets, swung their packs onto their backs and picked up their weapons. They lined up in single file, ready to head down the hill, a tense, silent group. She stood beside them, waiting.

Just as they seemed ready to set off, Mack reappeared. He spoke in a low voice to the Sergeant Major and they both turned to look at her. Their faces were stern. She wondered what they made of her. Once upon a time, when she started all this, soldiers used to stare because she was long-limbed and attractive and they couldn't take her seriously. Now she was pushing middle age and they must think her a liability, an oddball maiden aunt who might need rescuing when the shit hit. She shrugged her flak jacket to a new position on her shoulders, switching bruises. She could move a lot faster without the damn thing. It didn't even fit properly.

Mack beckoned her towards him. 'Go if you want to,' he said. His eyes were thoughtful. 'But it's your risk.'

He spoke quietly, acknowledging that they both understood what might lie ahead.

'Of course.' She nodded. 'Thank you.'

The men around her were starting to move. She hesitated for a moment, steeling herself, then forced herself to press forward and join them before she could think any more about it. Mack stood, unsmiling, and watched her, binoculars idle on his chest. She fixed her eyes on Dillon's broad back and fell into step, stretching her stride to match her footprint to his. Hancock was behind her, his breathing as shallow as her own.

They threaded their way down the hillside and reached the bridge. The soldiers grouped there, the bridge builders, ran their eyes over her as she mounted the treads. The rush of the river rose from below. A broad, fast-flowing river. The Taliban must have thought an attack from this side was impossible. Her boots rattled on loose metal. The scream of a jet and a dull boom from the hillside ahead told her the bombs were still falling. When she reached the other side of the bridge, her boots hit earth again and silence.

She followed Dillon into the first field, into thick curtains of corn. It was high, ready for harvesting, stretching up above her head. Visibility was terrible. The corn cloaked everything. There could be a whole army out there, low against the ground. She steadied her breathing. The corn stank, a bland, cloying smell of dry grass. Flies were buzzing round her face. Her helmet slipped heavily back and forth as she moved her head, tugging at its chinstrap. Diagonally, through the crops, she could see muddy irrigation ditches. Good hiding places for fighters who knew the ground. Her ears thumped with her own blood and the swish of corn against her boots and body.

Dillon ducked suddenly to one side and she flattened herself into the corn behind him. The firm earth was a relief and absorbed the shake in her limbs. She thought of the layout of the satellite map. They should be approaching the first compound. Ahead, someone fired a shot. Silence. The scratch of a voice on Dillon's radio. He started creeping forward again, bent double. She followed, keeping close to him.

At the edge of the field, the land opened out. The next field was full of rows of low bushes. A dull, mud-walled building rose beyond it, a primitive house with a single round hole for a window. The walls looked thick. It must be black as night inside.

The Sergeant Major and Moss were crouching behind the low compound wall with their weapons trained on the black rectangle of the doorway. The Sergeant Major was hollering something in a Lancastrian version of Pashto. '*Raw-ooza! Raw-ooza!*'

A sudden movement to the side of the building. She swung and stared into the dopey brown eyes of a donkey as it stuttered into view from behind the corner. It reached the extent of its tether and was jerked back, its head jolted, its eyes rolling white, its long ears flattened in fright against its head. Dillon raised his gun and took aim. The donkey backed clumsily, as if it knew, and disappeared again with a toss of its head.

The Sergeant Major fired a high warning shot. Two men had appeared in the doorway, walking forward into the earth yard.

Their eyes were wide with terror, their hands high in the air. One of the men was elderly, tottering on bent legs. His beard was white and ragged. His lips were moving soundlessly, either in fright or prayer. The other man was stout and middle-aged, a fat belly bulging beneath his long kameez. Their clothes looked threadbare, pathetic. They shuffled forward in rope sandals, round hats perched on their heads.

Ellen had reached the cover of the wall now and threw herself down against Dillon, her helmet banging round her face. A moment later, Hancock bumped up against her on the other side. He and Dillon stuck their weapons along the top of the wall and gave cover as the Sergeant Major and Moss went forward and pushed the Afghan men down on their knees. They pressed them against the outside of the building, their hands splayed palm-out against the mud above their heads. Moss patted them down. Nothing. The Sergeant Major was shouting for a translator, signalling the rest of them forward. The back of the old man was shaking violently as he crouched against the wall.

'Clear.' Dillon had checked the building, looking for people or weapons. The Afghan translator was barking questions at the two men. They were shaking their heads, eyes downcast, foreheads flush against the wall. The old man's body was shaking so hard, he looked about to collapse. She thought of the whites of the donkey's eyes as they rolled in its head.

They left Moss guarding the Afghans and crept on. This time, Frank and Dillon were front men and she was in the middle, with the Sergeant Major and Hancock giving cover behind. They plunged back into thick corn. The sun was pumping out heat now, the warmth rising in shimmering waves from the ground. Her hair was slick with sweat, her helmet slipping forward over her eyes. Her hands were anxious fists at her sides, nails digging into palms. Her body was aching with the weight of the body armour and her rucksack. The fear took her in waves, as it had before in moments like this: maybe this is the time, here, now, when my luck finally gives out. Maybe, for me, this will be it.

They were steadily climbing, through gently sloping fields, cutting across irrigation ditches and mud ridges. The corn gave way to fields of stubble, thick-cut stalks standing low in the ground. They stuck her boots, bruised her ankles. At the sides, split pods here and there were littering the ground. She kicked them, then bent to look at them. Spent poppy.

It was hard to look up and forward as they climbed. She kept her eyes on her footing. She was sickened by a sense of how exposed they were. The stillness ahead was invisible. Hidden eyes all around might be fixed on her. Anyone could be lying in wait in ditches and gullies above them. Anyone could be on their belly in the undergrowth, getting them in their sights, ready to pick them off. Her legs were juddering with tension. How many more compounds ahead? She couldn't remember. The Taliban had controlled this ground for a long time. There'd be surprises to come. They were tough fighters. They never surrendered, even when the odds were hopeless.

Her blood swarmed in her ears. The small flies, buzzing round her eyes and nose, were nipping her skin. She lifted a hand to clear a strand of hair from her face, a normal everyday gesture to steady herself.

Just as her arm was moving back again, the ground to her left exploded with a sudden burst of fire and smoke. Instinctively she threw herself to the ground. A hail of debris rained down on her, pelting her helmet and back. Everything was bleached white. A pure light, couched in an almost holy silence. For a second, utter stillness. Life stopped. Then sound pitched back into her ears with a bang.

Dillon, to one side, was shouting. His voice shot through with curses. She blinked hard, trying to clear the whiteness. Shapes again, blurred. The rich smell of earth. Poppy stalks were sticking into her. Her pack had crashed down on top of her like a dead man, knocking her into the ground, winding her.

'Compound ahead. Enemy fire.' Dillon was next to her, flat in the cut poppy. He was twisting back, staring right at her, signalling to her, motioning her to the side. She nodded, crawled to her right through the corn. Her ears were whining with the blast. She half crawled, half fell into a ditch, an irrigation channel with a few inches of water. The water soaked her clothes. Its coldness shocked her skin. She crawled forward up the ditch, propelling herself with her elbows.

A burst of gunfire. She concentrated, trying to work out where it was coming from. It must be Frank or Dillon. Weren't they both further ahead? The static of radio talk. One of them must be near her. Silence. The swish of water as she crawled forward, the tumble of a dislodged stone, deafening. How far was she from the compound? She had no idea. She paused to listen. Nothing. Her stomach convulsed, bringing bile to her throat.

She crawled on. Ahead, the field ended abruptly. Open ground beyond. The compacted mud yard was scattered with cut poppy stalks, spread out to dry in the sun. On the far side, a small mud house, surrounded by a low boundary wall. Dillon was lying along the near side of the wall, his weapon in his hands. She crept to the edge of the field. Dillon was readying his weapon, raising his head a fraction above the wall. He started to fire. She pulled herself to her feet and ran across the open ground. She seemed to hang there, exposed, forever, her legs pumping like a cartoon character. She thudded beside Dillon against the wall. He'd kept up a steady stream of fire. The walls of the building were pitted with marks, mud smoke hanging in the air all round it.

Dillon ducked his head below cover again. He looked shaken. 'Enemy fire,' he said. 'That building.'

He was staring at her, his eyes unnaturally wide.

'You sure?' she said.

'You wanna knock?'

A crash. Something smashed against the other side of the wall. Further down. An explosion and a shower of mud. Fragments struck her helmet. The wall was so thick, it absorbed most of the blast. Dillon's face was ashen. He frantically motioned her back, sending her, scuttling, away from the blast, crouched low along the shield of the wall. Adrenalin propelled her forward. As they ran, bent double, the radio crackled. Dillon's voice, thin and breathless, gave their position. He was so close, his breath was hot on her neck. They half ran, half tumbled together along the wall, fell back into the ditch, crawled down towards the lower field.

When the jet roared overhead, they were pressed flat in the ditch. Ellen had one hand against the ground, the other pressing her helmet down on her head. Her face was in soil, steeped in the fetid stink of earth and rotting vegetation. Her limbs were shuddering with fear. The whistle of the bomb through the air. The moment stretched. Silence. An almighty explosion. It seemed to blow out her eardrums, shake the ground beneath them. Blast waves ran through her body, ripples through water. She lay rigid, too stunned to move. Mud and dust flew across her body, rattled against her helmet, filled her mouth, nose, ears. Silence. Stillness. Her chest moved under her. Air. She was still breathing. She forced herself to tense first her hands, then her feet. Thank God. Relief flooded her. Her body was intact.

The dust had turned the daylight to premature dusk. A swirling fog of dirt engulfed them. Dillon's warm, solid body at her side began to shift and move. He dislodged clumps of dirt and they pattered to the ground. He was raising himself onto his hands and knees and peering forward into the chaos. His jaw strained with concentration. A moment later, it loosened into a boyish smile. A single word: 'Bullseye!'

The bomb had hit the side of the building, reducing three of the four walls to piles of rubble. Dillon rose cautiously to his feet. He shielded his mouth and eyes from the swirling dust as he crept forward. He checked the ditches round the edges of the yard. Frank climbed out too and stood, peering into the debris, his weapon raised. All around them, dust was settling. Shapes were starting to form, emerging like ghosts out of the haze. Ellen, lagging behind them, walked on unsteady legs, blast-drunk. She pulled out her camera, trying to focus with shaking hands.

The back of the house was scattered with sour straw. Frank was kicking at something. The tail and back leg of an animal. Frank kicked it again. A goat. Lifeless. He pushed away the mud bricks round it. He prodded the inert body of another goat beside it. A third, more deeply buried, was still alive. Its hindquarters, crushed under the debris, twitched quietly, without hope. Frank put his pistol to its head. He looked away as he pulled the trigger.

Dillon sat on a mud boulder and lit a cigarette and Frank went across to join him. Their shoulders had slackened and their tone shifted as they talked in low voices. Frank let out a short laugh. They had half turned their backs on the site as if, for them, the bombing was already in the past. The radios spat static.

As she climbed over the debris, the heaps of broken mud shifted and settled under her weight. Her vision was jumping. She wanted to sit still with them, to concentrate on breathing evenly again and thank God she was alive. But she knew she must keep moving and capture what she could while the scene was still raw. She started to photograph the wreckage, looking for detail, for human clues. The fourth wall was still almost intact, the interior exposed, naked, to the outside world.

A cracked mirror in a simple wooden frame hung crookedly from a nail. Scattered hairgrips and a comb sat in the narrow shelf that stuck out from the bottom of the frame. Long black hairs were snagged in the comb's teeth. A dark bag and a woman's bright red scarf hung from a second nail to one side. She examined the scarf, without touching it. It was cheaply woven, the thread coarse, a typical rural *tikrai*, large enough to cover head and shoulders. It was thick with dust now but still carried the memory of heavy, spicy scent – homemade, perhaps. More pungent than the gentle rose-water that Jalil's mother liked to wear. She took a step away and photographed it all, item by item.

She climbed on, sensitive to the shards of broken wall and dirt as they crunched and gave way in sudden shifts under her boots. More photographs; remnants of possessions. The protruding corner of a battered metal trunk. The leg of an upturned wooden stool. A piece of cloth, a filthy shirt or torn tunic, lying limply. The page of a book, cheaply printed, splattered with grit. Then she stopped. She lifted the camera away from her face to look with her own eyes.

Sticking out of the great heap of broken brick, blown up against the remaining wall, was a hand. A small hand, the nails minute, the palm soft and pink. A dusty bracelet, a bangle that might have been silver or tin, showed at its wrist. The rest of the body was hidden.

Dillon and Frank, cigarettes in hand, had fallen silent. They were watching her but she couldn't speak, she couldn't look up, couldn't lift her eyes from the hand. A child. Maybe one of many buried beneath her boots. They'd cleared the area, they'd said. She breathed hard. They'd warned the civilians to leave. The small hand shimmered as she blinked and stared, as if its fingers were reaching towards her, begging to be clasped. She couldn't move.

A moment later, Dillon's feet crunched on the mud behind her. His step sounded businesslike, almost jaunty.

'You all right?' he said. 'What's up?'

She lifted her camera, zoomed in on the hand and took one picture, then another. She was preserving the hand as efficiently as she could, before the men took possession of it. Dillon, close behind her now, swore. He turned away and spat into the dirt, gestured to Frank.

They took her by the shoulders and made her stand clear as they prised away the top rocks with their hands, sending them tumbling down the tower of rubble. She stood, watching them, as they worked methodically. Corpses were slowly emerging at their feet, small bodies, with dust-encrusted hair, their limbs bloody and crushed. The girls' scarves pinned them in the earth, their necks and chests stretched back to boulders, the material twisted and filthy, slipping through the men's hands as they struggled to tug it free. Thick, clumsy fingers playing with dolls.

Dillon stopped, straightened up, looked across to Ellen.

'We were taking fire.' His voice was tense. 'You saw.'

He picked out a stout piece of wood to use as a lever. They prised off the larger boulders, sending them tumbling down the rubble. The stones were grinding under them. Sweating, they heaved and pushed. Deep in a crack, a flicker of movement.

'Stop.' She raised her hand, craned forward. Frank and Dillon stood side by side, tense and motionless. In that moment of silence, it came again. A low moan. A sound so faint she sensed it more than heard it.

She lifted her eyes to the two men who were focused on her, their nerves strained.

'Quick,' she said. 'Someone's alive.'

The woman had been trapped under an overturned bed-frame, one of the low wooden cots so common here. It had formed a pocket, protecting her upper body from the falling debris. She was still conscious when the lads dug her out. One of her legs was crushed, bloodied and split to the bone. Dillon covered the wound with a field dressing and strapped the leg to a piece of wood, a makeshift splint to keep her going until they could get her out to a medic.

While the lads were dressing the leg, Ellen poured water into her hand and washed dirt from the woman's nose and mouth. Her skin was leathery and lined by the harshness of the desert, but Ellen put her age at about forty. She had a determined face, her skin loose over strong cheekbones. Her lips were chapped and coated with dirt. Her hands, now motionless at her sides, were heavily calloused and ended in thick horn fingernails, as if she laboured outdoors. Ellen cleaned off her face, then dripped water into her palm and trickled it from between her fingers into the woman's mouth.

The woman's eyes opened. For a moment, they stared at each other. The woman's eyes were striking, a startling green, brilliant against her light brown skin. The woman's lips fluttered open and closed, dribbling with water, as if she were trying to speak. Ellen lowered her head to listen. The woman's breath rose sourly. She saw the woman raise her head a little, the veins in her neck bulging with effort. Then she spat. The woman's spittle fell back, splattering her lips and the side of her mouth and hung there, glistening. Her head sank back to the ground, as if the effort had exhausted her, her eyes again fallen closed.

Ellen watched her for a moment. Then she wiped the spittle gently from the woman's face and sat, crouched over her, stroking her limp hand between her own, until they brought a stretcher to carry her out.

7

By late afternoon, the troops had taken the village. They walked in through dirt streets that were rutted with cartwheels and pitted with stones. The place was deserted. The shoddy metal gates of the high-walled mud compounds hung open, banging emptily against the walls inside. The villagers had fled. Tethered cattle, hungry and thirsty, stamped in frustration.

Ellen and the other soldiers followed a convoy of Snatches into a large compound. Paint was peeling off the rusting metal gates. The mud walls were thick and about twenty feet high. As the vehicles drew to a halt, Ellen was engulfed in rising dust and the animal smell of fouled straw.

She went with the men to a corner. She brushed away loose stones and rolled out her sleeping bag on a flat piece of ground, littered with chicken shit. Dillon and Frank and the boys were already unpacking their rations. Ellen dug out antiseptic wipes and ran one round her face, neck and hands. It came away black. A headache was gathering behind her eyes. She sat for a while in the shade, sipping water, feeling suddenly limp. Her nerves were jangling, playing out the memory of the assault, unpicking the noise, the fear. When she closed her eyes, she saw again the small pink hand, reaching for her through the rubble.

After some time, she swallowed down aspirin, pulled out her notebook and went to look round the camp.

A third of the land inside the compound was taken up by a house with smooth walls, mud bricks rendered with a plaster of liquid mud mixed with straw, making it a foot or two thick. It was topped with a softly undulating mud roof, sculpted into a row of domes. To one side, a pile of burnt poppy, a jumble of blackened pods and dead branches, was quietly smouldering. The softly dispersing smoke turned the air acrid. Someone had made a hasty departure, she thought. And a recent one.

A dim tunnel ran the length of the building, forming a central corridor with doorways off to the sides. She walked through, peering into the dingy rooms that led off it. They were cool and smelt of animals and dust. In one of them, two Afghans, wearing cast-off army jackets, were setting out their bedding. Translators, perhaps. They looked up in surprise when they saw her in the doorway. She nodded and greeted them, hand on heart: 'Salaam Alaikum.' They hesitated, stared. As she walked on, the younger of the two called after her with a stumbling reply. Chickens ran past her legs in frenzied zigzags. A goat was tethered in a dark corner, chomping at straw.

Beside the building, soldiers had prised the cover off the well and were winding up wooden panniers of water. In the corners, more spent poppy lay in bundles like brushwood, their desiccated pods split where the resin had been drawn.

In the far corner, behind the gate, Moss and Hancock were digging. She crossed to them.

Hancock looked elated, buoyed up by survival. 'Shit pit,' he said, pointing to their work, and sniggered. Another soldier was banging in posts and hanging camouflage netting as a primitive screen.

The soldiers had been allocated the main part of the compound. Officers were congregating in the flat mud area in front of the house. Vehicles were pulling up with extra kit, mosquito nets and tarpaulin. Young privates were running to and fro, carrying wooden staves and building structures.

She sat on a ledge, her back against the mud wall and wrote notes, trying to capture the bustle of the camp, the rush to make order from chaos and to secure the surrounding area before night fell. She caught snatches of banter between the men, the laughter that came from relief after their earlier fear of the assault. She wrote too about the bombed house, the digging out of the three children's corpses and the rescued mother.

When the lads gathered and started to cook their rations, she went to join them. She sensed them watching as she sorted out her burner and lit it, dug out a foil meal and set her mess tin boiling. She'd had a few days with the Americans in Iraq and there'd been endless discussion about the pros and cons of the food each nation was issued. The US got chocolate and gum and self-heating Meals Ready to Eat and couldn't believe the British were still expected to boil up, the old-fashioned way.

Dillon was sitting with young Hancock, their backs against their packs. He squeezed army-issue jam out of a tube onto brown crackers, his hands engrained with filth. The trauma of the day, the bombing, the children, all firmly set aside. He brandished a cracker at Hancock. 'This, mate,' he said, 'is living the dream.'

She fished out her sachet meal, tore it open and started to poke into it with her fork. Thick steam enveloped her, a chemical version of cheese.

Dillon called out to her. 'Like the scoff?'

'My favourite.'

He grinned, nodded. 'What're you gonna write about anyway?' he said. 'About us?'

'Maybe.' She looked at his eager young face. 'What do you think I should write about?'

'Dunno.' He shrugged. 'About me? Me Mam'd like that.' He looked her over, thoughtfully, chewing. 'Why d'you do this anyway?'

'It's a job.' She smiled to herself. 'Been doing it a long time now.'

He nodded, considering. He was very young and she wondered what he made of her. War was still very much a man's world. She'd spotted one or two women supporting the assault, signallers or medics. No fighters.

'You married?' He was looking at her ring with curiosity.

'No.' She shook her head. 'Doesn't really fit the lifestyle. You?'

'Nah,' he said. 'Not me.' His voice was light. 'Only Moss over there, lard boy. He's hitched. Got a kid and all.'

They fell silent. She wondered if he too were thinking of the dead children who sat like ghosts beside them as they talked and ate.

The sun was bloodied and falling when Mack came striding across the compound, kicking up small stones with his boots. A sudden tension. The lads nearby stopped eating and looked up. Mack bent down to her.

'Care to join me?' He nodded back over his shoulder towards the compound building. 'Not awfully civilized. No cocktails. But I could stretch to tea.'

She followed him back across the sand, rich in the mellow light. She could feel the soldiers raising their eyes to watch as they passed. It was like being invited to the headmaster's study. Only here, she thought, I'm the same age as the headmaster, not the class.

An aide rushed forward to unfold a canvas camp chair for her. A cluster of junior officers had gathered with mess mugs of tea under the canopy of a camouflage net. The air was cooling, seeping its daytime heat. The cluster of junior officers looked up, nodded to her as they approached. Mack directed his aide to draw their chairs away from the group. She took a seat next to him in the deepening shadows.

'Bad business,' he said. His eyes were intent. 'That bomb.'

'Yes.' She let the silence between them lengthen, testing his comfort with it.

He waited longer than most men would, his eyes resting on her face, his elbows on the camp-chair arms. He made an arch with his splayed fingers. His fingernails were neatly cut, ridged with the dirt of the desert.

'The boys are upset,' he said at last. He tapped his arched fingers against his lips. 'Very upset. When a child gets killed.' He paused. 'Affects everyone.'

'I'd hope so.'

He inclined his head. The aide bustled forward, handing them both mugs of weak tea, then retreated.

'It gets to me,' said Mack. His voice was low, drawing her towards him to listen. He smelt of sunscreen and lightly burnt skin. 'You know why?'

'Because you have children of your own?' She heard the cynicism in her voice.

'An old line?'

'Very.'

He nodded, unsmiling. 'That's not it. And actually, I don't.'

She watched and waited. He was a powerful man, used to being obeyed and he had brought her across for a reason. He was watching her closely.

'They do it deliberately, you know. They use civilians as shields.'

She narrowed her eyes and kicked up sand with the toe of her boot. Black shards of burnt poppy rose and fell in the dirt. 'What are you saying? That militants were there? In that house?'

He lowered his voice further. 'The enemy was in the area. In some numbers. As recently as yesterday.'

'Evidence?'

'Satellite images.'

Ellen considered. So this was going to be the official line. That it was justified, in self-defence. Hard to believe. She raised her eyes. 'Can I see them?'

He grimaced. 'Difficult, I'm afraid. Operational security.'

'Of course.'

He sighed and sipped his tea. Even when he looked away from her, she felt his alertness. This is a man, she thought, who is never at rest.

'This enemy, you see,' he said, 'they have no morality.'

She thought of the bodies of the dead children and felt anger rising. He seemed so calm. She wanted to challenge him, to shake him up. 'Hard to play fair', she said, 'when your opponent doesn't follow the rules.'

He nodded. 'That's part of it.' His tone was even, his hands steady round his mug of tea.

'So how can you possibly win?' She heard her voice rise. 'They keep tying your hands behind your back. Those interfering politicians in London who don't understand a thing. Those journalists who traipse out here and criticize. It isn't fair. Right?'

He looked at her quietly and she had the feeling he was absorbing her, reading her feelings. It was disconcerting. He lowered his eyes after a moment, raised the mug to his lips and drank his tea. She watched the ripple of his throat. Her cheeks felt hot.

When he finally lowered his mug, he fixed his eyes on its brim. 'It's not a level playing field,' he said.

They sat in silence. She wondered if she'd overstepped the mark, if she'd offended him. He didn't look at her. His fingers gently tapped the sides of the mug, rhythmical and thoughtful. Behind them the voices of the young officers rose, erupted into laughter, then became again subdued.

Mack raised his eyes and leaned towards her. 'What we're doing here is right. I believe that.' His voice was intense, giving her the sense he was communicating a truth. 'But it's messy. It's not easy.'

'Killing children doesn't help.'

'It doesn't. I agree with you. I know how it looks.'

He was speaking seriously, without a trace of humour. He was so close to her, she could smell the milky tea on his breath.

'We can fight,' he said. 'We do it damn well actually. I've got good men here. The best.' He gestured vaguely across the compound at the young soldiers, sitting on the fast-cooling sand in loose groups; eating, smoking, lying back against their packs. 'We can secure villages and kill the enemy and take ground. But that's just one battle.'

'There's also hearts and minds?'

'Quite.'

He hesitated, as if he were choosing his words with care. His eyes were bright.

'People need to think,' he said. 'Think who's got their interests at heart. Who's building clinics and schools. Cleaning up wells. You know? Who goes out of their way to help civilians, not hurt them.'

'Not this time.'

He clicked his tongue. 'We don't do it on purpose. They do. You know that. Look what they've just done.'

'You mean Nayullah? The suicide bomb?'

He shrugged, lifted a hand, palm upwards, spreading the fingers as if to say: I rest my case.

She thought about the impact of a suicide bomb in a crowded market. The bloodshed, the shock, the fear. 'It's effective. I bet it frightened the hell out of people.'

'A sign of desperation,' he said. 'That's all.' His chair creaked as he shifted his weight. 'Suicide bomb? IEDs? Losers' tactics. They can slow us down. But the fact is, they can't take us on, man for man. Haven't got the numbers. Or the kit.'

The words jumped out at her. This then, she thought, was the man who'd fed John his lines. Over a cup of tea, no doubt, just like this one. She looked at him more closely.

'This suicide bomb,' she said. 'Was there nothing from your informers, no warning?'

He was studying her, his expression bemused. 'Informers? You've been reading too much le Carré.'

She tutted. 'Mack,' she said, 'as it happens, I rather like le Carré. But if we're going to talk, we might as well be frank.'

He let his face relax into a smile.

'Ellen,' he said, 'I get the feeling you're always frank.'

Dusk was setting in around them, sealing them off from the mud walls and the other soldiers. Beneath the camouflage net, there was movement, a shuffling of boots and chairs as men got to their feet. Time for stand-to, she thought, that old end-of-day ritual of warfare.

He too was preparing to move. He emptied the dregs of tea from his tin cup with a whip of his wrist, splattering thin dark lines across the sand. She saw a pattern in it at once, a pattern that disturbed her. The spurt of blood from a wound. She reached forward and put her hand out to delay him.

'Tell me about the Afghan who was killed. Jalil.'

He looked surprised. 'The turp?'

'What happened?'

He sighed. 'Hard to say.' He paused. 'He went out on a routine patrol. Not far from here. Then he left it and struck out on his own.'

'Why would he do that?'

He shrugged. 'Don't know. By the time they found him, it was too late.'

'Shot?'

'Through the head.'

'What weapon?'

'AK-47, I should think.' He put his hands flat on his thighs, bracing himself to get up. 'We didn't retrieve the bullet. Frankly, it was a mess. And pretty clear what happened.'

'Which was?'

He pushed his weight forward, his thighs thickening with muscle, and got to his feet. The chair struts creaked.

'Two theories. Maybe he'd crossed the line and done some deal with the enemy. Drugs. Information. When he went to meet his contact, he got more than he bargained for.'

She pursed her lips. 'Or?'

'Or he had a perfectly innocent reason for straying from the group and ended up in the wrong place at the wrong time. All turps take a big risk working with us. They know that. They're seen as traitors.'

She looked up at him, a dark shape against the sky, his face in shadow.

'And what do you think?'

He blew out his cheeks. 'Hard to know.' He fiddled with his belt, straightened his shirt, then stooped over her, low enough for her to catch the masculine musk of his skin.

'I'd like to think: wrong time, wrong place,' he said. 'I liked Jalil. He was a bright lad.'

He reached down a hand to her. She looked for a moment at the broad palm and long fingers, then put her hand in his and let him haul her to her feet.

8

Dust. Shifting. Falling. Raining on her cheek. Fine dirt in nose, throat, breathed deep into her lungs. The dry earth penetrating her, turning her to desert. Black shapes above shifting. Light bleeding in, hot drops of sun. Her skin twitched. Her eyes tightened at its sharpness.

She was on her side, pinned. Such weight on her leg. Crushing. Unbearable. She closed herself off from it, trying to disown the damaged leg. If she opened herself to that much hurt, she would suffocate.

But they were getting nearer. They were working towards her, looking for her. She was being unburied. She heard their heavy breath as they heaved and strained. Stones tumbled, crashed, settled. Fresh dust fell, exploded and rose around her face in clouds. She spluttered. They were rocking the weight that pinned her leg. Pain shot through her body in arrows of white heat. She tried to cry out but her moan was strangled. A man's voice gave a short command. It was efficient, bleached of emotion. He used their language. They will kill me, these men, these infidels. Better they do it quickly. End it now. May Allah in His Mercy protect me.

Sun burst over her. The weight was gone. She could smell the foreigners round her, their rich, rancid odour. They were talking. Foreign words. Now they would kill her. She braced herself. She thought of Abdul, of Aref. She told them goodbye.

Cold water shocked her face, splashed her skin, bringing her back to life. A hand was brushing water over her eyes, her mouth. It mixed with the dust. A finger dripped it onto her lips. Praise Allah for the bliss of water. Her lips parted, letting the moisture in. She savoured it in her mouth, down her throat. Someone was touching her leg. Indecent. Tearing her clothes to expose and humiliate her. She could not defend herself. She could not move. She felt their hands on her flesh, examining it, binding it. But here, at her face, cleaning off the dirt, it was a woman. It was a woman's hand.

She opened her eyes. The pale face of a white woman, shining with sweat, peered down at her. Her head uncovered. Her breath so close she knew it to be warm and slightly sweet. Her eyes were the dull green-blue of river water in shadow. They were keen, studying her. The woman, this enemy, bent her face a little closer, as if she expected something. What? A word? A kiss? Hasina glared at her. She gathered her strength and tried to spit. She was too weak. The spittle fell short. She let her eyes sink closed again, screening out the woman, the dust, the sky. She felt their hands on her, touching her, shifting her, taking her prisoner, and she fell back into darkness again.

Her body was lifted, swung sideways in the air, came back to rest on rough material. The pain in her leg was consuming her. Voices. Bright light and shadow crossing her eyelids. Her body was lightly bounced as they carried her. She could not open her eyes. She might be dreaming. She might be dead. Images, shapes, colours tumbled down on her like falling leaves. Darkness.

Some time passed. Minutes or hours? She was lying on her back. Her leg had died. The pain had left her. Noise. Low voices close to her. Louder voices distant. Foreigners. She would be tortured.

She opened her eyes. Another woman, thickset and fat, dressed in man's clothes. Army clothes, sand-coloured cotton. Her trousers showed clearly the outline of her large bottom and of her thighs. Hasina looked away. The woman's arms were naked. They were slick with dark hairs, like a dog. Her fingers were busy with some instrument. The woman turned and Hasina glimpsed a needle in her hand. She bit down as the woman took her arm, wet it, plunged in the needle. Sleep.

A man was lifting her arm, holding her hand, patting it. Abdul? She opened her eyes, dazed from dreaming. She stifled a scream. A big black man, skin shining with sweat like a dark polished pebble in a stream. The inside of his lips flashed wet pink when he spoke to her. Foreign words. She understood nothing. He moved to examine her leg. It was plump and white with bandages. They had done this to her. She tried to move her toes but felt nothing. It would wither and drop off now, this leg. She knew this. Her death would be slow at the hands of this black man.

She tried to twist her head away, close her eyes. Sheets of green material stretched round her, pinned up in the desert, separating her from the heat and sand. A tube was attached to her arm, with a transparent sack of liquid, raised, emptying itself drop by drop into her body. Sleep.

Early evening. Heat draining from the desert. She opened her eyes and they felt clean. The dust had gone. Who had done this to her and what else had they done while she slept? She tried to move her leg. Lifeless. She could not run away.

'May Allah be with you, Madam. I hope you are a little better, if God wills it?' A man's voice. A gentle voice. Speaking in Pashto. His voice was close. She sensed that he had been there some time, watching her as she slept. Waiting for her to wake. She turned her head.

'My name is Najib.' He looked older than Aref but his beard was short and thin. His face was a little plump. 'What is your good name?'

Her throat was too dry for her to speak. He leaned forward, dribbled a little water from a bottle into her mouth. She felt herself flooded with it. The water was clean and tasted of nothing, neither of stones nor of earth.

'What is your good name?' he said again, a little louder.

'I do not know you.'

'My name is Najib. I am from Kabul.'

'Kabul, is it?' She snorted. Now she knew. He was a traitor, a conspirator, taking foreign money.

'What is your good name?'

She closed her eyes, pretended to sleep.

'Madam,' he said. His voice was respectful. 'Maybe I can help you.'

She remembered the children. Now where . . .?

'Children?' she said. 'There were . . .?'

She knew at once from his face. No hope. Only grief, embarrassment. It could not be. How could such a thing . . .?

And Aref?

'Who else?' she said.

His eyes were full of confusion. 'The children,' he said. 'Three little ones. May Allah, His Name be blessed, bring you comfort.'

She let her eyes fall closed. May Allah forgive her. What had she done?

He waited a moment, then spoke again. 'You are safe here,' he said. 'They have good doctors.'

She didn't reply. What would they say, what would they do, Karam and Palwasha? Their children; all their children. The weight of it stopped her breath.

'They have some questions.' The traitor was speaking again. She kept her eyes closed. 'They want to know what happened here. Why were you in the house?'

She blocked him out. She lay still, her eyes closed, waiting for him to leave. She would not tell. Sleep.

Water was trickling down the back of her throat, cool and fresh. Her head ached. Her body was leaden. She was coming to again, finding herself on her back, immobile, sweating and uncomfortable. Something was wrong. No one breathing beside her. Her left side was not warmed by the heat of Abdul's body, by his breath, hot and stale in her ear. For every night of their many years of marriage, he had balanced her like a scale. Now she was alone. She forced herself to open her eyes but everything was blurred.

Now she remembered. The memory knocked her down. The bomb. The dust. The soldiers. She battled to focus. The Kabul man was there, bending over her. His face was kind. The rim of a transparent water bottle loomed large in her vision.

'Are you all right, madam?' he said. Stupid question. She gulped down the water inside her mouth. Not local water. The light was softening. The air was cooler. It must be almost evening. Where would they take her now?

'Can you eat a little bread? Drink some tea?'

She stared at him, incredulous. He was speaking Pashto but his words made no sense to her. Why was he offering her tea, as if she were a guest?

'What . . .' she managed to say. Her voice was croaky. 'What will they do with me?'

He smiled. His short beard waggled on his chin. 'They won't hurt you,' he said. He sounded almost merry. 'They are making you well again. No need to be afraid.'

'Afraid!' she said. He spoke the truth: she was terrified. Better she'd died in the house. Better they shot her where she lay. To be brought back to life and then killed, this was a far worse fate. Abdul, she thought. My own dear Abdul. My parents chose wisely when they married me to you. Thank you and bless you, wherever you are.

'Don't cry.' The man from Kabul was dabbing at her face. His movements were gentle.

Later, she sensed a woman, a stranger, hovering at the green curtain, peering down at her. She looked. That Western woman, the one with the river-water eyes. She wanted something. Hasina could smell her eagerness, hard and wolfish like hunger. The woman didn't come close, just stood there, watching her, taking her in. Her head was strained forward, her eyes on Hasina's face. Hasina closed her eyes.

After a few moments, there was whispering. Foreign words. One of the women in men's trousers came forward and bent down over her. The smell of antiseptic, of lemon. A cool cloth wiped her forehead. Soothing. Her limbs relaxed. Floating. Sleep.

9

The earth was breathing sand across her body, covering her face in a fine film of grit. Ellen pulled the upper lip of her sleeping bag a little tighter, her nose filled with the smell of dust and decay. Men, sprawled around her, were snoring and grunting in their sleep. The black silhouette of a soldier was standing guard on the gate, his cigarette a bobbing red dot. The moon was up. The outlines of the compound walls, the buildings, shimmered in the half-light. Outside the bolted metal gate, cattle were shuffling. Distantly, out in the desert, a wild dog howled. She tensed, listened. The Taliban howled like that at night, a covert way of signalling to each other. A dog or a fighter? No way of telling.

She turned on her side, shifting shards of stone, and imagined the scene here last night. The men of the family whispering, smoking, bolted inside their compound, discussing how to destroy the remnants of their poppy. Wives and children sleeping in those dark, dank rooms. Where had they fled to? Did they know foreign troops had taken over their home?

The soldiers had seen much less resistance than they'd expected. She read the relief in their faces. Hancock's jauntiness. Frank's swagger. They were pleased with themselves, pretending they'd never been afraid.

She was less confident that the ground had been so easily won. Mack had told her they had satellite images of fighters here. If that were true, where were they? Why hadn't they put up a fight? Perhaps they still might.

She checked her watch. After one. A few more hours and they'd be up again. She tucked her head into her chest and closed her eyes and saw again the dead children.

The youngest had been dug out with a deep gash across her face, a stain reaching from the inside corner of her eye down to her mouth. Blood had spilled, then dried across her cheek, blackened and clotted by dust. Ellen's first thought had been: that must hurt. Then: she'll need stitches. And, finally: they should clean that up before they bury her. The girl only looked about three. Patches of clear, delicate skin showed under the filth. Small hands, with creases of dirt in the palms and pink bitten-down nails. Fingers like a doll's.

Three kids in all. All dug out. Two girls and a boy, not one of them more than seven. The soldiers handled the bodies with exaggerated care, making their apology to the dead, avoiding each other's eyes.

She'd seen a lot of dead bodies in her time. The very first ones, years ago, had bothered her the most, haunted her even. Then she lost count. Mangled remains dug out of earthquakes and landslides. Disconnected body parts scattered by bombs. Corpses so disfigured by flood or fire they barely looked human. She wasn't immune to them but she always forced herself to look. She knew she had to see it to write about it, and writing about it was the only means she had of paying them respect. They were just dissolving flesh by then. Whatever life they'd had, whatever had made them people had gone. By thinking that, she shut them out.

But the deaths of the children were different. When she was crawling in the ditch, disorientated, they'd been close by, still breathing, still alive. It was a cock-up, clearly. She wanted to blame the soldiers but, the truth was, she felt responsible too. She'd been there. She was left with the lingering sense that maybe there was something she could have done, so the children might not have died.

The lads were upset. This kind of thing always caused shockwaves. It messed up the image they had of themselves, the belief that kept them going through all the danger, the misery of war. No one wanted to be a child killer.

'Collateral damage,' the Sergeant Major had said as they'd straightened out the bodies and wrapped them in dirty cloth they'd found. The small rolls lay there, side by side, in the dust. Frank and Dillon had refused to look at her.

'First rule of war,' the Sergeant Major said. 'Shit happens.'

A fresh breeze skimmed sand along the ground and made her cough. She turned over, onto her other side. What had that woman and her children been doing there? She knew there had been warnings. The Afghan translators had been hollering across the valley with loud-hailers from first light, warning civilians to get the hell out of there.

Mack had hinted that the family had been used as human shields. Could that be true? She didn't know. Someone had certainly attacked the troops. She remembered the explosions, the splattering of dirt. But if he were right, where had the fighters gone? The bomb had been a direct hit. No time for anyone to run.

The image of the woman came to her, with those green eyes. The dead were beyond pity. The bereaved were a different matter. The woman shouldn't have survived. The medics had sedated her for now but sooner or later she'd have to surface. She'd have to become human again. The horror she'd face then, the grief, would be suffocating.

She thought of Jalil's mother. Kneading her hands endlessly, staring wide-eyed at nothingness. Jalil's young brother, desolate, pressed into her side for comfort. The cool pride in his sister's eyes as she pushed the money back at her. She knew what had happened. It was her fault Jalil had come to Helmand, had placed himself in such danger. She was the one to blame.

She twisted quietly and reached for her rucksack. She felt in the darkness through her possessions, put her lips to her shampoo bottle and felt the seeping warmth of the vodka run through her body and numb her into sleep.

* * *

The next morning the lads were ordered to unload new supplies from vehicles: boxes of bottled water, telecoms kit and ammunition. Jets screeched overhead, sparking a distant boom of explosions. The offensive had moved on towards the next village.

Ellen watched. An Afghan man was hanging around at the bottom of the slope on the far side of the village. He was dressed in threadbare cotton, the long tunic and baggy trousers that all the village men wore, a traditional hat on his head. The cloth must have been white once. Now it merged into the village dust as if he were frightened of being seen. He wasn't a short man but he exuded a sense of smallness with a thin, malnourished body.

He seemed agitated, moving forward repeatedly towards the soldiers who were guarding the track from the low fields into the village. His shoulders were stooped, his hands imploring, his head tilted to one side. Whatever the soldiers said to him, it wasn't welcoming.

Repulsed, he then backed off again, his arms limp at his sides, his hands opening and closing in the empty air. After walking a few steps, he'd sink down to the dirt track and squat on his haunches, staring at his palms. A little while later, he'd get up and approach the soldiers all over again.

Ellen went across to the Sergeant Major and pointed him out.

'That man. I'd like to know what he wants. Is there a translator I can send down?'

He narrowed his eyes. 'A turp?' He looked round, shrugged. 'If there's one free.'

Ellen went across to the young Afghan who was standing in the shade, half watching the soldiers and shifting his feet in the dust. He was wearing shabby civilian clothes with army-issue body armour on top. The flak jacket was too big for him, sticking out beyond his shoulders. He seemed wary when she approached.

'*Salaam Alaikum.*' She inclined her head to him, placed her hand on her heart. 'My name is Ellen.'

He was the younger and slighter of the two translators she'd startled in the house the day before when she'd greeted them from the corridor.

He nodded, gave a shy smile. 'How do you do?' He bowed. 'My name is Najib. I am from Kabul.'

She remembered what Jalil's sister had said, that Najib and Jalil had been school friends. Najib's face was young, with a fresh stubbly beard. He held himself proudly but she sensed his awkwardness. As they spoke, his fingers worked the strap of the military helmet in his hands. Out here, he should be wearing it.

When she made her request, his expression changed to unease. She nudged him along, nodding and smiling so politely it was difficult for him to refuse. Finally he gave in with a sigh. He lifted the cotton scarf from his neck and wound it carefully round his face until only the strip of his brown eyes showed, strapped his ill-fitting helmet on his head and headed down the slope to nego- tiate with the soldiers. They spoke, shrugged, let him through. At the bottom of the slope, an irrigation channel ran from side to side. Najib approached the man with one eye on this ditch, scan- ning for movement.

Najib dwarfed him, not with his height but with his solidity, his years of good food. The older man seemed distressed, beating the air as he spoke. He took a step towards Najib and made to grasp his hands.

Najib's face was grave when he came back. The Sergeant Major walked across to listen.

'That man,' Najib said, 'he is saying his wife is disappeared. I am telling him: everyone is fled, no one is here. But he is repeating. He wants to come, to look.'

No one spoke. Najib looked embarrassed. 'He is saying he has bad feeling,' he added. 'Very bad. About his wife.' He shrugged, as if to apologize for the foolishness of villagers.

Ellen looked at the Sergeant Major. He was staring doggedly at his boots.

'Take him to see the bodies,' he said at last. 'We need to bury them.'

Najib looked uncomfortable. 'And about his wife?'

'See if the kids are his first. If they are, tell him we've got his wife. I'll ask the Major about letting him see her.'

They walked through the village in procession. Frank, sent along as protection, walked with his jaw hard, his eyes wary. The Afghan villager's stride was long and irregular as he hurried them forward. He was bombarding Najib with a nervous, machine-gun stream of words. Najib struggled to translate.

'Abdul,' said Najib. 'His name is Abdul. His house is on the far side. He was together with his wife when they heard news of the attack. Everyone was shouting to leave.'

'So why didn't they?' said Ellen.

'He did. He went to the desert. But his wife said first she must pack their belongings. Their cooking knives and pots and clothes. She said she would follow afterwards. But she never came.'

'And his children?'

'He has a grown son. He is . . .' Najib switched languages to check the details. 'He goes for work in Kandahar. Abdul is very proud. He is a . . .' Najib hesitated, tapping his palm against his forehead as if shaking vocabulary to the front. 'He is a learning businessman.'

'A business trainee?'

'Yes.' Najib's face lit up with relief. 'That is good.'

'What about the others?' She paused. She wanted to avoid the word 'dead' in front of their father. 'The young ones?'

Najib shrugged. He seemed too embarrassed to ask.

Ellen read the gentleness in Abdul's face. He was scurrying across the ground like a mouse, his eyes low, his body folded in on itself in the effort to shrink from them all. She looked away. She needed to stay detached, to protect herself. If she started to know him even a little, it would make his grief harder to withstand.

They climbed down the track from the top of the village and skirted the fields to approach the bombed house. When Abdul saw the small rolls of cloth, laid out on the mud, he let out a cry and quickened his pace to a lumbering run. He collapsed to his knees in front of them and tore at the material covering their faces. He emitted a low-pitched moan, slow and painful, as if his lungs were collapsing. He raised his arms above his head, his fists grasping at the air, opening and closing. Then his chest sank forward. He lay prostrate, his face buried in the children's bodies, his arms stretched out to the sides, gathering all three of them into his embrace.

Ellen imagined the feel of the bodies against his face, their awful stiffness, their sour-sweetness in the gathering heat. A familiar nausea gathered in the pit of her stomach. There was no smell as repulsive or cloying as putrefying flesh. It cut her to the quick. It brought back a decade of memories, returned her to the very first time, in a warm, wet field, where she'd stood to bear witness as forensic investigators had dug for evidence, watched by bereaved relatives standing, desolate, in a silent huddle.

Abdul's back and shoulders started to undulate, a convulsive motion. His moaning gave way to wailing. She looked away. Frank was standing guard at a distance, his weapon raised across his chest. He'd set his body at an angle, looking half towards Abdul and half out across the valley towards the distant ribbon of river.

Far below, close to the river, engineers were at work. They were putting in the foundations for a more substantial bridge, wide and strong enough to take supply vehicles. The soldiers, light brown figures in their desert camouflage, were directing the diggers, their arms signalling and pointing.

Najib appeared at her side. She sensed his need, his awkwardness in the face of Abdul's grief. 'Give him time,' she said, keeping her voice low. 'He's in shock.'

Najib nodded. He hesitated beside her a little longer, then crept back to Abdul and knelt beside him, reaching out his hand and gently patting his back, the way a mother might soothe a baby. After a little while, Najib started to speak. It was a rhythmical incantation that she knew, without understanding it, to be prayer. She found her mind running through the only prayer she knew. Our Father, Who Art in Heaven. It was absurd, of course. Hypocritical. She wasn't religious. But, even without faith, she always found comfort in the cadence of prayer.

The whole pitiful business took less than an hour. The Sergeant Major sent two men down with stretchers to carry the bodies away. Abdul stumbled behind, his hands groping after them like a blind man. The soldiers had dug small, bundle-sized hollows in the graveyard behind the village. The ground was as unyielding as rock and they ran with sweat. Lying once again in the dust, the rolls of cloth were already buzzing with flies.

When no one was looking, Ellen slipped back alone to the bombed house. It was eerily quiet. The corn sat neglected in the surrounding fields. From this side, the softly flowing water in the irrigation ditch, where she'd crawled in fear of her life, looked innocent. The sun was high overhead, bleaching the colour from the rocks and fields. The light wind, carrying in sand from the desert, rasped her face.

She knelt beside the low compound wall and examined the impact of the blast. The scars were clear. A crater surrounded by rough pockmarkings across the surface of the mud. The fragments of a grenade lay in the dirt. She turned them over. They didn't look Western. Russian, perhaps. She stood up, judged the distance from the house. A slightly firmer pitch, a higher angle of elevation and it would have had them. It had been close. She ran her hands over her face, feeling the bone beneath the flesh. Her legs trembled. Far too close.

She breathed in deeply and thought of Jalil. He had always been fatalistic. She heard his voice in her head, his quaint English. *When it happens, it happens. It is God's will.* His God had picked a strange place for him to die. A random patch of desert in Helmand, so far from his family. A place so barren, it didn't even have a name. He could have been in America now, walking across a college campus.

She imagined his emails to her, full of gratitude, of professions of friendship across the miles. His mother would have been faint with pride. But instead . . .

She shook the thought out of her head, walked back to the debris and picked her way through the broken fragments of mud brick. The goats had been piled to one side and were starting to rot. The rancid stink hung heavy in the air.

The soldiers had cleared what they could. A heap of belongings sat on the earth. She turned over filthy pieces of clothing with the toe of her boot. Broken chairs and stools. Two cots, sturdy wooden frames plaited across with layers of rope. One of them was stained where the woman's leg had bled against it. Fragments of pots, a metal ladle, a cooking spoon, a knife, a large blackened pan.

They were country-made goods, rough and basic. Judging by the debris, the whole house had only been one or two rooms, with the goats in a lean-to at the back. The fire-pit for cooking was in the open air, just outside. The earth was scorched and soft with fresh ash. She remembered the small windows that had looked down on them as they crawled up the slope. A dark home, then, well insulated against the sand.

Ellen looked round. A couple of days ago that Afghan woman had been sweeping here, feeding her goats, milking them into one of those pots. Chopping up her vegetables over there, with that machete of a knife, setting her blackened pot to boil here. And now she was lying injured in a military camp, her children buried, her home destroyed. And, despite the pain as they dug her out, she'd still found the energy to spit.

She walked along the sides of the clearing, looking at the ground. Their boots had trampled a path through the corn, ending in confusion along the low wall. She turned to compare with the far side. There the corn was still erect. Unblemished. Apart from one place. She went across to look. A narrow path had been gouged out. She bent down. The stalks were mature and freshly broken. Almost as if . . . She followed the path into the corn and through the field until it disappeared into a deep stony ditch. An escape route?

As she paced it back, a dark square caught her eye. A small brown book, lying off in the corn to one side. She picked it up. The print squiggle of Afghan script. It was a well-worn volume, the cover hanging off. The paper was brittle and the outer edge smeared brown with dried blood. She lifted it to her face. It smelt of stale spices and cheap ink. She put it in her pocket and turned to look back through the corn to the ruins of the house. It looked different from here, less sinister in the burning sun. Smaller. More pathetic. She walked back to the clearing.

A rusting metal trunk lay to one side, perhaps two and a half feet long and a foot across. Battered and dented but still intact. She pulled up the metal clasp to find a mess of books inside. Old school exercise books with missing covers. A few printed books in the same state, their paper speckled. She wondered who in the family had enough schooling to read.

Right at the bottom, some typed documents in a cardboard folder. And a photograph album. Its shiny cover was a gaudy design of bright red and blue flowers on an egg-yolk background. The pages inside were cheap peel-back plastic. The photographs had thick white borders and were arranged with care, four to a page.

Sweat was pricking her hair, her neck. She eased off her helmet, unzipped her flak jacket and settled down on a flat mud brick. Ahead the sweep of fields, the corn, stirred in the low breeze. Here and there, mud compounds were dark in the landscape. Beyond the river, glinting in the sun, the scrub and sand nothingness of the desert stretched to the horizon. It was land that had seen almost constant warfare for the last thirty years.

Her ears were buzzing with pumping blood. She let her shoulders sink and thought again of Jalil. They'd covered so many stories together, bumping down dirt roads on endless trips, sharing bottles of water. They'd crouched together countless times inside dark fetid mud houses like this one, skins filthy and slick with sweat, trying to coax a story out of some villager. Trying to make sense of fragmented scraps of news. There was a lot about

Afghanistan, about tribal rivalries and customs, that she understood now because he'd taken such pains to explain it to her,
creasing his brow, struggling to find the right words in his strongly
accented English.

You must understand my country well, he used to say. He seemed
to take her instruction as a matter of personal pride. *You must
report it well and tell the world the truth about Afghanistan.* The
truth? If only life were that simple.

As a traditional Afghan male, he'd been protective. So much
so, he saved her life once.

They'd been driving back from a village on the Shomali Plain,
north of Kabul, close enough for them to reach and return in
a single day. She was working on a story about the fate of
returning refugees. They'd flooded back in their tens of thousands,
drawn to their newly democratic country from cramped camps
in Pakistan and Iran. Communities of youngsters who'd grown
up as foreigners, seeing their mothers spat at in the street and
their fathers competing for menial, poorly paid work. Old people
whose bones ached for home, for the stark shadows cast by
sunlight on pitted Afghan mountains and the bleak expanse of
the desert.

She and Jalil had sat, cross-legged, on dusty floors while one
family after another had told them their troubles. The lack of work
here in Afghanistan. The hostility from neighbours who'd stayed
and endured the fighting and despised them for having left.

They had both been subdued and exhausted as they drove back,
Jalil in the front of the battered car beside the local driver, Ellen
stretched out across the back seat, her hair itchy and hot under
her headscarf. Dust rose in clouds along the roadside as the driver
weaved his way past overladen trucks and cars. He was aggressive,
leaning on his horn, eager to be home. The sun was low and falling,
a brilliant orange ball setting fire to the jagged mountains that
ran along the road.

The driver braked sharply and swerved, pulling in. He and Jalil
exchanged a word or two. The car came to a halt in front of a

row of shacks, selling pyramids of unevenly shaped oranges and pomegranates and soft drinks. The driver jumped out of the car and went across to one.

'Please. One minute.' Jalil twisted round to her in the back, holding up a finger to denote the minute and jumped out too, pursuing the driver. His face was tight.

Ellen tried again to press down the lopsided lock on her door, which had stuck at half-mast. The road was busy. Passing trucks and lumbering buses blew dust into her face through the cracks round the window and set the car rocking on the road. She was hungry and thirsty. She thought about arriving back at the guest-house, pulling off her dusty clothes and having a warm shower. They served wine in the basement bar. Poor-quality wine that guaranteed a headache. After her shower, she would go down there, order bread and hummus and a salad and let her senses be numbed by that cheap—

A sharp knock on the window, inches from her face, made her jump. A man, a dark shape in the gloom. His flat metal ring clattered on the glass. His face came low to the window, fogging it with his breath as he peered in. A thick dark beard and bushy eyebrows gave volume to a thin face. A flash of dirty teeth. She took hold of the inside handle and pulled the door taut. Useless, she knew, if he decided to jerk it open and the lock didn't hold. But what else could she do? Her headscarf slipped back on her head. His eyes were on her face.

The driver's door opened with a stirring of dust and air. For a second, she was relieved. Thank God. He's back. Let's go. Then she saw the head and broad shoulders pushing inside, the greasy hair of a stranger, and heard the scrape of fingernails against plastic as hands ransacked the inside of the car. A voice, raised, shouted something close to her ear. The intruder lifted his head, poked it to one side, his cheek level with the broken headrest of the front seat, and stared at her. He hesitated for a moment, taking her in, then smiled. She glimpsed the flash of light on metal and looked down to see a gun in his hand. Her mind was trying to process it, even as she waited to be shot. Not an AK-47, some part of her brain was deciding. She couldn't see quite what . . .

The man at her door was rattling the handle, trying to get in. The car rocked. Shouting. Footsteps, figures running. The intruder was suddenly retreating, twisting his neck back to see, scrambling to get out. A blow fell. Another. The car jerked. The dark shape at her door moved, letting in light.

Now the driver was falling into his seat, his hands trembling too hard to fit the keys in the ignition. She heard the jitter of metal as he scraped and failed, then tried again. A man fell sideways across the bonnet. His face, staring, pressed against the windscreen, squashing the flesh of his cheek. His eyes were open, stunned and unseeing. A trickle of blood smeared on the glass. Jalil pulled him off the car and there was a thud as the man hit the ground. Jalil was running round the front of the car and wrenching open the car door, jumping into his seat. He was shouting at the driver. The key found its slot and the engine started. They jerked forward into the road.

No one spoke as they drove back to Kabul. Ellen sat with her arms crossed, trying to hold her body and stop it from shaking. She felt sick. Images of the men's faces, of the gun, blurred her vision. The driver drove slowly, staying in lane, afraid to overtake anything. When he changed gear, his hand trembled on the gear stick. Jalil was rigid, his neck stiff with tension.

It was dark by the time they reached the guesthouse. The guards came out to them, guns dangling from their shoulders, and shone torches in their faces before they opened up the metal gates. Her legs buckled as she stepped out into the compound.

'Jalil,' she said. She hesitated. She wanted to invite him inside, into light and safety. But it was an overpriced place, designed for Western businessmen, aid workers and correspondents. He seemed uncomfortable there.

He got out of the car and stood in front of her in the darkness. Shame-faced.

'I'm sorry.' He didn't look her in the eye. 'These people.'

'Of course.' She didn't know what to say. She wanted to touch him, to pat him on the shoulder or take his hand and comfort him, but any such gesture, she knew, would only embarrass him more. She hesitated.

'Tomorrow,' he said. 'I will come at nine o'clock?'

'Nine o'clock.' She nodded.

Jalil leaned towards her and added in a whisper: 'I will find a better driver. I am very sorry.'

He got back into the car, slammed the door and they reversed out into the dark road.

It was only the following day, in proper light, that she saw the bruising around his eye and the cut down the side of his face. I should say something, she thought. I should thank him. But he seemed determined not to discuss what had happened and, as the day passed, it began to seem too late.

Now he's dead, she thought, and it really is too late. She lifted her hands to her face and rubbed them heavily down her cheeks. Her stomach was twisted with shame. She looked out across the valley.

Halfway down the hillside, a heavy brown bird flashed with sunlight. Its tail was fanned, its broad wings proud. It was hovering over the corn, straining to keep its stillness in the currents of air. She sat and watched it until it finally swooped and disappeared. Then she turned her attention to work, picked up the photograph album, wiped the dust from its cover with her sleeve and opened it out across her knee.

When she arrived back at the compound, Najib was waiting for her. His face was crumpled with anxiety.

'He is here,' he said, 'with his wife.'

He pointed to the medics' makeshift field hospital which had sprung up in one corner. Camouflage nets and ground sheets had been hung round for privacy but the dark, low shape of a man was visible, squatting on his haunches by a figure on the ground. Even from this distance, she could sense their stillness together.

His head was bowed towards his wife, his body tense. They'd found each other. She was no longer alone.

'How long's he been there?'

Najib shrugged. 'Twenty minutes,' he said. 'They are whispering, whispering.' He stamped his feet and looked self-important. 'Major Mack wants to speak to them,' he said. 'I will translate.'

Ellen sat on a flat stone against the wall and opened her notebook. She started to write a description of the bombed house and its contents before the details began to fade from her mind.

'The children are not theirs.'

She looked up. Najib had lit a cigarette and was quietly smoking. 'Not theirs?'

'The dead children, they are not theirs.'

He drew on his cigarette, blew out smoke.

'He said that?'

Najib nodded. 'After the burying. They are his older brother's children.'

Ellen considered this. 'So where's his older brother?'

Najib shrugged. A wasp was buzzing round them, close to their heads.

'He doesn't know,' he said. 'Everyone is fled.'

Ellen looked at him. 'It's his wife, though, isn't it?'

'It's his wife.'

She stared at him. Something wasn't right. This story smelt crooked.

'What do you make of them?' she said. 'Of the family?'

'Something strange.'

'What do you mean? Strange?'

Najib paused before he spoke. 'I don't know,' he said. Another pause. 'I don't trust them. They are hard people.'

'We just dropped a bomb on them.'

'That is true.' Najib finished his cigarette. Instead of screwing it into the dust with his boot, the way a soldier would, he walked over to the wall, stubbed out the sparks and crushed the end in his hand. He sat next to Ellen.

'My father was taken by the Taliban,' said Najib. 'He was a teacher. A good teacher. Someone accused him. They said he was irreligious. That he was teaching wrong things. He was picked up one day, on his way to the university, by the Ministry of Vice.'

Ellen leaned forward to listen. Najib's voice was barely more than a whisper.

'We waited long time,' Najib said. 'Painful waiting without word. My mother couldn't eat, couldn't sleep. It was too dangerous to go to the ministry to ask for him. I was just a boy. What could I do?'

Najib fell silent again.

'So what happened?'

'He crawled back to us in the night,' he said. 'More than a month afterwards. Both his legs were broken. He was so thin, so weak, it had taken him half the night to reach us.' He paused. 'His face was so bruised, I didn't recognize him. He lay in bed for many months before he could live again. He is crippled, of course.'

'Was it your father who taught you English?'

'Yes. He taught me many things. Including English.'

Ellen nodded. 'He must be proud of you.' Every Afghan family she met had suffered loss.

'I will make him proud.' Najib smiled. 'Isn't that what you are taught, when you learn about Afghan people? That we are very proud?' He spread his hands, still smiling, as if to say he admitted that this was so. 'That is why I hate Taliban, because of my father.' He paused. 'But these people,' he gestured back towards the medics' corner. 'I do not think they feel like this. I do not feel they hate Taliban. That is why I cannot trust them.'

Ellen let the silence settle. Najib was feeling nervously in his pockets, looking perhaps for more cigarettes.

'I think we have a friend in common,' she said.

He looked up.

'Jalil.'

He reacted at once. A sadness came into his face, mixed with something darker, with fearfulness.

'I saw his family in Kabul,' she said. 'Jalil used to translate for me.'

He nodded but he had turned his eyes away from her, towards the ground.

She waited, judging his silence. 'His sister said you were friends. You and Jalil.'

'We talked,' he said. 'He liked to talk about going to America. To study. His dream.'

Najib found another cigarette and lit it. They sat together as he smoked, the acrid smell of his tobacco heavy in the air. She wondered how much Jalil had told him. Her face felt suddenly hot.

'He didn't have the money,' she said. 'That's why he took this job.'

'Of course.' Najib drew on his cigarette, kicked the toe of his boot against the ground. 'The money is important.'

'Tell me, Najib. What happened?'

Najib sat on the ground beside her and stared at the sand as he began to talk. He kept his voice low, speaking hastily, as if he were afraid of being overheard. His words came to her scented with his cheap Afghan cigarette.

'He became worried,' he said. 'I don't know what it was. Something he knew. He was usually a happy person. But a few days before it happened, he changed very much. He wouldn't tell me. I knew there was something. But he told me it was better that I don't know.'

'What do you think it was?'

Najib drew on his cigarette, looked around cautiously. 'I don't know,' he said. 'But I think it was about the suicide bombing. In Nayullah. When we heard news of it, he was angry. I mean, of course, we were all angry. But his anger was something else. Something different. Bitter.'

Outside the compound, a convoy of heavy vehicles crashed past, proof that the engineers had strengthened the bridge. The roar enveloped them and they were both coated, even at this distance, in a light film of dust. Ellen waited for the noise to subside, then spoke again. 'Was he mixed up in anything? Drugs? Bad friends?'

Najib looked at her sadly. 'Jalil! I thought you knew him?'

'Did he tell you anything else?'

'He was going to leave. After the bombing, he told me he was leaving soon and going back to Kabul. He didn't care if he couldn't find another work, that's what he said. He couldn't stay here.'

Ellen leaned in towards him. 'Why?'

'Not his safety.' Najib looked up, realizing he might have been misunderstood. 'He wasn't worried about himself. He was brave.'

'Yes,' she said, 'he was.'

'And he liked the soldiers. He was always fooling around with them, playing football. And he very much liked Major Mack. He is like a father to me, he used to say. He has the heart of an Afghan.' Najib lifted his elbow and rubbed his eyes.

Ellen smiled. From Jalil, she knew, this was high praise.

'I don't know what happened.' Najib looked close to tears. 'He went out with the men that day and then he disappeared. They found him dead. Tied up like an animal. Shot through the head.'

He got suddenly to his feet, pressed his cigarette into spilled strands and wiped down his face with the palm of his hand. Mack was approaching across the compound, spraying sand. He gave Najib a curt nod and Najib ran towards him, falling into line at his heel. The two men set off together to the medics' corner.

She sat quietly, looking after them and thinking, breathing in the fragments of Afghan tobacco in the air around her, until it had dispersed completely into the desert air. It was the same cheap brand that Jalil used to smoke.

Moss, Dillon and young Hancock had set their mess tins to boil and were rifling through their ration packs. They didn't look up as she settled beside them, got her own kit out, lit the burner and started to heat some water.

'Torta-wotsit with three cheeses,' Moss was saying, waving a foil packet. 'Tastes like dog shit, doesn't it?'

Dillon pulled it out of his hand. 'Thank you, Jamie Oliver.

Gimme that.' He handed Moss a pack from his own rations. 'Spag bol. More your style.'

'More like pie and chips and a pint, mate.'

Ellen pulled out a vacuum pack of meatballs in tomato sauce and put it to boil. She squeezed synthetic cheese from a tube onto brown biscuits and rubbed them together to spread it. Her hands were black with dirt. She could feel Dillon watching her out of the corner of his eye. 'Are we still living the dream?' she said.

'Bloody right.' He grinned. 'Happy days. You signing up?'

Hancock sniggered, his head down.

'Bit old,' said Ellen. 'But thanks anyway.'

Moss was bent over his mess tin, prodding the sachet with his knife. 'Fucking sand,' he said. 'Fucking everywhere.'

'Language,' said Dillon. 'Ladies present.'

Ellen bit into a biscuit. The cheese tasted of chemicals. What could possibly have upset Jalil so much? He needed the job. He knew as well as anyone how scarce work was in Kabul. By Afghan standards, this job was dangerous but it was very well paid. The rest of the family depended on it. She thought about Jalil, about the kinds of thing that made him angry. He had strong principles. It would have to be something he found offensive or insulting to cause him to walk away from his duty to his family.

'Why haven't they put up a fight?' she said. 'The Taliban?'

Hancock looked round at the others. Moss, focused on his food, ignored her. Dillon shrugged. 'Dunno,' he said. He didn't look at her.

'An offensive like this, taking villages they've held for years. It's a real slap in the face.'

Dillon nodded. 'Well cheeky.' He and Moss were both fishing their hot foil packets out now, cutting them open and digging into them with plastic spoons. Steam rose round their faces. They ate hungrily, the packets up against their mouths as they spooned in the mush.

Ellen tried again, half thinking aloud. 'So where's the response?'

Dillon made a face through his food. 'Dunno,' he said. He pointed to her mess tin, now boiling hard. 'Don't leave it too long,' he said, 'or it tastes like crap.'

Mack finally re-emerged. He strode across the compound to the house and disappeared inside. Ellen spooned meatballs into her mouth; they were thick and tasteless but hot. She made a mug of tea with the boiling water and went back to her place against the wall to drink it. Her questions made the lads uncomfortable. The atmosphere had cooled.

It took her until mid-afternoon to get permission to talk to the Afghan woman. She was sleeping, the medics kept saying. Her husband's visit had tired her. She was still drowsy from the sedatives. Her leg wound? Nothing serious. Now it was clean, it should heal well.

She and Najib sat in the sand and waited. Najib spelt out the woman's name in her notebook in neat, sloping capitals: HASINA.

'Age?'

He wrinkled his nose. 'Maybe forty? Forty-five?'

'We'll ask her.'

'She won't know.' He jabbed her page with his finger. 'Write forty.'

Hasina was lying on a bedroll, a folded blanket under her head, a drip in her arm. Her headscarf was veiling her head and neck. Ellen knelt down beside her. The green eyes glared up at her, large and defiant.

'Tell her I'm a journalist, not a soldier,' said Ellen. 'I want to write about what happened to her. What happened to her family.'

She looked Hasina over as Najib translated. The dust that had coated her face and neck had been washed off and her skin smelt of disinfectant. Her lips were again pink with blood.

'What was she doing in the house, when the soldiers came? Why hadn't she left?'

'She was putting together belongings,' Najib said. 'Like her husband said to you.'

'Why were the children there?'

Najib translated. His tone was cool. Ellen sensed his suspicion of this woman.

'Playing,' he said. 'They hid in the house, she is saying. She didn't know they were there.'

'And who else was there?'

She watched Hasina closely as Najib asked the question. The green eyes were instantly wary.

'No person.'

'But someone threw grenades. Someone attacked the soldiers. Did she throw them? Or was there someone else there?'

Hasina's face seemed to close. Her eyes became expressionless.

'No. She says no person was there.' Najib leaned forward to add in a stage whisper. 'But maybe she is lying.'

'So ask her again: who threw the grenades?'

'She says she doesn't know about grenades.' Najib shrugged as if to say: what's the point? You're wasting your time.

The green eyes glared at her. Ellen held their gaze.

'She doesn't know anything,' Najib was whispering. 'She is just village woman. Not educated.'

Ellen opened her bag and brought out the bloodstained book she'd found in the cornfield by the house. She held it out word-lessly to show Hasina.

No need to ask if she recognized it. Hasina's alarmed surprise registered at once. She grasped the book from her and brought it to her mouth to kiss. She ran her fingers over the dark stains along the side, as if she were licking them with her fingertips, tasting the blood. Ellen saw the confusion in her eyes.

'That is Holy Qur'an,' said Najib. He looked disapproving. 'Where did you get it?'

'At the house.'

He shook his head. 'It's not good for you to take it,' he said. 'You are not Muslim lady.'

'Ask her: whose is it?'

Hasina's knuckles were white where she gripped the book.

'Her husband's, she says. It belongs to Abdul.'

Ellen shook her head. The woman was lying. She knew Abdul was all right because she'd just seen him. 'So why does the sight of it upset her so much?'

Najib pulled a face. 'I don't know. Maybe she is very religious.'

'Tell her I have photographs too. From the trunk. I'd like her to tell me who these people are. OK?'

Hasina had slipped the book under the blanket, still tight in her hand. Now she was shaking her head, speaking with passion. Najib shrank back a little, as if he were being scolded.

'She is saying these are her photographs, her family,' he said. 'You must give them back.'

Ellen tried to soothe her with a low calm tone of voice. 'Of course,' she said. 'Of course I will.'

Hasina had lifted herself onto her elbow, agitated. She turned to Ellen and glared at her as she spoke, fire in her eyes. Ellen remembered her weak attempt to spit at her when they were digging her out.

'Maybe you should give her the pictures,' said Najib. He seemed alarmed by her strength of feeling.

'Of course. They're hers.' Ellen kept her eyes on Hasina, trying to quieten her. 'No one's disagreeing about that. I just wonder if she could—?'

A medic appeared, stony-faced. 'What's going on?'

Hasina was struggling to sit up, her drip knocking to and fro above her. Her face was contorted, words hurled like missiles.

The medic patted her on the shoulder, steadied the drip. 'I think you'd better go,' she said to Ellen.

'She's saying: where are the photographs?' said Najib. 'They are hers. This is what she is saying, over and over.'

'Photographs?' said the medic. 'You can't take pictures in here.'

'I think perhaps you'd better give them,' said Najib in a low voice. 'She is very upset.'

'I can see that.' Ellen rummaged in her bag and handed over the few pictures she'd slipped out of the album. Stiffly posed family groups, set against mountains. Old-fashioned. Hasina and Abdul were in some, with others she didn't recognize. 'Ask her who these people are, would you?'

But Hasina had already snatched them from her and they too disappeared under the blanket.

'If you want to see a patient again,' said the medic coldly, 'you'll need my permission. Understood?'

As Ellen left, she paused and turned back for a final look. Hasina's eyes were on her, strong and clear but with an expression she couldn't quite read. Cunning or fear, or a mixture of the two?

10

The voices exhausted her. Their foreign words clattered like stones down a well. She had slept through the night, her body exhausted and drugged by their medicine. Now she was awake. The green material, strung round her, only shielded her a little from the sun. She lay, sweating, unable to move. Flies settled on her feet. Under the bandages, her leg ached. She was a prisoner.

Sometimes the camp was quiet. The soldiers' voices fell silent. Somewhere outside the compound, engines droned. The doctor, that black man, came to her in the morning, bringing that man from Kabul to translate. Her leg was healing well, he said. He pulled the needles out of her arm and took away the empty fluid bags. When he smiled, his gums made a red gash in his dark skin. She must try to walk today. Perhaps in a day or two, she could go.

Go, she thought. Go where?

The women in men-trousers, their hair scraped back, came to check her temperature. They were shameless, their heads uncovered for all the men to see, their fingers thick as bananas. No man would marry them. They bent over her, pulling back her clothes and intruding on her flesh with wet cloths. The liquid smelt of lemons but it was false, hard scent, not of the earth.

A shadow came over her face and she opened her eyes. Sad brown eyes were gazing down at hers. A rough hand stretched down to touch her face, its fingernails black with earth. The fingers traced the contours, chin to cheek to hair.

'I'm dreaming,' she said. His kind face swam as her eyes filled.

'Not dreaming.' He stooped down close to her, settling himself at her side. He took her hand. 'I have found you again.'

She was crying now, drowning in his familiar smell, of dust and of land. 'Abdul,' she said. He was squeezing her hand like a cloth, wringing it dry. 'Abdul. I have had secrets from you. May Allah forgive me. Terrible secrets.'

He nodded. She could read in his face the knowledge of the dead children, his nephew and nieces, his blood. She pulled on his hand to make him lean in closer, so close his breath was warm on her neck.

'I must speak to you of Aref,' she said. 'My husband, he is not in Kandahar.'

He sat silently beside her, his face close to her whispering mouth, as she told him the story of the boy fighters who had come to claim their son, about the suicide bombing and then her son's return, crawling through the corn to find help, and escaping again to it, when the soldiers began their assault.

When she had finished her story, Abdul sat silently, his hands folded in his lap. He was still for a long time. Hasina lay watching him, exhausted by the effort of speech. Her mouth was dry.

'They have buried the children,' Abdul said at last. His voice cracked. 'The house is gone.'

She nodded. 'We must get word to Karam,' she said. 'They must be searching.'

The traitor from Kabul appeared round the canvas. Abdul looked at her, his face pale. Could this stranger have heard?

'I am Najib,' he said. 'Major Mack wishes to speak to your wife.' He bowed his head to Abdul, showing the respect due to an older man. 'Perhaps it is better if you see him together?'

Abdul nodded. He helped Hasina raise her shoulders and fasten her scarf more closely over her head and neck. 'I will speak,' he whispered. 'You stay quiet.'

The Major didn't have a beard. He didn't look wise. He crouched by Hasina's knees as if he were about to milk a goat. If I kicked him, Hasina thought, he would topple right over into the dust.

Now he was low, she could see the thinness of his fair hair. His scalp was pink and mottled. He was strong but not a man built for the desert. The conspirator from Kabul stood behind him, his hands folded at his groin, and translated back and forth.

'Why was your wife in the house with the children?' he said. 'Why didn't she leave? We issued warnings.'

Abdul inclined his head. 'She went back to fetch our clothes and cooking knives,' he said. 'The children were frightened. Perhaps they followed her.'

The Major's face was impassive. His eyes were ringed by white circles but his nose and cheeks had been burnt red by the sun. 'Someone threw grenades at our men. Was it your wife?'

Abdul shook his head. 'My wife is a simple woman,' he said. 'A village lady. What does she know of weapons?'

The Major was looking at Hasina, his eyes thoughtful. He would be a handsome man, for a Westerner, if he grew a beard. Behind him, the traitor shifted.

'So someone else was there? A fighter?'

Abdul tutted. 'If there had been a fighter, you would have found him,' he said. 'Just my wife was there, with the children.'

The Major's voice became harder. 'We know there've been militants in the village,' he said. 'We have photographs. We've been watching the movement here for some time.'

Abdul said nothing but Hasina smelt the tension in his body. He bowed his head to the ground. Somewhere outside the compound, a machine started up and the noise kept the silence busy. The Major's eyes were searching, moving from his face to hers and back again. His red forehead had creased into a frown.

'You're lying,' he said. 'You'd be better off telling me the truth.' Silence. He craned forward, reaching his body towards them. When he spoke, he made his voice soft again.

'We are here to help you,' he said. 'To bring peace to the village.'

Abdul's face broke into a slow, sad smile. 'Peace?' he said. 'That is very hard for us to believe.'

They waited until the Commander had been gone some time

before they dared to speak. Abdul leaned close to her, clasping her hand and whispered.

'You must stay here for now,' he said. 'They say I can visit you. They've given me a paper.' He pulled it out of his pocket to show her. It was a small paper, with black handwriting in their language. 'See? I will come every day.'

He patted her hand. 'You must get well enough to walk.'

He picked up a plastic bottle of water from the sand, half full. 'Is this what you drink?'

She pulled a face. 'Foreign water,' she said. 'It has no taste.'

He unscrewed the top and helped her swallow a little. Her lips were chapped.

'You know where you are?' he said. 'This is Masoud's house. The soldiers have made it into a camp. The whole village is the same. They sleep in all the houses, in the compounds; even in the straw with the goats and chickens.'

He stopped and shook his head in disbelief. 'The corn is rotting in the ground. The animals are thirsty. What kind of men are these, who don't know how to care for a donkey, a hen?'

'Aref,' she said. 'You must look for him.'

He nodded. 'Of course.' He bent over to kiss her forehead. His beard scraped against the side of her nose. 'May Allah bless and protect us,' he said. 'We must have faith.'

A little food. The heat of the sun. Her head aching. Her skin, thick and wet as a dog's tongue. Sleep.

The next day, the uniformed woman came to her with metal sticks. She gestured to her to sit up and pushed her thick hands into Hasina's armpits. She grunted as she heaved her, lifting Hasina upright and slowly lowering her weight onto her legs. Hasina stuck the injured leg, in its white bandages, forward into the dirt, afraid. The green screen of material swam in front of her eyes. The woman kept her grasp tight. She was talking to Hasina in her foreign language: short words, spoken loudly in her face as if she were a fool.

'This is my country,' Hasina said. 'You should speak my language.'

The woman stared at her, not understanding. Najib came across and showed her how to use the sticks to walk.

'You must practise,' he said. 'Build up your strength.'

'Practise?' She looked round Masoud's compound, cluttered now with foreign soldiers and tents and hanging mosquito nets. The Commander was sitting in a chair close to the entrance to Masoud's house, papers spread out across his lap. Her head was clearer. She swung the sticks and propelled herself forward.

'I want to go back,' she said. 'To see my home.'

Najib looked shocked. 'Too far,' he said. 'You'll be too tired.'

She stared him out. 'I need to see it.'

She practised walking as the foreigners ran back and forth, discussing her request in their own language. Najib's face was pursed, his eyes anxious. She had embarrassed him, she knew that. Finally he came scurrying back.

'You may go,' he said. 'The journalist will take you. And one of the soldiers. And I will come too.'

'If that woman comes,' she said, 'tell her to cover her head.'

The state of the main street shocked her. She stepped out from the metal gate and stood there, leaning on her sticks, breathing hard. Not a villager in sight. The soldiers had driven military vehicles right against the walls of Masoud's compound. Young men sat inside them, dressed in their sand- and mud-coloured clothes, helmets on their heads, dark goggles over their eyes, staring down their guns at her. Masoud was such a gentle man. What would he say to this?

The foreign woman had emerged from the compound and was walking ahead, following just behind a soldier. The two of them paused at the end of the street, waiting for her. The soldier crouched low and trained his gun round the wall.

Hasina pushed herself forward. The street was otherwise deserted, apart from the parked vehicles and a bewildered wandering goat. There was evidence of soldiers in every compound, every house. Eyes watched her from tank turrets that slid in their sockets, following her, as she passed. Compound corners were covered with thick nets, spread out like spiders' webs. The life of the village had been snuffed out. No chatter, no gossip. No children, no women. Only foreign fighting men. By the time she reached the corner, the foreign woman and the soldier were already some way ahead.

Hasina's arms were starting to ache. She stopped often, wiping down her face with her scarf and shifting her weight on the sticks. Najib buzzed at her side, telling her it was too much, she should go back and rest. She swatted him away.

Her breath quickened as she took the winding track from the main street down to the house. She stumbled, setting stones bouncing and one of her sticks clanging to the ground.

'Slowly.' Najib picked up the dropped stick and handed it to her. 'You'll fall.' The soldier behind them stopped too, keeping a careful distance. She set off again, her eyes to the ground as she rounded the final corner and picked her way down the slope to the back of the house.

She smelt the change before she saw it. A thick odour of stale dust, with a sour note of decay. She had been told the truth but she stared, just the same, in utter disbelief. One wall was still standing, the interior exposed like innards. The decorated mirror her mother and father had given them as a marriage gift. Her best red scarf. To one side of the heap of rubble, their trunk, dented. Its lid was standing open. They'd looted it, of course. Broken belongings had been piled to one side. Blue-painted sticks from the stool. The battered cot she and Abdul had shared from the day they married so many years ago. Her cracked cooking pot and ladle. All picked over by these foreign vultures.

The foreign woman had stopped at the edge of the clearing and turned back to wait. Her pale eyes were on Hasina's face. Nothing moved.

Beyond the house, the land stood lush in the strong morning light, the corn shining as if it were aflame. She saw where boots had trampled down the crops and the ragged scar in the boundary wall where the small bomb had exploded, scattering mud.

Najib was at her elbow, his breath hot on her cheek.

'Madam,' he said, 'let me help you.'

When she had rested, she asked where the journalist had found Aref's copy of the Holy Book. They led her to the far side of the clearing, to a crumpled path that stretched out into the corn, pointing away from the house and the valley, across the fields. Hasina handed Najib the sticks and lowered herself to the earth, her legs trailing behind her, until she was lying with her body and face pressed against the ground. She filled her lungs with the deep rich smell of dust and vegetation, moving her arms above her head as if she were swimming through the corn. She rubbed the dirt into her hands, embracing the field. Let them watch. She laughed into the ground. Aref had been here. She could smell him. No blood. No sign of struggle. Just her boy, crawling this way to make his escape. He was alive and he was out there. Wherever he was, she would find him.

11

Ellen threaded her arm under Hasina's shoulder, lifting the hot, damp cave of cotton at her armpit. The bone was light, hollow as a bird's, and almost fleshless, riding on Ellen's own as she took her weight. Hasina's breathing was shallow against her ear. The sun was high overhead now, making their skin slippery as they clung together.

At the junction with the main street, Ellen saw a stretch of broken wall and lowered Hasina onto it. She stood back, rotating her shoulders and kneading the tight muscle. Frank had dropped to one knee, tense, pointing his weapon down the track. Najib was hanging back, watchful, his face anxious. She dug water out of her pack, tipped Hasina's head back and trickled some into her mouth. It spilled from the corners and ran in rivulets down her chin and throat.

The air reeked of petrol, wrapped in fine clouds of dust and the noise of a heavy engine. Further down the street, thickset Danish soldiers were working a mechanical digger, churning the dirt and piling it along the verge as fresh defences. Hasina's head had sunk to her chest. Ellen wondered how long it was safe to let her rest.

The Danes cut the engine. The air was instantly softer as animal sounds were restored: footsteps, voices, the cry of a bird. The Danes started to pile the earth by hand in a metallic scrape of spades and gentle male grunting. Ellen listened intently. There was another sound rising beyond them. The throaty chug of a diesel engine and, tangled in it, the subdued voices of women.

Frank swung to look as she strode off towards the sound. His face was tight with disapproval. She crossed the street before anyone could stop her and rounded a corner. The noise peaked at once.

A tractor was labouring up the slope towards her, driven by a thin Afghan man. He was pulling a simple wooden cart, laden with women and children. The colour had been washed out of their cotton clothes. They had a subdued air, as if they were wary or afraid. They clung together as a sticky mass, extended legs dangling over the side of the cart. Toddlers stood upright in the cage of their mother's arms, clinging to the top struts to keep their balance. The low murmur of voices fell silent as the women saw her.

Two young soldiers were walking alongside the tractor, weapons readied. She nodded to them as they all approached.

'What's this?'

The soldier nearest to her, a young Brit, shrugged. 'Women, ma'am.'

At the top of the slope, the tractor juddered to a halt. The women clambered off. They pulled their headscarves further forward, hiding their faces. Children were handed down to the ground, their noses encrusted, faces streaked with dirt. Dresses and shirts gaped with the memory of buttons.

Ellen saw their eyes shift to a place behind her and turned to look. Najib had come round the corner, followed by Hasina, hobbling on her crutches. A low murmur of voices ran through the group of women when they saw Hasina. Finally Frank appeared, his face sullen, his gun against his chest.

'We shouldn't be here.' Frank's tone was petulant. 'Let's move.'

Some of the young women, babies in their arms, looked to be teenagers. Their faces were thin with malnourishment, their cheekbones sharp. They drifted to nearby compounds and stood in clusters at the closed metal gates without knocking, visitors without hope. Some of the women sank to their haunches in the dust, eyes to the ground.

Ellen spoke again to the British soldiers. 'What's going on?'

One of them spat sideways into the dirt. His dark goggles hid the expression in his eyes.

'Dunno, ma'am,' he said. 'We was just told to let them come.'

The sun was starting to burn. The women crouched in the thin lines of shade along compound walls and waited. Hasina had reached them now and was leaning, her face pale, against a compound wall. Several women gathered round her and they spoke quietly amongst themselves, heads close together.

Ellen turned to Najib. 'Are the women from this village?'

He looked round. 'Of course,' he said. 'Must be from these houses.'

'Where are they living now?'

He waved his hand towards the vastness of the desert. 'Out there, maybe.'

Her eyes fell on a young woman whose eyes didn't flicker away. She was holding herself erect, her expression challenging. Her clothes stood out in the crowd, the colours brighter and made of finer cotton.

'Ask this woman,' she said to Najib. 'Ask her where she's living.'

Najib sighed as if to protest about the pointlessness of asking village women anything, then spoke to her. 'In the desert,' he said. 'I told you.'

The young woman ignored Najib when he lifted his hand to quieten her and jabbed the air with her finger, her voice angry.

'What's she saying now?'

'They have no shelter, she is saying.' Najib pulled a face. 'They are getting sick. They are not having clean water.'

'Which house is hers?'

'This one,' he said. He pointed to a grand compound behind them on the corner, its metal gates closed. 'That's what she says.'

Frank signalled to Ellen. 'That's enough.' He sounded rattled. 'Time we moved.'

Ellen kept her eyes on the young woman. 'Ask her what she's come for.'

Najib stared at Ellen as if she were stupid. 'We must go,' he said. 'Didn't you—?'

'Najib. Ask her.'

He sighed theatrically and threw out the question. The woman rattled off another angry speech.

'So many things.' Najib counted them off on his fingers. 'Blankets, pots, buckets, knives, stools, cots. And she has good clothes, she says. And carpets.' He was looking increasingly incredulous. 'Expensive carpets, this is what she says.'

The woman was still talking.

'They have goats, chickens, she says. If no one gives the animals food and water, they will surely die. This is all what she says.' He pulled a face. 'She is very bossy woman,' he added in a low voice. 'God's mercy on her husband.'

Frank put his hand on Ellen's arm, his gun pointed defensively at the women. 'Now,' he said. 'Time to go.'

Ellen considered for a moment, then walked over to the grand compound and banged her fist on the metal gate. Frank swore.

'Hey!' The grille made a satisfying metallic crash.

A bolt scratched and the inner gate opened a fraction. A gun butt poked towards her, inches from her head. Behind it, a Danish soldier with startling blue eyes and a sullen face.

'These women need their things,' she said.

The Dane's face was furious. 'Not possible.'

The feisty young woman pressed into her back, trying to peer past into the compound. Ellen felt the hard warmth of her body. The Dane scowled.

'They need cooking pots. Blankets.'

'This is a secure area.' The Dane's blue eyes were cold.

Ellen nodded to the angry Dane, preserving her smile. 'We'll wait. I'm a journalist, by the way. Ellen Thomas. *NewsWorld* magazine.'

The gate slammed shut in her face. The meeker women settled back in the shade and pulled children into their laps.

Frank had stormed to the corner and disappeared. Ellen turned back to Najib.

'Ask this woman about the fighters,' she said. 'Were they here?'

Najib shook his head in despair.

'If they come with guns, she is saying, what can we do? Now you have come with guns, what can we do?' He lowered his voice. 'They are lying, these village women. They all support Taliban.'

Najib spelled out the woman's name in Ellen's notebook: PALWASHA.

The metal gate opened. The cold-eyed Dane peered out, his weapon raised. A bucket flew out and splashed into the dust, followed by a bundle of cotton clothing and the crash of a metal cooking pot.

'Anything else?' Ellen asked the Dane.

The Dane glared back. 'You are welcome,' he said, then slammed the metal gate shut.

Ellen looked round at the women who were silently watching her. Hasina's gaze was the most intense. Her strong green eyes were locked on Ellen's, boring into her as if she were penetrating Ellen for the first time.

The Sergeant Major was waiting for them just inside the gate of their own compound. He poked a finger at Najib. 'Get a move on,' he said. 'Major Mack's waiting.' Ellen followed, uninvited, as they strode off.

Mack was sitting at his table under an awning, a mess mug of tea in front of him. He twisted round as they approached and smiled. Opposite him, flowing over the edges of a spindly camp chair, was a stout Afghan man. His rounded stomach, pushing out a long white tunic, was forcing him to sit back from the table. His face looked familiar. It was dominated by a white beard, which fell from his chin in ridged waves. His full moustache, in contrast, was a confusion of black, grey and white streaks as its colour turned. The hair on his head, visible in clumps beneath a round hat, was still a glossy black. So were his eyebrows, which hung over sharp eyes. They fixed on Ellen, stony, as she held his gaze, trying to remember where she'd seen him before. He had the hard stare of a man who has seen bloodshed and chaos and survived.

'Ellen Thomas. Quite a celebrity in England,' said Mack. He gestured her to a seat. 'Join us. We're nearly finished.'

Mack turned to Najib, who was standing with his head lowered.

'I was eager to find you a little earlier,' he said, 'but in fact Mr Karam speaks very good English, I discover.'

The Afghan man turned back to Mack. 'Just a little,' he said. His accent was thick but his voice strong. He reached forward to take a biscuit from the tin plate on the table and a chunky foreign watch flashed at his wrist.

'Mr Karam is one of the headmen here,' said Mack. 'We're talking about arranging a *shoura*, a village meeting. See what we can do to help.'

Karam inclined his head. 'Certainly that can be arranged. Perhaps in two or three days?'

Mack looked pleased. 'Any help you need, let me know.'

Karam rested his large hands on the table. The skin was smooth with long dark hairs bunched around the knuckles. A businessman's hands, not a farmer's.

'There is one thing.' He broadened his mouth into a smile that didn't reach his eyes. 'My wife is ill. As you know, the last days have been very difficult. And now, living without shelter in the desert – well, it is too much for her. I would be most grateful . . .'

Mack pursed his lips. He pressed his hands together, making an arch with his fingers, and tapped his chin. 'Difficult,' he said. 'Yes, I can see.'

'It would be a sign of good intention,' Karam went on, 'if we could have access to a small house. My compound is under occupation. I am host of the Danish troops, I believe.'

Mack cleared his throat. 'Well, I'm afraid I really couldn't—'

Karam raised his hand to stop him. 'But I have another house. A small place on the edge of the village. For servants and for storage and for the children to play.' He stopped, steadied his breath. 'Perhaps if we could go there, it would not be too inconvenient? A sort of village base, if you will.'

He paused. The air was heavy and silent.

'Where is it, exactly?'

Karam pointed in the direction of the river. 'Close to the house that was bombed,' he said. 'My brother's house.'

There was a moment's silence. Karam's eyes were empty, his smile controlled. As she made the connection, Ellen realized where she'd seen him before. In Hasina's photographs.

Mack nodded. He seemed embarrassed. 'I'm sure we can work something out,' he said. 'Access will be restricted. We can't allow other villagers here without permission. You understand. Security.' He paused, his eyes on Karam's face. 'But perhaps, in the circumstances, for you and your wife . . .' He pushed back his chair and stood up.

Karam too got to his feet, easing himself out of the small chair. At full height, he looked all the more imposing. The two men shook hands as the officers looked on.

As Karam turned and headed back towards the gate, Ellen pursued him, pushing alongside him to make him acknowledge her.

'Your brother,' she said. 'His name is Abdul?'

He stopped and turned to look at her. He was clearly not a man who was used to someone holding his gaze, especially not a woman.

'He was here,' she said. 'Yesterday. To see his wife.' She pointed to the curtained enclosure of the medics' corner.

'I know this.'

Ellen felt the challenge in his eyes as he tried to stare her down. His face was hard with power. Just by looking, they were circling each other like fighting cocks, each getting the measure of the other's strength. The silence grew round them.

'The bombing,' she said at last. 'They were your children?'

He did the last thing she expected. He smiled. 'They were,' he said. 'Is that what you are so anxious to know?'

'They know that?' She nodded back towards the officers, bent in conversation round Mack.

'They know.' The false smile was still on his lips. 'They offered me money. They pay per child, as I understand.' He gave a brusque nod. 'I declined their offer.'

Ellen tried to read his eyes, his tone of voice. He was giving nothing away. He turned and she walked slowly by his side across the sand.

'Unusual,' she said. 'To come from such a small village and speak such good English.'

'Not so good.'

'Where did you study?'

He paused before answering. 'In the mosque at first,' he said. 'Later in Kandahar. I was very fortunate about my teachers.'

They were approaching the compound gate. 'The poppy must have brought a lot of money to the village,' she said. 'This is good land.'

He turned to her, his face composed. 'Does it look like a rich village?' he said.

'No,' she said, returning his half-smile. 'That's what makes me wonder where the money's been going.'

He looked past her for a moment, gazing over the heaps of kicked straw and rows of army sleeping bags, the damp shirts draped along mosquito nets to dry, and at the soldiers themselves, stripped to the waist and sweating in the sun.

'Always in Afghanistan', he said, 'the rich get richer. And the money from poppy goes to guns, to fighting. This is the tragedy of our country.'

'And where are the fighters?' she said. 'Where have they gone?'

The square hat bobbed on its wiry pillow of black hair. 'You ask too many questions,' he said. His eyes were cold. 'You are in my country now, in Afghanistan.' He continued to stare at her and she felt the menace in his look. 'Life here is easily lost. You would be wise not to make enemies.'

She stood, watching him walk away, his back broad under his

cotton clothes. He was a powerful man and a dangerous one. She felt her heart rate quicken. You should be careful, she thought, making threats like that. I make quite an enemy too. She watched Karam gain the gate. He stood proudly as the young soldier there slipped back the bolt and let him leave.

The compound was fast turning into a barracks. The lads all had mosquito nets erected, draped with newly washed socks and damp cotton boxers. Young Hancock was lying on a mat, his head against a mud brick, his eyes closed. The wires of his iPod trailed from his ears. Frank, walking back to their corner, lit up a cigarette for himself. He tossed a spare one into Hancock's lap as he passed. Hancock half opened a lazy eye and a hand came out like a lizard's tongue to take it. The eye closed again.

Dillon and Moss were both stripped to the waist, winding up buckets of water from the well. Its old-fashioned crank moaned as they turned it. Their flesh shone white in the sunshine, Moss revealed in all his flabbiness and Dillon, narrow-chested, his arms and back branded with tattoos. Their desert sunburn stopped abruptly at shirt necks and cuffs.

Frank settled to smoke and shouted across to them. 'Burning some fat, Moss?'

Moss gave him the finger. They heaved out another load of water and sloshed it into army buckets. Frank lay back on his sleeping bag, smoking his cigarette and staring at the sky.

Ellen felt restless, eager to be alone, to sit and stare into the vast bleakness of the desert and mull over the puzzle of everything she'd heard so far. She paced along the inside of the wall for a few turns, then struck out across the compound and walked round the outside of the house. Household goods had been cleared from the rooms and piled up against the walls.

The first room she peered into had become a communications base, oozing wired kit. The second had been turned into a command centre. Satellite maps were stuck up round the walls and a large table dominated the centre of the room, scattered with more.

She took a quiet step inside. The first satellite map was of the area west of Nayullah. The second showed the land they'd just taken. The valley, with the river threaded through it. The rise to the village, each compound marked with—

'Looking for something?'

The voice came from the shadows behind her. She turned. Mack, his eyes lively, was crouched low in the corner, a pile of papers on the ground in front of him. His boots creaked as he swung himself to his feet.

'Maps,' she said. 'Can't resist them.'

'They're old.' He left the papers and beckoned her across to the table. His skin smelt freshly of army soap, his breath of coffee. He picked up a map and unrolled it on the surface, weighting the ends. 'This is the course we took yesterday.' He traced a route with his finger across the river and into the green zone.

She ran her eyes across the contours, measured the distances. He pointed to the dense cluster of compounds that showed the village.

'This is where we are now.'

He unrolled a second map on top of the first. This showed an area outside the green zone, where whole tracts of desert seemed no more than uninhabited wilderness. The only signs of life were scattered dots of compounds in the middle of nothingness. Hard to imagine how the families who lived there could survive at all.

'Pretty bleak.'

Mack nodded. 'Primitive,' he said. 'Unchanged for centuries.' He ran his hand slowly over the paper, reading its features. 'I think sometimes of the British soldiers who fought the last campaign here. Walking on the same sand. Facing the same heat.'

His expression was wistful. She thought of Najib's comment. That Jalil thought Major Mack had the heart of an Afghan.

'The ones playing the Great Game?'

'Not playing.' He tutted. 'Giving their lives for their country.'

She looked at the seriousness in his face. 'Maybe history's

131

repeating itself. Except this time, it's a proxy war against global jihad, not against the Russians.'

He lifted his hand from the map and it sprang back into its roll. He turned to face her. 'You're clever,' he said. 'But it's too easy to be cynical. Men's lives are at risk. My men. That's not for nothing.' His eyes were intense on hers. 'You have a great responsibility. You should be careful what you write.'

'Oh, I am.'

He turned abruptly back to the table, moved the map aside and unrolled a third. His cheek was flushed. She had annoyed him, punctured his sense of mission. She felt both amused and contrite. She had a tendency to be flippant without thinking, to deflate people. It wasn't always welcome.

She bent beside him to look at the third map. His fingers were long, efficient, as they smoothed and marshalled the paper.

'This is the area south of here,' he was saying. 'That's the river. There's the track we took to the ridge when the offensive started. And the ridge itself.'

She looked more closely. 'So tell me,' she said, 'where was Jalil found?'

'The turp?' He turned his head to look at her, his eyes surprised. 'What makes you so interested in him?'

'I knew him.'

His eyebrows rose.

'I worked with him. In Kabul.'

'I see.' He spoke to himself, nodding. 'That explains it.'

He bent back over the map. He pointed to a blank stretch of desert about ten kilometres away. 'I don't know. Around here, I suppose.'

South-east of the latest offensive. She judged the distance and the angles of the nearest tracks. It wasn't as far away as she'd expected.

'I'd like to go.'

'Go?' He re-rolled the map. 'There's nothing to see.'

'Even so.' She kept her voice firm.

He levelled the ends. 'Absolutely not.' He fastened the map with a paperclip. 'That's impossible. Final word.'

'But now you've pushed North,' she said, 'it must be more secure. That area—'

'I'm not risking my men's lives,' he said, 'on some fool errand.'

He dropped the map onto the table and turned away from her. His body had tightened. She watched, taking in the tension across his broad shoulders.

A young officer appeared in the doorway, saw her there and hesitated on the threshold. He coughed. 'Sir?'

Mack turned round. His expression was formal, with little trace of the friendliness she'd seen earlier. He motioned her towards the doorway. 'If you don't mind?'

'Of course.'

The officer stepped neatly to one side to let her pass.

She walked back through the tunnel that ran the length of the house, blinking in the gloom. The pattern of the map was clear in her mind. Jalil, she thought, I'd like to see where you died. She had an absurd image of herself laying a flower on the sand. Stupid, of course. But he'd been a kind friend and a loyal one. She would have liked the chance to say goodbye.

Two young soldiers careered into the passageway from the bright sunshine beyond and bumped into her, knocking her against the wall. One twisted back, shouting over his shoulder, 'Sorry, ma'am', as they ran on. The other lad, ahead, was spluttering with laughter.

She leaned her head against the brickwork, catching her breath. The mud plaster was warm and soft. A tinny radio was playing a high-pitched song, a man's voice climbing up and down the scale in Pashto. It reminded her of the bazaars in the cities she'd visited with Jalil, where a babble of music constantly spilled out of every alley, every shop, every café. Beyond the music, there was another noise, of feet shuffling in the dust. She moved forward, peered in round the half-closed door.

Najib. His hands were raised gracefully above his head, his arms

133

bent, his shoulders gyrating as he waved flexed fingers in the air. He was dancing with one foot extended, sashaying in small steps, his hips undulating to the wailing rhythm of the music. His eyes were closed. He seemed lost. When the song ended, his body slackened, the magic broken. His eyes opened as she clapped.

'Very good,' she said. 'Bravo!'

He beamed shyly, twisted his head away. Then he turned back, gave a slight bow, and gestured her inside.

'Please.' He reached down to snap off the battered radio. 'You are most welcome.' He motioned for her to sit on the mud bricks lined against the walls. 'You must do me the honour to take tea.'

She sat cross-legged on a brick as he shook a packet of crackers onto a dusty plate. 'Your radio?'

He nodded. 'We must listen,' he said. 'Sometimes the Taliban make announcement.'

'But not on that station.' She smiled. 'You're a dancer then?'

'My father loved music,' he said. 'He was a real dancer. Before Taliban, of course.' He poured a cup of strong green tea from a cracked pot on a tray.

'Did they really stop all music?'

'Oh yes.' He sat opposite her and sipped the tea. 'You cannot imagine to live without music. How dead the life is.'

'And you think these people support them?'

He shrugged. 'Maybe. Taliban made things stable. Not like now. That's what people say.' He urged her to take a cracker. It tasted stale and slightly damp. He was relaxed, sitting there against the wall. His beard was downy, his eyes proud. 'Many here say the British, the Americans, are like the Russian army. They are here for some while. They build some clinic but forget we have no doctor. Or open some new school with beautiful walls and forget the teachers have all fled. Then they too will leave.'

A fly came in from the dark corridor and buzzed between them through the room.

'And what do you think?'

'I think maybe they are right.' He spoke into the floor, then looked up at her cautiously, scanning her face for reaction. She sensed that she was the first Westerner to sit with him, share a cup of tea and ask his opinion. In his own country.

'What do your parents feel about you working for the British?' she said.

He drained his tea, stared for a moment into the empty cup. 'My father says it is good that I fight with a dictionary, not a gun.' He smiled. 'And my mother, she says: Najib, my son. I have a nice girl for you to marry. Come home at once before she gets too old!'

She shook the final drops out of her cup into the floor and placed it on the mud brick beside him. 'Thank you. That was almost as good as the *chai* Jalil used to make me.'

He looked pleased. 'You and Jalil were good friends?'

'We worked together.' She chose her words with care. 'And yes, we were friends. I hope so.' She paused, thinking of him. 'He was a good man. You must know that.'

He nodded. 'They say bad things about him now,' he said, 'the soldiers. I don't like that.'

'What sort of things?'

'That he was a traitor. Taking money. Even men who knew him, they say these things.' He shook his head. 'It is very wrong.'

The fly landed on a brick beside her. She watched the sheen on its wings as it walked, cleaned itself. She knew how army gossip worked. Once one person bad-mouthed an outsider, everyone did the same. An Afghan would be an easy target. Someone must have put the word round about Jalil after his death.

'Karam,' she said. 'The man who visited the compound earlier. What do you make of him?'

Najib whistled under his breath. 'That he is father of those dead children, this is very bad. He is a tough man. A vengeful man. I thought this even the first time I saw him. Now his anger is greater.'

Ellen looked up sharply. 'You've seen him before?'

'Of course.' He swallowed, blinking. 'The army held a big *shoura* earlier, in Nayullah. He was coming to this *shoura* and bringing men with him. I went with Major Mack to translate. He is a powerful man in this district.'

Ellen hunched her shoulders, her mind busy. 'When was this *shoura*?'

Najib considered. 'Two or three weeks, maybe. Jalil was there too as translator. Before the suicide bomb.'

'Thank you,' she said. She got to her feet and put her hand to her heart to say goodbye. 'Najib, that was wonderful tea.'

Outside, the light was rich with the fading afternoon heat. Dillon and Moss, their work done, were sitting on a sleeping bag, still stripped to the waist, talking together in low voices. Frank had cleared a flat space in the shade of the wall and was doing press-ups, his biceps hard as rope, his back muscular.

She sat on a rock and opened her notebook on her lap, then bounced the pen on the blank page and tried to think. So Karam had already been collaborating with the army? She thought of Mack and his passionate pursuit of hearts and minds. What a shock it must have been to him, to realize they'd killed the children of one of his most powerful regional contacts. No wonder he'd made such a strange concession and told Karam that he and his wife could live under army protection, inside the village.

But Karam? She thought of his cold stare and his warning that she should stop asking questions. What were his loyalties? His so-called ally had just bombed the home of his brother, killed his children. How could an insult like that go unavenged?

She twisted the pen in her fingers, clicking the point in and out, and let her thoughts stray to Jalil. She didn't believe for a minute he'd got mixed up in something underhand. It was so unlike him. He was idealistic, he always had been. If anything, she'd had to battle with him at times to get him to compromise. To slip a guard a bribe to let them through a security gate, instead of enduring a pointless argument with him about their rights.

She thought of his family, of their love of education, even though their country was poor. His father had been an archivist at Kabul Museum, in the years before the Taliban took power.

'He was a great scholar,' Jalil had told her. His pride was clear. 'A man of learning. History and objects of beauty were his passion. His life.'

He'd been the driving force behind Jalil's education, using money they couldn't afford to make sure Jalil had extra tuition and mastered English.

'He wanted very much for me to study in United States,' Jalil told her. 'To leave this country. He used to talk very much about this.'

Ellen had no idea, when he told her this, the first or second time they worked together, how desperately Jalil was still trying to pursue that dream.

His father had died when Jalil was a young teenager. A chill took him one Kabul winter, when the streets and roofs were thick with snow and the rooms of the houses, with their ill-fitting windows and shoddy doors, were just as icy. Quickly, for lack of medicine, the chill progressed to pneumonia. His final fever broke late one evening when a curfew was in place and his mother was too afraid to take him out through the streets to the hospital. Jalil described that night to her, his face set and angry.

'My father could not breathe,' he said. He put his hand to his chest and made a frantic gasping sound. 'Every breath was so much of pain.' He paused, remembering. 'What could I do? I didn't know what to do. I was a boy.'

His voice faltered. They sat quietly together as she waited for him to continue.

'My mother piled him with blankets. All the blankets in the house. She called me to put more wood into the stove until the heat was blazing. More wood. The room was so hot.'

She imagined his mother, beside herself, fighting to preserve her husband's ebbing life.

'It came before dawn,' he said, 'the end. Allah took him. Then, at last, he was at peace. In Paradise.'

He turned his face away from her. She had the sense that he had never spoken to anyone of this before.

'I'm so sorry, Jalil.' She got up and turned her back to him as he composed himself. He would be embarrassed, she was sure, if she acknowledged his tears. He hadn't mentioned his father again.

She shook her head. Jalil hadn't been tempted by drugs or corruption. She was certain of that. He'd been driven by a strong sense of honour. But he was always careful too about his own safety. She found it hard to believe that he would have left the patrol on his own and struck out into the desert. He must have had a compelling reason.

A thick shadow fell across the page. She looked up. Dillon, blocking the light, was bending over her.

'Scoff time,' he said. 'What you got?'

'Same as you,' she said, assuming he wanted to barter.

'I'm cookin' up now.' He was waiting for something. He put his hand out, pointing at her kit. His expression was all embarrassment. He looked as awkward as a schoolboy. Behind him, Moss was gawping.

'Gimme a rat pack,' he said. 'I'll boil it up with mine. You're working.'

She smiled, rummaged in her rucksack for a thick, brown, army-issue sachet. 'That's really kind,' she said. 'Thank you.'

'No drama,' he said. 'You gotta eat.' He looked down at her notebook. 'What're you working on?'

'Just piecing some things together.' She sighed. 'You know about that translator who died? Jalil? I want to figure out what happened.'

His eyes hardened. 'Him?'

She took in the abrupt change in his mood. Was this the result of the bad-mouthing Najib had warned her about? 'You knew him?'

'I was there.' His lips shrank to a thin line of distaste. 'Thought he was all right.'

She watched his face closely. 'And?'

'Can't trust any of them. They warned us about that, but him, well, he seemed all right.'

Moss was straining forward, trying to listen. Ellen could hear the tension in Dillon's voice. He sounded hurt.

'You were there, then? On that patrol?'

'Course I was.' He shifted his weight from side to side, his awkwardness growing.

'Why did he leave it?'

He spat to the side, a silver coin in the sand which slowly sank and disappeared.

'He'd been acting weird. Agitated. Must have had the whole thing planned but we didn't know that. He got down from the vehicle. Needed a slash or something, that's all I thought. Next thing we knew, he'd gone. Legged it.'

'And you left him there?'

He stared at her, his eyes angry, her ration pack dangling forgotten from his hand. 'We waited,' he said. 'Thinking he'd come back.'

'And?'

'And he didn't. We drove on a bit further. Can't go off the track. Too many mines. No sign of him. We'd had reports of enemy in the area.'

'So you drove away?'

'No, we fucking didn't.' His eyes were glaring. 'We turned back. Drove off the track, looking for him. Searched all over. Finally found a shack, some goatherd's shelter or God knows what. He was lying there, outside, behind it. In a right fucking mess.'

She nodded, keeping her eyes on his face. He was trembling, his cheeks moist. He was still young. She wondered how many times he'd seen the devastation of a gunshot to the head, the wet fragments of a face he'd known.

'Doesn't mean that he'd double-crossed you,' she said gently. 'Couldn't it have been—'

He shook his head. 'Then explain the cash.'

'Cash?'

'When they found him, he had a great wad of cash stuffed in his mouth. Like a warning.'

'What kind of warning?'

'Not to get greedy. Not to cheat on the boys. Who knows? A message from whoever he'd gone to meet.'

Ellen kept her voice low and even, trying to keep him talking. 'But a warning to who? No criminal leaves money behind.'

Moss had got to his feet, was walking heavily towards them.

'Whatever. Thing is, can't trust any of them. All on the take.'

Dillon jumped when Moss slapped his hand on his shoulder.

'Come on, mate,' said Moss. 'Gotta eat.'

Dillon nodded, shrugged. He stared round at the compound, at the camouflage nets draped with drying socks, the lads, stripped to their waists, clambering on the undulating mud roof of the house, erecting some communications structure. His eyes skimmed over it all as if he were struggling to register where he was.

'Anyway,' he said. He poked a finger into the air as he turned to go, trying to cover his feelings with a show of bravado. 'You wanna be careful. I'm telling you. You start poking yer nose in, someone's gonna shut you up.'

12

Hasina was lying in the heat when Abdul came. Her leg, propped up on a rock, was softly aching. He sat close by her on the sand and shyly took her hand in his. There was another patient today. A young soldier had collapsed. Voices, low but sharp, penetrated the green curtain. Two men had carried him into the compound on a stretcher, his arm hanging loose. Now he lay silently, as helpless as she had been a few days ago. The top of a transparent bag of liquid was just visible above the divide. If she and Abdul spoke quietly, no one would hear them in all the commotion.

'Our son,' she whispered to him. 'He's alive.' She squeezed his thin hand.

He frowned. 'Are you dreaming?'

'I went to the house.'

'How?' He looked wary.

'They gave me sticks.' She pointed to them. 'To walk with.'

He paused and considered. 'But why do you say he's alive?'

She pulled the battered copy of the Holy Book from beneath her pillow and placed it in his hand. The pages curled at the edges like a child's hair. The brown bloodstain lay along the side. It flickered and settled again as Abdul leafed through the pages.

'His?'

'Of course. From the foreign woman. But Abdul – ' she sat forward, breathing in his familiar smell of earth and sweat – 'she showed me the place. There was no trace of blood. No struggle.

Just a straight path through the corn and out the other side.' She watched his eyes. 'I think he escaped.'

Abdul kissed the Qur'an and handed it back to her to conceal. His forehead was crumpled. He sat still, looking at nothing.

'Maybe he found help,' she said. 'People would help him. Maybe he's lying low in the desert. Getting strong again.'

Abdul sighed. He patted her hand. 'Maybe,' he said. His voice had no hope.

'What?'

He lifted a hand to his face and stroked his beard. 'He needs help.' His eyes, when they met hers, were dull with despair. 'How can I look for him? The soldiers are everywhere. Not even Karam's friends can rescue him now.'

His beard had been as fresh as Aref's when she married him. Little more than a boy's downy fluff. Now lines ran up and down his cheeks, fissures in rock. He was a good man, she thought. A kind man. But somehow she must find the courage to find Aref for them both.

Najib put his head round the curtain. Abdul started and pulled his hand away from hers.

'A woman is asking for you,' Najib said. 'At the gate.'

They looked at each other. Behind the divide, the young soldier was starting to moan, stirring to life again. The nurses were speaking loudly to him.

'Your sister-in-law, she says.'

Najib was still standing there, awkward. He picked up the sticks lying by Hasina's feet and handed them to Abdul. 'The soldiers say you can go with her. To some other place. To visit.'

Abdul was staring at him. 'Visit?'

Najib blushed. 'Maybe', he said, 'another place would be more convenient for you both.'

Palwasha led them through the village without a word, her back straight and angry. Her scarf trailed over her shoulder, stained with mud. Hasina swung herself along on her sticks, her arms now becoming raw where they rubbed her skin, with Abdul beside her.

The worst of the day's heat had passed but the air sat heavy on their heads. The soldiers, watching them from camouflaged corner towers and gun-turrets, swivelled to follow them with their weapons. Their heads were encased in helmets, their eyes hidden by goggles. Diesel fumes hung in the dust.

They came to the end of the main street and turned down into the lane that led to Karam's servants' house. Palwasha picked her way along the hardened cart ruts. Hasina stopped and leaned against the wall to rest, her heart loud in her ears.

'Where are we going?' Abdul's breath was hot on her cheek. His tension spread from his body to hers. 'How is she here?'

Hasina shrugged. She remembered Palwasha's explosion of anger in front of the foreigners. Was this some trap they'd cooked up for her, for them all?

At the entrance to Karam's servants' compound, a foreign soldier was standing guard. Palwasha walked straight past him without a glance. The scrap of land around the house had belonged to the servants' forefathers. Barren land with sandy soil, rocks and no water. Even with irrigation ditches and hand-cut channels, corn failed there. The family had survived, for as long as anyone could remember, by begging work on richer men's land. Now Karam was that richer man. His money had bought the chickens and two scrawny goats bleating by the shabby mud house. In return, the family tended his poppy and laboured in his own large compound.

They passed the low compound wall and crossed the yard. Palwasha had disappeared. The figure of a man came into the doorway, half disguised by shadow. He was more thickset than the father of the family, Hasina could see that at once, with a large belly and proud shoulders.

'Karam?'

'Abdul brother.' He stepped forward to greet them. The men embraced. 'Come, sister-in-law.' Karam gestured to a rush mat set along the shaded side of the house. 'Sit and rest.'

Palwasha emerged from behind the house with a bucket of

water. It was a well-worn bucket, its plastic rim dented and scarred. She set it down hard and water sloshed out, drawing wet marks in the mud.

'No cups. Nothing.' Her voice was hard. 'What did you expect?'

The men cupped their hands together and drank first, then Hasina. The water was cool. It tasted of stone and of the earth. Better, she thought, than that bodiless water the foreigners brought. She drank again. Palwasha scowled round at them all and went into the house.

'These are terrible times.' Karam settled himself on the other end of the mat, slipping off his sandals and drawing his feet under him. He raised his kameez into a cotton tent with one knee and sighed. Abdul was standing a few steps away, his back half turned on them both. He was looking out over the barren piece of field as if his thoughts had flown down into the valley below. The silence stretched. A bird's whooping call cut through the space between them.

Karam's face was haggard, his eyes sunken in his flesh. Hasina had never seen him look so wretched. She waited for Abdul to take the lead and speak. The silence lengthened. Abdul was just standing there, gazing into the afternoon glare as if dazzled by the sun. Hasina wanted to catch his eye, to call him to his senses. How rude he was being, standing when his brother had asked him to sit. What was he doing, acting so strangely? Was he deliberately trying to provoke him?

'You are in my prayers, brother-in-law,' she said at last. She clasped her hands together respectfully and dipped her head. 'May Allah embrace your little ones and keep them always at His side.'

Karam nodded his head without looking at her. He raised his hand to his forehead and brushed his eye with the side of his fingers as he brought it down again. He is trying to hide it, Hasina thought, but the death of the children, of his son, has split him in two.

Silence. Still Abdul didn't turn to join them.

'Palwasha is a fine wife, Thanks be to Allah,' Hasina said. 'I pray she will bear you more sons. Many boys as fine as Yousaf.'

She thought of Yousaf's large eyes, round with fear, when he pressed himself against her lap in the darkness of the house. Of Sima, always the mother of the group, hugging her brother and sister to her as they cowered against the wall, their ears filled with the crash of bombs on the hillside and the foreign shouts of the advancing soldiers. Nothing compares to losing a child, she thought. Nothing on this earth is as cruel. Aref, my Aref. Where is he now?

'Sit!' Karam was patting the mat beside him, calling out to Abdul. 'I can't offer you tea, brother,' he said. 'But we can sit together in the shade.' He turned to Hasina. His tone was falsely hearty. 'Our foreign friends will let me live like a servant, at least. Very generous, nah?' He threw back his head and showed the long bearded stretch of his neck. 'What crazy times we are living in!'

Abdul turned to face them. He still hadn't come to sit down with Karam. Silence pressed in. He seemed hesitant, deep in thought.

'Brother,' Abdul said at last. 'I grieve for you.' The tension in his voice made Hasina's spine stiffen. She pressed herself against the wall of the house and tried to steady her breathing.

Karam seemed oblivious. He inclined his head, pointed again at the mat for Abdul to sit. 'You are thinking that I am angry with you,' Karam said. 'But I don't blame you or your wife.' He dropped his voice so low that Hasina could barely hear. 'I blame them,' he said. 'And I will have revenge.'

Abdul took a step towards him. His fists were balls at his side. 'My son too is lost,' he said. There was a coldness in his voice that made Karam look up.

After a moment, Karam shifted his weight, tucking his legs under him on the other side and settling again. He gave a short cough.

'Sacrifices,' he said. 'There are sacrifices a good-hearted young man is proud to make. A young man who brings honour to his family.'

Abdul's face was wretched. 'But my son,' he said. 'Your own nephew.'

Karam stretched out a hand. His eyes glinted with moisture. 'Now we are both the fathers of martyrs,' he said. 'We must continue the fight.'

Abdul didn't move. Karam's hand hung in the air.

'All my life, elder brother, I have respected you. Obeyed you. Loved you without question.'

Karam blinked. 'Abdul, you have been—'

'But you betrayed me.' Abdul's features were weighted by a seriousness Hasina had never seen before. She looked in consternation from him to Karam and back again to her husband. Abdul was standing tall and stern in front of them both. 'You deceived me,' he went on. 'You taught my son wickedness and called it duty.'

'Wickedness?' Karam's voice was uncertain. 'How can—?'

'You had no right, brother. How could you be so disloyal? Teaching my boy to become a murderer? And my wife a liar?'

Hasina shrank back into the wall. Abdul, her sweet-tempered husband, denouncing her in such a way? Insulting his elder brother, who had such power and influence in the village? It was impossible. He was possessed by madness.

'Abdul. Stop this.' Karam was heaving himself to his feet. He moved towards Abdul, his arm outstretched, and placed his hand clumsily on his brother's shoulder. 'May Allah be our witness, we have suffered enough,' he said. 'Brother, let us—'

Abdul knocked the hand from his shoulder. 'You are no longer my brother,' he said.

Hasina tried to get to her feet. Her leg collapsed under her and she fell back onto her side. Karam's broad back was blocking Abdul from view. His hand swung and the sting of a slap rang out across the yard. Silence. The air seemed drained. For a long moment, nature seemed to pause all around them. She held her breath.

The men fell on each other. They locked their arms round the other's shoulders and clawed as each clutched his brother in

146

the broad of the back. They staggered and clasped each other, swaying like a drunken man with two heads. Dust kicked up at their feet, lapping against their calves. The air was thick with panting and grunts. They wrestled on their feet. At first, neither made progress, their legs splayed and feet digging into the ground.

Soon Abdul was being pressed backwards. His feet groped further behind him, trying to get purchase on the earth. Karam seized his advantage and pulled free an arm. He punched Abdul in the stomach. Abdul, winded, bent double, his own arms still locked round Karam's neck, forcing down his opponent's head. His knee flashed upwards, crunching into Karam's lowered face. Karam let out a cry of rage.

'Stop this!' Hasina pushed herself forward onto her knees and, finally, up onto her unsteady feet against the wall. She cupped her hands and scooped up water from the bucket. She limped forward as the men twisted and turned in the dirt and threw it over them. The water erupted on the back of Karam's head, sloshing down his neck and splashing along his thick, muscular arms. 'Stop!' she shouted.

Neither man paid her any attention. Karam had wound his arms firmly round Abdul's waist now, tearing him sideways as if trying to snap open his stomach and break his hips. He was the stronger, heavier man by some measure, but Abdul was the more furious.

Sweat flew off in a spray of droplets across the yard as they grappled. They were both breathing heavily. Abdul's foot flashed forward. He hooked his ankle round his brother's calf, straining to pull it from under him and knock him off balance.

When the men fell, the goats strained at their tethers, tossing their heads in fright, eyes rolling. Karam hit the dirt first. Abdul crashed, sprawling, half on top of him. Their heads bounced as they struck the ground. For a moment, they lay still, locked in their tight embrace. Hasina wailed, her hands at her face, shutting out the sight. Karam would kill him, that bear of a man. Abdul was half his weight.

The men seemed to come to again. Karam moved first. He roared and raised himself, flipping Abdul over onto his back, pinning him to the ground and straddling him. He pounded his fist into Abdul's chest, again and again. Underneath the thudding, there was a sickening crunch from the hollow of Abdul's chest. Abdul let out a low moan of pain.

'Don't! Let him go!' Hasina threw herself across the yard and seized hold of Karam's arm. She latched onto it, trying to use her weight as a lever to hold it back. The yard span as Karam tossed her off and she fell, slithering across the dust, to one side. The impact left her dazed and winded.

The distraction had given Abdul a chance to rally. As Karam turned, Abdul pulled his arm free and pressed his hand into Karam's face, forcing back his head. Two fingers twisted deep inside his nostrils. His extended thumb strained upwards, stabbing at his brother's eye.

He will blind him, Hasina thought. She was too far away to stop it. Abdul's thumb was jabbing into the soft tissue of Karam's eye, his nail gouging. Allah forgive him. A trickle of blood was falling from Karam's nose and climbing down Abdul's straining hand. Karam's head was pressed back as far as his neck would twist, his hands flailing forward. His neck will break, she thought. She stared in horror. All her senses seemed concentrated in her eyes. The image of the grappling brothers was seared into her mind as if the world had stilled to slow motion.

The snap of a shot filled the yard. Tearing through them all. Deafening. Shocking. Hasina turned, feeling the fighting men slacken and look too in surprise towards the noise.

In the yard, just visible at the corner of the house, the soldier who had stood guard at the compound entrance was facing them squarely. His fired gun pointed out over their heads like a salute. He shouted something. A command.

Karam knocked Abdul's loosening hand away and rolled from him. He pressed his hand to his nose. Blood was oozing through his fingers and staining the dust brown. Ants appeared from nowhere to feast.

Abdul struggled over onto his side. He coughed, wincing as his chest heaved. A sticky mess of bloody saliva leaked from the side of his mouth. Water. He needed water. Hasina looked, exhausted, at the bucket. Too far away to reach.

Karam and the soldier were exchanging foreign words. Karam's voice was weary. The soldier sounded angry. A schoolmaster shouting at fighting boys. Abdul was still on his side, panting. His eyes stared out blindly at the sunlight. Abdul, you foolish, proud man. He was alive, God be praised. But now what? He lay in the dirt, breathing noisily, making no effort to move. He had fought his brother to defend his son. But at what price?

Behind Hasina, a figure stirred. She turned to look. Palwasha was standing, watching them all from the darkness of the doorway. A thin smile was on her lips.

'At last,' she said to Hasina in a low voice, 'we find our husbands are, after all, real men.'

The soldier had gone but the two brothers did not speak. Karam had crawled to the mat in the shade. He had soaked a cloth in the bucket and was sitting with his head tilted back against the wall of the house, the wet cloth pressed to his nose. When he moved forward to dampen the cloth again, Hasina saw the red puffiness of his swelling nostrils. Abdul's fingermarks were raised in weals and rising bruises on his skin, seared into his flesh like burns.

Hasina was afraid to speak to Karam. She must get Abdul safely away from him. Who knew what his brother would do to avenge himself? He had been insulted, his honour compromised in front of his wife. Hasina was light-headed. She could never have imagined such a thing. Never had she seen her kind, mild-mannered husband say so much as a cross word to his elder brother. He had never raised his fist to anyone, not even her.

Her hands shook as she wet the end of her scarf and wrung it out over Abdul's head. The cool water ran in rivulets down his face, meandering from nose to chin and dripping from his flesh into the dust. He didn't raise a finger to wipe the water away. His eyes were dull, looking out into nothingness. His breath was rasping. She ran her fingers over his limbs, his back, his chest, feeling for injury. He winced when she touched his ribs but her hands came away clean, not bloody. She sat, cradling his head in her lap and shielding him from the sun and watched him rest, fearing for what was to come.

As the sun grew weak, they staggered back to the compound. Karam had gone wordlessly inside the house. Palwasha was nowhere to be seen. Abdul moved by shuffling, bent over with his arms across his chest. His face was pale, his skin moist with sweat. At the gate, a young female soldier barked at them through the inner metal gate. Hasina could smell her nervousness.

'A doctor,' Hasina said. She pointed to Abdul. The young soldier raised her gun. Abdul slumped forward against the wall. 'Please. He needs a doctor.'

That night they lay side by side inside the medical corner of the compound. Abdul's chest was cleaned and bound tightly with a bandage. His breathing was thick and wet. The doctor had dismissed his injury as bruising when he examined him. Najib translated for them. Heavy bruising, he said, but no bones seemed to be broken. Abdul needed a good night's rest and water and he would soon recover. He could stay here with his wife for just one night and no more.

No one had asked them what had happened. Najib had been short with them. He repeated the doctor's words but didn't add any of his own. Hasina could see the suspicion in his eyes. He was wary of them both.

Now a light breeze was blowing sand across the surface of the ground. Hasina wrapped her scarf round her face to protect her eyes. She listened to the background music of the desert. The clatter of insects, the distant howl of dogs. Somewhere inside the compound, chickens were squawking as they settled to sleep. The foreign soldiers were talking in low voices, laughing. Someone struck a match.

She closed her eyes and tried to imagine she was safe inside their home. Instead of the stony sand, she was lying on their cot. Abdul's weight beside her was setting it creaking. At the end of the cot stood their wedding trunk. On the side wall, wisps of moonlight, creeping in through the window, passed across the surface of the mirror like ghosts. The lumps of stools were dark rocks. And Aref, of course. Aref was there too, his breathing light and young, barely audible beneath his father's. Twitching and turning on his cot as he dreamed. He had always had vivid dreams, ever since he was a—

'Hasina.'

The whisper was so low that she wasn't sure at first if she had heard it or imagined it. Aref? Her head, half in sleep, was full of shadows. She lay rigid on her back, her eyes closed, afraid to move and dispel the phantom. Where was she?

'Hasina.' The voice brought her to her senses. Abdul, of course. They were in the soldiers' camp. She opened her eyes and turned on her side towards him, stretching her fingertips to touch his skin. The bandage swelled his thin chest.

'I'm here.'

His fingers touched hers. He was straining to turn towards her. She could hear the pain in the catch of his breath. She moved closer to him and he put his mouth against her ear. His breath was hot and moist.

'I am going to tell them,' he said. 'Tell the foreigners.'

She drew back, trying to see his face. His skin shone pallid in the darkness. She was instantly afraid. 'Tell them?'

'About Aref.'

'No!' Too loud. She put her hand to her mouth. They would hear her. That traitor was everywhere, spying on them. She must be careful. She put her face against his and whispered. 'No,' she said. 'Husband. Don't say such a thing.'

Abdul's eyes were gleaming, looking straight into hers. He didn't speak.

'The soldiers will track him down,' she said. 'They will kill him.'

Her heart was beating in her ears. 'And Karam and his friends will kill you for betraying them. Don't talk nonsense.'

Abdul lifted a hand and stroked her cheek. His eyes were determined.

'If we leave him,' he said, 'he will die. They have control of the land now. They will find him for us.' He put his hand to her mouth as she opened it to protest. 'I won't tell them everything,' he said. He paused. She saw her own frightened eyes reflected in his.

'No,' she said. 'Please! They'll kill him.'

'I will tell them some story,' Abdul went on.

She listened with a sense of rising panic. She felt abandoned. He had been making this plan without her and now his mind was made up.

'I won't tell them about the training, the fighters, the market,' he whispered. 'But I can tell them that he was wounded. That you were afraid for him, because he is a young man and they would assume the worst. That he crept away to hide. Then perhaps, they will search for him.'

Hasina's eyes were wide. 'They won't believe you,' she said. She caught hold of his arm and pinched it. Her heart was pushing itself out of her chest. His skin was chilled. 'They will kill him,' she said again. 'Maybe they will kill you too.' She imagined herself, left behind, alone in the world. Her stomach was chilled with terror. 'Please, Abdul,' she said. 'Don't do this.'

Abdul shook his head. His eyes, on hers, became sad.

'On my own, I cannot find him,' he said at last. 'But if they look for him and I go with them, then perhaps I can.' He looked pained. 'They have tended us,' he said. He pointed to the bandage round his chest. 'Maybe they will save him too. What else can we do?'

She stroked his face. At the moment, his mind was made up. Tomorrow, she thought. Tomorrow she would try again to stop him. His eyes fell closed and his breathing thickened into sleep. She lay still, looking at the night sky. Aref was somewhere out there, wounded and needing help. She felt that as keenly as her husband. But what would the foreigners do if they found him? Tending an old couple was one thing. But a young man, a fighter? The foreigners would never believe Abdul's story. What if Abdul helped them to find him and then they tortured him, killed him? How could she bear that?

Her chest was fluttering with panic. And Karam. If he and his friends knew that Abdul had collaborated, they would kill him. He would be a traitor, no better than that man from Kabul. Her life would be over. Her forehead was wet with chilled sweat. She lay, trembling. She must stop him. Somehow, she didn't know how, she must find Aref herself.

She closed her eyes and tried to rest. Her head was spinning, dizzying shapes whirling behind her eyes. She felt nauseous. The soldiers' voices had fallen to a low murmur. Male snores rumbled across the sand. She started to slip, exhausted, into sleep.

Suddenly her eyes snapped open. A truth had come to her, from Allah himself perhaps. Of course. What a fool she was. Why hadn't she thought of it earlier? There was one possible place. A place where Aref might hide which was known only to the two of them. She knew.

She twisted to look at Abdul, afraid for a second that she had spoken aloud. He was lying still, hunched on his side, his chest steadily rising and falling. Dare she wake him and tell him what she was thinking? No. She steadied her breathing. He might tell the foreigners. If she were right, he'd lead them straight to Aref and put them both in danger. No. She must find a way to go there herself first and see.

She put her hands to her face and felt her hot cheeks. For a moment, she thought of hauling herself to her feet right now and creeping on her sticks to the gate and beyond. Nonsense. The guard would never let her out. The sentries and patrolling soldiers, watching from their stolen compounds throughout the village, would shoot anyone they saw creeping through the shadows at night.

Tomorrow. She must go tomorrow. She bit her lip and wrapped her arms round her body, hugging her secret to her chest. How would she do that alone? She needed help. That conspirator? She shook her head. No. She needed someone who had their own reason to take risks. Someone with a strong spirit who might conceal the truth from these soldiers. Had Allah sent her just such a person? Hasina smiled.

13

Mack looked like a soldier from another century. He was sitting in a camp chair, sipping tea, a floppy khaki hat shading his eyes. His nose and neck were bright with sunburn, his face bent forward over a sheaf of papers on his knee. His expression was thoughtful. It changed abruptly as she approached him and he looked up and smiled.

'Excellent,' he said. He jumped to his feet, one hand holding flapping papers, the other held out to her. His fingers were firm and warm. 'Civilized company.'

'I was summoned.' She settled into the camp chair beside him. 'Ordered by a commanding officer.'

'Invited, please.' He waved at a young soldier who picked up a tin mug and poured boiling water onto a tea bag. Mack waited until the junior soldier had withdrawn before he spoke. He folded up the papers and stowed them between his thigh and the side of the chair. His hands were capable and economical in their gestures.

'Truth is, I was a bit of a grouch earlier, wasn't I?' he said. 'That business over the maps. Hope you'll forgive me.' He grimaced. 'Too used to giving orders, I suppose. Soldiers don't answer back.'

Their legs were so close she could feel the warmth rising from his body. His thighs, knotted with muscle, were twice the width of hers.

'That's all right.' She watched his eyes, trying to work out what this was all about. He was a smart man. He hadn't called her over just to say sorry.

'That request you made,' he said. 'To go out and see where the turp died.' He nodded. 'Well, I can't promise. I've asked for a threat assessment. But it is possible.'

'Thank you.' She was surprised. He'd seemed adamant before. 'Very kind.'

'Well.' He shrugged, spreading his hands. 'Don't want you saying we didn't cooperate.'

She thought of the words he'd used before: that he wouldn't risk the lives of his men on a fool errand.

'You worry about the boys, don't you?' she said. 'Out here.'

He nodded without a trace of embarrassment. 'Of course. They're good lads. Every one of them.'

'You're from an army family?'

He gave her a keen look. 'How'd you guess? Father and uncle both. Never considered anything else.' He ticked off the countries on his fingers. 'Northern Ireland. Balkans. Two tours in Iraq. Now this place.'

She nodded. He struck her as a loner. But she believed too that he did care for his command. As she considered this, he raised his hand as if to wrest back control of the conversation.

'And you've been coming to Afghanistan for, how long . . .?'

'Since just after the fall of the Taliban,' she said. 'Two thousand and two.'

He nodded, thoughtfully. 'How does your family feel about that?'

She smiled, sensing that he was probing. 'I live alone,' she said. 'My sister's too busy with her kids to worry much. And my father's elderly now. I usually don't tell him. My friends stopped pestering me years ago about coming to war zones. They think I'm mad.'

'And why do you keep coming?'

She shrugged. 'It's addictive.' She thought of the dead children, of the invisible villagers who'd fled their homes and were camping somewhere out in the desert, waiting to see which place the soldiers or the Taliban bombed next. John wouldn't have bothered filing on them. 'And besides,' she added, 'someone's got to.'

He watched her, then looked away, and she felt his attention shift and move on. 'So,' he said, 'you've been coming for quite a few years. Tell me. What's changed?'

'You really want to know? I can speak plainly?'

'I'd expect nothing else.'

She sat forward and watched him closely for reaction as she spoke. 'A great wave of hope at the start. Excitement. Expectation. And there have been gains.' She marked them on her fingers. 'The elections. More children in school, a lot more girls of course. A new road here. A new park there.'

'But?'

'But the hope's turned sour. To disillusionment, even. Most people I talk to, Afghans, I mean, they don't feel safe. In many places, they're even less safe now than a few years ago. No point having a school if you're too afraid to send your children there. And then there's corruption.'

He bristled slightly. 'That's always been a problem.'

'All they keep hearing is how many billions of dollars are being poured into their country. But they look around' – she gestured round the compound, at the scratching chickens, the mud walls, the well – 'and don't see much to show for it. They feel cheated. By the warlords and drug-runners who've lined their own pockets.'

She sat back in her chair, feeling hot in the face. She seldom expressed her views. Men so rarely asked, and those who did so rarely listened.

'Takes time.' His eyes never left her face. 'Don't forget, they're starting from scratch here. After thirty years of war. There's a lot to build. Police force. Government. Army. Legal system. Doesn't happen overnight.'

She sipped her tea. She'd already said too much. She felt exposed. Debate about anything that mattered to her was a type of intimacy she'd almost forgotten.

'You're not convinced, are you?' His eyes were on hers, alert.

'I think we're getting it wrong.' She shook her head. 'There was a real opportunity here. A chance to make a difference. We're squandering it.'

'Ouch.' He tipped back his head, exposing his long throat. His teeth, as he smiled, glistened in the sunlight. 'You don't have much faith in us.'

She said nothing. He needs to believe in this mission, she thought. To believe wholeheartedly. How else can he lead young boys into battle, send home flag-draped coffins and yet carry on? But that doesn't make him right.

Somewhere beyond the compound, fresh construction work started up. The bang of steady, rhythmical hammering filled the silence between them. When he spoke again, his tone too was serious.

'It's not perfect,' he said. His voice was low, as if he were sharing a secret. He spoke rapidly. She had to strain forward to hear. 'Progress is slow. But let me tell you this.' He stabbed the air with a slow, deliberate finger. 'Every time the Taliban blows up a bus or bombs a market, people remember all over again what animals they really are. And they turn a little more against them and towards us. In the end, that's how we'll win this thing.'

His eyes were so close to hers, his pupils so large, she saw herself reflected in them, a tiny distant figure, her face distorted into bulging features. His gaze was resolute. She looked abruptly away.

'Win?' She shook her head. Military thinking. He was a man who measured success in bombs and bullets. She spoke almost to herself. 'This isn't about victory. Not for Afghans. It's about survival.'

The moment passed. He exhaled heavily, sat back in his chair, his bottom bulging in the soft sling of its seat, his shoulders pressed back against the metal frame. Outside the compound, an engine stuttered, then roared into life, competing with the hammering to fill the vast vacancy of the desert air. The energy between them was depleted, as if the effort of speaking with passion had exhausted them both.

A group of soldiers bustled past with packs on their backs, heading for the gate. It was some time before she continued.

'I want to know more about Jalil's death. There are things about it that don't add up.'

'Like what?'

'Like why he left the patrol for no apparent reason. Put himself in danger.'

Mack reached up a hand and scratched the back of his neck.

'Peculiar,' he said. 'I agree. None of the boys could shed much light on it.' He'd shifted in his seat and was staring out now into the thin morning light, scanning the air for answers. 'They didn't entirely trust him.'

Ellen waited. The engine cut to silence, leaving the hammer blows striking a steady beat.

'Maybe he was meeting someone?' he said. 'A contact?'

Ellen shook her head. 'How could he have arranged a meeting? He was a translator. He wouldn't even have known where they were going.'

Mack sighed to himself. 'True,' he said. 'Probably not.'

'He knew something.' She spoke carefully, watching his eyes for reaction. He was looking out into middle distance. 'He knew something incriminating. And someone shut him up.'

'Knew something?' He smiled to himself. 'I'm afraid you're getting back to your love of spy fiction again. The truth is usually far less—'

He was interrupted by a cough. Najib was standing a little way from them, trying to attract their attention. Mack looked up and nodded acknowledgement. Najib led Abdul forward to speak to them. Abdul was shuffling, looking gaunter than ever, his shoulders bowed. A red bruise crept along the side of his face like a disfiguring birthmark.

'Excuse me, sir.' Najib was red-faced as he addressed the Major. 'This man is insisting that he must please talk to you.'

'This is the man whose wife we've been treating, isn't it?' Mack

159

offered a seat but Abdul remained standing, his arms stiff at his sides. 'I heard you got into a scrape of your own?'

'Yes, sir.' Najib spoke for Abdul. 'But he's much better now.'

'Glad to hear it. So – what can we do for you?'

Abdul ran his hands down the seams of his shabby cotton tunic. His nails were stubby and black with dirt. He was standing with his chest hollowed, looking even shorter than he was. The smell of sour stale sweat rose from his body. His eyes were fearful and, when he began to speak, his voice was hesitant, barely more than a whisper.

'He is saying he has something important to tell you,' said Najib. 'About his son.'

'His son?'

Abdul paused, gathered his courage and continued.

'His son was injured, this is all what he is saying.' Najib looked increasingly uncomfortable as he translated. 'Injured in the offensive. That's why his wife, that injured lady,' he pointed to his leg, 'that's why she was not leaving. Their son was too afraid to give himself up. He was worried what the soldiers would do to him. So he is hiding somewhere in the desert. Wounded.' Najib leaned forward and added in a quieter voice, as if it were his own thought: 'If he is still alive.'

Mack was listening keenly. 'How was his son wounded?'

Najib questioned Abdul. 'In the stomach.' He touched his own midriff. 'Here, sir.'

'But how? By a bullet? A falling building? What?'

Najib scrunched up his face at Abdul's answer. 'He is a little unclear,' he said at last. 'Through explosion, he is saying.'

Abdul was staring miserably at the earth.

'So what does he want?'

'A search.' Najib was squirming. 'He wants soldiers to go out to look for his son and he will go too and help them find him.'

Mack shook his head. 'That's impossible,' he said to Najib. 'Please say I'm very sorry to hear about his son.' He was leaning forward in his chair, his eyes never leaving Abdul's face. 'We would like to help him. But I can't spare the men.'

Abdul's face contorted as Najib translated. He turned to Najib and put his hand on Najib's arm.

'His son may have good information for you, he is saying.' Najib shrugged off Abdul's hand. 'He may be able to help you.'

Mack's expression didn't change. 'Really?' he said. 'In what way can he help me?'

'If there have been fighters coming to the village,' Najib said. 'This man is saying that maybe his son knows about them.'

Mack formed a bridge with his hands and tapped his fingertips together. Abdul's own hands were trembling at his sides.

'Thank you,' he said at last. 'So he's confident his son may have information for us? If so, it may be possible for this gentleman to accompany a security patrol. I'll see what I can do.'

'I'd like to go too,' said Ellen.

Mack was getting to his feet. 'I'm afraid that's not possible,' he said. 'I'm sorry.'

He turned to Abdul to dismiss him. 'Terrible shame,' he said. 'About your son.' Najib led Abdul awkwardly away. Ellen watched the two men, young and old, shuffle across the sand.

Mack waited until they were out of earshot. 'See?' he said. 'Didn't I tell you? That family supports the enemy.'

'You think so?'

'Young man. Wounded. His family tells us nothing. Suddenly they need help and, lo and behold, he's got intelligence for us.' He shook his head. 'Whole family's involved.'

She pursed her lips. 'Even the dead children?'

'They used them. Shields. Wouldn't be the first time.'

No point arguing. She got to her feet.

She negotiated a bucket of water for herself from the well and found a quiet, level piece of sand. The lower rim bit into the earth, darkening it. The water in the bucket sloshed, flashed with sun, settled. She rolled her shirtsleeves up above the elbow and let her forearms sink down into the water, feeling the coolness, the delicious rush of water between her splayed fingers.

She cupped her hands, bent down low and brought water to

her face in a sudden shock of wet and freshness. Her soap sat beside her on a stone, pitted with grit but ready. She was just about to wet her face and neck a second time, savouring every slow sensation, when she heard a polite cough. Najib. She sensed him close by, waiting. No. Not now.

She rubbed her hands over her dripping face and raised her head. A hot, hard flannel of desert heat rushed in to scour her cheeks. Najib, radiating awkwardness, was standing beside her, wringing his hands.

'Madam,' he said, 'I need to talk to you.'

'Right now?' The water in the bucket was still moving, scattering shards of light.

'Yes. It is most urgent.'

She sighed, reached for her dusty towel.

Najib led her to a corner of the compound and crouched there, his back to the mud wall. Goat droppings lay scattered at their feet. The stink of dried urine rose all around them from the earth. Ellen stood in front of him, looking down at his anxious face.

'What is it?'

Najib looked past her, his eyes darting, checking who might hear. His manner had changed completely.

'That lady,' he said. 'The one with the cut leg.'

'Hasina? What about her?'

'She sends a message to you.'

'A message?'

Najib peered round again, as if for spies. His forehead was tight with tension. 'She wants to do mission with you. Mercy mission. For villagers.'

'A mercy mission?'

'Yes. Taking some food, medicine and whatnot.'

She rubbed her damp hands through her hair, already feeling hot again. 'She should ask the soldiers. That's nothing to do with me.'

Najib was gently wringing his hands. 'This is what I am telling her. But she wants you to go,' he said. 'Just ladies, she is saying. Not me even.'

Ellen shook her head. 'That's not safe, Najib,' she said. 'I doubt they'd even let me.'

Najib shrugged. 'I told her that,' he said. He pulled a face. 'She is stupid lady. Peasant only. She knows nothing.'

She looked at him closely. 'What does she mean? A mercy mission?'

'She says some ladies are hiding in a secret place. Without food, water. She thinks she knows where. They need help but they are afraid of the soldiers. She can't go alone. The soldiers might hurt her. But you are not a soldier. Maybe, if you go too, this is possible.'

She brushed sand off a large stone and sat down heavily beside him. 'Dangerous.'

Najib nodded. 'Too dangerous,' he repeated. 'I told her that too. She says no, you are a strong lady. You aren't afraid.'

She kicked at the sand and loose stones at her feet, disturbing a trail of ants. 'It's not about being afraid,' she said. 'I'm just not sure it's possible.'

'Of course.' Najib sat quietly for a moment. 'Also,' he said at last, 'she is not a good lady.' His voice was low, conspiratorial. 'They are not a good family, I think. Not for trusting.'

Everyone seemed determined to warn her about these villagers. She didn't see what basis they had for being so suspicious. She thought of the women who'd taken the risk of coming back to their village, despite the soldiers, desperate for their pots and clothes. If they were out there in the desert, without shelter and scrabbling for life, it could be a strong part of her story.

Najib pulled out a cigarette, lit it and drew on it quietly, blowing smoke into the cloud of small flies gathered round their heads.

'That business with her husband,' she said. 'What do you make of it?'

Najib wrinkled his nose in distaste. 'He is stupid,' he said. 'He is making trouble for everyone.'

'He seemed really frightened.'

Najib nodded. 'Very frightened,' he said. 'First he is loyal to Taliban. Now he's a collaborator. How can he live here safely again? One day the soldiers will leave and the fighters will come back.

Then – ' he lifted an imaginary gun with his hands, looked down the sights and pulled the trigger – 'bang! He is finished.'

Ellen nodded. She remembered the strain in Abdul's clenched hands. He had kept his eyes on his feet when he'd spoken to Mack. 'You think he does have a son out there? A wounded son?'

Najib shrugged. 'Maybe. But I don't believe him. Maybe he will lead the soldiers into some trap.'

'Maybe.'

Najib pushed himself upright again and stretched out his legs. 'So I will tell that lady that your answer is no.' He looked pleased. 'That is a good decision.'

He bent down to rub his cigarette butt into sparks in the sand and bury it neatly under a stone.

'Tell her yes,' she said.

Najib's expression collapsed. He put a hand out towards her and opened his mouth to argue. She spoke again before he could.

'Don't tell anyone about this, Najib,' she said. 'OK? No matter who asks you. Promise me?'

His face, as he nodded, was sullen.

She found Hasina lying with her eyes closed, her crutches crossed at her side. The tattooed junior medic was unpacking a box of kit. She nodded to Ellen.

'Sly old bird, that one.'

Ellen looked down at Hasina's face. The muscles of one cheek were twitching as if she were dreaming. Her skin was relaxed, her fine wrinkles erased. She looked uncharacteristically peaceful.

'Sly?'

'She's not that ill. I'd have her out but the boss won't let us.'

As soon as the medic moved on, Hasina's bright green eyes snapped open and settled on Ellen. They were sharp with anticipation. The two women held each other's gaze, then Hasina slowly smiled. She reached out a hand for Ellen to haul her to her feet. She walked stiffly, leaving the crutches behind.

Ellen followed her to the deserted corner of the camp and

watched her rummage through the kit piled there. Hasina started to lift roll mats and sleeping bags and scavenge through boxes.

'Hey.' Ellen kept her voice low. She looked round to see if anyone was watching. Dillon and Moss, the only soldiers in sight, were hunched over their clothes, pummelling and wringing. 'Stop that.'

Hasina was gathering plastic bottles of water in her arms. When she had five or six, she dumped them at Ellen's feet. The second time she came back to her with bright plastic packets of army food. Brown biscuits in green foil, boiled sweets, small tubes of soft cheese and strawberry jam, cold sachets of ration meals.

'They'll notice, you know.' Ellen frowned at her. 'They won't like it.'

The third time, Hasina brought back a bulky medical kit and a pouch of field dressings. She pointed to Ellen's rucksack. Her expression wasn't beseeching or even inquiring. It was an order. Ellen shook her head, sighed. Hasina was sitting on her haunches, her shoulders raised like a vulture's wings, her eyes sharp.

The young guard on the gate was slouching against the wall, trying to squeeze himself into a thin line of shade. His face was pink with sunburn. He levered himself off the wall to stand up as they approached. Hasina had brought just one crutch, stabbing it into the sand in front of her as if it were a walking stick. She'd pulled her headscarf forward over her eyes.

'We're together.' Ellen had slung the rucksack over her shoulder. She gestured back towards the house. 'It's OK. Major Mack knows.'

The young private hesitated and narrowed his eyes. He looked past them towards the house. The area where the officers usually gathered, with camp chairs and table, was depleted.

'I take full responsibility,' she said. 'Ellen Thomas. *NewsWorld* magazine.'

He gave her a sullen look. The metal bolt screamed as the guard unfastened the gate, then locked it behind them.

The mud roads outside were hazy with heat. Dust swirled in clouds as they walked. Ellen was very conscious of being without an armed escort. There were hidden military faces everywhere, guns swivelling as they tracked their movement. She put her hand on Hasina's arm.

'You know,' she said, 'maybe we should go back.'

Hasina shook her off, her eyes contemptuous. She spat sideways into the dust, adjusted her headscarf and walked on.

Ellen walked a step or two behind, hurrying to keep up. Hasina was lean and wiry, moving quickly despite her injured leg. She was looking straight ahead, picking her way deftly between piles of dried animal dung and loose stones. The earth fortifications and barbed wire, unfurled like giant rolls of tumbleweed along the ditches, seemed invisible to her. The metal flashed with sun as they moved past.

Ellen shrugged her rucksack into a new position, trying to spread the weight. It was rubbing her body in wet, sticky patches along her shoulders and down her back. Hasina, ahead, turned left and disappeared. Ellen hurried to follow. A narrow alleyway threaded its way between two compounds, slimy with rotting rubbish. Beyond, the lane contracted to a dirt track into a cornfield. By the time Ellen reached it, Hasina had been engulfed by the standing corn.

The ground sloped downwards. The earth underfoot was slippery with dry undergrowth and uneven with clods. Small flies hung in a cloud of dots round her head, buzzing in her ears and nipping her neck. She was starting to pant. The corn stalks scratched at her arms as she pushed her way through, raising red weals. Sweat had formed a stinging glaze across her cracked skin. The rucksack was a dead weight on her shoulders.

She was disorientated. Which way had Hasina gone? Blood banged in her ears. The stench of rotting vegetation rose from the ground. She started to push through the corn more urgently, not caring how much noise she made. The press of the corn around her made her suddenly claustrophobic. If she could only . . .

Hasina was suddenly beside her. Where had she come from? Her hand was gripping Ellen's arm. Her large green eyes were fierce. An ambush, Ellen thought. Betrayed. As she stared into

Hasina's face, noises broke through the field. The thud of boots. The dry crack of corn as bodies forced their way forwards. A low male voice.

Hasina put her hand flat on the top of Ellen's head, her eyes never leaving her face, and forced her quietly downwards into a crouch. They perched, stiff, on their haunches. Hasina's hand was still pressing down on Ellen's crown as if she were anointing her. Her damp skin smelt of the earth.

The boots came closer. Ellen's muscles were shuddering with the stress of the crouch. She gritted her teeth, closed her eyes, willing herself not to move. Could these be Taliban fighters, so close to camp? Or soldiers? The memory flashed back to her of the blind scrambling in the ditch, just before the soldiers had bombed the house. Hasina's house. The corn was trembling around them with each heavy step. The press of blood was painful in her chest.

And then silence. Hasina's hot hand stayed on her head. An eternity passed. Ellen opened her eyes. Hasina's eyes were closed, her face straining with concentration. Listening. Calculating where on this piece of land the men might be. Finally Hasina withdrew her hand. She opened her eyes and gave Ellen an unexpected smile.

They walked on. The ground twisted under their feet, turning for a while to the left, then sharply down, picking up a small trail through another set of fields. They left the standing corn behind. The further they moved from the river, the more lunar and desolate the landscape became. The backs of Ellen's legs were slippery with sweat. Ahead, Hasina drove forward relentlessly, using her crutch as a third leg.

Hasina turned abruptly to one side and threaded her way down a sharp slope, balancing her weight with her crutch. She was zigzagging into a small gully. Boulders clung to the sides. Ellen skidded as a rock beneath her feet suddenly gave way and went clattering down ahead of her. Its bouncing sent a ripple of echoes. Ellen paused, looking upwards. The slopes rising round them as they descended were steep and unforgiving. If anyone came to the rim, they'd be sitting targets. She hesitated, jamming her rucksack against the rock and sand and leaning backwards into it.

Hasina had reached the bottom. She stood, hands on hips, and stared up. Ellen pushed herself forward off the side of the slope and started to climb down again, testing each foothold with care before she committed her weight, her eyes on her feet. At the bottom, she rested, legs splayed, on a boulder and drank water. Her rucksack sat on the ground beside her.

Hasina was crouched in a corner, scratching at a clump of dead brushwood. It was piled behind a rock at the foot of the gully. She burrowed into it with her hands, then kicked away loose stones. Pashto words were tumbling from her, low and insistent. Ellen looked away, scanning the top of the hollow for movement. Suddenly there was silence. When she looked back, Hasina had vanished.

The brushwood had concealed a square hole, the width of a man's shoulders, set in the earth at ground level. Three sides were lined with weathered pieces of wood. Ellen climbed round the large boulder, less than a foot in front of it, to peer inside. She stretched out her hands to touch the wood. It was warm, alive against the stone. Inside the hole, deep in the blackness, she sensed movement. A scrabbling in the dirt. A thick animal smell rose to greet her, encased in stale air. She hesitated. Hasina must have crawled inside. Anyone going in would be defenceless, blinded by the darkness and framed by the sunlight. She went back to fetch her rucksack and dug out her torch.

The beam was powerful but narrow, illuminating a thin cone of darkness. The hole marked the entrance to a short passage, a crawl space just big enough for a small adult to force their way through. The beam dispersed before the passage ended. No way of knowing how far into the earth it ran. She lifted the beam to the roof and craned her head upside down to examine it. A single staff was embedded in the mud, running vertically from the entrance into the interior. The earth round it was dull and settled, as if the whole structure had been there for some years. It didn't look safe.

She put the torch between her teeth and pushed her rucksack into the hole, then her head and shoulders. The heady smell of compacted earth was at once overwhelming. When her hips followed, they blocked out the remaining shards of daylight. All she could see now was the wavering light of the torch in her mouth, swinging pale and weak in front of her as she inched forward. The mud seemed to clamp itself round her body, a hand squeezing her flesh. She wriggled forward, then stopped to breathe. Panic was rising inside her in waves, threatening to suffocate her.

She closed her eyes and tried to force her muscles to relax. She was losing her grip on the torch. Her hands, jammed by her sides, couldn't reach it. She tried to inch forward but her hips seemed stuck in the dirt. She kicked her legs like a drowning swimmer, her feet flapping against the earth.

The torch fell sideways out of her mouth. The beam arced and settled on a patch of mud a few inches ahead of her, to the right. It illuminated a large spider, threading its way round a rock. Ellen closed her eyes again and forced her breathing to settle. She lifted her chest on her hands and rammed her upper body forwards again. The earth seemed to be sweating with her, tight and close. If she made it too slippery, she thought, the tunnel might collapse. She would be entombed here, absorbed by the desert.

For a moment, nothing moved. Then, in a sudden rush, her hips skidded free and her head shot forward, a protruding rock grazing her cheek. Her chin overtook the torch, her neck extinguishing the beam and plunging her into blackness. Her eyes spangled lightning rods of yellow and green. She sniffed. The air had changed. The dank closeness of the tunnel was shifting. The air had a new note; not fresh, but somehow fuller, as if the tunnel were opening up at last. She inhaled gulps of it, drawing it deep into her lungs, then summoned all her strength and pushed forwards, nudging the torch in front of her with her nose and pushing the rucksack ahead of it all with the crown of her head, like a seal with a ball.

The scrape of her shoulders along the earth filled her ears.

Now she was moving again, in jerky, frantic movements, propelling herself forward, slithering and dragging her lower body. All she could think of was escape, of being free of this claustrophobic grave of a tunnel and being able to breathe again without the weight of the cool dark earth crushing her chest.

Her rucksack went first. It rocked, then tipped forward into nothingness. A crash as it hit the ground a second later. Air rushed in behind it. Her head was the next to plunge free of the tunnel. She opened and closed her mouth, trying to taste the new darkness. She was being squeezed out by the earth. The torch, knocked forwards, had already fallen. The beam had gone out. The blackness around her became total, stuffing her mouth and eyes. Her shoulders came close behind, until she hung, arms trapped under her, her upper body free of the tunnel and dangling into space. She slithered out in an ungainly forward roll, her hands finally free, groping for the floor. She lay, panting, on cool sand. Relief ran up and down her limbs in numbing waves. The air was moist and close but instinctively she could taste oxygen. Better air. She could sense it.

She was lying, curled on her side, relishing survival, when she realized what she could hear. Her body stiffened. Breathing. Close by. Human? Animal? The hairs on her neck rose. She wasn't alone. She spread her fingers and sieved through the sand and stones round her body, searching. Her fingertips finally knocked against the smooth plastic of her torch and closed round it. She pointed it away from her body and snapped it on.

The beam fell at once on the figures huddled in front of her. Hasina, dishevelled, her headscarf crooked on her head, was sitting against a mud and rock wall, her legs tucked under her. The upper body of a young Afghan man was stretched limply across her thighs. His eyes were closed, his cheeks hollow. His face was pallid and moist with drops of sweat. Hasina's eyes stared, wide in the torchlight, with the fierceness of a cornered animal. She was cradling the young man's head in her lap. Her fingertips stroked the contours of his face. Ellen ran the torch down the young man's body.

His cotton tunic was grey with dirt, smeared with patches of filth. His feet, a set of fine bones held together by cheap rope sandals, were twitching, fluttering weakly against the sand like the wings of a dying bird.

Hasina's son. Of course. Ellen's apprehension turned to a sense of triumph as, in a moment, a pattern that had been blurred suddenly shifted and sharpened into focus. No wonder Hasina had been desperate to pursue her so-called mercy mission. It was not a group of stranded village women who needed food and water so urgently, but her own son. Ellen nodded to herself. She couldn't make out the whole puzzle yet but she sensed that this youth was key.

Hasina crawled forward and fell on the rucksack, pulling out water, food. She sat, supporting her son's head, and dribbled water into his mouth, drip by drip. Ellen studied the contours of his face. The remnants of a handsome young man beneath the pale mask. She wondered how long he'd been lying here without food or water. Had his parents known this all the time? She frowned. Why had Abdul asked the Major for help in tracking him down? It could have been a bluff, of course. An attempt to lead the soldiers as far from his hiding place as possible. But if that were so, what did they stand to gain from it? Hasina was struggling to bring her boy back to life. Her concentration was intense.

Ellen looked over his body. A wound, Abdul had said, around his stomach. Another lie? She ran her eyes again over the thick stains on his tunic and realized they were more than just filth. She made out dried blood and crusted yellowing pus. She passed Hasina food and watched as she struggled to make him eat. Finally she pulled out the first-aid kit from her rucksack and crawled over to him to do what she could to clean and patch him up. It was a chance too to search him for whatever weapons he might have concealed in his clothing.

Afterwards, she sat back against the cool mud wall. Hasina and her son were awkward in front of her – she could sense that; but she didn't want to leave them alone. She didn't trust them. She switched off her torch, letting a torrent of darkness pour in. She waited, breathing evenly, forcing herself not to let claustrophobia get the better of her, her hand always on the cool cylinder of the torch.

After some time, Hasina's low voice started to murmur, gentle at first. Her son's lips smacked feebly as she tried to force him to drink. Finally he too began to speak, his voice little more than a whisper. What was he doing here?

Ellen thought about the injuries she'd seen across his torso. The wound was extensive, deep at his midriff, then tapering as it stretched round to his sides. The skin along the wound was yellowed and torn, shredded into fat and sinew and congealed in a putrid mess. It was hard to tell how many days ago he'd been injured, but her sense was that he wasn't healing well. There was little sign of fresh pink skin emerging round the sores. The sickly smell of the wound itself was underpinned by the acrid residue embedded in pock-marks in the skin: a cheap gunpowder or explosive.

She nodded to herself as she heard their voices strengthen and flare in argument. An explosion, Abdul had said. That might be true. But he was more likely the victim of some cheap Afghan device, not of the fallout from a British or American bomb. A revenge attack? She heard a light slapping break out, the slowly rising sounds of smacking flesh on flesh. She tightened her fingers round the torch, wondering whether to startle them by switching it on. Perhaps he had fainted and Hasina was trying to rouse him? Silence. Then, finally, the whispers began again.

She sat in the choking blackness and strained to follow their conversation as their voices rose and intermeshed. In all of it, there was only one word she could pick out, a word they used again and again. Karam. A name she already associated with danger.

14

Hasina knew him at once by his smell, even as she crawled into the chamber, her eyes staring greedily ahead into the darkness, searching for him. He was here. She was overwhelmed by his scent. He was alive, but barely.

His skin was cool and moist to her touch. She closed her eyes to seal off the darkness and felt her way across his body, her heart fluttering with panic. His fingers were limp, his legs dragged as she tried to pull him round into the softness of her lap. She buried her nose in his neck, inhaling him. The gunmetal of dried blood at his stomach where the rags sat bulkily. The animal filth that encrusted him. The richness of the earth in his hair, as if his grave were already hungry for him.

'Aref,' she whispered. 'My own precious son.'

He stirred a little and moaned. She stroked his damp hair and rocked him, trying to breathe life into him. My life for yours, she thought. Know how happily I would give it.

When the foreign woman appeared, spinning lines of light round the bunker with her torch, Hasina took water and dribbled it into his mouth. He coughed and began to swallow. Water, then biscuit, one of these hard foreign biscuits, crumpled into pieces and dampened. He chewed and ate.

She dipped the end of her scarf in water and mopped down his face, his neck, as he feebly tried to swat her away. She pulled up his tunic to flannel his body.

'She isn't a soldier,' she told him as the foreign woman cut away the rags and dressed his wound. 'Praise Allah you're alive.' His eyes rolled backwards in his head as the foreign woman poked at his flesh. Afterwards he slept.

The foreign woman, her face pale, had crawled back to the entrance and switched off her torch. The blackness engulfed them at once. Hasina ran her fingertips over the fresh cloth round Aref's body. Clean. The reek of blood and filth had been overlaid with chemicals. Now she must think. She rocked him, her arms filled with his chest, his shoulders, his lolling head. Think how to get back to him each day to feed and clean her boy, without raising the soldiers' suspicions. How to make sure the foreign woman wouldn't betray them. How to get Aref away from here and to safety as soon as he had enough strength to move again. She closed her eyes and swayed, drowning in his close sweet smell.

Aref had found the bunker when he was a boy. A lonely boy; always the odd one when the children played. Awkward with others. Maybe it was because he was an only child. Maybe he felt the absence of all those older brothers and sisters who never survived. He came into this world with the scent of death on him and the other children were repulsed by it. So, as a young boy, he ranged alone into the desert for hours at a time, playing imaginary games. That was how he'd found the bunker, chasing after some animal and crawling right inside it himself to curl and hide. He had told her about it and sworn her to secrecy. What friends did he have to tell?

It was left over from the days of the Russians, of course. The local fighters had dug networks of bunkers all over the countryside, turning the hills into ants' nests. They needed hiding places to lie low when the Russian soldiers came. They crept through the tunnels from village to village, invisible inside the earth, setting their bombs and laying their ambushes.

He stirred and woke, confused. She pulled out from her tunic the gift she'd brought for him and placed it in his hands. He felt his way round its contours, reading it with his fingertips, uncertain at first. Then she felt him lift the bloodstained Qur'an to his lips and hold it there for some time, his eyes closed.

'It was in the corn,' she whispered. 'You must have dropped it.'

He opened up the clogged pages and pressed the writing against his forehead with reverence. 'God is great,' he murmured. After a while, he tucked the book inside his shirt, reached for her hand and squeezed it.

'Karam Uncle,' he said. She put her face down to his lips. 'You must tell Karam Uncle I'm here.'

'No one must know,' she whispered. 'It's too dangerous.'

He was silent for a moment. 'Where is my father?'

'Searching,' she said. 'For you.'

Aref twisted his head and she felt his stale breath on her face. 'Searching where?'

'Everywhere. With the soldiers.'

He stiffened at once. 'No.'

'Not helping them,' she said. 'Using them. Their cars, their machines. Looking for you.'

He wriggled and sat up, pulling away from her. 'He is a traitor then,' he said.

Hasina felt for his shoulders and shook him. 'God forgive you,' she whispered. 'Ungrateful boy. Don't say such a thing.'

Aref shook himself free. 'Traitor,' he said again. 'My own father.' He paused. The darkness ran into the space between them. 'He is not my father.'

She raised her arm to slap him and caught his skin with the flat of her hand, a smack. 'Such trouble you've caused.' The words burst out of her. 'Don't you see? Messing about with those foolish boys. Their guns and bombs. Have you no brains?'

She reached for him, raining slaps on his fingers, his wrists, as he stretched his hands towards her to fend her off.

'Look at you. Curled in a hole like a rabbit. Half dead. All of us risking our lives to find you. To save you.' She sat gasping, depleted.

Silence. He was breathing hard. He shifted his weight on the earth.

She tried to touch him again, gently now, and felt him strain away from her.

175

'Aref. Stop this. Forget what your uncle said.'

'They've corrupted you.' He sounded like a sulky schoolboy. 'The foreigners.'

'Don't be stupid.'

'You're traitors, both of you. You and him. You are shaming our family.'

She closed her eyes. Please God, she thought, please stop this.

'These foreigners will kill us all. Steal our land.' He was working himself up. His voice was gaining anger. 'Why won't you help me make a noble sacrifice to defend this land, our forefather's land? To serve Allah?'

Karam's words. Aref didn't have the wit to think these things by himself. He was pulling himself to his feet, leaning against the wall of the bunker. Now what?

'My work isn't finished.' He was sounding feverish again. She sensed the trembling in his body. 'Karam Uncle will help me. I will die a martyr. I will bring honour to myself, to our family.'

'Stop that!'

'What do you know?' He spat. 'You don't know anything.'

He crawled from her into the darkness. She heard the soft trickle of liquid, then the smell spread, hot and steaming. Peeing in a hole like an animal. Foolish child. He was caught up in events he could not understand. How could she save him, if he were determined to fight, to sacrifice himself? How could she watch him every moment, protect him from his own craziness? Karam, she thought. Karam was to blame for this.

Hasina led the foreign woman back through the fields towards the village, her heart racing. It wasn't exertion, it was fear. Nothing she could say had changed Aref's mind. He was clinging to his notion of martyrdom as if it were his only mission in life. He spoke as if the rest of his life, that sacred gift from Allah, could be squandered without regret. As if doing battle against the foreigners were the only way of redeeming himself.

Too many young men; too many bodies blown into pieces.

176

She thought again of the bloodshed in the market. The stench of petrol and explosives. The screaming and running. The vile stickiness of blood underfoot. Aref had been saved once already. Hadn't he seen enough? How could he speak of a second time?

The corn was stirred by a light breeze, drying the sweat on her neck and cooling her skin. She set down her crutch and lowered herself to the ground, insects nipping her feet, to wait for the foreigner to catch up.

Better alive, she thought. These men with their talk of honour and death. They'd caused so much fighting, so much grieving. They weren't the ones who gave birth to these sons, who suckled them. Allah in His Wisdom didn't give women the chance to bear new life just so their children could destroy themselves. What honour lay in that?

The earth was dry and cracked between her feet. The corn, close to her face, was splitting. Even if the foreigners left now, she thought, the harvest was spoiled. Such a mess they caused, these men, whatever their tribe, local or foreign. Abdul wasn't that sort of man. She thought of his gentleness, his quietness. Aref was wrong to insult his father. Abdul was risking everything to work with the foreigners, just in the hope of finding his son. She must tell him. Somehow, without revealing too much, she must let him know that Aref was safe. Abdul should flee while he could and join their neighbours in the desert.

The foreign woman almost fell. She sat heavily on the earth, shrugged off her bag, opened it and pulled out water to drink. She drank too quickly, in gulps. Trickles ran from the corners of her mouth and dripped onto her shirt. Her face was puffy and burnt.

Hasina looked at the foreign woman's hands on the bottle as she lifted it to drink again. Pale-skinned hands with long smooth fingers and neatly cut nails. They had tended her son, those foreign hands, cut away with care the mess of filth around his wound and cleaned his skin. They had shaken foreign powder into his broken skin and dressed it with rolls of fresh white material.

Hasina shuffled painfully onto her knees. She ran her fingers under the trailing fabric of her scarf and stretched it across the flat of her hands. She knelt, proffering it to the foreign woman, palms uplifted, in a gesture of blessing and respect.

The foreigner took her lips from the bottle, watching. Her eyes were wary.

Hasina kept her scarf raised, honouring her with it, enveloped in the rich smell of the earth. She bent her head forward, her eyes falling on the foreigner's boots, their thick hard toes coated with dust.

'Thank you,' she whispered into the ground. '*Allah Mo Mal Sha.* May Allah bless you for the kindness you have done today.'

15

Ellen had put off calling London for as long as she dared. Before she did, she wanted to be clear in her own mind what she could pitch to Phil. At the moment, there were too many questions she couldn't answer. Phil, she knew, would cut straight to them.

The soldiers, back from morning duties, were lolling around in small groups, setting up their mess tins to boil rations and tea. The air was full of their ragging, insults flying back and forth. She sat apart from them, cross-legged on the sand, throwing the satellite phone from one hand to the other, and tried to straighten out her thoughts.

Najib had told her that Jalil's mood had soured just before his death. That unease, he thought, was somehow connected to the Nayullah suicide bomb. Jalil's letter to his family in Kabul suggested something had disturbed him so profoundly, he'd decided he must leave.

Then there was Hasina's son, lying injured in his burrow inside the earth. Hasina's fear of anyone finding him – and his injury – suggested to Ellen that he'd been involved in some sort of botched explosive belt attack, possibly the suicide bomb itself.

But why was Hasina's husband, Abdul, risking his life by collaborating with the troops to look for his son – when his wife already knew where the boy was? Was that just a bluff? If so, it was a bloody dangerous one.

And where did Karam fit in? She saw again Karam's hard eyes, the menace as he fixed her with his stare. He was a powerful man.

Did he suspect his own nephew was a suicide bomber? And if so, if he were allied with the fighters, what the hell was he doing collaborating with the soldiers, living under their protection? It made no sense. If anyone had a reason to hate the troops, it was Karam. They'd just killed his children. So why had he planted himself here, in the middle of army-controlled territory?

A stray word from the boys caught her attention. She looked up. A loud-mouthed lad from another section was talking about 'that Afghan'. She listened.

'Sodding waste of time,' he was saying. 'Wild-goose chase.'

Abdul? Someone made a remark she didn't catch and sniggered. She got to her feet and walked across. They simmered down as soon as they saw her. The loud-mouthed lad was spreading jam on crackers, the fingers round his knife thick and stubby with blackened, bitten-down nails.

'Can I ask you?' She crouched down beside him. 'Were you out with that Afghan man today? The one looking for his son.'

The two lads exchanged glances. For a moment, they looked about to freeze her out. The loud-mouthed lad shrugged.

'Yeah. So what?'

'What happened?'

The lad looked uncertain. He hesitated. 'Nothing,' he said. He stuck a cracker in his mouth and bit it in half, scattering crumbs. 'Didn't find squat.' He chewed. 'Waste of time.'

'Where did you go?'

He gestured vaguely with his jam-stained knife. 'All over. Saw people out there. Just not his son.' He swallowed and stuffed in the rest of the cracker. 'If he's even got one.' His mate looked at him and grinned.

Ellen considered. 'Where is he now?' she asked. 'The Afghan.'

The loud-mouth looked indifferent. 'Left him out there,' he said. 'We came back. He wanted to keep looking. On his own.'

He turned his shoulder on her, stretching away to reach into his pack. The soldiers beside him lowered their eyes, sneaking furtive glances at each other and struggling not to laugh. She took the hint.

The young woman on gate duty let her out without question. Ellen tucked her notebook into the front pocket of her flak jacket. Her helmet slipped lopsided on her head, hot and heavy, as she walked. The main street was deserted, the ruts baked hard with the midday heat. Her boots beat puffs of dust from the hollows with every step. A gun-turret swivelled as she passed a fortified compound, unseen eyes following her. She felt exposed, all the more conspicuous because she was out alone.

She followed the mud street to the point where it crested the hill and dipped in its slow descent towards the valley. There she switched on the sat phone and turned in a circle until she found a strong enough signal to call London. She crouched in the shade, helmet by her side, pressed the phone against her hot ear and listened to the far-off ring in the editor's office.

'Phil?' The echo of her own voice came right back at her. 'Ellen here. Can you talk?'

'Ellen? Where are you? What've you got?' She pictured him leaning back in his swivel chair, looking out over the dull rooftops of London, his feet on an open drawer of the filing cabinet, his belly sagging sideways over his belt. He was an aggressive man and his manner was always abrupt, even to his senior news correspondent.

'Out with the troops. Saw John Long here. Is *The Times* carrying much?'

'Every day.' His voice was sloppy with food, as if he were slurping coffee at the same time as talking, the noise amplified by the receiver. 'Eyewitness bollocks. All colour. No new angles.'

She smiled. John was always prolific, but it didn't sound as if he'd found anything fresh enough to impress Phil. 'I'm working on something,' she said. 'Not sure what I've got yet.'

'Try me.'

She closed her eyes and tried to focus. Phil had the concentration span of a 3-year-old. She wouldn't get long. 'Something shady's going on. A translator's been murdered. One I used to work with.'

Phil interrupted. 'He wasn't working for us when—'

'No.' She knew the way his mind worked. Legal liability. 'He was with the army.'

'So who killed him?'

She paused. 'I'm not sure. But there's something else. A family. I've been on this big army offensive. They dug some dead kids out of a house they hit.'

'The army hit?'

''Fraid so. Three young kids dead. A woman survived. I'm still piecing it together but I think her family has something to do with the Taliban. And with a recent suicide bomb.'

Pause. 'And what's that got to do with the dead translator?'

'Well, there might be a link.' She sensed Phil's confusion. She was losing him. 'Between the suicide bomb and his death.'

The creak of his office door. Footsteps. A man's voice, low, too distorted for her to identify.

'Hang on.'

Phil's voice became muffled. He was speaking brusquely to someone, his hand on the receiver. She waited, listening to the backdrop noises, thinking of the life of the office, the gossip and rivalries and intrigues, being played out so far away. Another world.

Phil came back. 'So what's the top line?'

'At worst, the impact of the offensive on this Afghan family, caught in the middle.'

Silence. That, clearly, didn't grab him.

'But I'm hoping there's something sexier. Some real dirt. I'm digging.'

'I'm looking for a lead.' Phil sounded grumpy. 'Something hard edged, Ellen. Investigative. Forget the feel-good stuff. Heard it all before.'

'How long can I have?'

A rhythmical knocking. She knew what that was. He was bouncing his pen on the desk, calculating.

'Tomorrow would be good.'

'The day after?'

He sighed. 'Call me tomorrow.' He was already bored; she could hear it in his voice. Just before the line was cut, he remembered to add: 'And Ellen – keep your head down.'

She switched off the phone and headed on, taking the path to the right towards the bombed house. Ahead and far below, the river was running lazily in the heat, shimmering as it twisted. Its banks were dotted with the squares of military vehicles. A flash caught her eye as an armoured truck moved onto the bridge and crossed to the far side.

The stench of the decomposing goats greeted her before she entered the clearing, turning her stomach. The desert was already picking at their bones. Their carcasses were black with ants. She picked her way through the debris, looking without touching, hoping to find fresh inspiration in the fragments of broken furniture and trampled clothing. The innards looked bleached by the sun, their colours fading.

She widened her circle and paced round the edge of the clearing. She stopped when she reached the flattened path into the corn where she'd found the bloodstained Qur'an. The broken stalks were still clearly visible. She thought of Hasina's visit here, when she'd flattened herself on the ground as if imbibing its blessing. Now she understood why Hasina had reacted with such passion. The Qur'an must have belonged to her son: the sign she longed for that he was still alive.

She lowered herself onto her hands and knees in the corn, imagining his escape. With his incriminating injury, he would be afraid of the soldiers but too weak to flee with the rest of the villagers. The brittle corn scratched her sunburnt skin. She turned over and sat quietly, hunched in thought, swatting every few moments at the tiny flies round her face. There was so much she still didn't understand.

A noise. Footsteps, then the approach of Afghan voices, speaking in Pashto. Men's voices, low and secretive. People who didn't want to be heard. She hesitated for a moment, wondering whether to stand up and reveal herself. Her heart was pounding. They might be angry if they stumbled across her and thought she'd concealed herself deliberately. Perhaps she could crawl forward through the corn, retracing the route Aref had taken, and escape before they found her?

Too late. Corn was swishing against thighs and legs somewhere off to her right, boots thumping on dry earth. Two men were hurrying through the field and had almost gained the clearing. The sounds were already close and distinct. She lowered herself to her belly and tried to twist round in the narrow gap to see. Any greater movement and they'd hear. Anyone, she thought. They could be anyone. Even the remnants of the armed fighters Mack said they'd seen in the village. She froze, pressing herself into the ground and trying to choke back fear. Adrenalin was kicking her senses into life. She listened intently. The voices had steadied now. One was deep, the other younger and more timid. A voice, she realized, that she knew.

She strained to peer low through the stalks. A dark shape moved across the front of the house. She raised herself onto her elbows and inched forward, pausing every time the corn around her crackled. Her forehead and temples were slick with sweat. When she came within a few feet of the clearing, she sank again to her belly and pressed her chin into the earth, trying to make herself as invisible as she could.

Najib was facing her, his shoulders hunched. His words, tumbling from him in a nervous stream of Pashto, meant nothing to her, but she could tell by his tone that he was afraid. He was holding something in his hands, trying to push it towards the other man. She strained her neck to the side, struggling to see more. Najib turned and for a moment he seemed to look right at her through the corn. She closed her eyes and waited, listening to the thump of blood in her ears. Nothing. His nervous voice faltered and then continued with its pleading.

When she opened her eyes again, Najib had moved forward towards the other man, his arms still outstretched. She could see now that the object in his hands was a cloth bag, cheaply made and bulging.

The other man turned and paced back and forth, his hands striking the air. He was uttering only a few words but they were spat at Najib. She recognized the thick set of his neck and shoulders with a sense of the inevitable. Karam. His rounded hat was perched high on his head, his long cotton shirt tight across his back, the outline of his shoulders traced in dark, wet patches. Najib took a step backwards, his face stricken, his eyes fixed on Karam's movements.

When Karam finished and stood still, there was a tense silence. Najib's face was pale and slick. It might have been an illusion, the shimmer of the hot air, but he seemed to be shivering. Ellen felt the sudden burn of cramp in her foot and clamped her teeth tight on her lip. She shifted her weight a fraction, trying to arch the muscle to stretch it out. A bird flew, crying, overhead.

She looked again. Karam had vanished from her narrow field of view. Najib had crept a pace further to the right and fallen to his knees, holding out the cloth bag across the flat of his hands, as if he were making an offering at a shrine. His expression was strained almost to tears. As she watched, he set the bag on the mud, then lowered his head to the earth before it in an attitude of supplication or prayer.

She strained to raise her shoulders and see a little more. A hand, Karam's strong hand, moved forward towards the bag in a single decisive motion, swept it up and snatched it from view. His feet thudded on the mud as he left, pushing through the dry curtain of corn. She waited. Stillness settled back over the clearing. Najib was lying silent and prostrate, stretched out full-length in the dust, his back rising and falling with panting breaths. When he finally lifted his head and gazed after Karam, the emotion in his eyes was frightened relief.

16

The house looked deserted. The soldier was sitting on a rickety wooden chair. A looted chair, Hasina thought, stolen from a nearby house. She listened to his rasping breath as she walked past him, her head bowed and covered, and headed towards the building. On the far side, hidden from the path, Palwasha was sitting in the shade. She was staring out towards the valley, her eyes blank. She jumped when Hasina approached her; she looked embarrassed.

'What are you doing here?' Palwasha scowled up at her. Her eyes were red and sunken. She must be crying more for her children than she would admit. 'Getting bored of your grand foreign friends?'

'Sister-in-law.' Hasina opened the bag she was carrying and showed its contents. Two chipped cups, tea and a small cooking pot. Given to her by that man from Kabul, Najib. They were too useful to refuse. 'Shall I make us some tea?'

Palwasha shrugged. 'Tea?' She gestured vaguely back towards the house. 'If you like.'

They squatted side by side, flicking off flies and watching the water boil. Palwasha made no effort to speak. Hasina took small sideways glances as she prepared the cups. Palwasha looked suddenly different to her. The ghost of the old woman she would become was poking through her face. The tops of her arms were starting to lose their fleshiness. Her lips were chapped and bloodless.

They sipped the tea and looked out at the empty fields below. The low throb of a military engine rose distantly from the valley.

'How our lives have changed,' said Hasina.

Palwasha grunted and blew across her tea.

'Karam brother-in-law is away?'

She pulled a sour face. 'I wonder you dare ask,' she said, 'after your husband's behaviour.'

Hasina clicked her tongue. 'Husbands,' she said. She kept her voice low and even. 'Why must men always fight? We women manage our quarrels without shedding each other's blood.'

Palwasha gave her a wry look. 'If I were wronged, I would shed more than just blood,' she said.

Hasina sipped her tea. The warmth was comforting. 'You have the heart of a man,' she said. 'And the brains too.'

Palwasha shook her head. 'Karam acts so tough, like such a big man. But he cries like a baby. All night. He thinks I don't hear.' She scoffed. 'Cries and pounds his chest, wailing for the children. Cursing the foreigners. Promising revenge.' She gave a thin smile. 'I will have revenge,' she said. 'If my husband fails, I will take it myself.'

A bird swept low over the yard. They sat. The sun was hot. Light pounded the bald earth in waves.

'Karam knows what Abdul has done.'

Hasina looked up sharply. Palwasha hadn't moved.

'What do you mean?'

'He knows.' Palwasha carried on calmly sipping her tea. 'He saw Abdul with the soldiers, riding in their vehicle with them.'

Hasina heard blood thick and loud in her ears. Had he gone so soon? Before they could even talk, before she could try again to stop him?

'He hid his face,' Palwasha said, 'like this.' She drew her scarf over her nose and mouth, covering the lower part of her face, then let it fall again. 'Did he really think we wouldn't know him? He's a fool.' She turned to face Hasina, her eyes cruel. 'You were a fool to let him. You want to lose him too?'

Hasina put her hand to her mouth. The yard was rocking in front of her eyes. Palwasha was suddenly far away, her voice faint.

She closed her eyes. A bang at her side. Her legs were burning, her skirt hot and sodden. She snapped her eyes open. The cup, fallen from her hand, was rolling on the ground beside her, the remains of the tea soaking in a dark splash into the mud. She pulled her skirt clear from her sore skin and fanned it.

Palwasha was leaning in towards her. 'Why is he doing it – turning traitor?'

Hasina shook her head.

'If you plead with my husband, maybe he can help. But why is he doing it? For money?'

Hasina let out a cry. 'Money? How can you think such a thing?'

Palwasha shrugged. 'Then what? What can the foreigners give you that's worth risking his life, worth betraying his own people, his own brother?'

Hasina thought of Aref, lying in his dark lair inside the ground. Her brain was exploding inside her skull. What parent would not give their life for their child?

She put her lips close to Palwasha's ear and whispered.

'Aref,' she said. 'He is still alive.'

When he first came back, Karam refused to speak to her. He turned away at once, wrinkling his nose as if she repulsed him and disappearing inside the house. Palwasha waited with her. Silence.

'Perhaps I should leave?'

Palwasha shook her head. 'Wait.' She got to her feet and followed Karam inside. Hasina heard their low voices murmuring through the wall. She should creep back to the foreigners' camp, she thought. Just leave. Her head was so heavy. She wanted to lie down, to sleep.

Palwasha came out. 'He's upset,' she said. Her tone was more scornful than sympathetic. 'I've talked to him. Go in and try.'

The house was small and cramped. Hasina took a step inside the doorway and was engulfed at once by the darkness. The mud floor was cool under her feet. She stood still, listening and letting her eyes adjust to the gloom. She realized her legs were shaking.

She was afraid of Karam, of his anger. Then she heard a sound. A noise she least expected. A stifled sob.

She felt her way along the wall. Shapes were emerging in the blackness. A stool. A low table. Towards the back, a cot. A figure was lying there, hunched round into a ball, crying. Karam? She stopped and listened. The crying paused, as if he were holding his breath, listening too. Then another sob and it began again.

She should leave. Her eyes were strained with staring into the darkness. The house smelt musty. The straw at her feet was dull and limp as she swished through it. A good sweeping, she thought. If Palwasha would let her, she could have this whole place—

'Is it you?' His voice was thick. Angry? She wasn't sure. She stayed silent. A pause. He was breathing noisily. 'Hasina?'

'Yes, brother-in-law.' She didn't move. If he jumped up, she calculated, she could reach the doorway and out before he could get hold of her. Her eyes were adjusting better all the time. A bucket standing there against the wall. Cotton clothes hanging from a nail on the side wall, the shape of a tall, thin person. A square crate or box.

'Come.' He was holding out an arm to her. It was waving in the air like the branch of a tree. He is stronger than me, she thought. If he hurts me, no one will protect me now. He sniffed and swallowed. She remembered the sound of his sobbing and walked forward. She knelt down beside the end of the cot and dipped her head to him.

'Please,' she said. He was sitting up now, taking her hands and folding them in his. His fingers were hot and wet. 'Forgive me,' she said. 'Help me.'

She sat stiffly, waiting to see if he raised his hand to hurt her. Instead he bent his head forward over their entwined hands and started to sob again. His shoulders were shaking with his breaths. His hair, close to her face, smelt of block soap. His thick tears and mucus ran into their cupped hands and soaked her palms.

She leaned forward, inching towards him little by little, alert to any sudden movement, and gently withdrew one of her hands from his. When she put her arm round him, he moved nearer at once, pressing himself into her arms, and let himself be comforted. She stroked his hair and rocked him, crooning in a low voice: hush, my dear, hush now.

That night, Hasina couldn't sleep. She lay on her back in the foreign soldiers' camp and stared up at the night sky. After all the walking and climbing of the day, her leg was seized with a shooting nerve pain like toothache. She shifted, trying to get comfortable. Somewhere near her, a young foreign soldier was moaning in his sleep.

Her head was aching. Thoughts were pressing down on her brain, too many thoughts. Was Aref sleeping now? The bunker would be hot and airless at night. There might be rats biting him, attracted by the stench of blood. Ants and flies crawling on him. He might be unconscious again. What if he'd run out of water, too weak to care for himself? She bit down on her lip. Somehow, she didn't know how, she must get back to him but make sure she was never seen.

And what of Abdul? He hadn't come to see her. Was he away, sleeping somewhere distant with the soldiers as they travelled and searched? Or had something terrible happened? The place beside her, where he'd slept last night, was large with emptiness. She closed her eyes and tried to imagine his steady breathing, his familiar smell.

Karam's distress frightened her much more than his anger would have done. He had cried in her arms until he was limp. For his children, of course. But also for Abdul.

'Why did he do it?' His voice was hardly audible at first. 'Why? My own brother.'

She had thought at first that he was weeping about the fight and the vehemence of their falling out. 'You can make it up,' she said. 'Hush now. Even the closest of brothers sometimes fight.'

His eyes turned on her, red-rimmed and wide in the gloom.

'Not that,' he said. 'Working with the infidels. So publicly. The fighters have eyes everywhere.'

Her stomach turned to ice. 'What will they do?'

He shook his head, blew his nose on his cotton tunic. 'I can't stop it,' he said. 'How can I? They suspect me too. After all these years.'

Her hand on his shoulder started to tremble. 'But you've sacrificed so much,' she said. 'Your children. Your only son. Surely if you . . .'

He shrugged. 'I must lie low. We all must.' He looked at Hasina strangely. 'And you,' he said. 'You must quit the foreigners' camp.'

'Quit?'

'Of course.' He stared at her. 'Leave them. Go into the desert and hide. If you stay with the soldiers, those people will kill you too.' He gave her a hard look. 'Especially if they find out about your son's failure.'

Hasina slowly withdrew her arm and sat back on her heels, her hands limp in her lap. So Palwasha had told him. He knew Aref was alive. Would he tell his friends? How could she take food and water to Aref now, knowing she might be watched? She might lead them straight to him.

'Maybe,' she said in a small voice, 'we could all leave. Leave together and start again in another place.'

Karam shook his head. His eyes bored into hers. 'If they want to hunt us down,' he said, 'we can never hide. No matter wherever we go. They will find us.'

Hasina looked at the pouches of swollen skin round his eyes, his cheeks. His beard was matted at his chin. Just a few weeks ago, their lives had been peaceful and whole. She had lived in a good house on land she loved like her own child. Now her family was in danger, her world destroyed. What had become of them? What had they done to deserve this?

'There is one way,' he said. He leaned forward and lowered his voice.

She trembled, sensing what he was about to say.

'If your son tried again. If he made a true sacrifice in the name of Allah. A sacrifice that would prove his loyalty.' He patted her hand. 'Maybe then, we could all be safe from harm.'

Karam's mouth was smiling but his eyes had turned hard and distant and made her afraid.

17

Dillon was lying on his back, dozing, his knees bent, a T-shirt across his face. Moss was propped up against the wall beside him, staring at a battered paperback book.

Ellen sipped at a bottle of warm water and stared out over the sleepy camp, puzzling about Najib's secretive meeting with Karam. Najib had seemed so afraid. He must realize what a risk he'd taken, an army translator sneaking out to see a local Afghan leader. She opened her notebook and bounced her pen on a blank page, willing answers.

The Sergeant Major strode across the compound towards them and gathered a group round him. Dillon, Moss and the others in their section scrambled to wake up and pay attention.

'Listen up.' His voice was effortlessly commanding. 'Increase in threat.' He stabbed his forefinger at them to underline each point, as if he preferred movement to words. 'Nonspecific intelligence. Increased risk of attack.'

The young faces turned to him were impassive.

'High alert. Got that?'

'Yes, sir.'

The Sergeant Major looked at his watch, barely visible on a forearm cluttered with tattoos.

'Fifteen hundred hours local,' he said. 'Sections B and C assemble at the gate for patrol briefing.' He looked round the group and pointed at Ellen. 'You. You're coming too. Major's orders.' Sunburnt faces turned to stare at her.

The lads heaved themselves to their feet and gathered their kit. Ellen heaved on her flak jacket again, feeling the weight settle into the bruises along her shoulders. They assembled. The Sergeant Major spread a recent satellite map across the sand, small black squares, shadows and lines on thin white paper.

'Three-vehicle convoy.' He traced their route across the map with a stick. 'Here, then along here.'

Ellen looked at the route, down the hillside to the river, across the bridge and out towards the south-east, into open desert. A broad loop into nothingness. Of course. Now she knew where they were heading. She thought of the map she'd viewed with Mack on the ops room table. He was keeping his word, taking her out to the patch of desert where Jalil had been shot. She looked up at the Sergeant Major.

'Patrol objective. To show presence in the area.' The Sergeant Major was looking round the faces. He avoided catching her eye. He wasn't a man who showed emotion but she felt he was particularly stony-faced. 'Latest reports suggest enemy in the vicinity.'

The men loaded up the Snatches and checked comms. Ellen was waiting with Moss and Dillon, getting ready to climb into the first Snatch, when Mack strode across and beckoned her out of line.

'Second vehicle,' he said to her, pointing to the vehicle behind. 'Safer.'

She hesitated. She wanted to say something about the patrol. To ask: is this a responsible decision? Don't risk lives for me, to help me to lay my own ghost to rest.

His eyes when they met hers were stern. 'That's an order.' He turned and walked smartly to the final Snatch himself.

She sat in a corner against the metal back door of the second Snatch in line, inhaling the sickly mix of oil and diesel. It lumbered off, rocking and pitching. The soldiers ignored her. The descent to the river was steep. Her body, corseted in the flak jacket, bounced off the metalwork, and her helmet clipped the roof struts. Through the square of bombproof glass, she watched the bonnet of the next vehicle as it rolled through thick dust. Mack must be inside, perhaps in the front seat beside the driver. She couldn't make out his face. She felt a surge of gratitude towards him. She realized how much she wanted to see the place where Jalil had died. To sink onto her knees in the sand and sift it for traces of his blood, just as Hasina had pressed herself into the corn for her son. It was irrational. Ridiculous. But she wanted to tell his mother, his sister, that she'd made the journey there to say goodbye to him. To know that, despite everything, she'd risked her own life to do so. It was a small redemption.

They reached the river bank. The driver was revving up, ready to take a run at the steel platform that led onto the bridge. The engine's vibrations shuddered through the seat. The air was ripe with petrol fumes. There was a crash of metal as they hit the bridge and clattered across the surface. Through the window, the bank receded. The third vehicle was still parked there, watching, waiting its turn.

From here, it was open desert. The third vehicle caught up and they set off again, the engines spurting and spitting as the vehicles struggled up banks of sand. The view from the back window was a brown blur of dust and stones and endlessly stretching sand. Whatever tracks they were following were barely visible.

She gripped the roof strap tightly and tried to focus her thoughts on Jalil, imagining him taking the same journey. Had he been frightened, wondering if he'd succeed in slipping away from the men, as he'd planned, to carry out his clandestine meeting? Did he have any idea, as he sat cramped inside the Snatch, that he was already so close to death?

Shouting. A lad on top cover, his feet right next to her, was shouting. His screech gave away his alarm. Something sighted. Enemy? She couldn't make out the words. The radios were crackling but the sound was too fractured for her to hear. She pressed her face against the window. A sudden blinding flash lit the desert. Luminous red and yellow rods stabbed her vision. A fraction of a second later, a bang so loud she felt the throb of it more than heard it.

The vehicle accelerated, turned sharply, throwing her against the back door. An acrid smell reached her. Explosives. Or smoke. She put her hand on the metal handle, looked down at the ground speeding under them. The inside of the vehicle was sharp with panic.

The soldiers' radios were screaming. A mush of barked orders. Their own vehicle was intact. Everything around her looked normal. The soldiers were scrabbling, groping under seats. But they were OK. Alive. No one hurt. They hadn't been hit. She pressed her face against the glass again. One of the other vehicles had taken it.

The Snatch swerved suddenly, pitching her off the seat onto the floor. She fought to get up. They were veering off to the side, bouncing over rough ground. She was cursing, banging knees, elbows, weighed down by her flak jacket, trying to pull herself back on the seat. She tasted bile. What the hell was going on?

The Snatch swung in an arc and jolted to a sudden halt. Her forehead, in its helmet, smacked against the window. She got herself back onto the metal seat and stared out. They were pointing back across the desert, across track marks. The other Snatch was there in the sand, smoke pouring from under it, a black streamer unravelling across the desert.

Someone was lying on his back in the sand. Another soldier was crouching beside him. A stout figure. Arms were moving, pulling out a first-aid kit. The blunt white of dressings flashed in the sun like bone.

Now the soldiers with her were snapping open the back door and jumping out, medical kits in their hands, joining the rush across to the smoking vehicle. She climbed out too and leaned back against the vehicle, sun in her eyes, feeling light sand blow across her face. The air reeked of burning fuel, hot metal, scorched cloth. She shook herself and ran, keeping her head down, towards the vehicle, wondering who it was on the ground and who else was injured.

Hancock. His boyish face was streaming blood, running from

his forehead, his nostrils. One of his eyes was a pulpy mess. The blood was bright and viscous, thickening and congealing like egg yolk as it dried. Mack was crouching beside him, wrapping gauze round his face. There was dust and dirt on Hancock's skin, blown into the cuts and wounds, and now sealed into the bandage. The eye, a soft, twitching mess, was being rapidly parcelled and hidden from view. Mack's expression was utterly focused, his hands capable. As he worked, Hancock's legs were quivering where they lay on the sand, his knees jerking in spasms.

At the back of the Snatch, she found a second casualty. Moss, his face pale and sweaty, was leaning his weight against the wheel hub. Frank was bending over him, cutting the fabric from his leg. His skin glistened in the sun. The angle of his leg was wrong. His trousers were black with blood. Flies were buzzing on the wet patches, round the skin beneath. When the material came away, the bone was revealed, jutting out cleanly through the flesh. Startlingly white in a bed of blood and torn skin and muscle.

'What the fuck is she doing here?' Someone had turned to her, waving his arms, shouting. 'Get her back in the fucking vehicle.'

Hancock was moaning and coughing. His head was bandaged now from his forehead to his nostrils. Blood was running down under the gauze into his mouth. Mack was forcing him to sit up, supporting him from behind in his arms. Hancock was choking, coughing. A sticky trail of blood and spittle dropped to his chest. Mack prised his mouth open, used a finger to hook out blood.

A soldier headed towards her, blocking her view. His arms were outstretched, his chest pushed forward, as if he were herding cattle. He put his hands hard on her shoulders and turned her, drove her back towards the other vehicle. He lifted her to get her up into the back and slammed the door.

She sat on the metal bench seat, staring out at the tableau of soldiers. The figures were moving feverishly. Arms waving, faces pallid with shock. The third Snatch had started to circle them, its guns trained outwards. She drank water, pressing back the memory of the soft pulp of Hancock's eye. They wouldn't save his sight and whatever had pierced the eye might have penetrated further, into the brain.

She thought of the way he'd sat silently just a few days earlier, grey with fear, as the lads had waited for the offensive to start. Of the way he'd horsed around with Moss when they reached the compound, giddy with relief that he'd made it through alive. She shook her head. He was just a kid. She thought of his family in England and the telephone call to come. Finally, the distant throb of a helicopter swelled. It sank onto the desert, blowing up a sandstorm as it landed, then lifted again with the casualties, evacuating them to base.

18

'You cannot report that. Not yet.'

Mack's face was pale. His voice was steady but she saw the distress in his eyes. They were back in the compound.

'Casualties. There's a procedure. We need permission from London and that'll take twenty-four hours. At least. Maybe forty-eight.' He spoke quickly, his tone detached.

'Of course, Mack.'

He ran a hand across his forehead. He looked stricken. She wanted to reach out to him, to say something wise or comforting. But there was nothing to say. He wouldn't even look her in the eye.

'I know the drill,' she said. 'Don't worry.'

He was staring past her, his mind elsewhere. The soldiers were traipsing in through the gates in small groups as each Snatch unloaded outside. Their backs were bowed under kit. No one spoke. She watched them discharge their packs sideways onto the ground, dropping them from a shoulder. An uneasy silence hung over them all.

Mack hadn't moved. He seemed to have forgotten she was there. She wondered if, in his head, he were running through the procedures to come. There would be a chain of calls that would end with sympathetic military voices talking to the families in England. There'd be reports to write too. He'd need to explain the reason for the patrol.

She remembered what he'd said before. *I'm not risking my men's lives on some fool errand.* She leaned towards him and put her hand lightly on his arm. The army cotton was coarse-grained against her fingertips. The heat of his skin leached through. Awkward, she lifted her hand away again.

He turned and looked at her and for a long moment neither of them spoke. All she could think of was Hancock and Moss and their injuries. Moss had a family, Dillon had said. She felt sickened by it all; by the war and the endless violence and the random nature of the suffering. The patrol had been in her name. Was this something else she should feel responsible for?

'I'm sorry,' she said.

Mack roused himself. He shook his head and raised a hand, commanding, as if to stop her thoughts. Her face must have shown her anguish.

'It's not your fault,' he said, then turned on his heel and walked towards the house.

The day's warmth was draining rapidly. The sun was already falling, the shadows cast by the high mud walls darkening and cooling the sand.

Dillon, his face hard, was bending over Hancock and Moss's kit, stuffing sleeping bags, books, roll mats, mess tins into their rucksacks. He worked methodically, without a word. A young soldier from another section came to help. They slung the packs over their shoulders and carried them out to the gate. The sand was ironed flat where the roll mats had been. She sat on her own sleeping bag, her knees drawn up, and considered the empty spaces. She wanted to sit still but her hands were too full of tension, drumming an agitated tattoo on the sand.

Dillon came back and sat on a stone a short distance from her, lying back against the wall, his long legs sprawling. He took a cigarette from a pack lying near him, lit it and inhaled deeply.

'I'm so sorry.' She heard the shake in her voice. 'Really.'

He acted as if he hadn't heard. He drew again on his cigarette, his eyes blank, staring ahead at nothing. The acrid smell of cheap smoke drifted across to her. She hadn't seen him smoke before.

'Maybe the injuries look worse than they are,' she said.

'What do you know?' He kept his eyes on the vacant air in front of him.

She let it go. He continued to ignore her, smoked his cigarette. A thought hit her. I should have been in that Snatch. If it hadn't been for Mack's intervention, I might be in a helicopter now, surrounded by medics. The skin along her hairline contracted.

Dillon twisted away from her, his cigarette in an unsteady hand.

'What did they see? Before the blast.' She watched his face, knowing he was listening. 'I heard them shout.'

'A lad.' Dillon wouldn't look at her. 'Running. Must've planted it.'

She tried to make sense of that. They'd been driving across a vast tract of desert. How could anyone have known a patrol was planned or which route it was taking? They'd been following no more than a goat track.

'How could they know?' she said.

Dillon drew on his cigarette, making the stub glow red, then crushed it into the sand, spraying sparks. 'Maybe they just got lucky,' he said. 'Or maybe someone dicked.' His voice was cold.

'Informed?' She shook her head. 'Come on.'

Dillon pulled out a second cigarette and lit it. 'Why were we there at all? The enemy's all over that heap of sand, everyone knows that. Why did we go?' Dillon shifted and turned at last to look at her directly. His stare was hostile.

'Jalil,' she said. Her cheeks were hot. 'It was where . . .'

'I know.' He scowled at her. 'I went the first time, remember?' He blew out a volley of smoke. 'Frankly, ma'am,' he said, 'the things the boys are saying about you right now. Well, they're not very nice.'

Ellen couldn't speak. She thought of Jalil and the blackening of his name after his death. He hadn't deserved it. Maybe she did.

No one tried to stop her when she left the compound. Either they're too much in shock, she thought as she stepped through the metal gate into the empty street beyond, or they no longer feel the same need to keep me safe. She tightened the strap of her helmet to stop it slopping from side to side and strode out down the dusty road. It was already after five. The anger had faded from the sun and the stark white light of a desert day was mellowing to yellow. The corn rose before her, rich and illuminated. She veered away from the path to the bombed house and struck out instead through a jumble of deserted outlying houses.

After several twists in the road, the graveyard opened up in front of her, a cluster of jumbled monuments climbing the hillside to the left. She stopped abruptly. A man was standing with his back to her, midway up the hill, his arms outstretched, his palms upwards. The low incantation of his prayer drifted down to her, his deep voice rising and falling in rhythmical waves of sound. She stood and listened. The graves in front of him were small and freshly dug and still unmarked by a headstone.

He missed the burial, she thought. The burial of his own children. His head, topped by its embroidered Afghan cap, was bowed. She walked to a boulder by the side of the road and leaned against it to wait, noting the heaviness in his body as he knelt and then prostrated himself, forehead to the earth.

When he finished praying, he stood silently for some time, looking down at the earth. His hands rose to his face and wiped it. He turned quickly, his eyes on the ground. She was now clearly visible to him, below on the path, but he didn't raise his eyes to look at her. She had the impression he had known all along that she was waiting there, even when his back was turned. He picked his way briskly through the graveyard, descending between the rows of crooked gravestones to the path. She stood, her hand on her heart, blocking his way.

'I'm sorry.' She bowed her head to him. 'What happened to your children was wrong.'

Karam stared at her, his eyes hard. 'That is for Allah in His Wisdom to judge,' he said. 'Not you.'

Ellen unfastened her helmet and took it off, setting it on the rock beside her and drawing her cotton scarf up from around her neck to cover her head. Her hair was clammy with sweat. 'Karam-jan, may I speak to you?'

He hesitated, then turned on his heel and led her further down the road to a flat piece of earth with the ruined remains of a broken mud-brick wall. He perched on it, his long cotton shirt billowing around his stomach and thighs, his feet sticking out in rope sandals from his baggy cotton trousers. The fabric flapped loose, stained brown with dust from the knee down. Ellen sat beside him, kicking aside the dried pellets of animal droppings at her feet.

Karam leaned back against the wall. His hands were folded in his lap, a string of amber beads entwined round his fingers. 'Well,' he said. 'Speak.'

'Tell me,' she said, 'what happened at Nayullah?'

He shrugged. 'There was a bomb. A terrible thing. There will be more.'

'Who were the bombers? Local people?'

Karam's eyes narrowed beneath his bushy black eyebrows. 'You must ask the police these questions,' he said. 'They are the investigators.'

'But Karam-jan, I think you know more than they do.'

His weight shifted against the wall as he made himself a little taller. His gaze, fastened on her face, was unyielding. She sensed that he was trying to intimidate her and she steadied her breath, refusing to let him.

'Your own nephew was there, wasn't he, Karam? He was one of them.'

The air sat hot and heavy. He looked taken aback, then his expression darkened. She watched him closely. My God, she thought. I've hit my mark.

'You did know,' she said. 'You sent him, didn't you?'

His body tensed, and for a moment he seemed about to strike her.

'Why would you do that?' she went on. 'For religion? Or just for money?'

Her own hands were sweating at her sides, the nails clenched against the palms. Then the muscles in his arm slackened and he was still again, staring at her with such intensity that she felt her chest constrict. She concentrated on keeping upright against the wall, conscious of her taut muscles, of the tremor in her legs. She tried to think quickly, to read his anger. She needed him to speak.

'I know more than you think,' she said. 'Much more.'

His eyebrows rose. 'You know nothing.'

'Who paid you? Tell me. The Taliban? Foreign fighters? From Pakistan, from Chechnya?'

He turned his head and spat in the dust.

'This isn't Afghan, this madness of suicide bombing,' she went on. 'We both know that.'

'No,' he said, 'it isn't Afghan, is it?' His tone was sarcastic.

He pushed back against the wall until he had reached his full height and towered over her. She could smell the sourness of his breath in her face, the traces of rancid meat and yoghurt. His expression was pure disdain. She stood firm and held his gaze. Afghan men despised weakness.

'What about Jalil?' she said. 'How did he find out? Were you afraid he'd tell?'

A shadow passed over his face, a look of confusion. 'Jalil?'

'The translator. Did you shoot him yourself?'

He shook his head, tossing his white beard. For a moment, he looked offended, then snorted and the anger flowed back into his eyes. He raised his hand, the string of beads clicking at his wrist. His palm and fingernails were brown, encrusted with dirt.

'You know nothing,' he said again. His tone was venomous. 'You are blind.'

He took a step towards her until he was so close that his breathing rasped her skin. His chest was hard against her body and when he spat out the words, his spittle sprayed her cheeks. 'You should be careful with your life,' he said. 'You are not in England now.'

He turned abruptly and walked away, the outline of his body broad and strong under his cotton clothes. Ellen leaned back into the wall. She watched him striding away from her, feeling the blood hard in her temples. He was a vindictive man, one who had killed in his time, she was sure. His anger when she had pressed him about Hasina's son and the suicide bombing had been clear. Now she was certain he'd been a key player in recruiting and planning the attack. But Jalil's death? She shook her head. His puzzlement had seemed genuine.

Once he was out of sight, she turned back up the road and climbed onto the hillside to pick her way through the graveyard. The land was jagged with cracks under her feet, dusted with light dirt which had accumulated in drifts against the base of the gravestones. She thought of Karam's raised hand, engrained with filth, and quickened her pace.

The shallow graves of the three children were distinct in their row, darker in colour than their neighbours because the earth had so recently been disturbed. Ellen stood quietly with her back to the road in the same place where Karam had prayed and ran her eyes over the low mounds. The graves were small, dwarfed by the adult plots around them, their edges rough hewn with picks and spades.

She walked slowly round the edge of the plot, her eyes low, scanning the earth. A thin crust had already formed where the dirt, newly exposed, had hardened in the sun. She crouched down and skimmed the tips of her fingers across its surface. The dirt had formed into granules and it took firm pressure to break through its skin. She paused, breathing in the fine desert dust. A movement above made her look up. A solid, broad-winged bird, its head straining forward as it searched for prey, was rising and falling, riding a current of desert air. She stopped to watch as it mirrored the contours of the fields, then dived suddenly out of sight.

She reached the final grave. She imagined the youngest child lying beneath the earth with her small pink fingernails and child's bangle. At the far end, where the mound joined the level ground, there was a difference in colour. Ellen squatted down to examine the surface. The earth looked newly disturbed, dark and light dust mingled together and scattered to disguise the change. She moved closer. Her fingers traced the surface. No fine crust here. Her fingertips dug in and sifted through loose sand and earth with little resistance. She let out a breath, looked around the graveyard and down at the road below. No one.

She sank her fingers deeper into the dirt and sensed her way through the earth, eyes closed, feeling the scratch of sand under her fingernails and against her mother's ring. Suddenly the tips of her fingers made contact with cloth, buried flat just a few inches below the surface of the child's grave. She opened her eyes and scrabbled to unearth it, to find out what had been buried in a place so sacrosanct no one might think to dig – and a place so private that only a grieving father might visit.

That evening, she cooked and ate alone. The general mood in the camp was subdued and it was clear in her corner that no one wanted to speak to her. Dillon and Frank sat huddled together. They spoke in low voices and averted their faces when she passed. Ridiculous, she thought. They're behaving like schoolboys. But as she sat on the cold sand and watched the darkness thicken, she felt wretched just the same.

Finally Mack's young officer came across the compound. He knelt down on one knee in front of her, as if he were about to propose, and whispered.

'Major Mack wondered . . .' he began. He didn't look her in the eyes. His gaze was fixed instead somewhere on her forehead. '. . . He wondered if you'd like to come and see him.'

It was absurd, she thought, to feel so pleased about the fact someone was still willing to relate with her.

Mack was in the comms room, bent over the makeshift table and the latest crackling rolls of satellite maps. He looked up and nodded when she appeared in the doorway, then waved her towards a canvas chair.

'Good,' he said. 'I'll be with you in five.'

She sat and watched him, taking in his brisk movements as he studied outlines, measured distances and made observations to the young officer who was now hovering at his side. His junior was in awe of him. She saw that in his scramble to please. Everything she knew about Mack told her that he was a soldier's soldier, quick to make decisions and focused on results. His sense of command was reassuring. She thought of the way he'd knelt beside Hancock and bandaged his bulging eye, of the calm efficiency in his hands.

After some time, he sent out the young soldier, rolled up the maps and turned to her. 'Now,' he said, 'how are you?'

She felt his attention settle on her. He dropped into the canvas chair beside hers and waited for her to answer. He was so close to her that she could feel the warmth of his thigh alongside her own. His physical presence was a comfort. She looked at the debris of half-rolled maps and pens.

'I've had better days,' she said. For a moment, she thought she felt tears rising. She swallowed. She could feel his eyes on her and turned her head away.

'Yes,' he said after a moment. 'I think I could say the same.'

They sat in shared quietness. She looked down at her feet, crossed at the ankle in front of her. Her boots were desiccated and coated with a film of brown dust. The laces were starting to fray. She imagined being at home in her own kitchen, newspaper spread out on the floor, cleaning them. She listened to Chopin when she cleaned. A Nocturne, perhaps, for boots. A lyrical passage came to her, flooding her head, and she sat with it, listening. There is a world beyond this, she thought. There is still beauty and peacefulness. Just a long way away.

She realized that some minutes had passed. The silence would be broken soon. Mack would speak. It was inevitable. But, for now, she was grateful for the quiet. She poured herself into it, utterly exhausted, overwhelmed by all that had happened. The Chopin rose and fell in her mind.

I have no idea, she thought, what music Mack would listen to. No idea at all. She turned to look at him, thinking how little she knew. He looked so tired. His eyes were bloodshot, the skin at their corners dry and creased.

'It's your decision,' he said, 'but I think you should move on.' He was speaking slowly and carefully, his voice measured. 'There's the chance of a place on a helo up to Rounell on Thursday. In the north. I could get you back to base on a convoy tomorrow. No guarantees. You know how it is. But it's a hot story up there. Lot of contact with the enemy. Lot of construction.'

She paused before she spoke, taking time to register what he was saying. She realized she was dismayed. She didn't want to leave. The idea fluttered in her mind, trapped, and beat out the last of the music. It smacked of defeat. In the face of the men's hostility, it seemed cowardly to go now. Dishonourable, Jalil would say. And there was so much she still didn't understand. She felt dragged down by weariness.

'Is this because of today?'

He shook his head. 'I put the request in yesterday, just in case. You've seen the worst of it here. It's quietened down.'

She turned her shoulder to him and forced herself to think. It was true, in terms of military action, that the story had gone quiet. She was also falling behind. Phil had told her to get back to him today to say exactly what and when she'd be filing. She hadn't. She couldn't. She didn't have the answers. She needed more energy and more time. She sighed to herself. Maybe Mack's instinct was right. If she promised Phil a fresh location, he might give her another couple of days.

'But after today,' Mack was saying, 'I'm all the more convinced you should leave. It was a close call. And the whole business has left the lads shaken up. You can understand.'

'They blame me,' she said. 'Some of them.'

He tutted. 'That's absurd.' He shifted forward in his seat to look at her. 'You know that's nonsense?'

She paused, letting the question hang.

'So what did happen?' she said at last. 'I mean, what do you make of it?'

He exhaled, blowing out his cheeks. 'They're a threat,' he said. 'Of course. A constant threat. Explosives are cheap. Effective.'

'But out there? In the middle of nowhere?'

He shrugged. 'It's happening a lot.'

Silence. He was sitting still, one hand resting curved in his lap in the open palm of the other. He seemed reluctant to talk. She thought of the passion with which he'd spoken before of protecting his boys. He'd organized the patrol for her, to accommodate her request. She felt guilt sitting heavy as a stone inside her. As their commanding officer, he must feel ten times worse.

'Do you think,' she said, 'they knew we were heading out there? Knew in advance?'

He didn't raise his eyes. 'It's possible.'

'Any idea who could've told them?'

He paused. 'None of my men, clearly. And there are so few others here.'

She swallowed. She felt neither of them wanted to come out and say it.

'The only Afghans,' she said, 'are the two translators. And the family. Hasina, the woman from the house. And Karam and his wife.'

He lifted his hands, then let them fall again. 'We don't know enough,' he said. 'These are serious allegations.'

She breathed hard, trying to decide how much more to say. She felt utterly miserable. If there was a chance that it might do any good at all, she felt she must confess to him the little she knew.

'I feel very responsible for what happened,' she said.

'No, please, not at—'

She lifted her hand to stop him as he tried to interrupt.

'If I hadn't been here, the patrol wouldn't have gone to that area. Don't deny it. I'm not saying it's all my fault. It isn't. But you can see, I feel some responsibility.'

'Well, if anyone—'

She kept on speaking. 'Karam,' she said. 'I think he was involved with that suicide bombing.'

'Nayullah?' He turned to her with a look of surprise. She held his gaze. A moment's stillness engulfed them both. Then he seemed to make a decision and his manner changed. He swung his chair round to face her.

'Speak quietly,' he said in a low voice. 'Voices carry.' He pushed in close to her until their knees touched. 'Now. Tell me. What makes you say that?'

Ellen felt the keenness of his attention. 'I think he recruited local boys. Possibly he planned it too. He doesn't deny it.'

'You confronted him?' He ran a hand over his mouth, looking at her with concern. 'You should be careful.'

'The Taliban's paying him off,' she went on. 'I'm sure of it.' She thought of the cloth bag she'd pulled from the grave and the soil that had fallen from it. Of the bundles of notes packed inside. 'I found money he's hiding. A lot of money.'

Mack nodded, his head bobbing as he processed this, his eyes sharp on hers.

'He's said to be a rich man,' he said. 'Who knows what business he dabbles in? Drugs, maybe. Guns.' He paused, watching her. 'But what made you think he's connected with the suicide bombing?'

Ellen dropped her eyes. She remembered Hasina, sitting with her arms stretched round the crumpled figure of her son in her lap, stroking his filthy hair. Of her lying prostrate, her fingertips touching Ellen's feet, her eyes imploring.

'I can't give you details,' she said. 'Call it a hunch.'

Mack formed a steeple with his fingers and rested his face against it, rubbing his nose with his index fingers. She wondered if all this was new to him or if he already had suspicions about Karam. He sat silent and thoughtful, half hiding his face with the lattice of his hands.

'There is something else,' she said at last. 'Najib. The translator.'

He looked up. 'What about him?'

She hesitated. 'I don't want to get him into trouble. It's just . . .'

'Go on.'

'I saw him with Karam earlier. Outside the compound.'

Mack looked taken aback. 'Doing what?'

'Najib gave him a bag. The one I found, full of money. He seemed frightened.'

'Why?'

'I don't know.' She paused. 'Maybe they've known each other longer than we think.'

Mack pushed back his chair and paced to and fro across the room. She waited. She had no sympathy for Karam but she was worried about the consequences for Najib. Mack came back and sat in front of her again, his head thrust forward.

'You did right to tell me,' he said. 'Thank you.'

The young officer had appeared in the shadows of the doorway, his face anxious. Mack got to his feet.

'The convoy's due out around lunchtime tomorrow,' Mack said. 'You'll need to pack up in the morning.'

He stopped at the threshold and held out his hand to say goodbye. So I never will find out, she thought, what music you like. The pressure of his fingers was warm and firm. She looked down at his hand as it enveloped hers, at his square knuckles and neat nails. She thought of her father's hands, marred now by arthritic joints, but still comforting. You're the only person who's touched me, she thought, all the time I've been out here. Through the offensive, the deaths of the children and now the bombing. She remembered the warm pressure against her body when Jalil's mother had embraced her. It seemed a long time ago.

'Good to meet you.' He smiled, already moving on. His tone was again becoming formal. 'Ellen Thomas. Now I can put a face to the words.' He nodded. 'It's been a real pleasure.'

'It has.'

The young officer was waiting to escort her outside. Mack, having dismissed her, was turning back to the room, to his papers. She hesitated, watching him. She was reluctant to move. You're a good man, she thought, and a complicated one. The young officer's arm was extended in front of her, leading her away. I'll miss you, Major Mack. You're another reason it's hard to leave.

That night Ellen lay in the darkness, listening and thinking, as the thick breaths of soldiers rose round her. The night breeze across the sand was cool and she pulled her sleeping bag up round her chest. Somewhere out in the desert, dogs were howling.

Her eyes made a slow adjustment to the low gloom of the stars and the thread of moon behind the clouds. The guard was slumped against the metal gate, half dozing.

She closed her eyes and tried to match the rhythm of her breathing to that of the soldier next to her. The breeze blew a fine spray of sand into her mouth and made her cough. She twisted onto her stomach, buried her face in the fabric of her sleeping bag. It was rank with sweat and dirt. A soldier snorted, spoke some incoherent words in his sleep, then turned heavily and settled again.

My last night here, she thought. Most people would be excited to get back to base. The prospect of hot showers and better food and an army cot. But she didn't want to go. She felt restless. She'd failed here. She still didn't understand Jalil's death. She'd let him down. She didn't have a decent story to offer Phil. Most of what she had was half-story, without proper substance. Her only hope now was of building something from the Rounell trip as soon as she got there. She turned onto her side, shielding her face from the sand with her hands. The boys' hostility upset her too. It was hurtful to know she was leaving on such a sour note.

She thought of Moss and Hancock. Their families would know by now. They would have packed bags and started to travel, steeling themselves for frantic flights to medical bases in Germany or Dubai. They would ache to see their damaged sons for themselves.

Finally she gave up, unzipped her sleeping bag and pulled on her fleece and boots. There was solitude in the darkness and she welcomed it. She felt for her spare shampoo bottle and its dwindling supply of vodka. She diluted a sachet of orange energy drink

212

in water and mixed a desert cocktail. She wanted to escape the compound, to walk and think, but at night, she knew, that was impossible.

In the silence, every sound was heightened. A stick of dried poppy cracked under her foot. The chickens, imprisoned for the night under an upturned basket, shuffled and set up a brittle chatter as they heard her pass. She placed her feet with care as she walked the narrow corridor through the building. In the comms room, a young soldier was stretched forward over the table, his face turned sideways on the wood. His eyes were closed, his skin a sickly silver in the moonlight, his mouth open and glistening with spittle.

As she turned back from the doorway to the dimness of the corridor, she almost stepped on a body, a torso sitting up against the wall with its legs stretched out. An Afghan man, wrapped round in a coarse wool *patou*. She crouched to look.

'Najib?'

He raised his eyes to her, dull with fatigue.

'What are you doing here?'

'I cannot sleep.'

They peered at each other, faces a few inches apart, eyes shining in the gloom. He looked tormented.

'Did you hear it?' he said. 'My job is finished.' His voice was edged with panic. 'Major Mack says I must leave. Why? I did everything he asked. Everything. I am a good worker.'

She felt hot, wondering exactly what Mack had told him. The young soldier in the comms room lifted his head, stared out at them bleary eyed, then turned his head away and settled again.

'I'm sorry,' she whispered.

His eyes showed his confusion. They held each other's gaze. She didn't know what to think. He'd seemed a kind man when she first met him. Good-hearted. But in Afghanistan, so few people were really what they seemed. She crouched down beside him on the ground, her back against the corridor wall. Najib made room

213

for her, wrapping his *patou* round his upper body, his arms inside its cocoon, and flicking the end across his shoulder.

She raised her shampoo bottle. 'Alcohol,' she whispered. 'Do you mind?'

He shook his head but didn't reach for it. A good Muslim. Jalil too had always refused, even frowned if he caught her drinking. 'It is not good thing,' he used to say. 'Especially not for a lady.'

She tipped back her head and tasted the orange, then, at once, the warming vodka kick. I would give anything, she thought, for the chance to do it all again and set things right.

'I am afraid.' He had leaned in close to her and his voice was quivering. 'Major Mack is angry.'

'What did he say?'

'Just now. Before sleeping. He said I was no longer needed.' Najib lowered his voice even further. 'I think the other translator has been speaking against me. You know him? He is not a good man.'

Ellen sighed. He has the right to know, she thought, but is it for me to tell him?

'Najib,' she said. 'Why did you meet Karam?'

She felt him shift nervously at her side. He didn't speak.

'I found the bag you gave him. And the money.'

When she twisted her head to look at him, his eyes flashed with desperation. He reached out a hand and seized hold of her wrist.

'I cannot tell you.' He could barely get the words out.

His fingers were digging into her skin. She tried to pull her hand away.

'You shouldn't have got mixed up with Karam.'

He pushed his face into hers. His breath was hot, his eyes pleading. 'Would you tell Major Mack not to send me away? Please?'

'Najib.' She prised the claws of his fingers away from her skin, embarrassed. 'I can't do that. It's his decision.'

He pulled away and sat stiffly beside her, his features obscured. The silence and the awkwardness grew.

'Major Mack is in charge here.' She tried again. 'You know that.'

Silence. She drank back the orange and vodka. The night sat heavy on their upturned faces. Through the arch of the building, she could see a drifting wisp of cloud, covering one star, then another.

Somewhere out in the desert a donkey started to bray, a jagged, sawing sound. She tensed, wondering what had disturbed it. At night, in the still air, the distance of sounds was hard to judge. They sat quietly, side by side, listening to the braying, then to the emptiness that followed it.

'Have you found the answer?' he whispered. He spoke almost to himself, his head tilted backwards against the wall. 'To your question about Jalil.'

'No.'

'But you will?' His voice was tense, his breathing shallow. She couldn't tell if he were faking concern or if he really did care about Jalil. 'And you will write it in your magazine and all the people who read it will know?'

She hesitated. It would be easy to shut him up, to say: yes, she would do that. Jalil would have justice, of a sort. She drank back the vodka. The light from the stars cracked into white lines across the darkness when she blinked.

'How can I?' she said at last. 'I don't know the truth.'

'In Afghanistan, there is no truth,' he said. 'No law. Only gun.' He shook his head. He leaned in close to her and lowered his voice again to a whisper. She smelt his fear. 'You must leave. Soon. You are not safe.'

He turned to face her. His features were distorted by the half-light and shadow, twisted into something grotesque. Was he warning or threatening her? She wrapped her arms round her body.

'I am going. Tomorrow,' she said.

It was time to end the conversation and leave. She got to her feet, aware of Najib's eyes following every movement.

'What will you do now?' She meant it as a polite formality, but when he answered, his tone was intense.

215

'I will find another job. I will work hard and save money. I will care for my parents and, when I take a wife, I will be a good father to my children.'

Your parents must have had the same hope, she thought, and your grandparents before them. But the peace they longed for never came.

'*Inshallah*,' she said. God willing. 'Whatever you've done, Najib, good luck. Keep safe.'

'Why do you say that?' He sounded puzzled, his face upturned, staring at her. 'Why do you say: whatever you have done?'

She shrugged and said nothing. He continued to scrutinize her for a moment, his face a mixture of confusion and defiance. Finally he looked away and they parted without exchanging another word.

19

Sickness woke Hasina. She lay, drowsy with it. The sickness was not in her stomach but deeper, in her gut. She lay, still clouded with sleep, and felt dread. Something had happened.

The sheet shielding her was torn aside and two soldiers stared down. One had his arm round the other's shoulder, his foot raised from the ground. A mangled ankle or foot. His face was pale and sweaty with pain. Like Aref, she thought. My boy. Their eyes met for a second, then the sheet fell back into place and the voices moved on.

Please God, she prayed silently. Protect my family this day. I will give you everything. Stay with us. The red pain in her gut made her twist onto her side and gasp as she waited for the spasms to pass.

After some time, a nurse came, helped her to wash and to swallow a cup of water. The dressing on her leg was changed. The fetid stink of the wound had gone now. The flesh was raw and pink but clean. Instead of applying a fresh bandage, the nurse peeled paper off a pink piece of tape and stuck it to her wound.

Outside there was commotion. An engine started up, more throaty than Karam's tractors. A foreigner was shouting. She lay still. Soon Abdul would come. Yesterday he had never come. But today she would comfort him, tell him that Aref was found, Aref was alive. Maybe he would find a way of taking food and water to him. He was a weak man but a kind father. Praise Allah for the gift of a good husband.

The black man came. He stood over her, blotting out the sun, his dark skin dotted with sweat. He bent to inspect her leg, touching her skin with his black fingers, his palms as pink as lips. His smell, of alien male sweat, repulsed her. Najib stood behind him.

'Do you have a place to go, the doctor is asking,' he said. 'They will help you leave. Your leg is much better now.'

She turned her face away. Go? Where could she go? Not to Karam. If she left the soldiers now, how would Abdul find her?

Najib was speaking softly. 'You can't stay here,' he said. 'You understand? They've done what they can for you. Now you must leave.'

When they'd gone, she turned on her side and closed her eyes. Come quickly, my husband. I am bursting with news about our son. I need you. The pain in her gut was twisting, consuming her. A new machine was humming. Outside the compound. A machine with a deep, throbbing tone. She must have slipped at last into sleep.

Someone was shaking her. A foreign voice. Whispering her name: Hasina! A woman. She opened her eyes. The non-soldier with solemn eyes. She was pulling her shoulders, dragging her to her feet, pushing the sticks under her arms, pressing her forward. Talking at her. Urgent foreign words.

Hasina pulled her scarf up around her head and neck and they came together from behind the hung sheets into the compound. A soldier was standing there, his gun across his body. His expression was stern. They're throwing me out, she thought, is that it? Kicking me out like a dog. What more did I expect?

The soldier followed them. The foreign woman had taken hold of her arm, forcing her to walk more quickly than she could. Out through the compound gate. An army vehicle waiting there, its back door standing open. The metal step was too high for her. Karam's warning came into her mind. Stay away from the soldiers. Don't let the fighters see you with them.

She tried to pull back but already the foreign woman and the soldier were pushing her up, propelling her into the vehicle.

The seat was hard with a torn cover, spilling foam. The inside was dark and thick with the stench of engine grease and petrol. A ribcage of metal bars running round the roof and back were painted a dull green. The foreign woman climbed in too and they squashed together on the seat. The soldier pulled the back door shut behind him, plunging them into twilight. He picked his way between their legs and stood with his head sticking out of the roof.

A prisoner, she thought. They were nursing me back to health just for this. The foreign woman put her hand on Hasina's knee. A hot hand. She looked down at the square-cut nails, the dirt-encrusted skin. The hand that tended Aref. Fear took her. Had this woman led them to Aref? She looked up quickly at the foreign woman's face. She was looking back at her, her large eyes watchful. The vehicle shook as the engine started and they set off, shuddering and bouncing, across the desert. The red pain in her gut smouldered, stoked by fear.

The air inside the vehicle was stale and, as they drove, the petrol fumes rose in waves. She felt dizzy and sick. The vehicle kicked them to and fro, knocking each other's hips, shoulders. Finally they circled and drew to a halt. The soldier clambered past them and opened the back door, saying something to the foreign woman.

Out of the back door, a triangular patch of desert was visible. Open desert, somewhere beyond the river. They had travelled not along the track to town but in the opposite direction, into wilderness. Hasina craned forward to see. Another army vehicle was parked alongside them in the dirt, its back doors standing open. The air was thick with flies.

Najib appeared. He had wound his scarf round his head so completely that only the narrow strip of his eyes could be seen. He climbed into the vehicle and sat opposite them. He looked first at the foreign woman, then at her.

'Well?' she said. Were they about to kill her? If Allah wills it, she thought, so be it.

Najib opened his mouth to speak and then closed it again.

'Well?' she said again.

'Your husband,' he said. He was about to say more but stopped, seeing it was already enough. The pain stopped her breath. Najib's face shimmied in front of her. Oh Abdul. Karam had warned her. What had they done to him?

'Where?' she said. 'Where is he?'

His body was lying crumpled in the back of the foreigners' other vehicle. Twisted on the floor like an animal, flies hanging low around his head. She crouched there beside him and ran her fingers over his forehead, his nose, his sightless eyes. How bruised he was. His hair, his beard, were matted with dried blood and sand. She pressed her face into his cold neck, licked the folds of his skin with the tip of her tongue, tasting him for the last time. His fingers were stiff at his sides as she tried to weave her own between them.

She hung over him, put her head to his chest and closed her eyes, willing him back to life. My husband, my own dear husband. Her body vibrated with a low moaning that came to her distantly but that she knew to be her own. She sensed the presence of the soldiers, watching her with blank faces. She spread her arms over his body and lay across him, protecting him. His own familiar smell, clinging in traces at his neck, in the crook of his limbs, was already fading in the desert air.

The vehicle creaked. Najib climbed in after her and crouched at Abdul's feet.

'It wasn't the foreigners.' He spoke softly to her. 'They found him. Here in the desert. This morning.'

She lay with her ear against Abdul's chest, listening for the heartbeat that had lulled her to sleep a thousand times and hearing only emptiness.

'May Allah in His Mercy comfort you.' He started to pray quietly, his lilting voice surrounding her like an embrace.

Soldiers were shouting. A radio flared and faded. The vehicle darkened as someone shut and bolted the back doors, then shook as the engine started. She lay on its bare metal floor beside her husband, holding him still and steady in her arms, cushioning his head from the hardness of the metal as the vehicle bounced back to the village.

In the village, a team of soldiers was preparing a grave. As the vehicle doors opened, they stood back from the shallow trough they'd dug, spades in hands, shirts soaked with sweat.

The foreign woman held her upright as they wrapped Abdul in a sheet and laid him in the ground. Hasina's own body slid downwards with his, formless as water. Let me vanish into the earth with him. Be covered by the dirt of our land, of our fathers and their fathers before them. An end to all this. Abdul, my Abdul. How could you leave me? Now what will become of me?

The dirt pattered down on him. Her breath came in gasps, her eyes barely able to see. Never again, she thought. Never see him. Never taste him. Never smell him.

When the soldiers pressed their boots on the mound and turned away, she spread herself across the fresh earth and filled her fists with dirt, groping for him.

Palwasha was there. Hard hands threaded themselves under Hasina's shoulders and tried to lift her. 'Come away,' she was hissing in Hasina's ear. Palwasha's arms were strong, levering her upwards, her thighs taking her weight. 'Get up,' she was saying. 'Sister-in-law. Come away.'

Hasina opened her eyes and saw Palwasha's fierce face close to hers, her head covered, her eyes sharp.

'Karam is waiting,' she whispered. 'Too dangerous for him here. But come now.'

Too dangerous? Hasina pushed the thought away. Unreal, her mind was telling her. This whole business is unreal. It cannot be true. Just sleep and wake again and this whole nightmare will have ended. Her feet moved forward across the ground, Palwasha pushing her as before the foreign woman had done. What difference did it make? She was sleeping; when she awoke, everything would have healed.

'Aref,' she whispered to Palwasha. 'He wasn't here. A father has the right to be buried by his son.'

Palwasha stared back at her, round-eyed and impatient, as she half carried, half dragged her towards Karam's makeshift house.

20

Last time Ellen had stayed at the base, on the way into the offensive, it had felt basic and small to her. Now, in contrast to the makeshift camp in the compound, the bustle and vibrancy were striking. She hauled her kit from the vehicle drop-off point; it was thickly coated with dust after the drive. Her boots clattered on the honeycomb walkway as she passed the cookhouse and chapel, turned down to the women's tent and unzipped the heavy canvas. The interior was dark and cool and hummed with air conditioning. She stood quietly and let her eyes adjust. It was late afternoon but two of the women were sleeping, curled on army cots. Above them hung the same array of towels and stiffly dried camouflage shirts and trousers.

Ellen dropped her rucksack at the foot of a bare cot and rummaged for her dirty clothes and wash-bag. The female ablutions block across the walkway was deserted. She tried to shrug off her guilt about the boys who were still covered with sweat and dust back in the compound and enjoy the luxury of a clean, stainless-steel flush toilet. The physical pleasure of punching the metal button in the shower cubicle and standing naked under a stream of lukewarm water. Of lathering herself with soap and shampoo and watching the water run brown with desert grime at her feet.

Afterwards she filled a metal sink with water and pummelled her clothes. She was back in civilization. The face looking back at her in the mirror was weather-beaten. Her lips were cracked and peeling, her nose and cheeks sand-scoured. While her hands worked, soaking and wringing, her mind was busy.

She thought of Hasina and the way her thin, hard body had sagged and drained itself of life as the battered remains of her husband were lowered into the ground. She thought of Najib's pleading eyes, large in the moonlight, as he begged her to intervene for him. She looked into the eyes in the mirror. They were uneasy. I had to tell Mack what I saw, she told herself. What he does with the information is his business.

She opened the taps and let another layer of desert dirt splash out of her clothes. She squeezed them into folds, then felt them swell between her fingers again, plump with water. Her mother's ring shone clean on her hand. Professional distance, she thought. It's the only way I'm going to survive this. Don't get involved. Don't cross the line.

She saw John as soon as she walked into the cookhouse. His dusty fleece stood out against the uniforms. He was sitting with three soldiers, holding forth about something, his sauce-stained knife stabbing the air for emphasis. Telling them how to fight the war, probably. She saw their tired expressions. They were listening with polite discipline, heads down, sawing at their meat and potatoes with plastic cutlery.

He was still there after she'd gone through the hand-sanitizing drill, loaded her plastic plate with food and come back into the dining area. The soldiers looked up with relief as she approached, taking her arrival as a cue to scrape back their chairs. Only John didn't look pleased to see her.

'Well,' he said. 'Look who's here. How was desert storm?'

The soldiers were cleaning off their places with antiseptic wipes and gathering up their debris, saying perfunctory goodbyes to John as they made their escape.

'Dusty,' she said. 'You?'

He gave her a supercilious look. He never used to be this

pompous, she thought. He was getting worse as he aged. Maybe they both were.

'Bloody hairy up in Lamesh. Filed every day. London can't get enough.' He pushed a buttered bread roll into his mouth and continued to speak through a churning cement-mixer of dough. 'You filed much?'

'Not yet.' She feigned a smile. 'Still working on a top line.'

'Blimey.' He looked smug. 'All right for some.'

Two young lads took their places at the far end of the trestle table and hunched over their food, shovelling it in. John looked at them, then leaned forward to Ellen, his jaws still working bread.

'One more location,' he said. 'Then I'm done. Be glad to get out. A shit-hole, this place. Going to hell in a hand-basket.'

She thought wearily that she should read through his pieces online. She ought to know what he'd been filing before she wrote her own article, but she wasn't looking forward to it. This would be yet another country he'd consign to the dustbin of history, without speaking to a single Afghan.

'Where's your last stop?' Please not Rounell in the north where she was heading. She couldn't bear it.

'Nayullah.' He looked furtive. 'You haven't been, have you?'

'Not into town, no. Why?'

He looked round with exaggerated care for spies from rival papers. 'Great story,' he said. 'Progress. For once.'

'Good news?' She smiled. 'You'll never get it into print.'

He leaned forward, his face low over his slice of cheesecake. 'That suicide bomb. Turns out it's just what they needed.' He nodded sagely. 'It's really turned things round.'

She set down her knife and fork and looked at him closely. 'Turned things round?'

He nodded. 'The coalition worked their nuts off trying to get a deal with the elders before the bomb. Not a sniff.'

She thought of the *shoura* that Najib had mentioned as part of Major Mack's diplomatic offensive. 'And?'

John's eyes gleamed with triumph. 'Then the bomb happened.

Local women and kids blown to bits. Policemen, all local lads. It's scared the hell out of them. Now they'll agree to anything. Falling over themselves to inform. Anything to save their skins.'

Ellen remembered Mack's voice, speaking so earnestly when he talked about the impact of the suicide bomb. *People need to think who's got their interests at heart,* he'd said. *Who goes out of their way to help civilians, not hurt them.* She blinked, considering. His words had been more prophetic than she'd realized.

'The Brits are wetting themselves,' John was saying. 'Can't believe their luck. Nayullah's small but it matters. That bomb. Could be a turning point.'

Even if it isn't, she thought, you'll hype it up so much in your copy, it'll sound like one. She considered. 'What's your source on all this?'

He tapped the side of his nose with his finger and looked pleased with himself. He stuck a plastic spoon into his cheesecake and brought a messy dollop to his lips. He's already regretting telling me so much, she thought, but he's such a big mouth, he can't help himself. She watched him chew, the corners of his mouth sloppy with confectioner's cream. Besides, she thought, he doesn't really see me as competition. It doesn't matter to a man like him what awards I've won. It's only a magazine. And I'm only a woman.

Ellen lowered her eyes and turned her attention to the stringy chicken and vegetables on her plate. Her head was buzzing. Something inside her was screaming and she longed to get away from John to think it through. As he droned on about the wonderful stories he'd filed and what Afghans really needed, she screened him out, swallowing her food and nodding. He wasn't a man who could tell the difference between interest and endurance. Finally he scraped back his chair and got to his feet.

'Fancy a smoke?' he said.

'Thanks but I'd better work.' She tried to sound disappointed. 'Any way of getting on the Internet here?'

'Not officially,' he said. He was already tapping a cigarette out of his packet, eager not to lose a second's smoking time. 'But they've got computers.' He grinned down at her, fleshing out his double chin. 'So if you bat your eyelashes and ask nicely . . .'

Two actions, she thought, of which you are incapable.

And then, thank goodness, he was gone.

The Internet connection was frustratingly slow. Ellen had been escorted by a self-important young media officer down a flight of wooden steps into a protected area, a dimly lit operations room built out of sand-filled hessian walls. He led her to a fold-up chair and table in a corner and hovered behind her, watching every move, as she started to search and read.

It was a secure comms area, the kind of portable field office that made her think of old Second World War films, only nowadays computers had replaced radio sets. Young men in uniform were hunched at similar desks and tables, writing reports and memos and bouncing emails to and from the provincial head-quarters. Above her own table, there was an official chart with lists that showed—

'Eyes forward.' The media officer leaned over her and tapped on her computer screen to focus her attention. For heaven's sake, she thought. I've seen more classified military info than you've had hot dinners. She nodded and smiled: Was there any chance of a cup of coffee? She'd be so grateful. He hesitated, then disappeared to make one.

She pulled up the site for *The Times* and started to scroll through John's pieces. Phil had been right. John had filed a steady stream, much of it embellished with melodramatic first-person accounts of the action he'd witnessed and hardships endured while serving at the front with 'our boys'. Each report was illustrated by a photo by-line, taken some years ago.

His report on the Nayullah suicide bomb was short. She could just imagine his conversation with the guys on the foreign desk – 'no Brits killed, only Afghans, a few hundred words?' He might regret that since he'd now decided it was such a pivotal event.

When she'd had enough of John's prose, she went back to the search engine and started to browse. She wanted to find out more about the way the Taliban paid off people like Karam. They had the money. The drug trade saw to that. But she needed concrete details to flesh out her theory.

She tried to narrow her search with a string of words about Afghanistan and dollars. It still pulled up several hundred finds. She began, at a maddeningly slow pace, to click through them, one by one. Most were useless. Pages about Afghanistan's finance ministry, the Kabul government's various budgets and adjustments to the scale of the international aid package. She struggled on, without knowing quite what she was looking for.

'Found what you wanted?' The young officer plonked a poly-styrene cup of milky coffee on the desk beside her and peered over her shoulder. 'What's that?'

'Just checking a few facts,' she said. 'Nearly done.'

He made an exaggerated point of looking at his watch.

'How much more do you need?'

'Half an hour?'

He shook his head. 'Twenty minutes max,' he said. 'Sorry.'

She scrolled down, scanning the sites, conscious that her time was running out. The budget statements continued, followed by a raft of references to pledges at a recent conference.

Just as she was despairing, a media article opened that made her stomach contract. She glanced round quickly to see if her media minder was watching. He had his back to her, chatting in a low voice to a colleague. She turned back to the screen.

Its title was: '*What price freedom?*' A clip from a newspaper in the United States. God bless that journalist, she thought. A proper piece of reporting at last. She scanned through it as fast as she could, expecting to be prised away from the computer at any moment.

It detailed a recent development programme, implemented by the American military in Kandahar, which was using funds approved as part of the aid budget to buy the loyalty of local commanders. Sometimes this was quasi-legitimate, the article said. An agreement to site a new school or well or clinic, for example, in the spot chosen by a sympathetic local commander and to his advantage. So it might benefit his supporters or relatives more than their neighbours and serve the purpose of shoring up his local influence.

But at other times, the piece argued, aid money was being spent on more explicit bribes. Bundles of dollars, sometimes substantial amounts, were being used to line the pockets of local men of influence and convince them to back the coalition rather than the Taliban. Did the public in the West, the reporter asked, realize how their tax-funded development money was being spent? What value did loyalty have if it were bought in this way? And didn't this covert strategy fly in the face of international commitments to curb corruption in Afghanistan?

An American military official was quoted, giving a standard denial. But the report ended with a Washington-based analyst. Such a strategy, he said, was perfectly plausible. Even, he argued, an effective use of funds.

'The government routinely divides the enemy into three categories,' he said. 'Tier three is the lowest threat. That might be local people who are sympathetic to the enemy, who give food or shelter but aren't actively involved in violence themselves. These people are typical targets of hearts and minds campaigns.

'Tier one is at the other extreme. They're hardcore militants. Fanatics who've been recruited and trained as fighters and are ideologues. They're usually impossible to convert.

'But that leaves the middle: tier two. Opportunists. Pragmatic local leaders who are willing to do deals for cash. Buying their support may be a good investment.'

Karam. She sat, staring for a moment at the open page, feeling the skin along her hairline tighten, her cheeks flush. The young officer was scuttling back to her, barking some instruction to finish up now, right now, he really had to insist. He reached forward, peering over her shoulder as she quickly closed down the page and deleted the search words that had led her to it. Suddenly she felt keen to cover her tracks.

'Phil?'

With his meetings and other calls, it had taken her three attempts to catch him. Here darkness was already pressing in, turning the desert into a menacing emptiness as she peered out at it through the thick perimeter fence. In London it was late afternoon, almost the end of the working day.

'Where the hell've you been?' He sounded bad-tempered. 'I thought you'd call yesterday.' He grunted. 'What've you got anyway?'

'A scandal. I think they've used aid money to buy support from a local leader. A thug with connections to a suicide bombing. And we're giving him taxpayers' money to sweeten him up. A shed-load.'

A pause. She heard the tap, tap of his pen bouncing on the surface of his desk. He exhaled heavily. 'What evidence've you got?'

She clicked her tongue. 'I'm building a case.'

'Which means what?'

'I've seen the money.' She was thinking quickly. 'I think it comes from the coalition.'

'Can you prove that?'

She hesitated. Truth was: not yet. It was taking shape right in front of her – she was sure she was right – but there were still pieces missing.

Phil was sounding impatient. 'I need it now, Ellen. You're out of time. Can you stand this up or not?'

'Almost,' she said. 'There's a man—'

He cut in. 'Almost isn't good enough.'

All I need, she thought, is one strong interview that confirms it. That ties the loose ends together. Even off the record, if that's all I can get. Phil's heavy breathing reached towards her down the line.

'You've got a backup, Ellen? Tell me you've got a backup.'

'One more day. That's all I need. Twenty-four hours.'

The second phone on his desk started to ring, echoing down the line like an alarm. He cursed them both.

'Phil. Have I ever let you down?'

He grunted. 'Twenty-four hours. But it'd better be good.'

A dull click as the receiver went down. She stood for a moment, looking at the pale stars emerging from the gloom, and wondering how on earth she was going to deliver this time.

The officious media minder intercepted her as she walked back to the tent. He looked angry, tapping his watch.

'Nine o'clock,' he said. 'Briefing.' He turned on his heel before she had a chance to reply. 'Hurry.'

She was ushered into a cramped bunker room. A strip light buzzed overhead. A white board was mounted on a bare wall. It was clearly a reception room for outsiders, stripped of any sensitive information. Three officers, including the Base Commander, got up from the central table and shook her hand. Smiles all round and jokey pleasantries. The famous Ellen Thomas, they said. They were honoured. The Commander claimed he always read her pieces. While they effused, a minion ran about behind them, making coffee.

One of them, a youngster with bloodshot eyes, had just come down from Rounell where he'd been based for the last three months. He'd be travelling back up with her tomorrow, they said. First thing. She saw the exhaustion in his face. A man, she thought, who desperately needed an evening to himself. A few hours to think about nothing. Hot food, a long shower, and a chance to sleep. Instead he was being rolled out by his boss to meet the media.

When the general chat subsided, the Commander turned to the fatigued young man and prompted him to begin. He cleared his throat.

'I'd like to give a short presentation about the operation in Rounell,' he began. He clicked through a series of computer graphics, projected onto the white board. He came across as nervous, embarrassed in front of his commanding officer. He faltered and repeated himself.

The presentation stretched on. A succession of facts and figures about Rounell, read off laboriously, line by line, from the screen. A geographical explanation of the surrounding area, with details of the indigenous communities. The Commander nodded encouragement.

Ellen sat, watching politely, but didn't hear a word. Her mind was miles away, processing and calculating. She started with Major Mack. He was unusually smart. She knew that. He was in a different league from most of the soldiers she met, even amongst commanding officers. He struck her as an individual, with strong principles and a mind of his own. Someone willing to take controversial decisions and risk operating outside the chain of command. Exactly the sort of person the military might select for a special operation. It seemed perfectly plausible to her that he'd been given the authority to identify tier-two leaders and quietly strike deals with them. Her heartbeat accelerated. The more she thought about it, the more it rang true. Given his passion for the safety of his boys, she could see that any strategy that cut corners and protected soldiers from danger would be something he could justify to himself.

The young officer turned to address her. 'Any questions so far?'

She shook her head and smiled. 'No, thank you,' she said. 'That's perfectly clear.'

The Commander looked pleased. The young officer, heartened, clicked on a new chapter. *Rounell: The Scale of the Challenge.*

'Strategic objectives,' he said, and started to read out a screen of bullet points. Next he moved onto an evaluation of progress on key objectives, including establishing power lines and digging wells. More bullet points. Ellen faded him out.

If the money came from the military, she thought, why had Najib been sent to hand it over? Why such secrecy? She felt suddenly sick. *Major Mack says I must leave.* She remembered the panic in Najib's eyes. *But why? I did everything he asked.*

If Najib had just been following orders, why had he been so afraid? Why hadn't he explained that to her and defended himself? And why had Mack decided to get rid of him so abruptly? She took hold of the edge of the table to steady herself. In the background, the intoning voice faltered, uncertain, and came to a halt. The Commander gave hearty thanks, then turned to her.

'Now, Ellen. Anything you'd like to ask?'

She looked round at their eager faces and took her courage in both hands.

'I'm so sorry,' she said, 'but I need to request a slight change of plan.'

The officers stared at her blankly.

'Could I possibly defer Rounell for now? I need to get back to the offensive tomorrow. As early as possible. To Major Mack's camp.'

The media officer rose to his feet, his expression indignant. The exhausted youngster stared at his fingernails. The Commander watched her through narrowed eyes.

'I am sorry.' She looked round at them all. 'But there's something very important there I need to do.'

21

The Danish supply convoy skidded to a halt in a swirl of dust, which poured in through the open top hatch and flooded the vehicle. Ellen coughed and drew her scarf more tightly across her mouth. The Danes were standing now, their blond heads submerged in helmets, goggles and layers of scarves. When she blinked, watching, the dust from her eyelashes drifted lightly onto her cheeks.

A clatter as the back doors were prised open. Fine particles hung in columns in the falling shafts of light. She lifted a hand to say a silent thank you to the Danes and clambered down, feeling compact earth again under her feet after the lurching ride. She walked down the dirt street to the familiar compound gate.

Inside, the compound was quiet. She stood, looking over the tents and makeshift structures, checking for change. The camp was intact but almost deserted. She ran a hand across her sweaty face. The sun was high, flashing on the walls of the building. The men must be out on a day-long operation. She walked across the sand with a sense of disquiet and checked the officers' sleeping area and the comms room. No sign of Mack.

She stood inside the doorway of the translators' room and looked round. Pieces of crumpled clothing belonging to the fat-bellied translator were strewn around the room. His bedding was piled in a messy heap in the corner. But all evidence of Najib had been expunged. His neatly arranged, battered books, his tea tray and cracked cups, his folded cotton shirt. Nothing remained.

She sank onto a mud brick against the wall, her head falling forward into her hands. She'd been certain that if she insisted on coming straight back, she'd catch him. Her challenge, she'd been sure, would be to make him open up to her, to draw out of him the details and testimony she needed to seal the story. It hadn't occurred to her that he'd have left so soon. Her palms were hot and damp against her cheeks. Now what? This was as far as her hasty planning had taken her.

Najib, she thought. The room stared back emptily at her. She wondered where he'd gone now, how he'd find work and whether he'd ever realize his dream of settling with a wife and being a good father to his children.

Outside, an engine started up. She lifted her face, specks of light dancing in her vision, and looked at her watch. It was after one. Najib was gone. She only had a few hours left before she had to send something to Phil. She had a lot of work to do.

The rucksack chafed her shoulders as she strode out down the main street and cut through the corn, trying to retrace the route Hasina had taken her. The sun was intense, glancing off the hard earth and setting the crops ablaze. Flies nipped at the soft skin of her neck, found their way into her trousers and fed on the soft wetness behind her knees. By the time she reached the gully and started to slither, dislodging stones, down its steep sides, she was lathered in sweat and panting.

She moved the dead foliage and pushed the rucksack ahead of her through the narrow tunnel, trying to control the waves of panic that rose inside her as she felt the clay squeeze of the earth round her body. The stink hit her when she was halfway through. A putrid smell of rotting mixed with human waste. At the end of the tunnel, the rucksack disappeared, falling forward and smacking onto the invisible ground. The stench hit her full in the face. She gagged and stopped to pull her scarf across her nose and mouth.

In the torchlight, his skin looked pallid and waxy. His eyes were closed. Dead, she thought at first, then heard the shallow rasp of his breathing. She stood for a second, looking him over. His body was slumped along the ground, his head on one side in the dust. His clothes were filthy, the bandages round his wound mauled as if he'd clawed at them in pain. His lower body was discoloured with dried urine and the dark stains of shit. An animal, she thought, which has crawled into its burrow to die. Whatever information she hoped to get out of him, it wasn't going to come for a long time.

His wrist showed a weak pulse. She unpacked the rucksack round her, the torch between her teeth, then eased him round and forward, using her own body as a lever as she raised his upper body from the waist until he was slumped upright against her. Once she opened the first bottle, she started to trickle water between his lips. At first there was no response. Water ran in rivulets from the sides of his mouth. Some seeped down into his throat without resistance. After some time, when she tried to increase the flow, he jerked, coughed, spluttered for air.

She mixed up a sachet of energy drink and dribbled it patiently into his mouth, trying to inject life back into him, drop by drop. When he couldn't take any more liquid, she wrapped her arms around him and let his head drop against the soft pad of her shoulder. The darkness closed in around them. He was breathing more comfortably now, as if he'd drifted into sleep. She tightened her arms around his chest and held him to her, thinking of the way Hasina had embraced him as she protected him so fiercely from death.

As she sat still in the intense blackness, her eyes straining to find a shape, a speck of light, time seemed to be suspended. The events of the last few days pressed in on her and she felt again a guilty sense of dread about her own part in the suffering. The boy in her arms was fragile and hot with fever. She pulled him close. He must be just a few years younger than Jalil. He at least still had a hope of life. It seemed like a God-sent second chance. This time, she thought, I'll do everything I can to save him, whatever he's done.

She closed her eyes and thought about Jalil. He'd been such a serious young man. But when he did have fun, it was usually boyish and always made her smile.

Once, she'd been sitting in the back of the car as they made some endless, bumpy journey. She'd been deep in thought, listening to the wheeze of the broken air conditioning and watching the skeletal brown mountains run level with the road, when he and the driver had burst out laughing, chortling like naughty schoolboys.

'What?' She'd sat forward, tapping the back of the seat to get his attention.

The driver's eyes had slid into the rear-view mirror to meet hers, then darted away.

'Very funny joke.' Jalil, giggling, had twisted round to explain. His face was flushed. 'This is very funny Afghan joke.'

'Try me.'

Jalil looked delighted. He'd launched with gusto into the business of telling the joke a second time, in English.

'Two women were doing gossiping,' he said, 'and one woman said: oh, look at your costly gold bracelet! So nice! Your husband is very kind man. How I wish I had such a kind husband!'

He'd broken off, giggling in anticipation.

'So what did the other woman say?'

'The other woman said: No, no, you are very fortunate and you don't even know it. This gold bracelet is not from my husband. It is from yours!'

When he got to the end, he and the driver had set each other off again while she'd watched, bemused, from behind.

Now, thinking of it, she smiled, shaking her head in the silence. In many ways, he'd been little more than a boy. She should have taken better care of him. She opened her eyes and the blackness rushed in. How could she have known that the few thousand dollars he wanted would have bought his life? She imagined him in another future, studying in Pennsylvania, taking classes with American students who called him 'the Afghan' and asked him a hundred times: which one's your country again? All of it, only in her mind.

Aref moaned and twisted his head against her chest. She felt along the ground for water and put the bottle to his lips. He was murmuring something. She reached to his face and stroked the clammy hair from his forehead, soothed him until he slipped again into sleep. He was feverish and had so little strength. She didn't know how long he had left. She thought of Hasina. She must find her.

The return to the desert blinded her. She stood blinking, drinking in the fresh air. The open land stretched in front of her, silent and bleached in the sunlight. She hurried along the track from the gully towards the village, sweating and breathing hard in the heat. Her mind was working frantically, her eyes fixed on her dusty boots. She would have to salvage something from the information she had. There was no other way. Phil was right. However strong her hunch, she couldn't go with a story so full of holes and conjecture. The lawyers would pull it to pieces. But what did she have left? An anecdotal tale of an assault on an Afghan village. They could dress it up as something but it wasn't a lead. Phil would be furious. *When have I ever let you down?* she'd said. Well, the answer was now.

22

The driver of the pickup must have seen her as soon as he crested the rise. The grunt of his engine was suddenly magnified. He came down the slope towards her with gathering speed, surfing on a cloud of dust. She turned to look, shielding her eyes. It wasn't a military vehicle but a battered local one, its metalwork flashing with sunlight. She strained to see who was inside. The driver, a man, was alone.

She stepped back off the track and into the corn. Her sight of the road was veiled now and she focused instead on the sound of the engine, a cheap diesel cough. The truck approached. As it got closer, the power of the engine was cut and it slowed, then, almost level with her, finally stopped. Silence. The drone of the flies around her head. Her own blood, loud in her ears. The metallic click of a safety catch. The truck door unlatched and opened and the heaviness of a man dropping to the ground. Should she run? If he had a gun, he'd shoot her anyway. He was already so close. No, she thought. He may be as nervous as I am. I'll face him. Footsteps, stealthy, made their way towards her.

She stepped out onto the track and the man turned at once to face her. A solid, broad man with an old-fashioned automatic weapon readied in his hands. He was wearing a dusty white salwaar kameez whose wide cotton trousers flapped at his ankles, and, on his head, a traditional square hat. The waves of his white beard and streaked moustache glistened with sweat.

'Yes,' he said, 'I thought it was you.' He smiled, but not pleasantly. 'What a surprise.'

'Karam.' She looked at his hands on the weapon. He hadn't relaxed them. She put her own hand on her heart and greeted him politely. '*Salaam Alaikum.*'

He didn't make the usual polite reply. Instead he gestured her towards the truck and ushered her forward. He opened the passenger door for her and stood guard while she took off her rucksack and climbed into the cab. The plastic seat was torn and spilling its innards of perished rubber. He slid into the passenger seat beside her, forcing her to move across until she was jammed against the gear stick, her pack at her feet. His thigh pressed hot against her leg. He pulled the door closed, forcing them more tightly together.

She used the driving mirror to look over her shoulder into the open back. It was loaded with belongings. Chests fastened with rope. Tightly rolled carpets. Small pieces of furniture – stools, a carved table, a large decorated mirror in a wooden frame.

'You're leaving?'

'Of course.' He had rested his gun across his knees, pointing towards her, his hands close to the trigger. His sharp eyes never left her face. 'What did you expect? To stay here? I'm a rich man. As you know.'

How much did he know about her suspicions? She couldn't read him. His expression was cunning but gave nothing away. Had he concealed himself and watched her, as she unearthed his money? Or had someone else told him what she'd found?

'I am sorry about your brother's death.' She kept her gaze level. 'He seemed a kind man.'

'He was my brother,' he said. 'But he was not like me. He was a simple man.'

'How is Hasina?'

His eyes narrowed. 'What do you expect?'

'What will happen to her now?'

'Now she is part of my family.' He spoke as if he had acquired a new goat. 'I am responsible for her. This is our culture.'

'But you're leaving?'

'She is coming also. With me. With my wife.'

Ellen hesitated. She didn't believe him. She knew Hasina's passion for her son. She wouldn't leave him willingly, knowing he was ill and helpless. This must be some trick of Karam's.

'I have heard you are a powerful person.' He was looking at her oddly. 'In your country.'

She shrugged. 'Don't believe everything you hear.'

'I have heard your writing is respected by important people. By people with influence.'

She didn't reply, wondering where this was leading. The area was deserted. The chance of anyone coming past and seeing them was minimal.

'You should write the truth.' He lifted one hand from his gun and wagged a finger at her. 'Only the truth.'

'That's what I'm trying to do.'

'Sometimes the truth is a dangerous business.' He looked forwards down the dusty track, at the cornfields, the stoop of the hill. His broad bulk squashed into her. The cab smelt of his stale sweat.

'And what will you write,' he said, 'about your friend, the Major?'

She felt her pulse quicken. His tone was serious. 'What should I write?'

'He is a murderer.' He was watching her closely for reaction. 'Will you write that?'

She tried to keep her voice calm. 'You mean he was responsible for killing your children,' she said carefully. 'Your son.'

'Not just them.' He smiled. 'They will call that war. I mean killing your Afghan friend.' He lifted his hand and mimed pulling the trigger of a pistol against her head. The smile was still on his lips. 'Because he found out the truth.'

For a moment her heart stopped. She shook herself.

'Jalil?' she said. 'The Major didn't kill him.'

'Really?' Karam threw back his head and laughed. His throat bobbed, making his beard wag. His eyes were screwed up into lines, submerged in his fleshy face. She waited, watching him. This was the last thing she expected. His laughter seemed hard-edged but genuine and she was perplexed. Finally he wiped his eyes and turned to face her. His cheeks were red.

'Why do you think the Major paid me?' He was looking at her as if she were a fool, but the laughter had erased some of the tension from his face.

'He wanted your support. Your loyalty.'

'My support?' He looked at her almost fondly, as if any danger he had seen in her as an adversary had dissipated. He picked up the gun and stood it upright between his leg and the inside of the door. He put his fingers together in an arch, his hands supporting his chin. He stayed like that for a long moment, thinking. Then he turned to her abruptly.

'I am leaving,' he said. 'I will tell you the truth and you must write it. Tell your people what sort of man they have sent to my country. Tell them everything. The deal he made with me, such a big secret from everyone, even his own commanders. That he killed your friend for knowing too much. And that he killed my children.'

Ellen shook her head. She wanted to cover her ears, to shut out his voice. She ran her eyes across the peeling plastic of the dashboard, faded by the sun. It was pitted with marks, littered with the shrivelled remains of flies. She couldn't bring herself to speak. Instead she sat silently beside him and listened.

'He wanted a suicide bomb. A big shock for the people of Nayullah. A shock to make them welcome the Western soldiers. It would look like the work of the Taliban and frighten people. That's what he paid me for. To find foolish young men loyal to me and eager to become martyrs. To make bombers out of them.'

She raised her eyes to meet his. He was staring at her, his eyes glistening, watching her confusion.

'That's ridiculous.' Her thoughts were in turmoil. 'He'd never do that. He just wouldn't.'

'Wouldn't he?' He was smiling now. 'Who'd stop him? Who'd even know?'

She bit her lip. Mack was a decent man. Jalil thought so. His men did too. The fog of war was one thing. But paying suicide bombers to blow up civilians? Mack would never do that.

'No one knew.' Karam had leaned in close to her. His sour breath was warm on her cheek. He seemed to be relishing her distress. 'Your Major is an unusual man. Not a man who follows rules. You think Afghan lives matter to him? Not at all. Only British lives. His men in uniform. So – a few policemen and local women die but his men are a little safer. You think he worries about that?'

She eased herself further away from him. 'And Jalil?'

Karam spread his hands on his knees. 'He used him,' he said. 'Just as he used that other one, Najib. He needed someone to run back and forth to me, to take messages and hand over money. Much safer to use an Afghan than a Westerner who might make trouble.' He sighed. 'But Jalil was clever. When the bomb went off, he understood at once.' He turned, looking at her through narrowed eyes. 'Mack couldn't let him live.'

'Prove it. Any of it.'

'How can I?' Karam shrugged. His voice was quiet and serious. 'I swear to you, by Allah Himself, it is the truth.'

Ellen shifted her weight away from Karam and started to climb over the gear stick into the driver's seat, dragging her rucksack behind her. He didn't stop her. She had to throw her shoulder against the door to force it open. He was already climbing out of the passenger side, his gun in his hand. She felt too dazed to run.

When he spoke again, his voice was lighter. 'Hurry back to the village,' he said. 'Write your news.' He pointed out beyond the fields towards open scrubland. It was a more exposed route but less circuitous than the one Hasina had shown her. 'Allah will decide.' He laughed to himself. 'Will you write the truth and bring your own countryman to justice? We will leave that to Allah.'

He inclined his head politely and walked round the front of the vehicle to the driver's door. He revved the engine and drove, bumping, past her down the track, his eyes forward, his belongings swaying and knocking in the back.

She stood at the roadside, enveloped in the dry brown dust that the tyres were beating into rising clouds. It made her eyes sting as she stared after him. The vehicle began, slowly, to lose its form, merging into the blur of dirt all around it. The rough assault of the engine slowly faded as it pulled further away into the desert. She watched the dust-cloud shrink, until, finally, all that was left was an echo and a thick tail of quietly settling earth.

She sank to the ground and sat propped up against her rucksack, her legs crumpled under her. He had gone. She had survived. She ran her filthy hands over her face, tracing her nose, her cheekbones, her jaw. She was alive.

She closed her eyes and let her shoulders sag. She wanted to erase Karam. To dismiss everything he'd said. It was malice. His way of trying to destroy the Commander who'd allowed a bomb to fall on his family.

But as she turned over what he'd said, the allegations he'd made, she felt a profound unease. Mack was a maverick, that was true. He was a man who disregarded rules and would do anything to safeguard his men. What if, just possibly, Karam's story were true? She sat in the dust for a long time, her head in her hands, too exhausted to go on.

The sun was starting to lose its power when she finally pulled herself to her feet, shouldered her pack and started to walk back. Her limbs were heavy, her thoughts confused. There must be a way she could prove for herself that Karam was wrong. It was too late to ask Jalil. Najib had already disappeared. Karam claimed that Mack had struck a deal secretly and independently, without the army's knowledge. So who else was there to ask? She was worried too about Aref. If he didn't get help quickly, his chances of survival were poor.

She took Karam's advice and left the corn and other planted fields behind, striking out instead across the arid piece of wasteland, dull with low-lying scrub and coarse grass. It was a vacancy.

No sign of boots or animals or any attempt to cultivate. She was walking quickly, her head down, deep in thought, when she sensed movement ahead. She looked up.

A large dog was trotting towards her, picking its way along the natural contour of the desert. It made a small detour through the scrub as it advanced and paused to lower its snout and snap, its ears pricked. She heard the clash of its teeth and its low growl as it foraged. Then it lifted its wolfish head and resumed its trot. She stopped and stood silently, watching its progress. The light was thickening, making the dog's saliva glisten where it hung in ribbons from its half-open jaw.

The air was still. She couldn't tell if the dog had caught her smell yet or seen her. She looked around, wondering how to hide and seeing only scrub. She shrank, inch by inch, bending down into a crouch, the weight of her pack pulling her backwards, her fingers groping in the dust around her for a stone. Her eyes stayed always on the dog.

It was coming steadily closer. The dog was near enough now for her to make out its ribs through matted grey fur and hear the rattle of its breath. It was powerful and thickset, its body ridged with muscle. She sensed meanness in it, and danger.

It stopped abruptly. She held her breath. It raised its snout and sniffed the air. It shuddered, then swung its head and looked directly at her across the open ground. Its eyes were bulging. Her fingers closed round two small pebbles and she tested their weight. Running was useless. Her crouch, low on her heels, put her at eye-level with the dog. Its look was feral, as if hunger or sickness had maddened it.

She turned her shoulder to the dog and dipped her head. She tried to look away, to avoid challenging it, but her eyes, afraid, slid back. It was stock-still, drool cascading from its jaws, its eyes on hers. Neither of them moved. She could hear its low panting and the wheeze in its chest. It swallowed and flicked its thick tongue.

With her sideways glance, she could read the strain in the dog.

It was alert, its limbs tense, watching her and considering. Its tail twitched. Under the dirty fur, its ribcage swelled and shrank rhythmically. She tried to slow her own breathing, to appear calm and persuade it to forget her, to turn its snout and trot away.

The dog burst suddenly into motion, catching her by surprise. In a second, it went from tense stillness to catapulting across the earth towards her. Despite the heaviness of its limbs and its wretchedness, she was struck by its grace as it ran flying towards her. It was pounding the scrub, its feet raising dust. She lifted her hand and hurled the pebbles, one by one, and watched them bounce useless in the dirt around it. She froze. She had no means of defending herself.

There was nowhere to hide. The dog was now just yards away, its jaw spraying flecks of saliva. In a moment, it would be upon her. She pulled her pack in front of her and brought her hands to her face, pressing her palms into her eyes and nose, bracing herself for the impact, for the moment it crashed into her, for the dull weight forcing her backwards, for hot sour breath in her face and the tearing teeth.

An intense burst of light. The brightness turned the fingers at her face into pink flares. A wave of noise followed, striking her in the head, the ribs, knocking her to one side. The explosion sucked the air from her chest. She gasped, stunned, fighting for breath. Her hands flew to her ears and she pressed her palms against them, her eyes screwed shut. The echo of the blast burst in her head. Her ears were buzzing with pain and shock, making her dizzy.

As the pumping of blood in her head began to subside, she became aware of the silence pressing in all around her. She concentrated on breathing. Her body came slowly back to her. Her legs, bent under her, were juddering. She eased her hands from her ears. No sound rushed in. She steadied herself, opened her eyes and dared to look.

The dog's head was lying a few feet from her. It was on its side, fixing her with staring eyes. Its mouth was open, its long dark tongue limp across sharp yellowed teeth. Beneath it, the severed neck was a mess of spurting blood, darkening the scrub and sand in slowing pulses. The rest of its body, the legs, the stomach, had been torn into fragments and lay, scattered, across a distance of several feet. The air reeked of the explosion and of singed flesh and fur.

She felt sick. The dog's flesh was already stiffening. The pools of blood were congealing on the ground. As she watched, its head blackened and buzzed with gathering flies. Her eyes moved slowly across the dirt, taking in the small fragments of twisted metal all around. Her legs started to shake under her, making her whole body tremble. A mine. She put her arms round her pack and clasped it. God help me. I'm in a minefield.

Panic fluttered inside her. She wanted to get to her feet and run, to sprint across the earth and escape, whatever the danger. She closed her eyes and forced herself to breathe deeply. Stop it, she told herself. Whatever I do, I must keep still. As long as I don't move, I'm safe. She stayed, petrified, her hands locked round her rucksack. She tried to think.

Once she managed to regain control of her breathing, she opened her eyes. The blast had knocked her sideways onto one thigh. She eased her weight back onto her feet and hung in a crouch. The sand around her looked unbroken. It was covered with a thin crust and dotted with scrub. Maybe there was just that one mine and that was it? She shook her head. It was possible but unlikely. Mines were usually laid in clusters. She peered out at the fragments of charred metal. There was no way of telling their age. The mines might have been laid recently, in the last year or two, planted as defences by the Taliban. Or they could have been lying here, hidden, for many years, left over from any one of the recent conflicts. Mines, she knew, were patient weapons. They could lie in wait for decades to find their victim.

The muscles along her thighs and calves were already aching. She eased herself slowly to her feet, careful to keep her balance, and rubbed her legs. Perhaps someone had heard the explosion.

Someone might come. She cursed softly. Of course. This was why Hasina, who knew the ground, had carefully taken her a longer route. This was why Karam had sent her in this direction. What a fool she'd been to listen to him. *Allah will decide,* he'd said. Was this what he'd meant? She remembered his thin smile.

She sank back to her haunches. There were thin scratch marks in the dirt around her where she'd groped with her fingers for a stone to throw at the dog. She sifted through these loose surface grains with her fingertips, feeling lightly for metal. It took more pressure than that, she knew, to detonate a mine; nevertheless it was dangerous, slow progress. Working laboriously, inch by inch, straining to keep her senses keen, she finally cleared an area of about a square foot around her and lowered herself to a sitting position, her arms circling her knees. She pulled her scarf over her head to shield her face and neck from the sun, opened up her rucksack and dug out her sat phone. She barely had to twist her body to find a signal. She stared at the phone for a minute or two before she dialled, trying to delay the humiliation of making the call, struggling to come up with another way of saving herself. There was none.

Phil picked up on the second ring, giving his name in his usual gruff tone.

'It's Ellen,' she said. 'I need help.'

Mack came in person to rescue her. She saw the dust rising from the convoy of vehicles all the way across the desert. They disappeared into the corn for some minutes as the track twisted and fell, then emerged again, larger and closer.

The vehicles finally skidded to a halt and a soldier jumped down from the front seat of the lead Snatch. She recognized at once the broad shoulders and confident, commanding manner. Mack. She felt a flush of relief. Mack would get her out of this.

He set the men from the first Snatch patrolling up and down the edge of the wasteland, then moved forward himself to the last line of safe ground and started shouting instructions to her.

She focused all her energy on doing exactly what he said. Crouching on her knees and using her pen to push down into the earth in front of her at an angle, alert for the slightest change or hard resistance. If she found nothing, she marked the spot with a couple of pebbles or mound of dirt, then started on the next section of ground, alongside. When she'd finally cleared an area the width of her knees, she crawled forward onto it, breathed deeply and started all over again.

Her body was hard to control. It was shaking from shock and the mental strain of staying constantly alert. Her hands were slick with sweat. She struggled to keep a tight grip on the slippery plastic pen. Mack's commands were a constant commentary from the sidelines. Occasionally she stopped, wondering if she were making progress at all, if she'd ever make safety, if she should just take her chances, get up and run and, as Karam had said, let Allah decide. Then all she heard, cutting through her lethargy, was his wry encouragement. 'Come on. We haven't got all day.' Or: 'Get a move on. Dinner's nearly ready.' Somehow he kept her focused.

When she jumped over the final strip to join him, she was close to collapse. He put his hands out to receive her and she thrust herself forwards, bumping up against him. He caught and steadied her, his broad hands cupping her elbows. His body was muscular and solid and warm and, as she inhaled him, her eyes closed, her face inches from his chest, she smelt safety.

The soldiers, milling round them, stood watching. Dillon was amongst them.

'Blimey, sir,' he said. 'What it takes to get a date round here.'

23

Hasina was outside. She wanted to be left alone. She had the strengthening sun on her face, the smell of the earth, the grass. A fly landed on her chin, buzzed, walked, flew again. She didn't move.

Palwasha was tending her. She forced Hasina's head into her lap and put a cup of hot, sweet tea to her lips. She and Karam were talking about her over her head, as if she were deaf.

'Shock,' Palwasha was saying. Now she was forcing the cup back to her lips. The tea was scalding but a comfort as it slid down her throat. Palwasha was rocking her, her knees moving like an earthquake, swaying her head and shoulders. 'Not even an Imam at the burial,' she was saying now. 'Just the foreigners standing round and the Afghan traitors with their prayers.'

Abdul's burial, she thought. Had it really happened? And when? She had lost all sense of time. Her own Abdul. Her eyes closed, lulled on Palwasha's lap.

The noise of crying woke her. Gasping. She couldn't breathe. Her body was shaking, jerking in convulsions. Strong arms, Palwasha, struggled to hold her still, to contain her. Her eyes were emptying themselves into the cloth at her face. Her nose was running. Drowning. She let out a scream. The sound of it shocked her. Look at me, she thought, making such a noise. Palwasha was bending over her, murmuring. Bringing her down again, to stillness, to quietness again. Her eyes were streaming, her breath coming in gulps. Her legs were banging against the ground. The hard dirt. Her ankle bones knocking.

'Hush,' Palwasha was saying, her face down close in a whisper. 'Hush.'

Her eyes closed and she whimpered, letting go of every muscle, every fibre that had held her in the form of a person. Water. Spilling into Palwasha's lap. Soaking into the dust beneath. Darkness.

Afternoon. Shade. She opened an eye. Her head was resting on soft cloth. In front of her, a piece of wood, lit by the sun. A line of ants, crawling. A table, put on its side. A screen, shielding her from the heat. Who had done that? Her neck, when she tried to move her head, was stiff and sore. Her eyes encrusted.

'Water?' Palwasha's voice. Nearby. Palwasha's cool hands, capable and alive, reached for her shoulders and pulled her upright. Everything ached; every knot of her spine squealed. She sat, lifeless as a doll, and stared. The wood grain of the table danced to and fro. Palwasha brought a wet cloth to her face and wiped her forehead, her eyes, her nose, her dry mouth. No strength to resist. The cloth chafed her, a cold, rasping tongue on her skin. She sat, her shoulders drooping, as Palwasha bustled. Food. A bowl of cool soup, ladled into her mouth, spoon by spoon. She spluttered as she tried to swallow. When did Palwasha make soup? Hasina tried to focus her thoughts. Abdul, she thought. My Abdul, cold and rotting in the ground. How can it be? Her lips crumpled and her mouth gave way, spilling the soup in rivulets down her chin.

As she slept, she heard the dull engine of a vehicle. Coming here, to the house. It stopped and there was a slamming of car doors, footsteps, voices. Karam and then Palwasha. She fell back into sleep.

When she woke again, it was late afternoon. Her body ached. Behind, in the house, people were moving. Palwasha's voice, low and angry. The clatter of cups.

After some time, Karam came out to her. He nodded down at her, his shoulders black against the sun.

'Sister-in-law.' His voice was tense. She didn't move. He hesitated, then sat down beside her, his legs crossed. He is frightened, she thought. This man who thought himself so much stronger than my husband. He is afraid for his life.

'We must leave,' he said. His voice was low. He spoke to her slowly as if she were a child. 'The foreigners won't protect us. It's too dangerous here.'

Hasina thought again of Palwasha's words: it was too dangerous for Karam to see his own brother buried. Such a man. She pursed her lips.

'We will drive this evening for Nayullah,' he was saying. 'Then go north to Kabul. I have friends there. And I have money. I will try to get a message out, to the fighters. To say sorry to them for this mistake Abdul made.'

Hasina listened. Her body was inert. She was too exhausted to move. But inside she was angry. Karam was a fool, a coward. So he'd rather make peace with these fighters and save his skin than avenge his own brother's murder? Abdul, she thought. You were twice the man. Karam was rocking himself, his face agitated.

'Palwasha has already packed our things to go,' he said. 'Can you travel?' His voice was uncertain.

Hasina slowly shook her head. 'I cannot leave.'

'The soldiers will let us leave.' He nodded his head back to the gate where the foreign guard was sitting in the shade, half asleep on a chair. 'They won't make trouble.'

Hasina looked away. The sunlight was failing, bathing the edges of the upturned table in a golden haze. A good time of day, she thought. When the day's work is almost done. A time for thinking. A time for prayer.

'I cannot leave,' she said again. She was shocked by her own defiance. 'I won't come with you. I cannot.'

Karam shook his head, only partly listening. As his brother's widow, she was under his protection now. It was unthinkable that she would refuse to obey him.

'You must,' he said. 'We must save ourselves. We are all tainted now. It will be safer in Kabul. I have enough money for us all. Allah will protect us.'

She turned and looked at him coldly. 'I cannot leave,' she said again. 'I have lost my husband. I will not leave my son.'

He sighed, examined his fingers, then got to his feet. After a few paces, he stopped. He came back and crouched by her, his face thoughtful.

'Aref – you know where he is?' he said. 'You will see him?' He handed her a bundle, heavy with clothing, tied up with a cotton sleeve. 'Give him this from me.'

She shrugged. Karam couldn't be trusted.

'He must fulfil his mission,' he said.

His eyes were compelling. He seemed to have a new confidence, a new reason to hope. This is the way he persuaded my son, she thought, with his passion and fine arguments. My poor son, who lacked the brains to defend himself.

'He must,' he said. 'If the fighters find him, they will kill him for sure. Once for failing in his mission. And once for being the son of a traitor. You understand?'

Hasina held his gaze. 'He is not the son of a traitor.'

Karam nodded. 'Of course I know that,' he said. 'But they will see things differently. You don't know these men. They have no mercy.'

Behind them, Palwasha appeared in the doorway, shaking out a scarf and folding it. Karam looked back, watching her. He waited until she had gone inside again before he spoke, leaning closer to Hasina.

'He will die anyway,' he said. His voice had fallen to a whisper. 'Would you rather he died like a dog in the desert? In disgrace? Or with honour, as a precious martyr?'

His eyes were on hers. 'And you,' he said. 'If you are the mother of a martyr, they will honour you. Protect you. That too would give Aref comfort.'

She closed her eyes. How dare he talk to her like this of martyrs and missions? Hadn't he done enough? They should go, leave her. She would tend Aref. She would stop his foolish ideas. She would nurse him back to health and together they would escape this madness.

'There is a way. Listen, sister-in-law. Listen with care. I can help him.' His eyes were shining. 'You must help him too. Don't try to stop him. Do you really think you know better than I do? And than your own son? It is his will to do this. And it is Allah's will.'

He paused, remembering. 'Those foreigners killed my son,' he said. 'My only son. Does that mean nothing to you?'

She sat stiffly against the wall of the house as he poured his poison into her ear. The sun was low in the sky, falling quickly now, drawing streaks of blood through the clouds.

Once Karam and Palwasha left, the foreign soldier came inside the compound. The thud of his boots made the ground shake. He started when he saw her, then pointed his weapon. He spoke to her, foreign words she didn't understand, then spoke again into his radio. He squatted on his heels, studying her as she half sat, half lay against the house. She gazed into the distance.

More soldiers arrived. An Afghan man was with them, a stranger, tall with a fat belly. 'What are you doing here?'

She shrugged.

'You should leave. Go.' He made shooing motions with his hands, herding a goat. 'Get up. You can't stay here.'

'I can't leave,' she said simply. She made no effort to move. Let them carry her if they wanted. Let them shoot her. What difference did it make?

The men talked, back and forth. A soldier spoke again to his radio. Answers crackled back. She closed her eyes. It was all untrue. She would sleep and wake and this nightmare would be over.

A man's hand gripped her arm, shook her. 'Get up.' The fat Afghan man. 'You're a stubborn woman.' He had coarse features. Behind him, the soldiers were giving him orders. He pulled her to her feet and held her there at his side. His breath in her face stank of stale cigarette smoke. 'Do you think these men want to waste time on you?'

I have buried my husband. My Abdul. She opened her mouth to spit at him but her tongue was too dry.

He was pulling her forward. 'I've seen you, hopping around on those crutches. You're not ill. You've got used to comfort, that's all.'

One of the soldiers kicked at the bundle lying beside her. The bundle for Aref that Karam had packed for her. She snatched it from the soldier, cradled it to her chest.

The Afghan man was still grumbling. 'They're taking you back,' he said. 'Just for tonight. Then that's it. You're out on your own.' He was walking beside her, his hand on her upper arm. His fingers pinched into her flesh. 'You can look after yourself, like everyone else.'

They marched her back to the compound between them, like a prisoner.

She slumped against the compound wall, holding Karam's bundle on her lap. He and Palwasha would be in Nayullah now. She ran her hands over her face, feeling the skull inside her slackening skin. She was growing older. Her husband was gone. She knew the fate of widows. Without the protection of in-laws or powerful brothers, they were outcasts, pathetic creatures who had to beg to survive.

She wiped off her cheeks with her scarf. She wouldn't be a burden to Aref. She wouldn't accept the humiliation of being the object of pity amongst the women at the well, each thinking secretly to herself: Please, Allah, may that never happen to me.

She twisted onto her side, dabbed at the sweat on her forehead and neck, wrapped her arms round her middle. Aref must be saved from himself, from Karam and his own foolish ideas. She imagined him, lying hunched on the floor of his earth burrow, hungry and thirsty. How he must be suffering. She brought up her hand and stroked her own cheek, thinking of his. She'd longed so much for her boy, after all the lost babies, the grief. Her own dear Aref. She let her face loll against the ground and closed her eyes.

My son must live. Blessed Allah, You made me a mother. How could I not do everything in my power to keep my son alive? To restore honour to his name and give him a second chance?

Her body shook. May Allah forgive me, she whispered. A trail of saliva oozed from the side of her mouth to the ground. As she tried to flick it away with her tongue, she caught the taste of the sand, gritty and harsh. She swallowed it down. Blessed God, please give me the courage to do what I have to do.

24

Ellen had never been so glad to see the compound. She sat in the sand, her back against her rucksack, her eyes closed, while a young soldier, under orders from Mack, boiled water for tea and cooked up rations for her. Her nerves were raw. All she wanted to do was crawl into her sleeping bag, have a nip of vodka and sleep. She wrapped her hands round the mess mug of tea and sipped. Sleep, she knew, would be impossible for a long time yet.

Hasina was back in the compound too. A lonely figure, sitting on her haunches against the wall, close to the gate. It was an area they all avoided, spiky with dried split poppy and pungent with dung. She had folded in on herself like a penknife, her spine crooked, her head sunk in her hands.

Ellen thought of Hasina's collapse at the graveside and the way the strength had leached from her as Abdul's body was lowered into the earth. Without a husband, Ellen knew, life would be hard here. Being taken into Karam's family might be more curse than blessing. There was no question what a burden she would be. She thought of the unknown women in faded burqas who sat hunched by the side of the road and begged.

Hasina's headscarf was limp, her hair sticking out from under it in matted strands. On her lap, a tattered cloth bundle lay like a dead child, protruding beyond her thighs.

She had leaned forward, rocking herself gently as if to dull pain. It was a steady, rhythmical keening.

Ellen pulled herself to her feet and went across to sit beside her. She put her hand on Hasina's bony shoulder. When she slipped her arm further round across her back, Hasina moved sideways into the fleshy pad of her shoulder. Ellen pulled the headscarf forward again where it had slipped back.

They sat quietly for some moments. Hasina's rising breath was stale and fetid and her skin had a greyish hue.

'Aref,' Ellen whispered to her. 'Your son. He's very ill.'

Hasina raised her head at the sound of her son's name. She couldn't have understood the words but she did respond to Ellen's tone. The green eyes fixed on her, then she reached out to grasp Ellen's hand, plaiting her calloused fingers into Ellen's long ones and folding them together.

Just before dusk, Mack came striding across to find her. His eyes were lively.

'Tea?'

She followed him across the compound to the building, past the growing military village of bedding rolls and mosquito nets. His shoulders were squared, his uniform taut across his back. Twin lines of sweat lay like wings along his shoulder blades. She thought of the relief she'd felt when she'd seen him getting out of the vehicle to save her. She'd been right. He was the man you wanted around in a crisis.

The comms room smelt of stale cigarette smoke and feet. Mack's young assistant was sitting at a low, makeshift desk, pen in hand. He got up as Mack led her in, shuffled his papers into a pile and left. Mack fussed over polystyrene cups and hot water, dunking tea bags. He pulled out a chair and motioned her into another.

'So,' he said, 'you came back.'

'Unfinished business.'

He raised an eyebrow. 'Really?'

She looked at his broad, open face. His lips creased into a smile. She looked past him to the sprawl of papers on the main table, weighted with stones. She lifted her cup to her lip.

'I've heard some serious allegations,' she said. 'About you.'

He laughed. 'That doesn't surprise me.' He was sitting back in his chair, one leg crossed over his knee. His position was relaxed but she sensed his alertness.

'I knew Jalil,' she said. 'He was straight. Always. And loyal. I don't believe for a minute he was mixed up in something crooked.'

Mack nodded, watching her. 'I liked him too. Fact is, we may never know.'

Outside a young soldier's voice rose, calling to a colleague, then a piece of machinery crashed.

'So tell me. What are these allegations?' His tone was cordial but she could hear too an edge of impatience, an early warning that his willingness to be friendly had a limit.

She kept her eyes on his. 'That you killed him. Because he found out too much.'

His eyes became dead, blank spaces for an instant. Then he gave a short laugh and half turned away. 'Honestly,' he said. 'If that's—'

'That the suicide bomb was your idea. A strategic move. Use the deaths of a few Afghans as a weapon and turn people against the Taliban.'

'Nonsense.' He spoke too sharply. He uncrossed his leg in a single angry movement and twisted in his seat, turning his shoulder on her. The atmosphere had shifted and changed. 'That's absurd.'

She looked down into the swirling foam of dissolving milk powder which was rising and falling on the surface of her tea. She steadied her breathing. She thought of this man she had come to admire, a man with such ability. She was seized by sadness. She opened her mouth to speak, then quietly closed it again. She thought of his passion to protect his men, a passion which, it seemed, had brought his own destruction. The silence stretched, separating them.

Finally he got to his feet. He was holding his body stiffly. 'That's not even worth a response,' he said. 'As for you, you should be careful what you say.'

He turned, his face hard with anger, and walked quickly out.

She was left, staring after him, her tea cooling in her hands. So, she thought, Karam was right. She was so heavy with disappointment, she couldn't find the strength to move. She sat silently in the deepening shadows, staring across the debris of military maps and memos into the rich golden light slanting obliquely through the square mud window to the floor.

25

That night she lay on her back in the cocoon of her sleeping bag and tried to think, as the soldiers around her grunted and snored. The drama of the minefield had bought her another day with London. Even Phil wasn't heartless enough to turn the screw so soon after a near-death experience. But tomorrow really would be the end. She had to file something. The question was: what?

She realized she'd clung to the hope that Mack would convince her; that he'd prove in some way that Karam was lying. In fact his abrupt denial had only confirmed to her what, at some level, she'd already known. But what could she file? She had no evidence. Mack knew that. Phil would never print such serious allegations against an army officer, based on the word of one Afghan. She knew now what Mack had done. But she couldn't touch him.

Finally, giving in to sleeplessness, she crawled out of her sleeping bag, pulled on her fleece and boots, tucked her shampoo bottle in her pocket and walked.

The compound was silvery in the moonlight. The guard on the main gate was slumped forward over his weapon, dozing. She walked round the edge of the walls, past the shit pit, past the well, towards the back of the compound. A small group of officers was sitting together in front of the building, lit only by the glowing cigarettes in their hands. Five or perhaps six solid black outlines against the mud wall. Their voices were a low murmur, breaking occasionally into laughter which they quickly suppressed.

She looked up as she walked. There was an ocean of stars above.

The night sky was spectacular, clearer here than she'd seen anywhere in the world. She remembered something Jalil once said. 'In Afghanistan, when it is hot and we cannot sleep, we go onto the roof. The stars comfort us.' They had stopped at a roadside tea-stall during a long road trip one night and stared at the beauty above. 'They are Allah's way of saying sorry,' Jalil had said. 'Saying sorry for the sorrows of Afghanistan.'

She stood back and looked up at the roof of the compound building. The front section was dotted with military antennae but the rest was deserted. It would be cool up there and quiet. There were footholds cut into the mud bricks by the open stove and she scaled them. The wall was rough against her hands as she pulled herself up, pricking her palms with fragments of embedded straw. A soldier, standing guard along the compound wall, tipped his head to watch her as she climbed, then lost interest and looked away.

She picked her way along the narrow gully between the undulating mud domes of the roof. When she reached the middle, she arched her back and leaned into the pillow of the slope and the thick, forgiving mud.

The stars above were stabs of light in the blackness. As she stared into them, she felt herself tipped upside down, weightless. The stars became white holes, falling endlessly into the darkness. She pulled out her shampoo bottle and sipped the vodka, feeling warmth and numbness enter her blood.

At least I know, she thought. I know what happened. I can tell Jalil's family a little more. That he was killed for trying to do the right thing. For refusing to go along with something he knew was wrong. It isn't justice, she thought, but it may comfort them.

But what could she write? Hardly a thing. She couldn't even explain the link between Karam's money and the military. Mack would deny it all. She sipped again at the vodka and watched the stars start to blur. Whatever watered-down version of the truth she managed to concoct, she was in trouble. Phil would be furious. The silence and solitude of the Afghan night seemed safe compared with the explosion she could expect back in his office. She let her head loll back against the roof and spin with the stars.

Mack, she thought. You fool. Just when I thought I'd found a man worthy of respect. She sighed and closed her eyes, twisting her mother's ring round and round on her finger. The feeling of weightlessness took her again, dropping her through the night sky.

She must have dozed. The breeze was cool and gritty on her cheek when she came to. Her neck and spine, stretched back against the curving roof, were stiff and her mouth dry. She pushed herself upright and kneaded her shoulders. Something had woken her. It was darker now, the moon obscured by drifting cloud.

She crept closer to the front of the roof to get a clearer view of the compound below. Three men, officers, were still sitting together in the darkness. A single cigarette glowed. At the gate, the guard was slumped to one side, asleep. But something else down there was moving. More shadow than person. A stooped Afghan figure, draped in cotton, making its way stealthily across the sand towards the building below.

The figure was short, moving with its shoulders forward, holding something across its chest. The camp was silent in sleep. She craned forward to see more clearly. She felt a sudden chill. Her instincts about this moving shadow made the hair on her neck prick and rise.

She looked back along the narrow gully. She could pick her way to the far end of the roof and climb down. But that would take time and the figure was moving quickly. Instead, she twisted her body round and lowered herself onto her stomach, wedged into the sharp angle between the two rising domes. She shuffled further forward on her knees and elbows, the rough surface grating her skin. Within a few minutes, she'd positioned herself at the very end, pinned between the slopes and hidden by their contours from the people below. If she raised her head, she could watch without being seen.

The figure was almost across the compound now, keeping to the deepest shadows and gliding weightlessly. It was approaching the area where the last few officers were still sitting. Ellen saw it raise a pale hand and pull the scarf more closely round the face. Hasina. Of course. It struck her at last. She hadn't recognized her. She was walking with such silent intent and barely limping. Skimming across the earth like a spirit. The bundle of clothes was cradled in her arms. As Ellen strained to watch, Hasina paused, looked around as if taking her bearings, then moved forward again.

In front of the building, one of the seated officers paused and turned his head. He was alert, listening. Ellen craned forward, straining to see in the low light. She heard the blood in her ears, the low hum of a night breeze across the surface of the roof. The man waited.

The cloud, making its slow path across the sky, dissolved a little and the moon lit him more strongly. Mack. The pale skin of his throat and face gleamed. The muscles in his face were taut, as if all the energy in his body had flowed to them and were concentrated there.

He pushed back his chair and got to his feet in a single fluid movement. Now he stood, listening and peering into the darkness. Hasina had disappeared. Ellen craned her neck to look down into the shadows. She must be there, right below her, pressed back against the wall of the building. Had Mack seen her? She couldn't tell.

He took a step towards the wall. Ellen saw something shift in the blackness. Hasina, still some yards from him, had moved forwards. Mack was gesturing to her now, his hands outstretched, palms turned upwards in a gesture of appeasement. Hasina stopped. The bundle filled her arms. She stood, facing him. Her frame was rigid with tension.

He took another step towards her, his hands reaching out, and light ripped through the blackness. The world turned white. The shock of the gunshot, magnified in the silence, bouncing off the curves of the roof and crashing into her ears, made Ellen reel. She clutched at the edge of the roof, blinded by images fringed with light. The rounded top of the wall. Her own hand gripping the curving mud. She blinked, refocused.

Below, Mack had crumpled. The force of the bullet had swung him sideways, knocked him down onto his knees. His hand was on his chest, his palm pressed against it, his fingers splayed. Between his long fingers, blood was flowering, a dark stain across the front of his light shirt. His legs were buckling, his heels twitching. His eyes were still staring at the figure in front of him. For a moment there was a silence so intense it stopped Ellen's breath. She stared down, transfixed.

A second blast of fire. A third. From other officers. One was on his feet now, his weapon pointing at Hasina like an accusing finger. The other was crouched, down low beside the table. The acrid stink of residue and of burning fabric rose. For a moment, silence settled again. Just her own breathing, hard and short in her head. Her own hand pressed so hard against the edge of the roof that the skin was white and bloodless.

Commotion was breaking out through the camp. A scramble. The dull pounding of boots on mud. A male yell, close, and another, mixed with a distant shout from outside the compound. Torches snapped on, writing a scribble of weak light across the darkness. Ellen pressed her body deeper into the arms of the roof.

Below, Mack had slid sideways onto the sand. His pupils were staring out sightlessly. His legs were turned, one folded under him, the other stuck out in front, its boot spattered with blood.

The two officers who'd fired shots now ran to him. One lit his body with a torch as the other crouched, putting his hands to Mack's neck to feel for a pulse, then tearing open the front of his tunic to expose the raw bloody hole of the chest wound. Blood, pooling in his navel and in the folds of his stomach, glistened there. The wound itself was a noisy sucking mouth in the membrane of his chest wall, shining in the torchlight. The soldier pressed the heel of his hand into it and Mack jerked. His spine arched, forcing his head back, his eyes rolling. His heel slapped against the ground.

Behind them both, a young soldier stared, paralysed. His face was grey and sweating, his eyes full of fear. Mack's body choked and expelled a rush of air. It gave a final shudder and settled into stillness.

Ellen eased herself forward and stared into the shadow. Her eyes struggled to focus, to get purchase in the half-light. Far beneath her, Hasina was lying on the sand. Her headscarf had fallen back and settled in folds at her neck, revealing dark hair in matted tresses down her neck and shoulders. The bundle of ragged clothes lay across her stomach. The dull barrel of a gun was protruding from it, the metal circle gleaming. The air around her was rancid with smoke.

Hasina's body was still. The only movement came from a slowing pulse of blood as her veins quietly emptied themselves through the wounds in her chest and stomach. The flow was already faltering. The dark ribbon of blood, its surface starting to congeal, was bubbling and sinking back into the earth.

Her head had fallen to one side, a cheek pressed into the dirt. Her mouth, half open, was twisted. Her unseeing eyes were wide, glassy with reflected moonlight, as if she were already melting into the vastness of the Afghan night.

26

She had never known the camp so silent. Ellen sat with her back to the compound wall, and watched the sky slowly lighten, turning first grey, then a sickly white as the sun strengthened. It revealed the men sitting in small groups, leaning against their packs and smoking. There was none of the usual banter and stir. The camp was in shock. No one spoke.

Dillon and Frank, faces dull, were amongst those called forward to deal with the bodies. They moved with dead, robotic efficiency. Dillon arranged Mack's stiff legs while Frank and another soldier washed blood from his torso. Dillon stopped twice to wipe his face across his sleeve.

They wrapped Mack round in a groundsheet and carried him into the building, away from the gathering heat and flies. No one lifted their eyes to Ellen. The men were sealed against her in grief. She thought of Dillon's light-hearted friendliness when she'd first met them. I was a welcome curiosity then, she thought. Now I'm a jinx, perhaps even a danger.

She sat quietly and thought of Mack. Of his smell, that mixture of fresh sweat and army soap, and the pressure of his fingers when he'd enclosed her hand in his and pulled her to her feet. She remembered the humour he'd thrown out to her like a lifebelt when she was in the minefield, and the broad warmth of his chest when she'd finally flung herself towards him and he'd caught her, his expression amused. She thought of her sense of connection with him after the attack on the patrol, when they'd sat silently together, side by side, sunk in mutual despair. She tried to summon Chopin into her mind, to draw on its comfort. But this time there was only silence.

She looked at her pack, thinking of her notebook in the pocket. She should be writing. There'd be a news blackout on all this for a day or two. But she needed to have her pieces ready to print as soon as it was lifted. She closed her eyes, dizzy with tiredness. She had a story now. Phil would be happy. But how much of the truth could she really write?

Frank was using the edge of a spade to break up the earth where Mack's body had lain. He was stripped to the waist. His white skin glistened over muscle as he dug through the clumps of blood that clotted the surface, broke them into pieces and turned over the crust, burying them from sight.

They treated Hasina's body with far less reverence. They wrapped it in a tarpaulin and raised it at the four corners. It formed a lumpen roll that bounced and sagged as they carried it on the platform of their shoulders. They gathered at the gate and listened as an officer gave orders. Their rough procession from the compound began and ended with armed men, guns and eyes scanning for movement as they stepped out through the gate and started off down the dirt street.

Ellen walked with them out of the compound and through the dust. The air was still cool and thin and she drew it deep into her lungs. Two young soldiers from Eastern Europe were standing guard outside a neighbouring compound. They lifted their eyes to the procession, took in the sight of the rolled body, then looked quickly down and busied themselves with raising ridges of sand with the toes of their boots.

The graveyard had no shade. The guards took up position on high ground and cocked their guns. The soldiers bearing the corpse set it unceremoniously on the earth and started to hack out a shallow grave, grunting and grumbling. Ellen sat in the dust beside Hasina's body, keeping it company. She looked out over the crooked rows of headstones. She felt exhausted and the sadness of the burial sat heavily on her spirits. It was devoid of dignity, little better than the burying of an animal.

She understood the soldiers' animosity towards Hasina. She was an Afghan woman. They had sheltered and protected her and she had repaid them by murdering their Commander.

But she remembered too the light she'd seen in Hasina's green eyes. The fierceness when they'd dug her out of the bombed house all that time ago. The tenderness as she'd grasped her son to her body in the jumping shadows of the torchlight and rocked him. The desolation when she'd spread herself on the floor of the Snatch alongside her husband's battered body, pressed against it as if her own warmth could stop him from growing cold.

The soldiers dug in pairs. Those waiting their turn, watching and catching their breath, talked in low voices. There was a helo coming in, they said. The Brigadier himself might come. And the Padre. They wiped off their faces and scanned the bleached sky thoughtfully. If they lifted the Major's body back to base soon, it could be in England by tomorrow. No wife, someone said. No kids. The men's faces were closed, as if they were thinking of their own families back home, of the wives and girlfriends and sisters and mothers who would grieve for them, if the time came.

They heaved the body into the trough at last and covered it, pressing the thin, dry earth down on the flesh with the backs of their spades. One of the soldiers stepped onto the grave and walked back and forth across the surface, stamping down the earth with his heavy boots until it was compact. *Alhamdulillah*, Ellen said under her breath. Thanks be to God. It was all she had to offer.

When the men passed round a cigarette and prepared to leave, she told them she needed to stay for a while to take pictures. They exchanged uncertain glances. One tried to radio back to an officer for permission. No response. Finally they shrugged. Their faces seemed to say that they had more important priorities than battling with her about her own safety. They shouldered the spades and walked away.

She listened to the receding thud of their boots and felt the stillness of the land settle around her. She looked out across the graveyard to the slope leading to the river through the valley below. Her head was aching with sleeplessness and the weight of everything she'd seen. What could she write that was fair and true? She shook her head, wiped down her face with her hands, feeling the sharpness of her cheekbones, the slipperiness of her hot skin.

She crept quickly through the fields, tracing her route back towards the gully. Her movements were automatic and she had to fight to ignore the signals from her body. The chafing of her hot, dirty feet in her boots. The ache in her calves. The dull emptiness in her stomach. She focused everything on the thought: I must get water to him. It's too late for Hasina now. But for Aref? There might still be a chance.

Her feet were catching on corn stalks and clods of earth, tripping her up. Her senses were dulled by tiredness. Something was troubling her. An uneasiness she couldn't place. Her ears were full of her own thick breathing as she hurried, keeping her head low, slapping away the clouds of flies around her face and neck.

A noise. She ducked down into the corn and listened. Blood pulsed in her head. She had heard something, she was sure. Heard it or sensed it. Some movement, deep in the corn behind her.

She peered through the stalks. The corn was spoiling, desiccated and wilting, collapsing into a lattice of leaves that made it hard for her to see more than a few feet. It could be an animal out there. She thought of the lean dog that had tried to attack her in the minefield.

She listened to the stillness for a while longer. Nothing. She tried to shake off her fear, got to her feet again and hurried on. By the time she headed through the final field and down to the gully, the sun was climbing quickly, spangling her vision. Her hair was trailing wild and slick against her face. She was thinking of

Aref, entombed in the earth. She tried to imagine the horror of endless blackness. She would nurse him, press him to take water. But, as soon as she could, she must get him out and—

Some distance behind her in the corn, a stick broke with a resonant crack. She dropped to a crouch, heart pounding. Her instinct had been right. She was being followed. She strained to listen, afraid to make the slightest movement. Silence. Flies pressed in around her chin and neck. Whoever was behind her, they must be close enough to see and hear her as she thrust herself forward through the corn. Close enough to fall silent the moment she stopped.

She waited and tried to think. Her pursuer had all the advantages. They were probably also armed. She saw again an image of Mack in the moonlight, his hand pressed against his chest, trying to hold back the pumping stream of blood as life flowed from him into the dirt. All she had to defend herself were her wits.

She made a sudden run across the patch of open ground to the gully and threw herself just beyond the ridge. Loose stones tumbled round her as she skidded, spreading her limbs wide and swimming in falling earth and debris as she tried to slow herself down. When the earth finally settled, she lay with her face pressed into the dust, tasting its dryness in her throat. The world fell quiet again. She lifted her head and looked round for footholds. She crawled upwards, spreading her weight, until she was lying almost upright under the top of the loose slope, her eyes level with the gully's lip.

She looked along the open scrubland and into the corn. At first, she saw nothing. The landscape was colourless in the strong sun. All she could hear was her own breathing, the push of her ribs against the earth. She forced her eyes to stay open, to focus on the empty air, bent into shimmering waves by the rising heat.

Just when she was preparing to move again, her eyes caught a sudden stir of movement. She held her breath and strained to see. Yes. She could see him. The distant shape of a man, low in the corn, creeping forward towards her along the same path she had just taken. His head bent low to the ground as he tracked her.

His cotton trousers and long tunic flapped loosely round his body. An Afghan scarf was wrapped round his face, protecting his mouth and nose from the dust and hiding his features.

At the edge of the corn, he crouched and waited. She could feel every nerve taut as she pressed her limbs into the steep side of the gully, trying to hold in place stones that might dislodge and tumble. The man bowed his head as if he were listening or praying. She waited. She couldn't see a gun across his body but she couldn't see his hands. He could have a handgun in the baggy folds of his clothes.

When he moved from the cover of the cornfield to the gully, he came quickly, stooped as he ran. She had little time to think. She braced herself against the stones, tense, waiting to spring, her face turned upwards to the lip of the gully. His face appeared, hanging there moon-like against the sky, peering over the rim and looking straight down at her, his brown eyes large with surprise above his cloth mask. She sprang, her hands grabbing for the tunic at his neck. His arms jerked forward to fend her off but already her fingers had tightened round the thick cotton fabric of his collar and fastened themselves there, pulling him down over the edge and forward over her, trying to throw him clear in an arc across her body and down the steep slope below.

He seemed to teeter for a moment, then lost control and toppled, his hands grasping at the empty air, reaching through it towards her. His nails dug into her wrist as he locked onto her arm and already he was falling heavily, head first, sending rocks and stones cascading down the slope around him. Her arm was jolted in its socket as he tightened his grip on her wrist, pulling her down after him as she was thrown off balance by his weight.

Her breath was snatched from her mouth, her hands flailing. Sky filled her vision, then rock and shadow, a stone crashing past her face as they both turned, clutching at each other, half bouncing, half rolling off the sides as they plunged helplessly towards the bottom. When they were almost there, he crashed sideways into the stump of a dead tree, scattering a shower of brittle leaves into the air. Twigs scratched at her face and clawed her hair. His head struck the ground and his eyes closed. He was still. She pulled his fingers off her wrist and scrambled clear of him, untangling her limbs from his.

She was shaking. Her breath came in gasps. She ran her hands in shock over her head, her face, her ribs. Her fingers came away clean and dry. No sharp pains or jutting bones. She sat for a few seconds, flooded with relief at her own survival, thinking of nothing but the need to breathe slowly in and out and steady herself.

He still hadn't moved. She reached out a hand and tugged down the scarf covering his face. The eyes opened. Familiar brown eyes. They struggled to focus on her, blinking in confusion.

'Najib.'

His look of confusion turned to shame. He was lying twisted round the tree stump. He made to sit up, then grimaced and lay still.

'Why are you following me?' She reached forward and ran her hands lightly down his body, ignoring his embarrassment as she searched him for weapons. Nothing. She leaned back against the slope, aware of a dull ache growing across her back and shoulders. 'Who sent you?' Her legs were seized with a sudden juddering, and she unfolded them. 'Tell me.'

'Is it true?' he said. His voice was thin with shock. 'About Major Mack?'

Above them the sky was throbbing. The metal pulse of helicopter blades grew suddenly deafening. They tipped back their heads and stared up into the whiteness as the helicopter, flashing with sunlight, circled the desert, then dropped into it, close to the village, and disappeared from sight. A dust cloud rose.

Najib rolled carefully off the tree stump and lifted himself into a sitting position. He ran the flat of his right hand over his body, checking it until he was satisfied there was no serious damage. He got shakily to his feet.

'We will sit in the shadow,' he said. 'I will tell you everything.'

The word is shade, she thought, but didn't correct him.

They sat together against a boulder close to the entrance to the bunker and passed a bottle of water between them. Ellen could feel the heaviness in her limbs of rising bruises. Her cheek throbbed where the branches had cut her.

'I heard talk in Nayullah early this morning,' Najib was saying. 'In the bazaar. People were whispering. An attack on the Britishers, they said. A Commander was killed.'

He looked at her for confirmation, his eyes full of concern. She was stunned by the way news spread, reaching the gossips in Nayullah in a matter of hours. Nothing happened here, it seemed, without Afghans knowing at once.

'Killed by a woman, they said.'

She held his gaze. 'Hasina.'

He looked away. 'It was her then. Her burial.'

Had he been watching her since then? Where had he hidden? She looked at the thinness in his face. A new weariness she hadn't seen there before.

'He danced,' he said. 'On her grave. That is a very wrong thing.'

'Who did?'

'That soldier.'

She thought of the young man tramping across the earth, stamping it firm.

'No,' she said. 'It wasn't that.'

He drank back the water, holding the bottle clear of his lips, then wiped off his mouth on a sleeve.

'Why did you come back?'

He handed her the water without looking her in the face. 'It isn't true, what you thought,' he said. He spoke quickly, intent and embarrassed. 'Major Mack made me give the money to Karam. He forced me. If Karam took the money, he said, it showed they were still allies. That he wouldn't take revenge for . . .' He hesitated. '. . . For what happened to his children.'

Ellen reached out to pat his arm. 'I know,' she said. 'I was wrong. I didn't—'

'Then he ended my job.' Najib's eyes were desperate. 'I need my job. For money.'

The heat and silence sat heavily between them. The sides of the gully rose steeply, pointing to the sky.

'I was trying to get back to Kabul,' he went on. 'From Nayullah. In a cheap way. A truck driver, maybe. But no one had place. Then I heard about the Major. I thought if it is true about his dying, then maybe, *inshallah*, I can get back my job?'

Ellen nodded slowly. 'Maybe.'

He got to his feet and stretched his limbs. The colour was coming back into his face. He looked theatrically round the gully, then stooped over her and whispered. 'I followed you,' he said, 'because you are alone and that's dangerous. He is coming.'

She stared. 'Who is?'

'Him.' His eyes were large and fearful. 'Karam-jan.'

She crawled into the narrow squeeze of passage, leading Najib into the earth. He was so close behind her that his breath fell hot on her legs. The fetid stink of the bunker reached into the tunnel to meet her.

Aref was on his back on the floor in the darkness, his eyes closed. The light from her torch was weak, the batteries fading. She cursed and shook it. When she put her hand on his forehead, the skin was hot and moist. His eyes fluttered in the light, opened but didn't focus, then fell closed again. His breath, coming in slight wheezes, was rancid.

She sat with his head and shoulders propped up against her side and forced him to take water, a little at a time. His clothes were filthy, soiled with his own dirt, his face streaked with grime. As she tended him, Najib settled against the far wall with his legs drawn up under him and watched with narrowed eyes.

'He's Hasina's son,' she said. 'She brought me here.'

Aref spluttered and started to choke.

'They are not good people.' Najib's disapproval was clear. 'Why are you helping him?'

Ellen took the bottle from Aref's lips. She lifted his shoulders and waited for his coughing to subside. 'Because if I don't,' she said simply, 'he will die.'

Najib didn't speak. He was hunched, uncertain.

'I don't think the soldiers will come out here to get him,' she said. 'Given all that's happened. Not a good time to ask.'

Aref had settled again and she put the bottle back against his lips.

'But if I get him there. If I physically take him to the compound. I think then, they'd treat him. They'd have to.' She looked at his pallor. His wrists and arms were pitifully thin, the bones as narrow and brittle as a bird's. 'It's his only hope.'

Najib lifted his scarf to his face again and covered his nose and mouth. She didn't need to ask why. The stench was overpowering.

'Now tell me,' she said. 'What's this about Karam?'

Najib studied his fingers for a moment, then, staring at the earth floor, began to speak.

'I was in the bazaar,' he said, 'looking for a driver who was heading north. Some boy came to me. Some ragged boy, doing work. He told me to go with him. A man had sent him to fetch me.

'I thought it was a driver. A man who'd heard I needed to go to Kabul and could help. So I went with the boy, through the narrow lanes into a small shop. A jewellery shop. And he was sitting there. Karam-jan. Big new rings on his fingers. Drinking *chai.*'

Ellen pictured Karam, his broad thighs squashed into a cheap chair, his expansive belly flowing over his groin, an excited shopkeeper fussing round him with snacks and *chai* and trays of jewels while a ceiling fan ground the air above them.

'How did he know you were in Nayullah?'

'How do people know?' He sighed. 'Some people talk and other people listen.'

'And what did he want?'

Najib grimaced. 'He had heard these rumours about killing in the Britishers' camp. He asked me: is it true that Major Mack is killed? I said: I don't know. He said: was he killed by a lady, an Afghan lady? I said: that is what men in the bazaar are saying.'

He lifted his head quickly to look at Ellen, then, when their eyes met, pulled his away, back to the floor. 'He asked me about you.'

She smelt his fear and felt her own insides contract with it. She bent over Aref and busied herself with wiping his cheeks, his mouth. Why is he asking about me? *I have heard you are a powerful person*, he'd told her. *I have heard your writing is respected by important people.* Was he frightened that word would get out in Afghanistan that he'd collaborated with the foreign infidels?

'He'd heard you had come back here,' Najib went on. 'He wanted to know why.'

'And you think he's coming to find me?'

Najib swallowed. 'I think so.'

He crawled forward towards her and lifted Aref sideways, out of her lap and into his own arms. 'If you do this,' he said, 'then it is my duty to help you.' He shrugged. 'Besides, it is right for an Afghan to tend his brother.'

Ellen handed him the bottle of water and watched as he forced open Aref's mouth. His hands were firm and gentle. He had warned her about the villagers from the start, she thought. Maybe his instincts had been right.

They stayed for several hours in the bunker, taking it in turns to care for Aref, trying to build back a little of his strength before they moved him. He slept shallowly, his body limp against them. The torch beam had faded to dim now and they sat mostly in darkness. The blackness pressed itself hard against Ellen's face and into her head. She let her eyes fall closed and tried to imagine she was outside, free and in daylight.

In the darkness, her thoughts found images of Mack. His broad shoulders outlined against the sun as he bent over her. His wry smile. His masculine scent and the heat rising from his bulky thigh against hers when they sat together. His physical presence. Already cold and starting to decay.

She shifted her back against the bunker wall, trying to find comfort. How did she write about him now? Did she paint him as a hero, as the army would? Or did she disgrace him? Denounce him as ruthless? She shook her head. Both were true. Both were also half-truths.

'He killed him, didn't he?'

Najib's voice was soft in the darkness. His words seemed to come from inside her head. She kept her eyes closed and didn't answer.

'Major Mack. He killed Jalil. Didn't he?'

She paused, and when she spoke her voice was weary. 'Yes.'

Najib let out a long, slow sigh. 'I thought he would kill me too.'

She didn't speak. She was beginning to realize how few of the facts she could expose. No one in the army knew what he'd done. No one would believe it. Discredit a dead hero? The army's top brass would destroy her. Worse than that, she'd never get the allegations past the magazine's lawyers. Already, knowing this, she was shamed by her own sense of failure and of collusion.

'What will you do?' Najib said. 'How will you tell people the truth?'

She opened her eyes and darkness flooded her senses.

'I can't,' she said. She thought of Mack's face, tight with anger, when she accused him. 'I can't prove a thing.'

Silence. She felt Najib's distress as another ache in her body. Soon, she thought, they would have to go. Somehow they must lift Aref between them. They must get him out of this place into the light and carry him back to the compound. She sat, exhausted, against the dry earth and tried to gather her strength.

They needed to leave. She knew that. Just by moving Aref, they would exhaust him, perhaps even kill him. But they had no choice. His need for medical attention was critical. Every hour mattered.

She put her hands to her face and pressed her eyes into her palms. Her hands smelt of dirt and decay. She was afraid. She was frightened of leaving the dark safety of the earth and venturing out again into the open desert where Karam was prowling.

27

They trussed Aref like an animal. He lay, insensible, his eyes closed, as they wound his clothes tightly round him and tied them firmly with a cotton strip. They worked in darkness, feeling their way round his body, conserving the dying torch. In the small space, the rising stench was overwhelming. From time to time, Najib's hands disappeared and low choking noises broke from him as he retched. Silence. Then his hands again joined hers.

Ellen pictured the form of a skeleton as she straightened him out, feeling the raised ribs and jutting hips. His trousers were stiff with dried filth. She scraped her hands against the bunker walls to wipe it off her fingertips and swallowed back the bile in her throat.

Inside the tunnel, he stuck fast. Ellen had gone first, crawling backwards, fighting panic in the face of the enclosing earth. She was making progress by wedging her hands in Aref's armpits and tugging him after her, inch by inch. Najib, invisible to her on the other side, was pushing. They had only moved a few yards when he stopped moving. She heaved at his shoulders, her hands digging into his muscle for purchase. His head flopped heavily to one side, his face turned to the earth.

She pulled until she ached, then lay, exhausted, her cheek pressed sideways in the dirt of the tunnel floor, and wept. I could just crawl backwards to the light and leave him here, she thought. Her sense of the tonnes of crushing land on top of her squeezed the breath from her body. She closed her eyes, screwed her hands into fists and tried to stop the fluttering in her chest. I could crawl backwards and leave. Aref is already close to death. He won't suffer. But what about Najib? He would never survive. She imagined him being buried alive, his escape blocked by Aref's swelling corpse.

She wiped the mucus from her face, spat out dirt and began to scrabble at the earth pressing round Aref's shoulders. Slivers of buried wood and stone pierced her nails and fingertips. Her ears were filled with her own straining. Earth pattered down and she brushed it off Aref's cheek and chin in the darkness.

She heaved again, her hands slippery with sweat and mud. She could hear Najib's low grunting as he pushed Aref's braced legs. Finally, with a flurry of falling earth, Aref – cork-like – came popping out of the constriction, his head and shoulders crashing into her head in a sudden rush. Please God, she thought, as they fell to moving him again towards the bright hot light of the midday sun. Don't let him die before we get him back.

Once they were outside, their progress was torturous. Najib hoisted Aref into a sitting position and pitched him onto his back. Aref's head and shoulders dangled from Najib's neck across one shoulder and his legs hung down from the other. Bowed down by the weight, Najib could barely move. He shuffled forward a short step at a time, panting hard. Ellen guided him up the steep slope and out onto the open ground. The strong light after the darkness spiked their vision. Najib's shirt was soaked through with sweat.

They were too exhausted to speak. The first time Najib stumbled and fell, he lay motionless, collapsed on his side. Aref, a weight round his neck, pinned him to the ground. She rolled Aref off him into the corn. His face in the daylight was waxy and pallid, his eyes lifeless. Maybe we should just leave him, she thought, then felt ashamed. Najib, hunched on his side, his head turned away from her to the corn, seemed just as defeated. Maybe, she thought, he was thinking the same.

They rested and then tried again. This time Najib struggled to walk backwards, grasping Aref's wrists. Ellen, facing him, lifted

Aref's ankles. His body sagged between them, swinging lightly as they moved.

Ellen was shaking with exertion and fear. They were conspicuous, noisy as they crashed through the dry corn, an easy target for anyone who wanted to hunt them down. The compound seemed an impossible distance away. Her scarf had slipped down to her shoulders and the sun sat heavy on her head. Sweat was running down her arms and making her palms itchy and slippery. It penetrated the broken skin on her face and stung her cuts. She was parched, thinking constantly of water. Imagining its soft silky passage through her mouth, across her tongue, down her throat.

At the far side of the cornfield, as they were about to step into open desert, they stopped again to rest. Ellen snapped the dry corn and bent it over in clumps to give Aref's face dappled shade. Najib lay on his back, his eyes closed, panting. This can't go on, she thought. We won't make it. Aref's nose and cheeks were already blackening with flies. She sat in silence, too exhausted to brush them away, and stared without seeing into the light.

The engine erupted suddenly in the stillness and grew as the truck turned a corner and accelerated along the rough track. She knew it at once. Karam's battered pickup, chugging with the gracelessness of a tractor. Najib, hearing it too, sat up. She put her finger to her lips. Stay here, she mouthed. Najib looked so much older. His face was drawn, his eyes dull with fatigue. She patted the air, gesturing to him to wait, then crawled forward on her hands and knees through the jungle of corn.

The truck approached their hiding place. He was sitting forward, peering through the dusty windscreen, one arm draped across the top of the steering wheel, the other invisible by his side. On his gun, she thought. She imagined it propped beside him. There was tension in his face. His eyes, narrowed and sharp, were scanning the land in front of him. His white beard fell in waves from his chin. She shrank down, pressing her body flat to the earth.

He passed her. Further down the road, still in sight, the pickup slowed and drew to a halt in a cloud of brown dust. He sat motion-less, a solid shape in the cab. Her heart thumped in her chest. He knows, she thought. It's as if he can smell me. Her eyes were fixed on him. She held her breath, waiting for him to move. Nothing. The silence settled as she watched. The sun was glancing off the metal roof in shafts.

After some time, the engine coughed again into life. Karam twisted in his seat, turning to look back over his shoulder. He ran the pickup slowly backwards, kicking up fresh dirt. She crouched flat. Her breath came in short bursts. He stopped a few yards from her and switched off the engine.

The metal scraped as he opened the battered door and stepped down. The light sprayed off the gun in the cab. He straightened his hat and flexed his knee, leaning his foot back against the bright, hot metalwork of the truck. It sighed and shifted on its wheels. He was settling himself there in full view, waiting.

She thought of Aref, semi-conscious in the corn behind her, and of Najib crouched there too. He mustn't find them. She steeled herself, afraid to move, then got abruptly to her feet. She revealed herself at once, stepping out into the track in front of him. He looked up at her and smiled without humour.

'I thought you would come here,' he said. 'I was slow to think of it the last time. The boy must be hiding near. I am right. Why else would you come here alone?'

She stood quietly, feeling the tremble in her knees. He was still leaning back against the pickup but his legs were tense, as if he were ready to push away from it and spring forward. He spread his thick fingers with slow deliberation and cracked the knuckles, one by one.

'Your countryman Mack. People are saying he had a very bad accident. Very bad.' He looked past her, into the corn, his eyes hungry. 'The boy was supposed to do it. Not her.'

Ellen thought of Hasina, moving quietly across the sand in the darkness, a bundle clasped to her chest. So it had been Karam who'd given Hasina the gun. Who wanted Mack dead more than Karam, still full of anger and grief for his lost children?

'She was a decent woman,' Ellen said. 'All she wanted was to save her son.'

He shrugged. 'Martyrdom is not a woman's path. I didn't ask that. But, *inshallah,* in Paradise she will be blessed.'

He pressed himself forward onto the soles of both feet and took a step towards her. Ellen's eyes strayed to the open scrub-land on the far side of the road. Somewhere here, Mack had waited, arms wide, and talked her safely out of the minefield. Somewhere here. She said: 'Why have you come back?'

'For the boy,' he said. He was still peering past her, looking low into the corn, his eyes sharp. 'He is a fool, but he is my fool now.'

She didn't dare turn and follow his gaze. Instead she walked further out into the road towards the open desert. Ahead, the dust was trampled, scuffed by military boots. She tried to see exactly where Mack and the soldiers had stood.

In the distance, the shattered remnants of the dead dog swarmed with flies. I can't fight him, she was thinking. Her mind was tumbling, trying to think how to survive.

'The boy is all alone now,' he was saying. 'Without me, he cannot survive. Take me to him. For his mother's sake.'

His movements were deliberate as he followed her. She had reached the edge of the scrub now, her eyes on the ground. I will not put Aref into your hands, she thought. I will protect him. But I need time.

'His mother wanted him to escape all this,' she said. 'To have a better life.'

'What do you know?' He shrugged. 'I was right about the Major, wasn't I? A man who cares nothing for the lives of Afghan people and everything for his own kind. A tribesman. I understood that.'

He had shifted his weight, turning his shoulder to watch her as she backed away from him along the edge of the track. His face was all suspicion. Her eyes, reading the dust, fell suddenly on a neat triangle of stones. It was one of her marks, a sign of safe ground.

She swallowed, blood pumping in her ears, and looked quickly away.

'And Jalil?'

He grunted. 'The traitor?' He shrugged his broad shoulders. 'He took their money. He knew the danger.'

The low vacant scrub reached out across the desert to her right, studded with forgotten mines. *Allah will decide*, Karam had said to her, when he had sent her into the minefield the first time. Now she must ask Him to decide again.

'What will you do with Aref?'

'He is a boy with no brains, no guts.' He grimaced. 'Just like his father. But he may be useful.'

She lifted her right foot and took a bold step backwards off the track, aiming for the small triangle of stones just inside the minefield. The muscles in her leg shook as she put her foot to the ground. Her heel found its place. She put her weight on it. Silence. Nothing. She brought her other foot smartly to join it and stood, swaying lightly from the knees with tension.

She turned her head and glanced back at the scrub. Wherever they lay, the mines were invisible, crouching below the surface, patiently waiting, camouflaged by dust and scrub. The dirt and stone marks that had led her through to safety were already being compromised by the shifting desert.

When she turned back, Karam was staring at her. His eyes had widened. He was flexing his fingers as if he were about to lunge.

'You Britishers,' he said, 'you are ignorant people. Some day you will realize the trouble you are making here with your money and guns.'

She shifted her weight. Sweat was trickling down her temples and dripping onto her shirt. She could feel panic rising. A bubbling urge to turn and run and, if she were blown to pieces, so be it, let it happen. The fear and imagining were far worse.

She breathed slowly and steadily and lifted her foot. She moved it back another step to rest on a tiny mound of dirt, half scattered by the wind. She put her weight on it. A soldier had told her once that mine victims didn't live long enough to hear the bang. The last thing they knew was a blinding light before shock closed down the senses.

'Forget the boy,' she said.

Karam was walking slowly towards her as he spoke. He was halfway across the track. He paused, looking at her with amusement.

'This is not good land,' he said, nodding to the scrub. 'Don't you understand that?'

She held his gaze and took another deliberate step backwards onto an X of crossed twigs. Her foot pressed it deeper into the dust. The ground held. She breathed.

'I'll take my chances,' she said. 'Won't you?'

He threw back his head and laughed. She saw the rigid waves of his beard ripple down his throat. She stepped again, glancing quickly backwards to find the next mark before forcing herself to place her foot squarely on top of it.

'They cleared it then,' he said. 'The soldiers.'

She didn't answer. He was still hesitating. He had reached the scrub now and was standing with his toes at the edge, as if he were on the shore of a dangerous sea. She was walking backwards now, one careful pace at a time, her knees weak with tension, gradually opening up the distance between them.

'Surely you're not afraid?' Her tone was taunting. 'And you call yourself a man?'

She took another step backwards, then froze. There was no sign of the next mark. She looked across at Karam. His eyes on hers were cold and appraising. She felt panic rise. She was afraid to move but she must. He was watching, waiting. She swallowed. It must be there. An unusual stone, a mound of earth, something. She flicked her eyes again over the ground behind her. Two full paces away, she could make out a cluster of stones, bunched together. But whatever sign she'd made next had simply disappeared.

'Wherever you go, the Taliban will find you.' She was stalling for time, trying to goad him. What did she do now? Risk stepping out into the unknown? Her steps hadn't always been evenly spaced.

'They killed your brother, didn't they?' she went on. 'For much less than you've done. He never took money from soldiers. You did.'

He glared at her. She had to keep moving. She had to distract him. Her eyes flicked from his eyes to his hands, clenched into fists at his sides.

'The fighters trust me,' he said. 'They know me.'

He took a step off the track onto the scrubland. His eyes were narrowed, his face dark with anger.

'Are you sure?' She held her breath, her heart painful in her chest. 'They'll still trust you when the word is out? Once they know everything? Karam, tell me, where will you and your money hide then?'

He was treading recklessly, taking broad strides towards her. He must have believed what he'd said, that the ground had been cleared.

She closed her eyes and stepped boldly backwards into the dirt, her nerves screaming. Silence. She opened her eyes. The next step took her to the cluster of stones, then the next, beyond, to a jagged stone, placed upright.

'I warned you.' He was calling to her, venomous. 'I told you to leave this place.'

A bird rose, squawking, from a bank of scrub to her left and flapped up into the sky. It startled her. She stood motionless for a second, shaking. Karam was gaining on her. She turned her back to him and stepped forward to the next mark, jumping to the next and the next. The rocks, scrub, dirt swam dizzily at her feet. The land was stretching on endlessly, an undulating sweep that curled down towards the village. Too far. Behind her, his feet were thudding. He was running, heavy—

A bang. Shattering. Splitting the air. Blast, striking her body, making her stagger. Panting. Her head a jumble of confusion. Her ears dull with the throb of the vibrations. Her body rigid. She was trembling where she stood, straining to listen. Silence. Then a great cry rose, a shrill animal cry of pain.

She sank to her haunches and pressed her hands on her ears, trying to shut out the screaming. Make it stop. Please God, make it stop. She tucked her head into her chest and closed her eyes. The screams pierced everything. She clasped her head. Her legs were juddering beneath her and she shook helplessly, unable to quieten them.

Finally she forced herself to twist, open her eyes and look. He was lying on his back, writhing in the dirt, his hands clawing the air round his lower body. His legs were tattered. One was severed at the thigh, the flesh hanging loose in ragged strips. Blood was spurting from the wound, pooling around him in the dust. His other leg was drumming the earth, his cotton trousers a mess of gore and sinew.

His eyes were wide, fixed on her, his face white and wet with shock. I can't move, she thought. I can't save him. It's too late. She closed her eyes and hunched again into a ball, her hands holding her head. She rocked herself. Gradually the screaming grew less shrill and less frantic until it faded at last to a low pulsing moan. In the end, that too gave way, and finally there was silence.

28

Ellen sat cross-legged on the worn carpet, her back supported by velveteen cushions. The fabric was so thin, the filling was bulging between its threads. Heavy drapes hung across the doorway, muffling sounds from the rest of the house. The television, on its stand, bled coloured light across the carpet as the picture changed. The volume was down.

She turned to the solid wooden dresser and looked again at the old-fashioned picture of Jalil framed there, his eyes veiled with self-consciousness. It was time to make her peace with him, she thought. To say goodbye and let him go.

Outside a car horn sounded, followed by an angry shout. A construction drill screamed. After Helmand, Kabul, with its rutted mud streets and traffic jams and rows of stalls and staring male crowds, seemed a step back into the chaos of the modern world.

The drapes were pushed aside. Jalil's little brother stood in the doorway, looking in at her shyly, using all his strength to hold back the curtain for his sister. She was carrying in a tray of *chai sabz* in a scratched enamel teapot, with two glasses for the tea. She folded herself beside Ellen on the floor and poured. Stray leaves swirled and sank in the light green liquid and pungent steam rose. She set out a glass dish divided into thirds, filled with raisins and almonds and hard white clusters of boiled sugar. Ellen took an almond. It was stale.

'How is she?'

Jalil's sister leaned forward and lowered her voice. Her hair was escaping in tendrils along her cheek but she didn't move to adjust her headscarf and cover them. Jalil's little brother had already disappeared.

'I've been very worried,' she said. She pushed a glass of tea an inch closer to Ellen. 'She's been like a dead woman. No life. No hope.'

Ellen nodded, lifted the hot glass by the rim and inhaled its richness.

'She never left the house. At night, she was awake, crying, walking from room to room. She thought I was asleep but I heard her.' Her voice had fallen to a whisper. She had poured tea for herself but it sat before her untouched.

'In the afternoon, she closed the curtains and slept. She wouldn't see even my auntie.'

Ellen listened. Jalil's mother was looking gaunt and pale. The deterioration, even since her last visit, worried her.

'How do you think she feels about this boy?'

Jalil's sister put her head to one side, like a bird. Her gold earring flashed.

'No one can replace Jalil,' she said.

'Of course not.'

'But she is distracted by him, by caring for him. It is giving her – .' she paused, reaching for the word – 'some meaning.'

Ellen looked at her fingers, idle in her lap. 'I don't know much about him, about what kind of boy he is,' she said. 'Your mother is very kind. But you must also be careful.'

'Of course.' Jalil's sister looked up, a half-smile on her lips. 'My mother is a clever woman. She knows that. He is a village boy, not educated.'

'He won't be able to work for some time,' she said. 'The army doctor said the wound on his stomach would take at least a month to heal. That's a long time for him to stay with you.'

Jalil's sister shrugged. 'Maybe it's a blessing,' she said, 'for us and for him.'

Ellen paused, watching the images flicker across the television screen. She let the silence settle for a moment.

'I'll pay for him,' she said. 'For his medicine. His food. Any other expenses.'

Jalil's sister hesitated. Ellen saw her eyes drop to her fingers, twisting in her lap. She reached out and covered them with her own hands, bunching the girl's fingers in hers.

'Once,' she said, 'Jalil asked me for money.'

His sister didn't raise her eyes. Ellen sensed her awkwardness.

'I was wrong,' she went on. 'I'm so sorry.' She paused. 'I'll regret it for the rest of my life.'

Jalil's sister shifted her weight and withdrew her hands. 'You must ask my mother.'

'Do you think . . .?'

'I know what she will say: Allah will provide.' Jalil's sister shrugged. When she looked up, her expression was calm. 'But I think Allah also provided you. So we should accept and be thankful.'

Ellen looked again at Jalil's face, staring out at her from the dresser. At what point had he realized that Mack, the man he respected like a father, had blood on his hands? Ellen closed her eyes. When had he realized how far Mack would go to keep him quiet?

'He has no relatives at all?' Jalil's sister's voice cut into her thoughts. Ellen opened her eyes, turned to face her.

'An aunt,' she said. 'That's all.'

Jalil's sister leaned forward to refill Ellen's glass and nudged the dish of snacks another inch nearer. She lifted her own glass of tea and drank, holding it delicately at the rim between her thumb and forefinger. Outside, horns blared as the traffic congealed.

Ellen was conscious of the time. She must leave for the airport soon and her flight home. This was her last chance to make peace.

'This Major.' Jalil's sister kept her head low. 'What kind of man was he? How could he do that to Jalil, when he worked for him, he was responsible for him?'

Ellen sighed. She thought of Mack, of his quick mind and strong character.

'In a way, he and Jalil wanted the same thing,' she said. She spoke slowly, choosing her words with care. 'Security. An end to this bloodshed as quickly as possible. And, like Jalil, he was a loyal person. But only to his own men.'

Jalil's sister lifted her head. Her eyes were clear, fringed with long dark lashes; her look was perplexed. I must be careful, Ellen thought. What I say now will set in her mind like amber.

'He did a terrible thing. A deal that led to the deaths of many innocent people. Somehow he justified it to himself. Convinced himself it was for the greater good.'

'And that's what Jalil found out?'

Ellen nodded. 'Yes,' she said. 'He found out. And after that, the Major couldn't risk letting him leave.'

The bedroom door was ajar, giving her a covert view of the scene inside. Aref was lying on a cot, his head and shoulders propped up by cushions, wool blankets tucked round his body. Jalil's little brother was sitting with him, a basin of water balanced on a towel across his lap and a damp cloth in his hand. He was dabbing at the soft skin behind Aref's ears and at the straggly beard on his chin and neck. The boy was concentrating hard, the tip of his tongue protruding from the corner of his mouth, his jaw set. Aref's eyes on the boy were gentle.

The staircase creaked. Slippered feet were rising from the ground floor. Ellen turned. Jalil's mother was coming along the landing, carrying a tray with a bowl and spoon and a platter of fresh bread. Heavy earrings swung in her ears, their weight stretching the lobes. Her headscarf was neatly tucked into folds at her temples and pinned so that every hair was covered. She smiled. Ellen held open the door and cleared a place on the low bedside table for her to set down the tray. The boy dried off Aref's face with his towel and, the job half done, got to his feet.

Ellen stood against the wall at the back and watched as Jalil's mother smoothed her long skirt and settled herself on the low stool at Aref's bedside. She shifted the tray across her knee and tucked a cloth round his neck as a napkin, then lifted the soup, spoonful by spoonful, blowing across it first herself, then taking it to his lips. His eyes never left hers.

The contours of his face were still stark, his cheeks hollowed, but already his eyes were starting to lose their dull, bruised look. His skin was pale but no longer grey. The sweat of fever had cleared.

Jalil's mother leaned forward to touch the edge of his mouth with her cloth where the soup had spilled. Ellen thought of Hasina, fierce with love, gathering her son into her lap as he lay, half dead, his eyes closed and his feet fluttering weakly against the sandy floor of the tunnel. She thought of the desert dust that now covered her and was already claiming her flesh as its own. She thought of the small hand with pink fingernails, emerging ghost-like with its tin bangle from the rubble of the bombed house.

Her task here was done. Phil had been delighted with the story she'd filed. The eyewitness account of the attack was both dramatic and an exclusive. She'd given a sense of Hasina as more than just some pro-Taliban fighter. She was a freshly bereaved wife. A mother. A woman who would defend her family to her last breath. Of Mack's betrayal, Jalil's murder and Karam's complicity she wrote nothing.

She looked now at Jalil's mother, patiently lifting each spoonful of soup to Aref's mouth. Her eyes were unsentimental. This was not her son and never would be. But he was an Afghan boy without a mother who needed soup. And she had soup to share.

Ellen stood upright from the wall and walked quietly to the door. No one seemed to notice her leave. The staircase creaked as she made her way slowly downstairs to the front door. Outside a car and driver were waiting to take her to the airport, her rucksack in the boot. She pulled her scarf up round her face and hid away her hair.

She had her story. Phil was happy. So why, now she was leaving, did she feel so weighed down by sadness? Everything she'd written was true. And yet, to the rest of the world, Mack had died a hero. Jalil's death was still a mystery.

She settled on the hot plastic of the car's back seat. The family's guard, his gun slung across his shoulder, dragged open the heavy metal gates and the driver nosed out into the street. The bleached brightness of the midday heat had passed and the first notes of gold were creeping into the sunlight.

At the junction, they pushed into the main road and its stream of honking traffic. She gazed out of the window at the passing scene. A young man, a jihadi scarf across his shoulders, was shovelling dates into thin plastic bags, his features blurred by the drifting smoke of a nearby brazier. Next to him, a cluster of stout middle-aged women, their faces veiled, were picking through a mound of second-hand clothes.

The driver sounded his horn, forcing his way between a lumbering cart and a truck parked crookedly in the gutter. A plump woman with a hooked nose and heavily powdered face was leaning in the open doorway of a beauty parlour, arms folded, surveying the street. A burst of children ran past her, barefoot, shouting. Two men were standing, gossiping, their pot-bellies lifting long cotton salwar kameez, their beards straggly and streaked with grey.

The driver crunched into a higher gear and urged the car forward. As they started to gather speed, Ellen's final sight was of a woman in a patched blue burqa, the cotton grid of her face bent low to a child. She raked his hair roughly with her fingers, then took him by the hand, guiding him as she picked her way patiently through a shattered pavement of broken stone and endlessly drifting dust.

Acknowledgements

Thank you to all at HarperCollins, especially to Patrick Janson-Smith, editor par excellence, and to Susan Opie. The Blue Door would never have opened for me without the wisdom and guidance of my wonderful agent, Judith Murdoch.

As a foreign correspondent, I've made many reporting trips to Afghanistan in recent years. I'm grateful to the BBC for those opportunities and to Afghan and British colleagues there, particularly producer Caroline Finnigan. Like Ellen, I've been embedded at times with the British forces in Helmand. I thank my military hosts of all ranks for their courtesy and kindness. Any negative portrayals are entirely fictional.

Special thanks to the members of my excellent writing group – Dorothy, Gabriela, Hilary, James, Maria and Ros – who nurtured this novel through early drafts and gave invaluable criticism. My thanks to the tutors on the MA in Creative Writing at Birkbeck College, University of London, in particular Julia Bell and Professor Russell Celyn Jones, for their ideas and support. Nageen Kargar gave informed comment on the book from the perspective of an Afghan woman.

And finally my love and thanks to my great friend, Dawn, and to my family: Sheila, for my first desk, first typewriter and much more; Ann, for wit and editorial wisdom; Nick for being a wonderful husband and my mother and late father, for a lifetime of love and great character stuff.